A Most Unsuitable Match

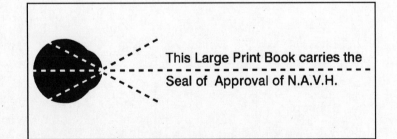

This Large Print Book carries the
Seal of Approval of N.A.V.H.

A MOST
UNSUITABLE MATCH

STEPHANIE GRACE WHITSON

THORNDIKE PRESS
A part of Gale, Cengage Learning

GALE
CENGAGE Learning™

Detroit • New York • San Francisco • New Haven, Conn • Waterville, Maine • London

GALE
CENGAGE Learning™

LIBRARY OF CONGRESS CATALOGING-IN-PUBLICATION DATA

Whitson, Stephanie Grace.
    A most unsuitable match / by Stephanie Grace Whitson.
        p. cm. — (Thorndike Press large print Christian romance)
    ISBN-13: 978-1-4104-4045-7 (hardcover)
    ISBN-10: 1-4104-4045-1 (hardcover)
    1. Steamboats—Fiction. 2. Frontier and pioneer life—Missouri River
Valley—Fiction. 3. Large type books. I. Title.
PS3573.H555M67 2011b
813'.54—dc22   2011027994

Published in 2011 by arrangement with Bethany House Publishers, a
division of Baker Publishing Group.

Printed in the United States of America
1 2 3 4 5 6 7 15 14 13 12 11

Dedicated to the memory of
God's extraordinary women
in every place,
in every time.

"Let her own works praise her in the
gates."

Proverbs 31:31

CHAPTER ONE

I water my couch with my tears.

PSALM 6:6

Sunday, May 16, 1869
St. Charles, Missouri

Kneeling before the tombstone, eighteen-year-old Fannie Rousseau retrieved the scrub brush from the water bucket she'd just settled in the grass. First, she attacked the dried bird droppings on the back side of the stone, then moved on to the deep grooves carving the name *Rousseau* into the cool gray surface. She'd just finished cleaning out the second *s* when a familiar voice sounded from across the cemetery.

"*Land sakes,* child, what on earth are you doin'? You'll ruin your hands. And put that bonnet back on. What will your mother s-s —"

When Fannie laid her hand atop the gravestone to steady herself and lifted her tear-stained face toward Hannah, the old woman stopped midword. Tucking an errant hank of wiry gray hair back under the kerchief tied about her head, she hurried to where Fannie knelt. Her voice more gentle than scolding, she said, "You know your mother would have my hide for letting you be seen in public doing such a thing." She nodded toward the red brick church just outside the cemetery fence. "And it's the Sabbath, little miss. What were you thinking?"

Fannie didn't have an answer. At least not one she wanted to say aloud. She scrubbed out the rest of the tombstone grooves before dropping the brush into the bucket and standing back up. The soil atop Mother's grave had finally sunk enough to be level with Papa's side, but the grass hadn't filled in yet. For now, the tombstone only told half a story. *Louis Rousseau, 1821–1866, Beloved Husband. Eleanor Rousseau, 1831–____*. The stonemason had yet to add the year 1869 to Mother's side. Fannie contemplated the words *Beloved Husband.* She supposed it was only right to add *Beloved Wife* to Mother's side. Even if she would always wonder if it was true.

Hannah picked up the bucket and, splaying her fingers across the rim, upended it, sprinkling the newly seeded side of the grave with water as she murmured, "I can't imagine what people thought when they saw you walking up here, scrub bucket in hand, bonnet dangling like a common servant. The very idea!" Hannah clicked her tongue disapprovingly. "And you didn't even attend services, did you?"

Fannie looked up at the church spire, then back at the tombstone. "I didn't want to face Mr. Vandekamp." That was partially true. She'd grown wary of the man handling Papa's affairs of late, what with his hints about her future and his coupling of her name with that of Percy Harvey. Percy might be heir to a considerable fortune, but he made her skin crawl.

Avoiding Hannah's gaze, Fannie shrugged. "Anyone who matters knows I'm not in the habit of avoiding church." She paused. "Maybe they didn't even notice me here."

Hannah looked past the rows of gravestones toward the street, then back at the ground at their feet. "They noticed."

Hannah was right, of course. People had to have seen Fannie on her knees here, scrubbing like a washerwoman. Papa had chosen the center of the graveyard for the family plot, and the slight rise in this part of the cemetery would naturally draw their eyes toward the name Rousseau every time someone ventured past. Of course, if the location didn't do the trick, Mother had made certain people would look this way when she ordered a life-sized stone angel to weep over Papa's grave.

There it was again, the increasingly frequent tinge of annoyance that always mingled with Fannie's grief. What good did a stone angel do? It was too late for Papa to know how Mother felt about him. And now it was too late for Fannie, too. Any chance she might have had to understand Mother was forever lost.

Lately, all Fannie's doubts and questions over the years seemed to have rolled themselves into a fast-growing, ever-darkening cloud of emotion she didn't quite know how to handle. This morning that cloud had been especially dense. And so, feeling confused and guilty about every negative thing she'd ever felt against Mother and not wanting to face the people at church, she'd come here. Tending a grave was something a good daughter would do, wasn't it? Something a daughter *should* do. She glanced up at the stone angel. Was Mother feeling just this way after Papa died? Did she have regrets? Had ordering the angel made her feel better?

"I want to plant rosebushes on either side of the tombstone," she said abruptly. "Yellow ones."

"That'll be nice," Hannah said, "but Mr. McWilliams will be happy to do that. You don't want him thinking you're displeased with his caretaking."

Fannie swiped at fresh tears. "I want to plant them myself. I need to do something." She gestured toward the new grave. "Something for her. Yellow roses were her favorite, and Papa never seemed to remember. He always gave her red ones."

Hannah's voice was gentle. "Red roses say *I love you.*"

She was right — again. Red roses meant love. Yellow meant friendship and fidelity. Was there some hidden meaning in Mother's liking yellow and Papa sending red? Would she always have these niggling doubts about everything? "Isn't the best way to say *I love you* to give what someone likes, instead of what custom dictates?"

"I see your thoughts, child." Hannah reached up and brushed one of Fannie's blond curls away from her face. "There was love in that house. They just didn't show it the way you wanted them to. That's all it was, little miss. They just didn't know how to show it."

11

Fannie pressed her lips together. Somehow, Hannah's tender touch made the longing worse. Why hadn't Mother ever done things like that? She cleared her throat. There was no point in bringing that up again. It made her sound spoiled and ungrateful. Maybe she was both of those things. She'd never heard her parents say a harsh word to each other. They'd given her everything she'd ever wanted. Mother had even been talking about a trip to Europe for them both. *You should be counting your blessings instead of feeling sorry for yourself.* Hannah was right. That feeling of being held at arm's length didn't mean anything. It was just Papa and Mother's way.

Hannah's gently insistent voice brought Fannie back to the moment. "Let's get you home so I can clean your skirt." She grimaced as she bent to inspect the smudges where Fannie's knees had met the earth. Then, bucket in hand, she gave Fannie a one-armed hug.

Dear Hannah. What would she do without her? Her hair might be gray, but her golden brown skin was smooth as glass, her back straight, her figure still the envy of anyone who noticed. Only Hannah's hands showed the years. And the stiff knees that kept her from gliding up and down stairs the way she used to. And now Fannie had made more work for her. "I'm sorry," she said as she bent to swipe at the smudges. "Maybe I can clean it."

Hannah caught her hand. "Let it dry on the walk home. It'll be easier to get off then." She arched one eyebrow. "I've slowed down, but I'm perfectly capable of getting a couple of smudges off a silk skirt." Apparently energized by her indignation, Hannah led the way toward the cemetery gate. "You listen to what I say, little miss. Your mother loved you. She wasn't much for talking about it, but that woman *loved*."

Fannie paused at the gate to look back toward the grave. Maybe if she'd been a better daughter . . . she blinked back fresh tears and, looping her arm through Hannah's, headed home. If she'd learned anything in these past few weeks, it was that shedding tears didn't yield answers. In fact, crying tended to set her back on the emotional spiral that made thinking harder and decisions more confusing than ever. God said that faith was the evidence of things not seen. She needed to believe more and doubt less. Besides, she didn't have time for any more tears. There was too much to do.

"First thing in the morning, let's head to Haversham's and see what he has in the way of rosebushes." She gave Hannah one of her best smiles. "We can plant them together. Surely no one would gossip about a girl *decorating* her parents' graves, especially if I make you carry the shovel like a proper servant."

Hannah tried to look stern, but Fannie knew that look. The beautiful old woman just couldn't keep her mouth from curving up at the edges.

Bleak skies and a steady drizzle on Monday morning dampened Fannie's interest in rosebushes and gardens. When the sun finally came out after lunch, she and Hannah picked their way around walkway puddles to Haversham's. When Fannie tried to charge her two yellow rosebushes, the boy at the counter seemed to have a problem finding her account. Once he'd located it, he hesitated to add to it until Mr. Haversham himself authorized the purchase.

"Perhaps you'll want to speak to Mr. Vandekamp," Mr. Haversham suggested as he looked down his long nose at Fannie. "It has been some time since your account was reconciled."

Grabbing the tops of the two cotton bags holding the roses, Fannie mumbled something she hoped sounded like agreement

14

and hurried out of the store. "Speak to Mr. Vandekamp?!" Fannie groused as Hannah took the bushes from her hands. "Why doesn't Mr. *Haversham* speak to Mr. Vandekamp if there's a problem with my account?"

"Now, now," Hannah soothed as they walked home. "He's got to make ends meet, too, don't he? He didn't mean anything by it. You go see Mr. Vandekamp. He'll explain everything. After all, understanding how to run a household is part of growing up."

"Maybe so," Fannie protested, "but it's not a part Mother let me learn. She said we'd always have Mr. Vandekamp and it wasn't ladylike to know too much about such things."

When they arrived back home, Hannah hesitated at the yard gate before saying, "I'm sure your mama meant well when she said that about you not needing to understand about money. She just didn't realize you'd face what you're facing. The good Lord blessed you with a good mind, little miss, and that's exactly what you need to make your way through the life he's allowed. You'll be all right. You'll see." She headed up the brick path toward the back of the house.

Pulling the gate closed behind her, Fannie

ambled after Hannah, noticing for the first time that the white trim on the windowsill just beneath the portico was beginning to peel. She paused to look up. *All* the trim looked weathered. The once-shining black shutters on the windows had lost their luster. Weeds threatened to overtake the low hedge along the front of the house. When had all that happened?

Hannah dragged a bucket out of the carriage house and settled the two rosebushes in it near the well pump at the base of the back porch steps. As Hannah pumped water, Fannie looked over the yard, the carriage house, the kitchen garden. She pointed at the weeds. "Things are looking a little . . . run-down in the yard." She nodded up at the portico. "And we — *I* — need to have the trim painted." She frowned. "Have I been sleepwalking?"

Hannah shook her head. "You've been grieving, child. Feels like sleepwalking sometimes."

Was this how Mother had felt after Papa died? Fannie had just assumed she didn't care all that much. But that didn't fit with Mother continuing to dress in deep mourning, did it? *Maybe the stone angel was more about grief and less about showing St. Charles how much money we have.* Once again, the things Fannie didn't understand about Mother pressed to the forefront. Hannah's voice brought her back to the moment.

"Walker's been feeling poorly of late. I believe I mentioned it to you last week." She paused. "I told him to keep up with the grounds as best he could." Hannah put her hands on her hips and gazed up at the house. "But you're right. He's let things go. This won't do. Miz Rousseau would have *both* our heads if she could see what's happened." She looked toward the garden. "I expect Walker'll show up directly. Should I tell him you need to talk to him?"

Fannie took a step back and put a palm to her heart. "Me?" She shook her head. "Can't *you* talk to him?"

"That's not my place. Walker wouldn't appreciate my putting on airs that way." Hannah reached out to pat Fannie's arm. "It's time you took the place over, child. The fact that you noticed those weeds and things is a good sign. You're growing into handling the changes around here." She smiled. "Old Walker dotes on you. Offer to hire him some help. He'll see it as a kindness, not a scolding." She paused. "Once you've spoken to him, you can walk up to that bank and schedule a meeting with Mr. Vandekamp and talk to him about the Haversham account and such."

Fannie glanced around the lawn. Weeds threatened wherever she looked. The lower leaves of Mother's roses sported black spots. She walked toward the garden. Reaching for the tallest weed, she grabbed it and pulled. When it didn't give way, she grimaced, grasped the stalk with both hands, pulled again, and was rewarded with the distinct sound of something ripping. When she let go and inspected her palms, she realized she'd torn a hole in her black gloves.

"I'm going inside now," Hannah groused. "Hand me the gloves. Just what I need, filet crochet mending." Fannie peeled the gloves off. She could hear Hannah's knees creak as the old woman turned to leave. "Make a spectacle of yourself to the neighborhood if you must, but I'll not be watching." Grunting with the effort, Hannah mounted the stairs to the back porch. The kitchen door slammed behind her, punctuating her mood.

Making a spectacle of herself? By trying to pull one stubborn weed? As she looked around, Fannie realized how truly shabby things looked. The second-story windows were filthy, and one of the shutters was hanging by only one hinge. Was that a seedling *tree* sprouting out of that loose gut-

18

ter? She knew she'd been in something of a fog since Mother died, but this was ridiculous. All of this couldn't have happened in only a few weeks — could it?

Of course it hadn't happened in a few weeks. Mother hadn't been herself since the buggy accident last fall. But Mother had assured Fannie that Mr. Vandekamp was taking care of everything. *But if he were taking care of things, the account at Haversham's would be current.* Clearly, Mother had been wrong.

Fannie headed inside, her sense of dismay tinged with outrage. Mr. Hubert Vandekamp was paid very well to take care of Papa's affairs. Fannie was certain of that. After all, Papa was a generous man. It was unseemly for someone they'd trusted to take advantage. Mr. Vandekamp needed to be reminded, *encouraged,* to do his job. Still, the idea of facing up to him made her heart lurch. He would bring up the topic of suitors again. And Percy Harvey.

Dear Lord, help. Please. I don't know what to do.

Stepping inside, she untied her black bonnet ribbons. Hannah sat at the kitchen table, crochet hook in hand, squinting down at Fannie's torn gloves. She didn't even look up as she said, "You might as well give me

19

that skirt, too."

"I will," Fannie said, "but I have to do something down here before I change."

Bonnet in hand, she headed through the kitchen, up the hall, and into the sumptuously furnished room Papa had always used for an office. Little had changed here since his death. Mother had looked completely out of place sitting at Papa's massive burled wood desk sorting papers. Had she even *read* the business mail? Maybe all she'd done was open it and take the stack to Mr. Vandekamp. *Maybe she was in a fog like the one you've been in.*

The enormity of facing life alone washed over her. If she trembled at the prospect of scolding Walker about the weeds outside, how would she ever face Mr. Vandekamp? To fight off a wave of near panic, she crossed the room and raised the window shades. Sunlight filtered in. *These things aren't Papa's anymore. They're mine.* She put her hand on the back of the desk chair and pulled it out. Mother couldn't tell her to get out of her father's chair now. Nor could she remind Fannie that "a lady doesn't concern herself with business."

Fannie perched on the edge of Papa's chair, her back straight. Placing both palms atop the desk, she closed her eyes. *Are you there, Papa? Do you see me? I'm all alone now. I can stitch the finest sampler in the state, and Jamison Riggs says I dance more gracefully than any of the other girls in St. Charles. I finally learned to play that étude by Mr. Chopin. I played it for Mother before she . . . left. She smiled and said I did a lovely job, and you know that Mother was very hard to please when it came to Monsieur Chopin.*

Fannie opened her eyes. Mother had been hard to please when it came to just about everything. Let Fannie show an interest in anything remotely . . . *challenging* to her intelligence and Mother got that look on her face as she said, "And how, exactly, would it help a young lady to know about *investments?* There isn't a single acceptable suitor in St. Charles who would find such an interest anything but appalling."

Fannie reached for the top envelope on the waiting pile of mail. She supposed Mother was right — for the most part — about what eligible men expected from eligible ladies. Be that as it may, she couldn't let it stop her from doing what must be done. She was the sole heir of something. It was time she discovered exactly *what.*

Fannie perused the contents of the first envelope. She might speak French, but clearly she did not speak Business. *Ton-*

nage . . . cargo . . . capstan engine . . . administrator's sale. The only thing she really understood were the words *urgent* and *projected loss.* The dollar amount next to that last phrase was impossible. Wasn't it? If that number was accurate, her problems with Mr. Vandekamp were much worse than weeds and peeling paint.

Fannie made her way through the remaining pile of mail, but with each unpaid bill, her spirits lagged. Finally, as the aroma of boiled beef wafted in from the kitchen, memories of Hannah Pike's creaking knees and the gardener's woes combined with the words in Papa's mail to send a frisson of true fear up her spine.

CHAPTER TWO

A friend loveth at all times, and a brother
is born for adversity.

PROVERBS 17:17

Monday, May 17, 1869
St. Louis, Missouri

"We're a full crew," the grizzled roustabout said, and nearly knocked the carpetbag out of Samuel's hand as he brushed past, headed for the waiting mountain of cargo. Samuel gazed toward the battered steamboat crowded against the St. Louis levee. The painted letters spelling out *Delores* had faded to the point that the name was barely legible. Peeling paint made the hurricane deck railing more gray than white, and the hull had obviously had more than one encounter with sandbars and snags. Just about every single steamboat taking on cargo today looked more promising than the *Delores*. And yet, Samuel knew she was piloted by Otto Busch, and no one knew the river better. Because of Busch, the *Delores* held the current record for ascending the Missouri to Fort Benton. Over two thousand miles in thirty-two days. Peeling paint didn't matter. Samuel needed speed.

Another roustabout — an older, wiry man — hoisted a sack of flour and limped back Samuel's way. "Heard you asking Isaac about work." When Samuel looked down at him, the man's pale blue eyes crinkled at the corners. "Isaac was right, as far as it goes. But I'm thinking any captain worth his salt would at least consider making an exception for someone your size." He nodded toward the steamboat. "If you've got muscles underneath that black coat to match the looks of you, you might just want to talk to the man climbing down from the wheelhouse."

Samuel nodded. "Thank you, sir."

The old guy chuckled. "Don't thank me, son. Cap'n Busch isn't what you'd call an easy man to work for. Threatens to toss me in the river at least once a day. One of these days he'll likely do it." With a laugh and a grunt, the old man shifted the sack on his shoulder and got in line with the crew headed up the gangplank and on board.

As Samuel watched, the captain made his

way from the wheelhouse, between the smokestacks, and then down to the hurricane deck. Taking a pipe from his coat pocket, he lit it, then leaned against the railing, puffing and watching his crew.

Samuel slid his hand into his pocket and touched the bit of paper he'd taken off Pa's desk before leaving home. He didn't want to use his father's name. Not unless he had to.

As he stood thinking about the best way to convince Otto Busch to hire him, the kind old man who'd pointed the captain out reached the end of the gangplank, but when he went to step aboard the ship, he staggered and almost lost his balance. Samuel glanced back up toward the captain just in time to see Busch take his pipe out of his mouth and begin to yell at the old guy.

Somewhere between the words *worn-out* and an ugly reference to the man's race, Samuel leaped across the narrow strip of water separating the steamer's deck from the levee. Once on board, he hurried to the wide stairway leading to the hurricane deck above. In no time he was at the top of the stairs, staring at the broad back of the angry man threatening to toss the old guy in the river.

"I'm looking to earn passage upriver,"

Samuel called to the captain's back.

Busch didn't even turn around, just said over his shoulder, "And I'm thinking that when you talked to him on the levee, Davis told you I have a full crew. Unless you're proposing to take Davis's place."

Samuel crossed to stand beside the captain at the railing. "I don't want to take anybody's place, but I need to travel fast, and the *Delores* holds the record."

Busch turned and looked Samuel up and down while he puffed on his pipe. Finally, he said, "Do I know you?"

"No, sir. My name's Beck. Samuel Beck." He held out his hand. Busch ignored it and turned away to watch his crew. "You know how many thousands of fresh-faced young fellas like you I've hauled north, their eyes blinded by visions of Montana gold? No idea what's waiting for 'em. No idea how many more go 'bust' than 'boom.' No thought of the Blackfeet." He swore softly. "Young fools." He shook his head. "I've a full crew, and I'm hauling freight and *paying* passengers this trip. Period."

"But I —"

Snatching his pipe out of his mouth, the captain let out a stream of epithets so vile they almost made Samuel wince. He followed Busch's gaze to the levee, where Mr.

Davis was bending over a sack he'd apparently just dropped. A flour sack, Samuel guessed, from the white powder scattering over the cobblestones. Busch pounded the railing. Spittle flew as he swore at the "dad-blasted, slack-jawed, stone-deaf son of a willy-walloo" who'd caused the mess.

Inspiration struck. Samuel set his carpet-bag down and shrugged out of his long black coat. He thrust the coat at Busch to draw his attention away from the spilled flour. "I'd be obliged if you'd put this someplace safe. It's my only coat. I hear the winters are fierce up north. Wouldn't want to be without a coat."

Busch threw the coat down and stomped on it, glaring at Samuel with such untainted animosity that Samuel's iron will almost wavered. Almost, but not quite. Samuel launched himself back down the stairs, across the deck and gangplank, and to the wagon, where Davis was struggling to hoist another bag. "Here," Samuel said, and took the bag on his own shoulder. "Give me another one." When the old guy hesitated, Samuel nodded. "It'll be all right. Just do it."

With a fifty-pound sack on each shoulder, Samuel got in the line headed on board. Stacking his two bags in the hold, he again leaped across the narrow swath of muddy river separating ship from landing. Quickly, he got another roustabout to hoist two more bags onto his shoulders. When he finally dared to look up, the captain had put his pipe back in his mouth and was standing motionless, Samuel's black coat folded over the railing next to him.

Samuel strode back on board, unloaded his second two flour sacks, and hurried up the stairs. Hoping he didn't sound desperate, he said, "You can see how strong I am. I'll work harder than anyone you've ever hired."

The captain peered at him for a moment before saying, "I expect you think you're worth more than the average."

"All I want is fast passage up the river. Food enough to keep body and soul together would be nice." Samuel lowered his voice and added, "And please don't fire the old guy for dropping that flour sack."

Busch arched one eyebrow. "How do you know Lamar Davis?"

"I don't. But when he heard me asking about work earlier, he was kind enough to point you out. And he seemed a little worried about keeping his job."

The pilot harrumphed. "How I treat Lamar Davis is none of your affair. But in case you're sweet on the old boy, suffice it to say I promised someone a long time ago I'd keep the old coot on, and while I may be a foulmouthed, whiskey-loving, woman-izing so-and-so, I am also a man of my word." He handed Samuel his coat even as he groused, "I expect you *eat* twice as much as most men, too."

"I'll eat whatever's offered, sir, and I won't complain."

Busch tilted his head. "You running from the law?"

Samuel shook his head. The captain's eyes showed suspicion, but Samuel remained quiet, willing his hands to stay loose. Balled-up fists could be misinterpreted, and he had nothing to hide. At least not anything that would make Busch's letting him earn passage north a problem.

After what seemed like an eternity, the captain thrust his lower jaw forward. "All right." He punctuated his next words with pipe flourishes in the air. "But I don't care if yer Goliath himself, if I find out you lied about the law, I'll put you ashore in Indian Territory and not look back."

He waved at a wagon just now pulling up to the landing. "Let's see how fast you can unload that. There's china teapots and perfume bottles and all manner of dainty whatnots in those crates. They're promised to a customer in Sioux City who won't take kindly to damaged goods. Drop one and you're fired."

"Yes, sir," Samuel said, trying to keep the triumph from sounding in his voice as he grabbed coat and carpetbag and headed below.

"And don't let Davis near those crates!" Busch shouted.

Samuel couldn't help but smile as he saluted the captain and hurried to unload the wagon. He paused on the main deck long enough to tuck his coat and bag out of sight atop a tall stack of crates and to roll up his sleeves. He'd heard stories about Otto Busch, but none of them had prepared him for the man in the flesh. Lucky for Samuel he was used to being called names, used to being sworn at, and used to being threatened. For all the pilot's blustering profanity, Samuel saw no evidence that he punished his employees with a blacksnake whip applied to shirtless backs.

This job would be easy compared to living with Pa.

"You can't fool me, Fannie Rousseau," Minette said, giving the swing a push. "You didn't come next door two hours before dinner and drag me out to the garden just to hear the latest news about Daniel and me. Something's happened. I can hear it in your voice. So . . . tell me what's bothering you."

When Minette held her hand out, palm up, Fannie grasped it. There was no use denying Minette's intuition — or whatever it was that enabled the girl to see more than most of their sighted friends did when it came to people's true feelings.

Minette squeezed her hand. "I gather it's something you don't want everyone to know, or you wouldn't have led me to the swing behind the gazebo. So . . . unless someone's lurking nearby who might over-hear . . . tell me."

Fannie glanced about them. "There's no one," she said, forcing a smile she hoped Minette would hear. "Unless we have to worry about Jake. But he's asleep at the mo-ment, curled up over there under the serviceberry tree. In fact, a white blossom just landed on his ear . . . and he flicked it off. And now," she said with a chuckle, "he's on his back, all four legs splayed in different directions."

Minette giggled. "Not very dignified for a watchdog, is he?"

"Calling Jake a watchdog is like calling

me an heiress." Fannie gave a little squeeze and let go of her friend's hand.

"Uh-oh." Minette frowned and turned Fannie's way.

It was unsettling to know those lovely hazel eyes couldn't actually see what they were pointed at. "Uh-oh what?" Fannie shifted on the swing and then gave a little shove with one boot to get the two of them in motion.

"Uh-oh you're considering not telling me everything." Minette tugged on Fannie's sleeve. "When you take away your hand, it removes one of the ways I read your mind. That's not playing nice. How can I give good advice if you aren't going to tell me everything?"

"I didn't know they taught you mind reading at that school."

Minette reached up to sweep her dark curls back off her shoulder as she tossed her head. "You know they didn't. They did, however, teach me to be aware of tension. And when your fingers start to curl or your palms sweat, I know something's up. So tell me what's troubling you."

"Besides everything, you mean?"

"Define the part of *everything* I don't already know about." Minette frowned and pretended to glare at Fannie as she said,

"Now."

Fannie sighed. She began with the awkward moment when she put the rosebushes on her account at Haversham's. "You'd think they were afraid they weren't going to get paid!" She sighed. "But that's only part of it. I don't know when it all started, but the house is threatening to fall down around me. Peeling paint, weedy gardens, rusted gates. Hannah says Walker's too old to keep up. She says I need to hire someone to help him. And the truth is, the grounds are only the beginning. Hannah isn't really keeping up inside, either." She leaned close and muttered, "Today I noticed cobwebs in the corners in Papa's office."

"Cobwebs?!" Minette gasped in mock horror. "Oh no! Whatever will you do? It's a travesty! A tragedy of outrageous proportions!"

Fannie laughed in spite of herself. "All right, all right. Granted, cobwebs aren't the end of the world. But they are a symbol of the general decline of all things Rousseau." She recounted going through the pile of mail on Papa's desk. "I looked up some of those shipping and business terms in the dictionary."

"And?"

Fannie shrugged. "Problems. Serious

ones. The thing is, knowing what the words mean doesn't solve anything. I need to know what to *do*." She rushed ahead before Minette could speak. "And before you say, 'That's why you have Mr. Vandekamp,' I should tell you Mr. Vandekamp has been hinting at all of this for a while now. I just haven't been paying attention, mostly because of the solution he's suggesting."

"Which is?"

"A certain eligible bachelor with the initials P.H."

Minette frowned, then her arched eyebrows shot up. "You wouldn't! You can't!"

"I won't." Fannie sighed. "But all I seem to know lately is what I *don't* want. I haven't any idea what I do." She glanced at Minette. "Why can't I be more like you? You and Daniel have your future all planned out. I can't seem to see past peeling paint and dirty windows. Mother never really pressured me about anything. She definitely didn't encourage ambition. Then Papa died and we just . . . I don't know. We just existed together, I guess. I couldn't imagine leaving her alone, and then after her accident . . . and now . . .

"I haven't a beau, I'd probably be a terrible teacher, and I hate to sew. But I have to do something, Minette. I can't just . . .

exist in that house. That's what I've been doing for months now. Resisting Mr. Vandekamp's advice and wandering through the days like some listless character in one of the novels I've been reading." She paused. "It's like I've lost myself."

Minette was quiet for a moment. Finally, she smoothed her dimity skirt and said, "Why don't you begin by asking Daniel or Papa to look into the business matters for you? I know Daniel's just begun his career, but Papa says everyone agrees he has a very promising future, and while Mr. Vandekamp may not be inclined to want to discuss business with you, he'd have to take a man seriously." Minette's voice warmed with pride as she said, "Daniel negotiated excellent terms for Papa's next shipment to Montana Territory on the *Delores*. With Otto Busch. And you know that man's reputation."

Fannie knew. Stories about Otto Busch had rippled all along the river and up from the St. Charles landing and into the dining room of every family involved in any business that relied on the treacherous waters of the Missouri River.

Otto Busch had once hired two men to chase down roustabouts who'd abandoned ship midvoyage in protest against harsh treatment. Busch had them hauled back on board and — Well, Fannie had never been allowed to know the rest of that story. But she knew the men finished the trip. Sparring and winning against Otto Busch said a lot about Daniel's business acumen. It could, however, also mean that Mr. Vandekamp would see Daniel as competition for the Rousseau Line accounts. Which would make him angry. Imagining herself the object of Mr. Vandekamp's anger made Fannie hesitate. "I wouldn't want to impose on Daniel."

"Meaning you're afraid."

"I am *not* afraid of Hubert Vandekamp. Exactly." Fannie's voice wavered. "I'm just . . . confused."

Minette stopped the swing with her foot and reached for Fannie's hand. "Who wouldn't be confused with everything that's happened to you lately." She put her hand on Fannie's arm.

"But you're smart. And you're going to be all right, Fannie. Truly. You'll see."

"It's easy to seem smart when the biggest decision you have to make is the color of your next ball gown." Fannie swallowed. "Sometimes I feel like I'm groping about inside a dark cloud. I know that sounds dramatic, but sitting at Papa's desk this afternoon and making the list of things I need to attend to —" She broke off.

Minette squeezed her hand. "Maybe Mr. Vandekamp has been trying to be thoughtful. Maybe he didn't want you having to deal with painters and gardeners and a bustle of activity around the house until you had time to come to terms with your loss."

Fannie resisted the idea of sour-faced Hubert Vandekamp being thoughtful. Still, he'd known Papa and Mother since before Fannie was born. "I suppose I should at least give him a chance to explain what's been happening before I call in reinforcements. Thank you, though, for offering Daniel."

"I'd do anything for you, Fannie. You know that. I owe you . . . so much. You gave me back my life. I'll never be able to repay you."

"Don't be absurd." Fannie shook her head. "The Missouri School for the Blind gave your life back, not me. It was obvious you were going to be all right from the first time you came home on holiday from that place."

"Not true," Minette insisted. "I was confused and afraid. But you stood by me. In fact, you were the *only* one of my friends who didn't toss me aside like a broken doll."

"You were the only one of *my* friends who

liked making mud pies," Fannie teased.

"You've forgotten Polly Bannister."

"But Polly wouldn't *taste* them." Fannie laughed. "And you even pretended to like them."

Fannie set the swing in motion again. "What's it like, Minette?" she asked after a few minutes.

"What's what like?"

Fannie nudged her friend's shoulder. "Love."

Minette didn't answer for a moment. Finally, she said, "It's like hearing an echo. As if I've been calling for something for all of my life without realizing it . . . and at last someone answered back. And what he said filled part of me I didn't even know was empty."

A flash of jealousy rose up. Minette had never wondered about being loved. Her parents doted on her. And now she had Daniel and a promising future. *Envy is a sin. And you love Minette. You know you're happy for her.* Feeling guilty, Fannie forced a laugh. "Well, no matter what Mr. Vandekamp says, I don't think Percy Harvey is my echo." She giggled. "Unless I want someone to echo my choices in fashion and lace. And perfume."

Minette pretended to fan herself. "He

does sometimes need corrective scent."

Just at that moment Jake came fully awake and in one quick move was on his feet, head erect, tail wagging. With Daniel's name on her lips, Minette jumped to her feet.

Fannie glanced at the street. "You cannot possibly have seen Jake get up. So how can you know —" Daniel strode into view. "How — ?"

"Didn't you hear him whistle?"

"Whistle? He *whistles* for you?"

Minette nodded, even as she reached up to smooth her hair. "He whistles *for* me," she said. "That's different from what you just said. One tune tells me we're alone. Another signals we aren't."

Fannie didn't require further explanation for the musical code between the two, for just then Daniel called out a hearty greeting — to Jake. Fannie watched as Minette turned her head toward her fiancé, hesitated for a moment as if thinking very hard, and then, without hesitation, ran into Daniel's arms.

Fannie smiled even as she felt a pang of longing as she saw the joy on Daniel Hennessey's face as he gathered Minette up and swung her about. A whistled summons wasn't necessarily a bad thing. More like an echo, really.

CHAPTER THREE

The robbery of the wicked shall destroy
them.

PROVERBS 21:7

When Daniel Hennessey suggested he and
Minette walk Fannie home after a fashion-
ably late supper and lingering conversation
at the Beauvais residence, Fannie resisted.
"There's a full moon and I'm only next
door. Minette and I could navigate the way
between our two houses blindfolded." But
then Minette leaned close and whispered
an intense plea. Feeling like a dunce, Fannie
quickly changed her mind and took Daniel's proffered arm so that he could guide
her across the lawn she truly could navigate
blindfolded — after all, Minette had made
her do exactly that after losing her sight.

As she bid the couple good-night and they
headed back toward the overgrown archway
separating the Rousseau and Beauvais

lawns, Fannie lingered, watching them. Just as they reached the archway, Daniel laid his open palm at the small of Minette's back. At her fiancé's touch, Minette reached for his hand and pulled it to her waist so that his arm encircled her. When they stepped into the shadows just past the archway, they paused. Long enough for . . . Long enough.

That's it. That's what I want. She wanted the kind of love Minette had described earlier that evening . . . the kind that made one heart echo back to another. The kind that would carry a woman into a future she couldn't see with a sense of hopeful joy. Fannie pulled the door closed and stood in the dark hall, listening to the quiet house. She was feeling a little better, thanks to Minette, her parents . . . and Daniel Hennessey.

First, after discussing the matter over supper, Mrs. Beauvais had agreed that Walker would welcome help with the grounds. Mr. Beauvais and Daniel had both said they would help Fannie prepare for a business meeting with Mr. Vandekamp. They even offered to go with her if she needed them, although Mr. Beauvais didn't seem to think she did.

"You'll do fine," he said, winking at his wife as he said, "in fact, Mrs. Beauvais and

I have said more than once that you're much too smart for your own good." He teased Fannie about all the trouble she'd masterminded when she and Minette were young.

Best of all, when Fannie mentioned Percy Harvey as Mr. Vandekamp's idea of "a suitable match," both of Minette's parents sang out "Nonsense," in a duet that warmed her heart.

Now, as she headed upstairs, Fannie could smile. Maybe the Beauvaises were right. Maybe she could navigate the muddy future successfully. Opening the door to her room, she swept inside, lit a table lamp, and posed before her dressing mirror, elbows bent, hands folded loosely before her. *That's it. You look relaxed but firm. Like a lady.*

She spoke to her own reflection, practicing what she would say to Walker. "No one raises more glorious roses than you. It only makes sense for you to be training someone new. Mother would want you to have help." With a nod, she turned away from the dressing mirror, then looked back over her shoulder at her reflection. If only she could manage to look and sound this confident when she met with Mr. Vandekamp.

She'd just unbuttoned her waist and pulled it out of her skirt when a thud sounded downstairs. *What on earth is Hannah doing up at this hour?* It was nearly midnight. With a tug and a gasp, she unfastened the skirt, stepped out of it, and draped it over the dressing mirror. Next came two petticoats, her waist, and the corset cover. Finally, she could unhook her corset — and take the first deep breath of the day.

Another clunk downstairs made her jump. Hurrying to undo the rest of the corset hooks, she laid it aside and pulled her nightgown over her chemise and drawers, then lit the bedside lamp. She hesitated at her bedroom door, listening carefully. Finally, lamp in hand, she tiptoed down the hall toward the back of the house and the steep narrow stairway connecting kitchen to back hall and back hall to the third floor servants' rooms.

Another thump. This time Fannie wasn't certain if it came from downstairs or if it had just echoed from the front of the house. Glancing behind her, she continued down the back stairs, calling softly, "Hannah? Hannah, whatever are you doing down —" The next word died in her throat as she reached the bottom stair.

The side door was standing open. Moonlight streamed in, casting shadows — ominous shadows. She took a step backward. Up one stair. Her heart hammering in her chest, she paused. *The wind. You didn't close it all the way and the wind blew it open.* But it was a calm, moonlit night, and the side door was a heavily carved affair boasting leaded glass and intricate brass hardware. It would take a mighty wind to blow it open.

Extinguishing her lamp, Fannie stood in the darkened stairway, afraid to move, nearly afraid to breathe. Listening. Somewhere in the night a cat yowled. Sweat broke out on her forehead. Perspiration trickled down her back. She reached out with her free hand to steady herself even as she glanced toward the hall ceiling. Was Hannah up there asleep? Terror shivered up her spine. She bit her lip and then — someone stepped onto the stair behind her. Put a hand on her shoulder. Fannie opened her mouth to scream . . . but no sound came out.

By the end of his first day as a roustabout, Samuel Beck had learned more than he had ever wanted to know about freight, the hold of the steamboat *Delores,* and Otto Busch. Nothing affecting his boat escaped Busch's practiced eye, and to him, an empty inch in the hold or an extra minute on the levee meant lost revenue.

"If you still want to be on board when we pull away," Lamar said at one point, nodding at the crates Samuel had stacked into the hold, "you'd better get that straightened up and tucked in." Davis showed him how to move things around so that an extra grain sack fit into the space Samuel had called full.

It didn't take a practiced eye to realize the captains on the waterfront were rivals in just about every aspect of steamboating. The *Delores* couldn't win when it came to size, but Busch made it clear as he bellowed orders throughout the day that he expected to win the race to be underway. Late in the day, when two other steamers pulled away ahead of them, Busch called one of the mates up to the wheelhouse and gave him a talking-to heard by every single one of the crew. After that, no one told a joke or said a word lest the mate accuse them of lollygagging.

The captain's cheeks burned with resentment when the *Sam Cloon* pulled out, its decks crowded with uniformed soldiers hooting and hollering insults at the *Delores* as their steamer chuffed into the Mississippi's deep channel and headed north toward the mouth of the Missouri.

45

The last crate had barely been settled on the *Delores*'s deck when Busch was backing her into the middle of the wide river, yelling, "Fill her fireboxes, I want more steam!" He gave chase after the *Sam Cloon,* but when they reached the Missouri and it was nearly dark, Busch nosed the vessel up against a wharf for the night. When Samuel wondered why they didn't keep going, Lamar gave him a lesson on the ways of the river known as Old Misery.

"Compared to the Mississippi, it's little more than flowing mud, son. Studded with dead tree trunks and broken up by sandbars. Just when a captain thinks he knows her, she cuts a new channel, throws up a new sandbar, drags a few more trees down into the water, and there's a whole new river." Lamar pointed up toward the wheelhouse. "He's the best there is at reading the water, but you've got to *see* it to read it. He won't risk the *Delores* just to catch the *Sam Cloon.* At least not yet. There's plenty of river ahead of us and plenty of time for proving who's fastest."

As night gathered, some of the men produced fishing poles and cast lines into the murky water hoping to snag a catfish. Others struck up card games. Most slept. One group gathered around a southern boy and

46

listened while he played his mouth harp. Samuel took a lamp and settled near the wagon he intended to sleep beneath. Bracing his back against one of the wheels, he dug his mother's Bible out of his carpetbag and set to reading. It had been days since he'd opened the book, and as he followed the fine print with his finger, he felt pangs of guilt about his failure. Ma had found something on these pages that seemed to be almost as vital to her as a cool drink on a hot day. Samuel needed to find what it was.

Lamar found him reading. "You got yourself a good book there, son."

Samuel shrugged. "Can't seem to make much of it. Just a bunch of *begats* on this page. Can't figure why they'd put that in."

Lamar smiled. "Can't say as I know. But I will say it'd be somethin' to know your line all the way back to the very first man." He nodded at the open space beside Samuel. "Mind if I join you?"

Samuel moved over and Lamar sat down beside him, his back against the other half of the wheel, the hub between them. Once he'd settled, Lamar said, "You know all the bee-gats in your family line?"

Samuel thought for a moment. "My pa used to expound on how his father was with General Jackson in the Battle of New Orleans and so on. If he wasn't lying, I guess we go all the way back to the Declaration of Independence. Pa always claimed one of our blood relatives even signed it. Can't remember his name, though."

"Hoo-ee," Lamar said, shaking his head, "now that's impressive."

"What about your begats?"

"Now, son, you know how it is with us. I was born in Tennessee at a place called Belle Meade. Don't know who my papa was. Mama's name was Grace. She worked in the kitchen. I don't recall it real well, except I know something bad happened when I was barely old enough to talk. All I remember is screaming. I'm thinking she got burned. Anyway, after she died, an old groom name of Henry found me crying in the stable one day. I grew up helping him and trying not to get kicked or stepped on. Mostly I succeeded. Soon as the Federals arrived in Nashville, I took the opportunity to offer my services to a General Scofield. That's where I met a young officer name of Otto Busch. Dragged him off a battlefield and to a surgeon and been trailing him ever since."

Samuel turned to look at Lamar. "You saved Captain Busch's life?"

The old man shrugged. "He seems to think so." He chuckled. "If he didn't think that, I'd have been kicked off the *Delores* a long while ago."

Samuel closed the Bible, leaned back, and closed his eyes just as thunder rolled in and the skies opened. A couple of the horses tethered nearby seemed nervous. Lamar got up to calm them, and Samuel followed suit. As the two men stroked the animals' broad necks and spoke to them, water poured off the upper deck in a torrent that made Samuel feel like he was on the back side of a waterfall. Then, just as quickly as it had begun, the storm ceased. The animals whickered softly, and if he didn't know better, Samuel would have thought they sounded relieved. When he said as much, Lamar chuckled. Someone opened a door above them on the hurricane deck. Feminine laughter spilling into the night made Samuel think of Emma.

A freighter Samuel had questioned on the levee early that morning remembered seeing her. "Red hair, pale green eyes, you say?" He spat a stream of tobacco juice onto the cobblestones. "Saw her with Major Chadwick. They boarded a steamer bound for Fort Rice just a few days ago." The freighter squinted up at Samuel. "Too bad about that scar."

It had to be Emma. Just thinking about it

made Samuel reach up to touch his cheek. He would have to get off at every stop along the way north. Emma had famously dark moods because of that scar. If Major Chadwick decided she was more than he could handle — The idea of Emma's being abandoned at some woodlot or village between St. Louis and Fort Rice was enough to keep Samuel awake half the night.

"Let me by, little miss."

Relief at the sound of Hannah's voice made Fannie weak in the knees. She turned, pressing her back to the wall so she could look up. How had Hannah made it all the way down the stairs so quietly? The old woman slid past her and, as moonlight illuminated her profile, Fannie saw Hannah raise her left hand and brandish a — curtain rod?!

She grabbed Hannah's arm. "We should just slip out the door," she whispered, and bent down to set her small lamp on a stair. Apparently that was what Hannah had had in mind all along, for without a word, she reached for Fannie's hand, and together, the two women padded outside. Fannie longed to run, but she couldn't leave Hannah behind. "Give me that," she said, and reached for the curtain rod.

Hannah resisted. "No offense, little miss, but if we're to face a criminal, I'd trust my own right arm before yours."

Hannah was right. Fannie couldn't imagine doing violence to anyone. From the look on Hannah's face, the older woman would be disappointed if she *didn't* get the opportunity to swing at someone. Grateful for her bravado, Fannie followed her across the side yard toward the archway that led into the Beauvaises' garden. The further they got from the house, the more ridiculous Fannie felt. "We're going to feel like fools when it's discovered that the wind blew that side door open."

Hannah didn't seem to hear her at first, but when they'd gone under the archway, she paused behind the tangle of vines and peered back toward the house. Fannie followed her gaze. A cat strolled up the brick lane from the street. Making its way up the stairs toward the door, it paused, nose in the air, one front paw lifted.

When something wet assaulted the palm of her hand, Fannie gasped, then realized that Jake had come to say hello. She laid an open palm atop his head, then snatched it away when a low rumble emerged from deep in the dog's throat. *Poor old thing. He's grown grouchy in his old age.*

Fannie had just opened her mouth to speak to the dog when the rumble became a full-fledged growl. Jake focused on the Rousseau house and then, in a furious charge that belied his age, launched himself through the gate and toward the shadows from which emerged a human form, crouched low, coming out of the Rousseaus' side door and slinking toward the narrow alley behind the house. Assaulted by an eighty-pound ball of fury, the burglar went down with a shriek. At the sound of a window opening above her, Fannie looked up just in time to see Minette's father appear and then quickly disappear from view.

Hannah charged back through the gate, curtain rod at the ready, shouting, "You'd better stay put!"

Fannie stood rooted to the spot, her fingertips pressed to her mouth, even as Mr. Beauvais rushed past her shouting for Jake to leave off. The dog obeyed but backed away only a few feet, head erect, teeth bared. Mr. Beauvais brandished a pistol as he ordered the criminal to get up — slowly. Fannie's knees went weak. She swallowed bile.

Mr. Beauvais called her name. "Fannie? Are you there?"

She nodded.

"Fannie?"

"Y-yes," she croaked. "I'm here. By the garden gate."

"Would you be so kind as to rouse James and tell him I require his assistance? I'd ask Mrs. Pike to go, but, frankly, I rather like the idea of her and that curtain rod at my side."

Fannie relaxed enough to move. Managing a reply, she scurried across the lawn toward the carriage house and up the outside stairs to the doorway to James's quarters before realizing she was definitely underdressed to be summoning the Beauvais family's coachman. She pounded on the door even as she felt a blush creep up her neck. Thankfully, James couldn't see her blazing cheeks as she blurted out what had happened and delivered Mr. Beauvais's summons.

"Right away, miss," James said and closed the door.

Fannie had barely gotten halfway back down the flight of stairs before he swept past her at a run, tucking in his shirt as he crossed the lawn. She was at the bottom stair when a combination of terror and relief swept over her and finally conquered her will to remain standing. Leaning against the brick wall of the carriage house, she slid down it, mindful of the sound of her sleeve ripping as she collapsed.

CHAPTER FOUR

Shall not God search this out? for he
knoweth the secrets of the heart.
                                PSALM 44:21

"There, now, little miss. It's all right now.
You're safe. All's well that ends well."

At the sound of Hannah's soothing voice,
Fannie opened her eyes. Blinked. When she
raised a hand to her forehead, someone took
it. Fannie turned her head. *Minette.* She
looked about. Someone had apparently carried her into the Beauvais parlor. When she
glanced down and saw deep green uphol-
stery, she realized she was reclining on Mrs.
Beauvais's fainting couch. *How appropriate.*
Embarrassed, she moved to sit up. Glancing
across at Hannah, she asked, "Are you all
right?"

Hannah's face crinkled up in a smile. "Fit
as a fiddle and enjoying a moment of short-
lived fame." She chuckled. "Along with

Jake, that is." She nodded at the dog curled up at her feet. "It seems that an old dog and an old woman *can* learn new tricks, after all. Who would have thought the two of us could foil a jewel thief the authorities over in St. Louis have been after for weeks."

Fannie frowned. Jewel thief? Her hand went to her throat.

Minette squeezed her hand. "Calm down. Hannah, Jake, and James held him at bay while Papa went for help. And your mother's amethysts are none the worse for having been stuffed into his pocket," Minette added. "Papa has them."

"Here, my dear." Mrs. Beauvais approached and set a tea tray on the table beside the divan. When Hannah moved to get up and serve, Mrs. Beauvais waved her away. "It seems to me you've earned a moment to sit and have a cup of tea yourself, Mrs. Pike." She chuckled even as she shook her head. "Why, I wouldn't be surprised if Mr. Donovan titled his news article 'Notorious Jewel Thief Captured by Curtain Rod.' " She poured a cup of tea and offered it to Hannah.

For the first time, Fannie realized that both she and Hannah were still dressed in their nightclothes. Hastily offered shawls notwithstanding, Fannie felt her cheeks

56

blaze anew. Minette lifted her own teacup in a toast. "You're going to be famous."

"For what? Fainting? If anyone deserves fame it's Hannah." She nodded at the dog. "And Jake." When the old dog lifted his head and thudded the floor with his tail, Fannie spoke to him. "What would it take to get you to stand guard next door every night?" The dog tilted his head as if pondering the question. "I'd pay you in beefsteaks."

Mr. Beauvais strode into the room. "You don't need a guard," he said. "St. Charles is far from being a haven for the criminal elements. The thief seemed truly terrified. In fact, he expressed concern for your well-being when we all realized you'd fainted. Had he known the house was inhabited, he probably wouldn't have stepped inside."

He thought the house was uninhabited? It looks that bad? Fannie looked over at Hannah. "How *did* you get down those stairs so quietly?"

"I don't rightly know," Hannah said as she settled her cup and saucer back on Mrs. Beauvais's silver serving tray. "I suppose the Lord undertook the problem of my knees."

"Yes. Well." Fannie took a deep breath. "I'm thankful the Lord undertook the problem, and I'm going to undertake the problem, as well. We are going to get you a new room. On the *main* floor. No more stairs."

Mr. Beauvais took a small pouch out of his waistcoat pocket, nodding as he handed it over. "Monetary value aside, I imagine these are far too precious for you to contemplate losing them. I'd suggest you gather up your mother's jewels and ask Mr. Vandekamp to keep them in his safe." He cleared his throat. "You'd do well to do the same with any cash that might still be in the house."

Fannie nodded. With trembling fingers, she untied the ribbon and opened the pouch. With more confidence than she felt, she said, "Thank you. I guess it's time I grew into the life I've been handed." *Whatever that means.* She paused. "I'll gather Mother's jewelry first thing in the morning. And Papa's cashbox."

"Let me know when you're ready to make the transfer and I'll drive you to the bank," Mr. Beauvais said. "And now, if you ladies will excuse me, James and I are to meet the sheriff to assist with a thorough search of your house, including the attic. I'll come back 'round after we've finished." He hesitated. "Unless you ladies would rather stay here for the night, in which case I'll just lock the house and bring you the key."

Fannie longed to once again be a girl sleeping beneath the roof of a home with a father and mother in charge. But she shook her head. "Thank you, but no. We'll go back as soon as you've checked things." She did her best to sound brave.

Fannie woke with a start. Sunlight poured through her bedroom windows. What time was it? She'd only managed to fall asleep after bracing her dressing table chair beneath the doorknob. Even then, she'd slept fitfully, newly aware of every sound, imagined or real. Had the house always been so noisy at night?

Tossing aside her yellow silk duvet, she slid out of bed. She had a full day ahead of her. First, she and Hannah would clear out that storeroom off the butler's pantry and get Hannah moved down from the third floor. Mrs. Beauvais was sending Tommy Cooper over around noon to talk about his helping Walker with the grounds. And then . . . then she'd get Papa's cashbox down from its hiding place . . . and, finally, tomorrow morning . . . she'd go to Mr. Vandekamp. But only after Mother's room. She wasn't certain what she dreaded facing most, Mr. Vandekamp or the memories in Mother's room.

Her black silk skirt was still where she'd left it draped over her dressing mirror in the night. Taking it down, she laid it across the bed, pausing to study herself in the mirror again. *You're all grown up now.* Stepping out of her nightgown, she pulled on a chemise, hesitating when it came time for the corset. It was going to be a workday. She needed to breathe. She would forego a corset today.

Going to the wardrobe on the opposite wall, she pulled out a lavender calico day dress. She supposed it was shocking to depart from full mourning when Mother had only been gone a few weeks, but it was only while she and Hannah cleaned out a storeroom. No one important would even see her. That wasn't disrespectful. It was sensible.

She began to hum as she buttoned the row of jet buttons marching up the front of the dress and tucked her blond hair into a snood. She pulled the chair away from the door. Returning it to the dressing table, she saw the jewelry pouch and opened it. Mother's amethyst earrings sparkled in the morning light. Fannie put them on, turning her head from side to side and admiring herself in the mirror.

Unbuttoning her dress, she tucked the facings back to create a décolletage and donned the necklace. Reaching up to feel the texture of the large faceted stone in the center, she envisioned the periwinkle blue ball gown Mother always wore with her amethysts. How she'd longed for gowns like that. Mother had unbending and hopelessly outdated ideas about what a "young lady of high moral character" should and should not wear. At times, Fannie had despaired of ever getting to wear beautiful gowns like Minette's.

She studied herself in the mirror. As soon as she put off mourning, she'd be able to wear what she wanted. She touched the cool stone at her throat. Was it disloyal to look forward to yards of ruffles and imported lace . . . to blush at the idea of using a parasol or fan to flirt? Was it wrong to lament all the black and gray, mauve and purple in the months ahead?

She turned away from the mirror, removed the jewels, and buttoned back up. The dark cloud threatened again. Maybe if she hurried downstairs she could outrun it.

Hannah had been up just long enough to cook oatmeal, and as the two women ate breakfast, Fannie teased her about defending them with a curtain rod even as she made fun of herself for fainting. Together, she and Hannah planned the new room off the kitchen.

"I'll ask James to bring some things down from the attic this morning," Fannie said. "I remember a rag rug that might look cheerful on the floor. Minette and I used to stage our attic tea parties on it. And there's a comforter Mother had sent over from France. I think I remember matching draperies that just might fit your new window."

Hannah got up to wash the dishes. "There's no need to bring anything down from the attic. Nothing's wrong with my things. Your mother wouldn't approve of me putting on airs with fancy draperies and carpets and such."

"I know for a fact that Dr. Eames believes cold air makes joints hurt worse. He told Mother that more than once. It only stands to reason that whatever we can do to keep you warm will only make you a better housekeeper, and Mother would most certainly approve of that."

Fannie cleared her throat. "I don't know what I'd do without you, Hannah. I *need* you here. And I want to make your room comfortable so that —" she forced a grin — "so that I can torment you for many years to come." She nudged Hannah's arm. "How old are you, anyway? A hundred and twenty?"

Hannah nudged back. "I'll have you know I'm not a day over seventy-five." She lifted her chin. "I swaddled you when you came into this world, and I plan to swaddle your firstborn, little miss."

"Good." Fannie nodded. "Until you're needed to swaddle my firstborn, I think you should have a thick comforter swaddling your stiff old knees."

Waving her hand in the air, Hannah relented. "Fine. Have it your way. But make sure James does the transporting. I'll not have you breaking your neck tripping over something on those narrow stairs."

"I'll head up there right now and get the comforter I was thinking of before Walker arrives to talk gardening. I can manage that, but I'll let James do the rest." Hurrying up to her own room, Fannie pulled a leaf of paper, a pen, and a bottle of ink from her writing desk. She would make a list of things for James to bring down and take the comforter out back to air. Until Walker and Tommy Cooper arrived, she and Hannah could work together, emptying the room off the kitchen of drying racks and brooms, mops and cast-off dinnerware.

As she lifted her skirts and made her way up the attic stairs, Fannie realized she had successfully outrun that dark cloud, at least for a little while. She felt hopeful. Almost happy. It felt *good* to take charge. Especially when taking charge was going to make things better for Hannah.

Later that afternoon, an exhausted Fannie paused at the bottom of the front stairs before ascending to face Mother's room. Tilting her head, she listened carefully. Was Hannah humming in her new room . . . or snoring? They were both tired, but it had been a good day. Hannah's new room had turned out even nicer than Fannie had envisioned. She'd hired Tommy Cooper to help Walker rescue the grounds, and just as both Hannah and Mrs. Beauvais had said, Walker appeared to be relieved at the idea of having help. As Fannie slowly climbed the stairs, sunlight shining through the leaded window on the landing studded the wall with rainbows of light. Her stomach growled. She hoped Hannah didn't nap for long.

She hesitated in the doorway to Mother's room, peering into the shadowed space like an intruder sneaking into forbidden territory. This room had always been off limits, unless Mother expressly invited Fannie in. Even the carriage accident hadn't changed that rule. Mother kept a little bell at her bedside. She would call if she needed anything. Later, when she grew weaker, she hired a nurse. Again, the message was clear. *Stay away unless invited.*

Stepping inside the doorway, Fannie took a deep breath. Mother always wore a sachet tucked into her pocket or sleeve. Was it her imagination, or did the faintest aroma of roses still linger in the air?

Clearing her throat, she padded across the room and opened the drapes, then stood watching as the afternoon sun bathed the room in light. The decor was hopelessly outdated, but Mother didn't care. She loved her periwinkle blue floral wallpaper and the pale blue chairs beside the tea table. Fannie could still hear Mother's sniff and her studied reply to Fannie's enthusiastic endorsement when Minette's mother redecorated their home in the most fashionable of reds and greens.

A woman has very few rights in this world, Fannie. The right to surround herself with the things she loves — especially in her own private quarters — is one of them. If I have anything to say about it, this room will be this very same color the day I die.

Remembering those words gave Fannie goose bumps. Rubbing her arms briskly, she headed for the dressing table. As a child, she'd thought it the most enchanting piece of furniture in the world, with its beveled mirrors framed with gilt carved wood, its painted china drawer pulls, its array of cut-glass bottles and silver-rimmed jars.

Perching on the striped cushioned seat, she looked into the mirror, then down at the daguerreotype of Papa that lay to one side. He looked young and brave in his blue uniform. Fannie looked around, taking stock of the exquisite oil paintings hanging from velvet ribbons. Papa's image was the only one in the room.

Lifting the faceted glass stopper out of one of the bottles, she inhaled, the aroma bathing her in a surprising amount of sorrow and longing. She replaced the stopper and gazed about the room again. Why did Mother like these colors so much? Why did Fannie never feel . . . relaxed in this place?

With a sigh, she opened the center drawer. Calling cards . . . a button hook . . . a ladies' mending kit . . . a small basket of buttons . . . a bit of silk ribbon . . . and, tucked in the far back corner, a ring box. Opening it, Fannie gasped with surprise at the size of the amethyst stone surrounded by tiny diamonds. She slipped it on her ring finger and, extending her hand, watched as light danced across the surface of the jewels. She couldn't remember Mother ever wearing it, and yet it was a perfect match to the earrings and necklace the thief had tried to steal.

The rest of Mother's best jewelry was kept in the compartments of a box in the lower right-hand drawer. Fannie lifted it out and opened it, taking note of the empty top compartment. Odd, that the thief had put the jewelry box back in the drawer. *Odd, but smart.* If she hadn't come home and startled him into hurrying, if Hannah hadn't heard him, this room might have remained undisturbed until Fannie married or decided to sell the house. The missing amethysts could have gone unnoticed for years.

Relief coursed through her when she lifted out the empty tray and saw the garnet necklace and earbobs right where they belonged. The intruder must have heard Hannah coming down the back stairs and decided to be happy with what he already had in his pocket. Mother's cameo brooch lay nestled in its compartment, as did the pearl bracelet with the porcelain disk boasting a hand-painted scene that Mother said was somewhere in France. Fannie couldn't remember where. Mother had promised to tell her a story about that bracelet someday. *I wonder if Hannah knows it.*

Finally, she took up her mother's locket. Opening it and expecting to see Papa's image again, she blinked back unexpected tears as she stared down at the image of herself, dressed in the elaborate christening gown she knew to be stored away in the attic along with her dolls and the china tea set Papa had brought from Paris. Knowing Mother kept a photo of her as a baby somehow eased the hurt over Papa's being the only one visible in the room.

She closed the locket, but the latch didn't quite catch. As she fiddled with it, a second compartment opened and a small key fell out. She wondered at the wisdom of keeping the jewelry box key inside the jewelry box. As she reached over to try the key in the lock, the amethyst ring slid from her finger. It hit the carpet with barely a sound but must have bounced, for Fannie heard the clatter of metal on wood as the ring encountered the floorboards along the wall. With a sigh, she got down on her knees to duck beneath the dressing table. Retrieving the ring, she slipped it back on her finger, grimacing when she bumped her head against a bottom corner of the dressing table.

Frustrated, she stood up and reached for both ring and jewelry boxes, intending to take them to her own room, where she could return the stolen amethysts to their compartment. She paused. If Mother kept a valuable ring stowed away in an odd place, she'd better be thorough.

Sitting back down, Fannie opened another drawer. This one held an assortment of elegant handkerchiefs . . . and a dark brown, almost black envelope made of some kind of leather. A small lock held the flap firmly closed. Glancing toward the hall, Fannie hesitated. Silly as she knew it was, she felt guilty. As if Mother would appear in the doorway at any moment. With a little frown, she retrieved the key from the locket. Her hands trembled as she inserted it into the lock. It didn't work. She tried again. Finally, with a faint *scritch-scratch,* the lock gave way.

Had the intruder's heart beat like this as he opened these very drawers? Had his forehead grown damp when he heard footsteps in the hall? Surely he'd heard Hannah coming down from the attic. Why else would he have left without the rest of Mother's jewelry? The idea that a stranger had lingered in this very spot while she went past on her way downstairs made Fannie tremble with new terror.

With a last glance toward the hall, she

opened the envelope and pulled out a stack of papers wrapped in a yellow ribbon. Atop the papers lay a cabinet portrait of Mother, dressed in a stunning evening gown. Fannie recognized the amethyst necklace, but nothing else about the portrait made any sense at all. The form-fitting sweep of the gown, the dangerously low décolletage, the bare arms, the tiara-studded coiffure. And the pose. She was flirting with that painted fan. *Flirting.* This was not the woman Fannie knew. She turned the portrait over. Someone had written a name on the back. *Edie.* When had Mother ever been called Edie?

Setting the portrait aside, Fannie untied the ribbon. *Letters* — each one addressed to Mrs. Eleanor Rousseau. With another glance around the room, Fannie opened the envelope, removed the letter, and read.

Dearest Eleanor,

I know you long ago stopped hoping to hear news from me in which you could honestly rejoice, and I do understand how that would be. I understand, as well, how it is that you haven't seen fit to answer my correspondence these past years. And yet, while you do your best to forget me, I remain stubborn as always. Be angry if you must, but know that I cannot let any of you go. As far as I have traveled, part of my heart has always remained in St. Charles. With you all.

There is news. Good news. Can you imagine? I, who have bowed before kings and known the favor of princes, am about to embark upon a journey into the Montana wilderness aboard the Bertrand. I believe you know it. I am told that the captain, Otto Busch, has quite the reputation. I have also been warned that he will try to refuse passage to a lady traveling alone. Of course the Otto Busches of this world have never stopped me from getting my way, and that will never change.

If God smiles on me, dear Eleanor, I will soon be in a position to show my devotion to you all. Do not fear. I know that any chance I had to repay you in person is gone forever. With all there is to regret, it is good to know at least one man in St. Charles upon whom a lady can rely. Hubert will inform you when the promise of gold has been fulfilled. While I am far from his favorite person, I still trust him to act in your best interest. He will be the conduit through whom I prove my devotion. Until then, I send greetings to Louis and Fannie.

Likely, you won't forward those greetings. And yet . . . I hope.

Ever your sister, Edith

Dumbfounded, Fannie sat immobile, staring down at the signature. Mother had a sister. A *twin* sister who knew Papa . . . who knew she had a niece named Fannie . . . and who also seemed to know that Fannie had never heard of her. Aunt Edith had journeyed on the very steamboat whose sinking was mentioned in that pile of papers downstairs on Papa's desk. Papa had been heavily invested in the *Bertrand*'s cargo when it sank back in '65. Had Otto Busch been the captain when the *Bertrand* sank? Had he met Aunt Edith? With a little frown, Fannie looked toward the doorway. What did Hannah know about any of this? She glanced down at the letter in her hand. And was the *Hubert* Aunt Edith wrote about Hubert Vandekamp? She couldn't think of another Hubert among their acquaintances here in St. Charles.

Taking up the bundle of letters, Fannie went to the window seat facing the river. Her hands shaking, she slipped another of Aunt Edith's letters from beneath the yellow silk ribbon.

CHAPTER FIVE

It is required in stewards, that a man be
found faithful.

1 CORINTHIANS 4:2

"*Land sakes,* child, didn't you hear me calling?" Hannah hesitated at the door to
Mother's room.

Fannie looked up from the letter she'd
been reading. "I found . . . these." She
pointed to the pile of letters next to her.
She held her hand up to show Hannah the
amethyst ring. "And this." Why did Hannah's silence make her feel like a naughty
child caught misbehaving? "I wasn't snooping. I had to check all the drawers to make
sure I had everything."

Hannah crossed the room and, sitting
down next to her, took Fannie's hand and
peered down at the ring. "I never saw her
wear this."

"It matches her necklace and earrings. I

found it in a separate box tucked toward the back of the middle drawer."

Hannah pointed at the jewelry box sitting atop the dressing table across the room. "Was everything else still there?"

"As far as I can tell." Fannie picked up the leather envelope. "This was beneath Mother's handkerchiefs. Filled with letters. And this."

Hannah took the cabinet portrait Fannie held out. "My, my," she murmured. "Your mother was a stunning woman." She shook her head. "I never knew her to dress so . . . stylish."

"Turn it over," Fannie said. "See the name? It isn't Mother." She grabbed the stack of letters. "These are all from the woman in the photograph. She's my aunt." She couldn't keep the accusatory tone out of her voice. "I can't imagine Mother keeping something like a twin sister from you for the better part of twenty years."

Hannah stiffened. "Well, imagine it, little miss, because I'm just as surprised as you." She handed the photo back and stood up. "I'd never stand by while you were burying your own mother and let you think you didn't have another living soul in this world to turn to." Her chin trembled. She waved a hand at the letters. "I've never seen those in

74

all the years I've worked in this house and I never heard a word breathed about anyone named Edith. Not a word."

Fannie reached for her hand. "Please, Hannah. Don't be angry with me." Her voice wavered. "Of course I believe you. It's just — I don't understand. She sounds wonderful." Hannah sat back down. "In every letter — in every single one — she mentions something breathtaking. A ball given by the queen of Spain. A gondola outing in Venice."

Fannie touched the ring. "Do you think I could keep this? I mean, wear it?"

"I don't know why not," Hannah said. "It belongs to you, now. Of course it'll have to wait until you're out of mourning." She gestured toward the jewelry box. "Best to put it in there with the rest and let Mr. Vandekamp watch over it for now."

Mr. Vandekamp. Hubert. Fannie reached for the letter and read it aloud. "Do you think Aunt Edith's *Hubert* could be Hubert Vandekamp?"

Hannah shrugged. "I suppose that would be a question for Mr. Vandekamp. And out of respect for your mother, I'd suggest that be a *private* conversation. She clearly had her reasons for not wanting anyone to know about any of this."

As Fannie gazed down at the woman named Edith, her stomach growled.

Hannah rose again and headed for the door. "Unless you want cold stew for supper, you need to lay aside all of that business and follow me downstairs."

After supper, Fannie spent the better part of the night alternating between reading Aunt Edith's letters and gazing at her photograph. As the night wore on, confusion transformed into dismay. By the time the indigo sky began to blush with pink, dismay had blossomed into full-blown resentment against the parents who'd robbed her of a chance to know such a fascinating woman. If Mr. Vandekamp was, indeed, the Hubert mentioned in Aunt Edith's last letter, he would have answers to Fannie's questions. And she intended to ask them. Today.

As soon as she heard Hannah stirring below, Fannie summoned her help with petticoats and buttonhooks, corset lacing and hairdressing. When she vented her resentment over the secrets her parents had kept, Hannah chastised, "Don't be so quick to judge, little miss. Letters only reveal what the person writing them wants us to know. I'm not speaking ill of this Edith woman.

I'm just saying that your parents must have had their reasons. All you really know is that there's a lot you don't know."

Fannie finished buttoning her black silk mourning dress as she said, "I've lost count of the number of times Mr. Vandekamp has told me I'm all alone in the world and dangled his list of 'eligible bachelors' as a cure for my 'difficult circumstances.'" She pinned a mourning brooch in place over a button. "If he's known about Edith LeClerc all along, I want to know why he didn't tell me about her. Especially since *she* seems to regret all the secrecy." She reached for the black gloves she'd torn pulling weeds. Only a practiced eye would ever see they'd been torn at all. She could always trust Hannah to take care of things like that.

Trust. She'd always trusted that Mother and Papa were doing their best, both for each other and for her. She'd assumed she could trust Mr. Vandekamp because they did. But for all her trust, her world was falling apart, one broken shutter at a time, one niggling doubt at a time, one business ledger at a time, and now . . . one revelation at a time.

Fannie's eyes had barely adjusted to the dark interior of the bank when the clerk she'd asked to announce her to Mr. Vandekamp returned. Pushing his glasses up on his nose, he squinted up at her. "I'm sorry, miss, but Mr. Vandekamp is with someone. He said to tell you he'll be available right after lunch."

Fannie stared past the clerk at Mr. Vandekamp's imposing office door. She wasn't certain her courage would last until after lunch. She needed to see him now.

The clerk mopped his brow. "I'm truly sorry, miss."

Fannie nodded. "May I leave a note?"

"Of course, miss, of course." He led Fannie to a desk. She wrote, *I have questions about Miss Edith LeClerc.* She blew on the ink to hasten its drying, then folded the note and handed it to the waiting clerk. Thanking him, she turned to go.

She'd just reached the exit when there was a stirring at the back of the bank. Someone called her name. She turned around just as a well-dressed gentleman exited Mr. Vandekamp's office. Vandekamp shook his hand even as he looked Fannie's way and beckoned her to come near.

Clutching the leather envelope containing Edith LeClerc's letters, Fannie headed back across the bank, newly mindful of the man's ability to intimidate with his set jaw, thin lips, and perpetual scowl. He didn't speak when she came near, but merely stepped aside and waved her into his office. As the door closed behind them, Fannie did her best to ignore the chill tracing its way up her spine. Crossing the room, she perched on the edge of one of the sumptuous chairs facing Mr. Vandekamp's massive desk.

Taking up his station behind his desk, Mr. Vandekamp reached for the crystal decanter positioned on a tray at his right and poured himself a glass of water. Gulping it down without a word, he set the empty glass down with a thud. Finally, he leaned back in his chair and, lacing his fingers together, said, "The name you wrote on your note intrigues me, Miss Rousseau. Am I to conclude that someone has contacted you to make a claim against your father's estate?"

Why would the very mention of Edith LeClerc's name make him so suspicious? Fannie shook her head. Explaining how she'd found the brown leather envelope, she took the cabinet portrait out and laid it between them on the desktop. "At first I thought this was Mother. But then —" she turned it over — "then I read the name on the back."

Vandekamp unlaced his fingers and leaned forward. He glanced down at the photograph. Two spots of color appeared on his cheeks.

Fannie held up a letter. "This last letter mentions a Hubert, and I wondered if that might be you. Would you like to read it?"

Mr. Vandekamp took the letter, unfolded it, and read. The edges of his mouth curved downward. "What is it that you want from me, Miss Rousseau?" He laid the letter next to the photograph. "None of this changes anything about your current situation."

Fannie frowned. She swallowed. "It changes everything. I'm not alone in the world. You haven't read all the letters yet, Mr. Vandekamp, but she speaks fondly of me. In every single one." She paused. "The last one was posted from Fort Benton, Montana, just last spring. I'd like your help finding her. Don't you think she would want to know about Mother?"

Taking a deep breath, Vandekamp poured two glasses of water. Setting one before Fannie, he took a sip from the other before saying, "Letters, however poetic, can be misleading, Miss Rousseau." He peered at her from beneath two bushy gray eyebrows. "I daresay that, had he only to write letters to win your heart, Percy Harvey would have succeeded in making you his betrothed long ago. But, as it turns out, Mr. Harvey's *let-*

ters and Mr. Harvey's *person* are very unlike each another. Wouldn't you agree?" He pointed at the most recent letter. "That is dated a year ago. Whatever it says, you can be sure that Edie is no longer in Fort Benton."

Edie. "You knew her," Fannie said, doing her best not to sound accusatory. "You *are* the Hubert she mentions in this letter."

Pink spread from the two bright spots on Mr. Vandekamp's cheekbones across his entire face. Curling his fingers toward his palms, he pulled both hands into his lap. "I did know her, and nothing good ever came of it." He looked away. "The only thing about Edith LeClerc that you need to know is that she *never* stays in one place long enough to take responsibility for anything." He met Fannie's gaze. "Even if she did hear from you and respond, there would be an ulterior motive behind it. Which is why I asked if someone had contacted you about your father's estate. That would be very like her."

"What possible motive could she have?" Fannie stared down at the elegant woman in the photograph.

"*Money,* Miss Rousseau. At one time, your father had quite a lot of it." He paused. "Unfortunately, that is no longer the case, and the last thing you need is someone like her wheedling their way into your affections in order to take advantage of your ignor—" He broke off and cleared his throat. "Hoping to take advantage of your *inexperience*."

"But you meant to say that she might take advantage of my ignorance." Fannie took a sip of water. "Is she evil, then? Is that why Mother never spoke of her?" She grasped the stack of letters. "Did Miss LeClerc lie for twenty years?"

Mr. Vandekamp rested his elbows on the arms of his chair and tented his hands, matching fingertip to fingertip. "I'm sure I have no idea."

Fannie tucked the letters and the photo back into the brown envelope. "I'm going to write in care of general delivery in Fort Benton. She deserves to know about Mother."

Mr. Vandekamp leaned forward. "Has it occurred to you, Miss Rousseau, that if Edith LeClerc were truly interested in her family, you wouldn't just now be learning of her existence?"

Of course it had occurred to her. But then, that question had been surrounded by all the others that had been circling through Fannie's mind for most of her adult life. So many questions, and the only answer was the one Hannah had offered in the cemetery Sunday morning. A stubborn assurance that Mother loved. Fannie trusted Hannah to speak the truth as she saw it. But increasingly, what Hannah thought just wasn't enough. *If Mother loved . . . why didn't I know it? If she loved . . . why didn't I ever meet my own aunt? If she loved . . . why didn't she show it?* And why was Mr. Vandekamp so upset right now? What was he hiding?

"Actually," Fannie said, "I think I'd like to meet her. Perhaps I'll invite her to visit when I write about Mother."

"Nonsense." Mr. Vandekamp dismissed the idea with a wave. "She isn't *there* anymore, Miss Rousseau. The gold rush in Montana Territory has nearly played itself out. Even now, we are noticing a huge decline in river traffic." His lip curled as he said, "Edie was never one to wait around when the excitement faded." He paused. "It would do your mother's memory a great disservice for you to go in search of someone she took great pains to protect you from."

"I'm not talking about *going.* I only want to write a letter. Surely Mother would understand that. She might even be grateful. I'd think she'd want her only sister to know about her passing."

Vandekamp rose from his chair. "Think

83

whatever you like, but I promised my friend Eleanor Rousseau that I would see to things, and I intend to keep that promise. I must forbid you to attempt to contact Edith LeClerc."

Fannie stood up. Somehow, she mustered the courage to look him in the eye. "I beg your pardon, Mr. Vandekamp, but I am of age, and while I acknowledge that Papa and Mother trusted you, I don't believe you have the authority to forbid *me* to do . . . anything." Surely he could hear her heart hammering. Surely he knew her knees were quaking. And yet . . . he was the one to look away first.

"Please, Miss Rousseau. Fannie." He gestured at the chair. "Sit back down. Let's not war over this. You have far more important things that require your attention." When Fannie didn't move, he changed the subject. "Mr. Beauvais tells me that you've been poring over certain papers on your father's desk. That you have questions."

"Yes. As a matter of fact, I have an entire list of questions. But I don't want to talk about that without Mr. Beauvais and Mr. Hennessey present." *I don't trust you anymore, Mr. Vandekamp. You're holding back, and I just don't trust you.*

Vandekamp's jaw clenched. The spots of

color reappeared on his cheeks, but his voice remained calm. "Mr. Haversham has spoken with me in regard to your account at his establishment. I would imagine you've already deduced that your situation isn't getting any better."

Fannie nodded. "The question is, what's to be done about it. Which is why I'm grateful that Mr. Beauvais and Mr. Hennessey seem willing to lend their assistance. I believe I remember Papa saying something about there being wisdom in many counselors. I'm grateful those two gentlemen have offered to help us." She hoped the word *us* would smooth a few of Mr. Vandekamp's ruffled feathers. Something told her she didn't want this man as an enemy.

Vandekamp sighed. "The losses you saw represented in those papers on your father's desk tell only a small part of the story. This nonsense about finding a long-lost aunt is a most unwelcome distraction." He paused. "I believe I have a plan that will enable you to maintain through the end of the year until we can effect a suitable match — if only you will concentrate on the matter at hand and make a few adjustments."

"Adjustments? Why? And . . . what kind of adjustments do you mean?"

"If you delay past this season, it will

85

become readily apparent to all the most desirable suitors that not only are you *not* a young woman of means, you are, in fact, one who comes with a great many liabilities, not the least of which are a house and grounds in need of extensive repairs. Forgive me for being blunt, Miss Rousseau, but we are already facing the possibility of needing to sell some of your mother's jewels in order to maintain appearances through the end of the season." He paused. "I've heard that you hired Tommy Cooper."

Fannie couldn't resist defending herself. "Apparently the burglar thought the house was unoccupied. I cannot let things go downhill any further."

Vandekamp amazed her by agreeing. "Quite right. As I was saying, appearances must be kept up." He smiled. "I am only thinking of what is best for you, when I insist that you cease giving any energy at all to the topic of Edith LeClerc. You must concentrate on ensuring your own future. You cannot stay in that house indefinitely. It's unseemly for a young woman to live alone. I believe recent events have shown that it is possibly even unsafe." He cleared his throat. "Now, I realize you are in mourning, but I also believe we can find an acceptable way around that. If we are to maintain the impression that you are a young woman of means, you are going to need to entertain as a young woman of means. I don't think society would object if you hosted a garden party to honor your best friend on the occasion of her engagement. Unfortunately, Hannah Pike is far too decrepit to manage that kind of thing. I realize she's been faithful to the family for years, but she must be replaced."

Fannie took a step back. "Replace Hannah? You can't be serious. I couldn't."

"You don't have to," he said with a patronizing smile. "I'll handle it for you." He pulled his watch from his vest pocket. "And now, I'm afraid I have a pressing meeting with another client." He didn't wait for Fannie's reply. Instead, he cupped her elbow in his hand and guided her to the door.

It was all Fannie could do to keep from breaking down right in front of him. Hannah's beautiful smile was one of her earliest memories. Hannah's soothing voice, not Mother's, had calmed her childhood fears. When Fannie broke a toy or took a tumble, it was Hannah who made things right. Mother never seemed to want to be bothered about such things.

Replace Hannah? What on earth was the

CHAPTER SIX

To every thing there is a season, and a
time to every purpose under the heaven.

ECCLESIASTES 3:1

It took every bit of her self-control for
Fannie to make her way toward home
without sobbing in public. She hadn't realized it, but her life had begun to fall apart
four years ago with the sinking of the *Bertrand*. In spite of Papa's best efforts, the
business had never really recovered from
that loss. Then the icy disaster in St. Louis
had been the final blow. And then Papa
died, and still . . . Mother hadn't changed
anything. How could she have been so
uninformed? So willfully blind to the truth?

Brilliant as they were, Daniel Hennessey
and Minette's father probably weren't going
to be able to work a miracle. It was too late.
Mr. Vandekamp had so much as said so,
what with his return to the same old theme

of marriage. Only now that theme had an even more distressing side. She was supposed to delude some poor, unsuspecting someone. Lure some man into taking her on . . . before he had a chance to know just how large a financial burden she would be.

Minette said Daniel Hennessey filled a part of her she hadn't even known was empty. That was what Fannie wanted. That breathless feeling she'd seen on both Minette and Daniel's faces when they'd embraced on the lawn on Sunday evening. She wanted that — not the dry, lifeless *tolerance* displayed between Mother and Papa. Never that.

As she stumbled along the brick walkway leading home, the dark cloud returned. The future looked so very bleak. What was she going to do? In the midst of those gathering storm clouds, the mystery surrounding Edith LeClerc called to her, a persistent glimmer, an unspoken hope-laden promise. *I'm not alone in the world.*

The familiar sound of a steamboat whistle rolled up from the levee. Fannie looked toward the river just as the vessel paddled into view. She could barely make out the name. *Delores.* Where had she heard that . . . Minette! Minette's Daniel had negotiated "favorable terms" with Otto Busch, the captain who would pilot the *Delores* to Fort Benton with Beauvais cargo aboard. Fannie glanced down at the envelope in her hand. Aunt Edith had mentioned Otto Busch in that last letter. Something about his objecting to unaccompanied women on his steamers . . . but that *she* wasn't going to let that stop her. Might Captain Busch remember Edith LeClerc?

Taking a deep breath, Fannie headed toward the landing, where a mountain of shipping crates marked *Beauvais* waited to be loaded on board. As laborers scurried to tie up the steamer, she peered up at the wheelhouse and the man guiding the steamboat toward shore. With clatters and clangs, bangs and shouts, the *Delores* nosed up to the levee. A tall roustabout thrust a gangplank toward the shore. A dozen tough-looking men marched ashore to load cargo. In spite of his size, the tall one who'd cast the gangplank into place didn't look quite as rough as the rest. Fannie approached him and asked if she might speak with Captain Otto Busch.

The first thing Samuel did when the blue-eyed beauty looked up at him and asked about talking to Captain Busch was to snatch his hat off his head. The abundance

91

of black silk ruffles and the jet earbobs and gold mourning brooch spoke of money, and a good deal of it. What was she doing alone on the St. Charles levee? Before Samuel had a chance to say a word to her, the captain hollered, "Beck! Quit yer lollygagging and get to work!"

Samuel turned around and shouted back, "She wants to speak with you, sir!" He hoped Busch would spare the pretty little thing his usual profanity. Amazingly, he did, shouting for Samuel to escort the lady on board and meet him up on the hurricane deck.

Hearing the captain's invitation, the lady in question scurried up the gangplank, leaving Samuel in her rose-scented wake. Her black silk skirts rustled as she lifted them enough to mount the stairs leading up from the main deck. Samuel caught a glimpse of a finely formed, leather-encased ankle, as she glided up the stairs ahead of him and crossed to where Captain Busch waited at the railing.

To Samuel's surprise, Busch seemed to have evolved into a gentleman between the wheelhouse and the hurricane deck. He actually bowed as he introduced himself. "Captain Otto Busch at your service, *mademoiselle*."

The lady curtsied and introduced herself. "Miss Fannie Rousseau."

"Rousseau . . ." the captain murmured. "Of the Rousseau Line?" Yes, Miss Rousseau said, Louis Rousseau was her father. The captain offered his condolences over her recent loss. She thanked him and reached for the leather envelope tucked beneath her arm. At which time Busch scowled at Samuel. "Is there some reason you're standing there while the rest of the crew loads cargo?"

"N-no, sir," Samuel said. "Except y-you said —"

"I said to escort the lady to the hurricane deck," Busch groused, "and you have."

Samuel saluted and headed off, pausing at the stairs just long enough for one more look at the lady. In another life, he would have been thinking of how to wrangle an introduction. How to get his name on her dance card. But he'd left that life — mostly for Emma's sake. He'd never go back to it for his own. And it was time to get back to work.

Recognition flashed in Captain Busch's dark eyes as he looked down at Edith LeClerc's photograph, but his reaction was nothing like Mr. Vandekamp's. The captain

93

smiled as he looked back at Fannie. "Your aunt, you say?"

"Yes, sir. But I've only just become aware of her. She mentions you in one of her letters. Something about talking you into taking her to Fort Benton."

Busch nodded. "And she did. Against my better judgment and against every reasonable argument. But she convinced me she was an honorable woman, and it was clear she was going, come what may. I decided she might as well be on board my packet as another." He paused then and, taking a pipe out of his pocket, asked Fannie's permission to light it.

Fannie gave it before asking, "Do you think that if I wrote her in Fort Benton, a letter would have any chance of reaching her?"

"Impossible to know. She was gold crazy like the rest of the passengers on that trip. Although I will tell you that, were I a gambling man wagering on the chances of any woman having success in Montana, I'd wager on Miss Edie LeClerc." His eyes flashed with humor. "She was a caution, that woman. I can tell you she disembarked at Fort Benton. As I recall, she'd made arrangements to head for Alder Gulch with a group of miners she met on the way, and they were all intending to travel with a freighter one of them had heard about. A man by the name of Babe Cox."

"Alder Gulch?"

"The gold diggings there yielded ten million in '63 and '64. Your aunt," he said, tapping the photo with a fingertip, "was among those who believed there was still plenty to be had." He paused. "Of course, tales of rich veins tend to change with the wind, so where Edie might have ended up, who can say." He smiled. "If she's still in Montana, Miss Rousseau, I imagine she's made a name for herself. She is not a woman people soon forget."

"So . . . there might be a chance of finding her . . . if someone were to go looking."

Busch eyed her for a moment. "You thinking of hiring Pinkertons?"

If only I could. Fannie shook her head.

"I'll tell you what. Your father was one of the better men I've met on this river. He believed in me when I was a fresh young pilot and others didn't. You write your letter, Miss Rousseau. I'll see what I can do about helping it find your aunt."

Fannie thanked him. "When are you leaving?"

Busch nodded toward the piles of freight on the levee. "It'll take a few hours to load all of that. We'll pull out at first light in the morning."

How many hands would a letter have to pass through? How easily would a letter get lost or forgotten? Was that the best way to find Aunt Edith? Now that she'd heard someone talk about the woman, Fannie wanted to meet her more than ever. She didn't really want to wait for an answer that might never come.

"How much is passage?" The minute she'd blurted out the question, Fannie's heart began to pound with a combination of nerves and . . . anticipation.

Busch shook his head. "I said I owe your father a debt, miss. Hauling his only daughter to a place like Fort Benton is no way for me to repay it."

Fannie looked out on the busy levee. The tall roustabout who'd brought her up here to talk to the captain was helping an older man carry a huge crate on board. She put Aunt Edith's photo away. "Is there anything I could say that would change your mind?"

"Write your letter, Miss Rousseau. Bring it back before we cast off, and you have my word I'll do my best to see that your aunt receives it." The captain tipped his cap. "Now, if you'll excuse me . . ." With a little bow, he headed off up the walkway leading

96

alongside the cabins.

Something about the way the captain dismissed her reminded Fannie of Mr. Vandekamp's shuttling her out of his office. Oh, Captain Busch had been more tactful about it, but she was still being turned away. Shoved aside. Patted on the head like a child and told to let the adults in the room handle things.

Why did men do that? Shouldn't she have a say in her own future? Why shouldn't she be able to do what she wanted? What was so horrible about escaping St. Charles and its problems for a few weeks?

Escape. What a wonderful word. Escape to a place where looming debt didn't stare her in the face every single day; where she didn't have to hear monotonous hints about marriage and, best of all, where Mr. Vandekamp couldn't threaten to dismiss Hannah. *Because Hannah will go with me. I know she will.*

Fannie called after the captain. "Tell me, Captain Busch, if you thought I *was* going to head north . . . 'come what may' . . . would you prefer that I be on board a steamer whose captain felt a debt to my father . . . or on board some other vessel in the company of strangers?"

Busch turned around. He considered her

97

question for a moment. Walked back her way. Scrutinized her expression while he savored his pipe. "Are you telling me, Miss Rousseau, that that is your intent?"

"Papa's business is failing. I may lose my home. I'm being pressured to marry a man who —" she shuddered — "who is completely unsuitable." She held up the envelope. "Thinking about meeting Aunt Edith makes me feel . . . hopeful. I can't see anything wrong with leaving the problems I have for a little while. They'll all still be here when I get back. I'm the only one who can search for Edith LeClerc, because I'm the only one who cares to do it. I'm certain my maid will want to come with me. And the more I think about Aunt Edith, the more I care about finding her. Please, Captain Busch . . . won't you help me?"

Somehow, it was easier to meet this man's gaze than Hubert Vandekamp's. Maybe it was because Otto Busch had smiled at Aunt Edith's photograph. Maybe it was because respect — sometimes grudging respect — had been the common thread running through all the stories she'd ever heard about the man. Somehow, she knew he was a man she could trust. Why she didn't feel that way about Mr. Vandekamp, she would ponder over time. Right now, she had to concentrate on looking more confident than she felt while Captain Busch studied her.

"You really mean to go," he finally said.

"I do."

He considered for a moment more and then, finally, nodded. "Well then, Miss Rousseau. You'd better get packed. The *Delores* doesn't wait for latecomers." He paused. "I'll send Beck for your trunks at sundown."

Fannie could hardly believe what she was hearing. "How much does it cost?" *Please, God, let there be enough in Papa's cashbox. Mr. Vandekamp will never give me the money.*

Busch scowled. "Who said anything about a cost? Consider it final payment on the debt I owe your father. And never tell a living soul I let you on board without your paying. It'll ruin my reputation as a son-of-a-willy-walloo."

By the time Fannie swished through the creaking front gate at home and tripped up the side steps into the house, she had talked herself into believing that what some might call ridiculous and outlandish was also inspired. If only Hannah would see things her way. The knot of anticipation in her midsection made her voice tremble when she paused in the kitchen doorway and called out to Hannah, "I need . . . your help."

Hannah's body continued its rhythmic swaying as she kneaded the mass of dough on the breadboard before her. "Where you been, little miss? Didn't think it would take you so long." She glanced up and frowned. "I take it things didn't go so well with Mr. Vandekamp? What kind of help you need?"

Fannie shrugged. "I'll tell you about the bank meeting later. The *Delores* is at the levee. I talked to Captain Busch. He remembers Aunt Edith and he smiled when he saw her photograph. His steamer leaves for Fort Benton tomorrow and Captain Busch agreed to take me — us. Will you come?"

Hannah stopped kneading. "What do you mean he's agreed to take us? Take us *where?*"

"I told you. To Fort Benton. To find Aunt Edith. Please say you'll come."

"Slow down, little miss. Exactly how did we get from asking Mr. Vandekamp about your aunt, to going to Montana? That's a mighty far leap."

"If I slow down I'm afraid I'll talk myself out of it." In a rush, Fannie related what had gone on at the bank, how she'd ended up on board the *Delores,* and how she'd decided to head for Montana. "I know it's . . . a far leap, as you said —"

"That it is," Hannah said with a nod. She went back to working the bread dough. "You've had yourself quite a day. Let's just think things through a bit before —"

"I *have* thought things through." Fannie walked to the table. She watched Hannah's arthritic hands plunge into the dough, kneading, folding, turning, kneading, folding, turning. She sat down. "I've thought them through for the last few nights. I'm exhausted from thinking." Her voice wavered. "I told you. Mr. Vandekamp wouldn't tell me anything. He forbade me to even *try* to find Aunt Edith. Talking to him is like talking to someone with cotton in their ears. I might as well not open my mouth at all." Frustrated tears slid down her cheeks. "He threatened to dismiss *you,* Hannah."

Hannah looked up. "Did he, now?"

"He said I need someone younger to help me entertain." She swiped at her tears. "I can't *breathe* in this house anymore. Everything I thought I knew has been shaken loose." She paused. "But in the middle of the falling apart, there's Aunt Edith. And Captain Busch *smiled* when he saw her picture. He said all kinds of nice things about her. I want to try to find her. And then I'll come home and be a good girl."

"You're already a good girl."

"Tell that to Mr. Vandekamp." Fannie forced a laugh. "I am *not* getting married just because he says I should. And I am *not* replacing you." She looked toward the hall and murmured, "Maybe we could take in boarders in the fall."

Hannah ignored the comment about taking in boarders. "You know anything about this Fort Benton place?"

"Nothing very . . . charming."

"And how long is the trip?"

"Could be as much as ten weeks."

"There and back?"

Fannie shook her head. "Just to get there."

"So . . . this adventure of ours is going to take all summer and then some."

When Fannie nodded, Hannah returned to her bread making. She formed the loaves, then slid them into the waiting bread pans and put them in the oven. Finally, she turned around and, as she was wiping her hands, said, "Walker and Tommy Cooper are out back trying to rescue your mother's rose garden. I'll fetch them and send them into the attic after a couple of trunks. I don't expect you'll be needing ball gowns, so maybe one of those smaller trunks in the northeast corner will do. I barely need one, but then again, I don't suppose it would be a bad idea to pack our own bedding and some decent towels. And some books. And our needlework." She glanced at the oven. "Guess I'll give the bread to Walker and Tommy. From what I know about steamboats, they do serve decent food."

Fannie clasped her hands. "You'll go?"

"Can't see as I have much choice. With Mr. Dandy-VandeKam planning to get rid of me anyway, I might as well hightail it along with you." She shrugged. "And besides that, I cannot imagine facing your mother on the other side and having to explain how it was that I stood on the levee and watched you float away into the wilderness towards the good Lord only knows what." Her voice softened. "I've had my time of heading into the wilderness, little miss. I was young and as terrified as a body can be, but things worked out. If the good Lord undertakes for us the way he did for me back then, we'll do all right."

Fannie jumped up and threw her arms around Hannah. "Thank you." She kissed the old woman on the cheek.

Hannah hugged her back, even as she said, "See if you still want to thank me after we've been on that river for a month."

CHAPTER SEVEN

Abstain from all appearance of evil.
1 THESSALONIANS 5:22

The sun had just begun to streak the horizon with golden bars of light when the *Delores*'s whistle shrieked, and Fannie exited the cabin she and Hannah would share throughout the long journey. With a chorus of shouts from the roustabouts casting off her lines, the shabby vessel backed away from the St. Charles landing and headed into the river channel.

As the span of brown water between the deck and the shore grew wider, Hannah came to stand alongside her at the railing. Taking a deep breath, she said, "I do believe we're gonna have us a fine spring day. Would you look at that shore go by. I declare, it's almost like flying."

Fannie picked at a bit of paint flaking off the rail in front of her. "More like limping."

"Where's my adventure-seeking little gal?"

Fannie forced a nervous laugh. "Back on the levee." She blinked away tears as she looked toward home. "Do you think Minette will ever speak to me again? What will Mr. Hennessey and Mr. Beauvais think? What will Mr. Vandekamp *do?*"

"Mr. Vandekamp won't be able to do anything," Hannah said. "Not without Minnette's pa and fiancé agreeing to it. Those letters you left made that clear." She smiled. "As for Miss Minette, she will likely be upset. I believe this is the first foolish thing you've ever done without her. She won't appreciate being left behind."

Fannie choked back a laugh. Hannah was likely right about Minette. She'd be upset, but she'd understand. Minette always understood. The men, on the other hand . . .

Her voice wavered. "I've asked a lot of Mr. Hennessey and Minette's father."

"Nothing they didn't offer." Hannah chuckled. "I suppose it's wrong of me, but I can't help but enjoy the picture of Mr. Vandekamp learning the news. He's gonna hate having Mr. Hennessey and Minette's papa looking over his shoulder." She sniffed. "Wonder how *he'll* like being dismissed."

"I would never have let that happen to

you," Fannie said. "You do know that, don't you?"

"I do," Hannah said. "Besides, the man hasn't been born who can separate me from my little miss." She squeezed Fannie's hand. They stood quietly for a few moments. Finally, Hannah gestured toward the sun-bathed shoreline. "I never thought I'd see anything farther west than St. Charles, and here we are, sliding by all kind of places and headed for Montana. Indians . . . buffalo . . . tepees!" Her eyes shone with excitement. "We're gonna be just fine, little miss. You'll see."

"So . . . you don't think I'm a fool?"

"I didn't say that," Hannah teased. "But *land sakes,* child, if the good Lord couldn't use fools and foolishness, he wouldn't get much done."

Fannie forced a smile. She didn't know all that much about how "the good Lord" did things, but Hannah's enthusiasm did help her feel better. "I didn't think we'd be the only women on board," she said, gazing behind them and up the row of mostly empty cabins.

"I doubt that'll last," Hannah said. "How many stops are on that card the captain gave you?"

Fannie reached in the small silk purse

dangling from her wrist and pulled the card out. *Distances on Missouri River from St. Louis to . . .* Two columns listed stops along the way. "At least three dozen," Fannie said, and handed the card to Hannah.

"Eighty-nine miles to Washington," she read aloud. "Four hundred five to Kansas City." She looked up. "Bet we take on some ladies in Kansas City." Glancing back down at the card in her hand, she shook her head as she read off, " 'Two thousand, six hundred, sixty-three miles. Seems like Fort Benton must be halfway to heaven and back.' "

The whistle sounded again. Fannie wondered how many more she would hear before St. Charles came into view again. Before she saw Minette again . . . and had to face Mr. Vandekamp. Would she have met Aunt Edith by then? Would she have answers to some of her questions about her parents?

She looked down at the river, taking little comfort in the notion that the water wasn't deep. *Halfway to heaven,* that's what Hannah had said about the distance they were about to travel. Fannie only hoped she wasn't taking them halfway to Hades.

It was time to read Aunt Edith's letters again.

■ ■ ■ ■

Whether it was Samuel's size or Lamar's skin color that did the trick, none of the other hands or deck passengers challenged the two bunking beneath a wagon bound for Fort Claggett. It was the least crowded square footage on the entire main deck, and Samuel was not only happy to share it with Lamar Davis but also grateful for the old man's companionship. There was just something about the old guy. Something peaceful.

Hauling wood was hard on Lamar, and they had to haul a lot of it. The *Delores*'s three boilers had an insatiable appetite for the stuff, burning through so many cords a day Samuel lost count. The steamer stopped twice a day to take on wood. Even though Lamar's weathered face often contorted with pain as he worked, a low hum accompanied just about everything he did.

"How do you do that?" Samuel finally asked.

"Do what?"

"Take everything in stride. You never get riled. You keep calm no matter how much Captain Busch yells. I see you're hurting when we haul wood. But you hum. How do you do it?"

Lamar chuckled. "Wasn't always that way, son. I'm no saint. I just don't have the energy for grumbling." He nodded Samuel's way. "Can't say as I hear you complaining much, either, and I notice you've got nearly raw hands where you need callouses. I'd bet you've got a few aches and pains, too."

Samuel only shrugged. His propensity for complaining aloud had been erased long ago by the tip of Pa's buggy whip. But just because Samuel didn't make noise didn't mean he didn't *think* complaints. Lamar just plain didn't seem to be bothered by things. That was what Samuel wanted to understand, if only they ever had a chance to really talk. But Lamar was snoring seconds after the two of them settled beneath the wagon each night, and Samuel barely made it through a page of his mother's Bible before he followed suit. Some nights he didn't even make it that far.

In light of how quickly Lamar fell asleep, it was strange how attuned he was to the slightest change in the steamer. The first time they struck a sandbar, Lamar woke with the first tremor. Before Samuel had so much as raised his head, the older man was scooting out from beneath the wagon, tucking in his shirt, and hurrying off.

Samuel moved slower, knowing that it would be at least a few minutes before the crew knew whether they were going to grasshopper or double trip. Lamar, on the other hand, would be up in the wheelhouse conferring with the captain and his mate about what to do this time. Busch might grumble and complain about the old man's slowness at hauling, but he respected Lamar's good sense and valued his opinion.

Delays were a normal part of the journey, but that didn't mean Captain Busch accepted them without a fight. As the days passed, Samuel learned firsthand just how many things there were to fight. Sunshine was pleasant for everyone, but at the right angle the glare could obscure the surface of the water. That made it difficult to judge the speed of the current and to read swirls and ripples indicating rocks and snags lurking below. Rain not only made everyone miserable but also erased any ability to read the water. Wind could actually topple the top-heavy shallow-drafted vessel. Captain Busch seemed to take all of nature's tricks as a personal affront, piloting with a combination of bravado and brilliance that had won him no small measure of fame in the river towns bordering the fickle Missouri River.

Samuel had just settled beneath the wagon one evening when Lamar came to fetch him. "Water level's high, moon's full, captain's going to take us into St. Joe by moonlight. I volunteered us to help mark the channel."

Pulling his suspenders back up, Samuel followed Lamar to the mackinaw boat where the mate was already waiting. The men shoved off. Samuel thrust a long pole into the river, seeking bottom and sounding the depth. Even loaded with two hundred tons of freight and thirty passengers, the *Delores* only needed waist-high water to navigate.

As Samuel poked the mackinaw upstream, Lamar and the mate marked a channel with lighted candles affixed to bits of scrap lumber. A length of rope and a stone weighted the floats so they'd remain in place as the steamer slid past, and paper cylinders set down over the candles kept the flames from blowing out.

There was little time to appreciate the aesthetics of the flickering lights marking a pathway for the *Delores,* but at some point Samuel realized that passengers had collected both on the prow and above on the hurricane deck to watch the spectacle. And it was a spectacle. The full moon had transformed the tawny river into a silver ribbon. In the moonlight, the belching ship almost looked romantic, like a timeworn lady of the night made beautiful by lamplight.

"It's called 'eating up the lights.' "

The deep voice came from just over her shoulder. Fannie jumped and whirled about, looking up into eyes so dark they were almost black. Perhaps it was the hour. Or the fact that Hannah wasn't there. Whatever it was, there was something about the man that made Fannie uncomfortable — in a fascinating kind of way.

He stepped up to the railing next to her. "E. C. Dandridge at your service, *madame.*"

Fannie had heard the name. Mr. Dandridge had come on board in Kansas City, but he hadn't seen fit to dine in the saloon yet. That fact alone lent an air of mystery to the man. Broad shoulders and expensive clothing did the rest. Socializing was an important part of life aboard the slow-moving steamer, and E. C. Dandridge was a regular subject of conversation among the half-dozen ladies who gathered in the dining saloon every afternoon.

Rumors about the man ranged from the

ridiculous — he was a desperado just a few steps ahead of the law — to the sublime — he was a widower seeking solace from the torments of grief with an endless cycle of travel. Whatever the truth, the fact that Mr. Dandridge was standing close enough for her to catch the scent of his after-dinner cigar made Fannie feel awkward and self-conscious, even as she enjoyed his attention.

"Please say that we will have the pleasure of your company for the entire journey, Miss Rousseau. It's been a long while since anything as lovely as you graced the decks of the *Delores*."

Thankful for the moonlight's ability to obscure her blush, Fannie stammered, "I-I didn't realize you knew my name." She glanced toward the cabin she shared with Hannah. And where was Hannah, anyway?

"Any man worth his salt would make it his business to inquire about a lady as lovely as you." Dandridge paused before adding, "I had you figured for an officer's wife bound for one of the forts upriver. Captain Busch set me straight on that issue." He paused again. "He seems to have taken you under his wing. I shall have to be very careful."

What did he mean by that? Careful?

About what? "I assume the captain told you that I am headed for one of the forts, though. Fort Benton."

Mr. Dandridge was quiet for a moment, then murmured, "Ah . . . Fort Benton. I assume this will be your first visit?"

How does he know that? And why was it so hard to look at him, even in the moonlight, without feeling flustered? She concentrated on the meandering pathway of floating lanterns on the river. "Isn't that lovely," she murmured.

Dandridge agreed, although Fannie didn't think he was looking at the river when he did so. Suddenly, he moved away slightly and said, "Miss Rousseau's companion, I presume?" He touched the brim of his top hat and introduced himself to Hannah. "I understand you two are bound for Fort Benton. My partner and I are opening a business there."

Hannah introduced herself. "Mrs. Hannah Pike. Nursemaid, housekeeper, traveling companion . . . and defender, when necessary."

Mr. Dandridge laughed. "I'll keep that in mind." He tugged on his mustache as he leaned toward Hannah and said in mock confidence, "I've noticed the lady has been the object of more than a little attention from belowdecks. It's good to know she has a friend looking out for her. I'd offer myself as a second if I thought there was a chance you'd accept my references."

"Happy to accept," Hannah said, with what Fannie thought sounded like forced pleasantness, "as long as the references include a minister of the gospel, a missionary, and a seminary professor." She touched Fannie's arm. "I do apologize for putting an end to a lovely conversation, little miss, but I'm certain Mr. Dandridge will excuse us." She nodded toward the river. "Looks like we're about to tie up for the night."

Indeed they were. Fannie hadn't really noticed, but the mackinaw was back alongside, most of the floating candles behind them now. Tipping his hat, Dandridge bowed and took his leave.

Fannie followed Hannah into their tiny cabin, where Hannah harrumphed. "What on earth were you thinking, taking up with a man like that?"

"I wasn't 'taking up' with anyone, and what do you mean 'a man like that'? He was . . . interesting. If he's opening a business in Fort Benton, he might have an idea of how I can locate Aunt Edith."

Hannah fluffed a pillow — although it looked more like punching than fluffing.

"You will encounter all kinds of *interesting* men on this journey, little miss. Men who are nothing like the boys who bowed and scraped to get the favor of a dance with you in St. Charles. A top hat and a stiff collar may dress up the outside of a man, but they don't change who he really is. And mark my words, the man inside Mr. E. C. Dandridge's fine suit is not a man you want to associate with."

"How can you possibly know that?" Fannie pulled the tiny purse that had been dangling from her wrist off and tossed it onto her cot. "We were just talking. He was passing by where I was standing watching the crew float those lights on the river. It would have been rude of him not to say *something*."

"It would have been rude of him not to tip his hat. It *was* rude to linger when you haven't been introduced and you were without an escort. He took advantage, and I'm quite certain he knew he was doing exactly that." Hannah sniffed. "You do recall that he stepped back away from you when I walked up? He knew he was being fresh."

Fannie rolled her eyes. "How on earth could standing at the railing in plain sight of everyone else and within a few feet of my 'nursemaid, housekeeper, traveling companion, and defender' be considered taking advantage?"

"It is none of that man's business where you are headed or why or with whom."

Fannie sighed and sat down on the edge of her cot. "But he might know something about Aunt Edith."

Hannah sat down opposite her. "If he's headed all the way to Fort Benton, there will be plenty of time for you to speak with him *when the two of you are in proper company.* It's not as if you're hard to find, little miss. We dine in the saloon three times a day. If he wants to be sociable, there is a correct way to do that. And that way is not to approach a young lady standing by herself in the dead of night, looking out on a romantic moonlit river bedecked with floating candles."

CHAPTER EIGHT

Forsake the foolish, and live; and go in
the way of understanding.

PROVERBS 9:6

Once the *Delores* left Nebraska City, the sky turned gray and the weather bleak. The journey took on a sameness that dampened Fannie's visions of a grand adventure. But then Mr. Dandridge began to dine with the rest of the passengers. He even condescended to read aloud to the ladies' sewing circle on an occasional afternoon while they knitted and pieced quilt blocks, tatted, and crocheted. For the first time, Fannie was grateful Hannah had seen fit to pack their needle cases and a few projects.

One afternoon, when Mr. Dandridge had concluded his reading of Mr. Dickens's *Great Expectations,* he asked Fannie to "take the air." Not unaware of the jealous glances some of the sewing circle ladies cast her way, Fannie accepted. Hannah had retired to take a nap, and as she and Mr. Dandridge paced back and forth along the hurricane deck, Fannie plied him with questions about Fort Benton.

"I'm afraid anything I'd have to say about the place might result in your abandoning the *Delores* at the next stop," he said. "To be quite honest, I can't imagine what Captain Busch was thinking to encourage you."

"He didn't encourage me," she said. "He merely realized he couldn't stop me." She was sounding much stronger than she felt, but something made her want to seem independent and decisive.

"I admire your courage."

"I'm not courageous," Fannie blurted out. "Half the time I'm scared to death. But every time I doubt myself I read one of my aunt's letters and it reminds me —" She broke off and asked Mr. Dandridge to wait while she went to get Aunt Edith's photograph.

When Hannah roused long enough to ask if everything was all right, Fannie reassured her with a very small fib about wanting to show Aunt Edith's photograph to "someone in the sewing circle." When Fannie handed Mr. Dandridge the photograph, something

119

flickered in his dark eyes. "Have you seen her, then?" she asked.

Dandridge looked up. "I can't say for certain. Her face reminds me of someone, but . . . Fort Benton's citizenry doesn't include anyone of this woman's obvious social standing. At least it didn't when I left last fall. It's still very . . . primitive."

There was no need to repeat what Captain Busch had said about Aunt Edie heading off into the mountains with a group of miners. At least not to Mr. Dandridge. And besides, who knew what romantic adventure a beautiful woman like Edith LeClerc might have encountered in a wilderness populated by Indians and soldiers. She could have found her one true love. "Couldn't she be an officer's wife?"

"There are no soldiers at Fort Benton, Miss Rousseau. It acquired its name when Major Culbertson of the American Fur Company oversaw the construction of an adobe stockade with three-foot-thick walls and a massive gate — for a fur trading post. If you were picturing a military stockade and a parade ground, I'm afraid you're going to be very disappointed." He returned the photograph. "I don't think there are more than a dozen white women in all of Fort Benton, and the ones I know are nothing like the refined lady in that photograph," he paused, smiling into her eyes, "and nothing like you."

When he put his palm at the small of her back, Fannie knew she should move away, but she didn't want to. It was . . . nice having someone care. What he next said proved that he only meant to comfort her.

"But please, Miss Rousseau — Fannie. Don't be discouraged. Fort Benton is growing. In fact, it has likely changed since I left last fall. Who knows but what you will find a few families living there when we arrive. There might even be a church by now. Heaven knows the good Lord is needed there."

A clap of thunder made Fannie jump — almost into Mr. Dandridge's arms. As rain poured out of the skies, they both laughed as they ducked beneath the hurricane deck roof, their backs pressed against the exterior cabin walls as sheets of water poured out of the sky, shattering the surface of the unpredictable river.

Dandridge leaned close and murmured an invitation to accompany him into the saloon to see if they could get another couple interested in a game of whist. Fannie happily accepted. Mother would be appalled at the idea of her playing cards, but except for meeting Mr. Dandridge, the trip was proving itself to be interminably slow and excessively boring. She'd read two books and finished knitting a pair of mittens she hated.

If only something *interesting* would happen.

Thanks to rain and sandbars and the leaking boiler, the *Delores* was behind schedule. At Omaha, Captain Busch discharged thirteen roustabouts. Samuel narrowly escaped being one of them. Lamar tried to avoid taking credit, but another roustabout told Samuel how the old guy had stood up for him, telling Captain Busch that Sam Beck was worth more than three men and the captain would be a fool not to know that. Samuel couldn't imagine anyone telling Otto Busch he was a fool and living to tell, but there it was again — Lamar had a unique place in Busch's life.

As for Samuel, the longer he was around Lamar, the more he learned. Lamar could recite impressive amounts of Scripture, and as the days went by and Samuel worried over Emma, Lamar spoke Scripture to those worries. Eventually, Samuel grew less anxious. He couldn't have explained why, but the words in the Bible imparted a strange kind of peace about the future. Lamar said that wherever Emma was, God knew, and God was in that place, too. Sam should keep checking in the river towns where the *Delores* stopped, pray, and sleep well, knowing he was doing everything in his power.

Samuel did his best to comply. He wasn't convinced that his own prayers carried much weight, but Lamar was praying, too, and God most certainly listened to Lamar Davis. The old man knew God better than he knew the river, and that was saying something.

The *Delores* was eleven miles north of Omaha when the strongest wind yet forced Captain Busch to lay up all night at a wood yard. Lamar showed Samuel how to position a lamp on the back side of the stairs leading up to the hurricane deck so that, between the woodpile and the stairs, they could keep a lamp lighted and play checkers.

When Lamar blew Samuel's plan of attack to smithereens with one black checker, Samuel just shook his head. He was setting up the board for another game when the horses tethered at the far end of the deck began to snort and stomp. Lamar got up to see to them, but when Samuel prepared to join him he pointed back at the board. "I'll get them calmed down. You just get the board set up so I can beat you again." With a chuckle, he headed off.

Samuel was studying the board, trying to replay in his mind exactly how Lamar had lured him to defeat yet again, when he realized the wind had died down. Voices overhead drew his attention to the top of the stairs.

"You see," a male voice said quietly, "if we sit right here we've a beautiful view of the river. The last time I came through this part of the territory I saw a white wolf at just about this spot. I'll never forget it. Not quite as amazing as a white buffalo, of course, but —"

"A white buffalo? Whoever heard of such a thing."

"You don't know the legend of the white buffalo?"

E. C. Dandridge. What was he up to now? Samuel hadn't liked the look of the man the minute he sauntered on board. He roamed the *Delores* with an air of self-importance that set Samuel on edge. More than once, Samuel had had to walk away to keep from landing a blow to the man's egotistical face when Dandridge called Lamar *boy.* And while he wasn't given to watching what went on up on the hurricane deck, it seemed to Samuel that in recent days, wherever Miss Rousseau was, Dandridge wasn't far away.

The man reminded Samuel of a wildcat stalking his prey. And now . . . he was just a few feet way convincing someone to sit on the steps to hear a story about a white buffalo . . . then saying she should move closer so he could shield her from the wind. *She.* It had to be Miss Rousseau.

Samuel's hands had already balled up into fists when the first muffled protest sounded. He stepped out from beneath the stairs then and glanced up toward the hurricane deck. One glance was all he needed. In an instant he was clearing the steps two at a time, grabbing Dandridge by the scruff of his neck, hauling him to his feet, and tossing him toward one of the smokestacks with enough force that when his body connected, all the air went out of him and he slid to the deck like a rag doll.

When Samuel finally turned back her way, Miss Rousseau was standing in the shadows with one hand at the row of buttons marching from her waist to her neckline. Even in the light of a half-moon Samuel could see stark terror registered on her pale face as she stared past him toward the limp form

125

crumpled on the deck. Samuel crossed to where Dandridge lay and bent to check on him before standing back up. "He'll be all right." He swallowed. "Will you?"

"I . . . I . . ." She gulped. "Y-yes. I think so." But just as she said it she hurried away to empty her stomach over the railing. The handkerchief she had tucked into one sleeve glowed white as she dabbed at her mouth.

Dandridge moaned. When Samuel looked over, he'd pushed himself to a seated position and was leaning against the smokestack. Miss Rousseau took a step back. Samuel held his hand up, palm out, and said, "Just — wait. There. I'll see to him. He won't bother you again." Miss Rousseau nodded.

Samuel started moving toward Dandridge, but before he could do or say anything, the dandy had scrambled to his feet and stumbled off toward his cabin. Samuel picked up the top hat he'd left behind. It felt grand to fling it overboard. When Miss Rousseau cleared her throat, he turned back toward her.

"I don't know how to thank you," she croaked.

"Let me walk you back to your cabin."

She didn't seem to hear him. He couldn't just leave her alone on the hurricane deck. A door slammed. She started. The moon came out from behind a cloud. Finally, Samuel crossed to the stairs and sat down, staring at the river. Miss Rousseau continued to stand only a few feet away. She was crying softly. What should he do? What could he do?

The faint scent of roses wafted his way. Unbelievably, a white wolf stepped out of the underbrush and padded to the edge of the water. "Do you see that?" he said quietly.

"I do." Her voice sounded stronger. "I suppose the white buffalo will come next. It is, after all, a night for all manner of varmints to be out and about. Preying on fools who put their trust in the wrong people."

"I'm told the river has a way of attracting varmints," Samuel said, "and that the closer we get to Fort Benton the more we'll encounter."

"Then I suppose it behooves the more naïve among us to be especially wary from here on out. Hannah's been telling me that for quite some time now. I didn't want to believe her."

"I'd say caution is something that benefits everyone, ma'am. It's my first time upriver, as well. I'm grateful I've had someone looking out for me."

They hadn't really looked at each another while they talked. Instead, they watched the white wolf as it lowered its head to drink and then pointed its nose toward the sky and howled. When the wind had carried the sound away, Miss Rousseau said softly, "You've looked out for him, too. I've noticed how you help each other. I've seen you carry more than your share to lighten his load." After what seemed a long while, she finally murmured, "Thank you for waiting with me. I'd be grateful if you'd see me to my cabin now."

Samuel leaped to his feet and offered his arm. He towered above her, and in that moment he thought of Emma, how she'd trusted him and how he'd failed her. How she would bear the mark of his failure until the day she died. Defending Miss Rousseau didn't make up for Emma, but he was glad he'd been able to do it, just the same.

She paused a few feet from her cabin. "I'd rather Hannah stay asleep if at all possible," she murmured. "She'd have my head if she knew —"

"There's nothing to know," Samuel said quickly. "Although I imagine she'd be fascinated to hear you saw a white wolf on your way to the necessary in the middle of the night."

She squeezed his arm. "Thank you, Mr. Beck."

Samuel watched her until her cabin door closed behind her. Then he made his way back down to the main deck. Told Lamar what had happened. Got the old man's advice, and went to wait by the ladder to the wheelhouse so he'd be there when Captain Busch emerged from his cabin before dawn.

CHAPTER NINE

Blessed be God, even the Father of our
Lord Jesus Christ, the Father of mercies,
and the God of all comfort.

2 CORINTHIANS 1:3

"You all right, little miss?"

Fannie leaned against the closed door of her cabin, her heart pounding, her entire body trembling. She gazed through the darkness toward Hannah's cot. *Go back to sleep, Hannah. I don't want to lie . . . but I can't tell you.* Moistening her lips, she croaked, "Fine, just . . . tired." Hannah mumbled something unintelligible, then returned to deep breathing punctuated by soft snores. Fannie moved to sit on the edge of her cot. Her fingers trembled as she undid the very buttons that Dandridge had — *Don't think about it. Just . . . be thankful nothing more happened. Be thankful for Mr. Beck.*

She unbuttoned her cuffs before returning to the buttons marching up the front of her dress. And focused on Mr. Beck's kindness. The concern in his voice. His strength. Clearly, the true gentleman on board the *Delores* wasn't dressed in fine clothing.

How could she have been so . . . stupid? Hannah wasn't overprotective. She was wise. Dandridge was exactly the sort of man Hannah had warned her against. And she'd been a fool. She was fortunate to have learned it with no less damage to her person than a slight tear in her silk waist.

Finally undressed and safe, lying beneath the mound of comforters Hannah had insisted they bring with them, Fannie inhaled the faintest aroma of home and closed her eyes with a thankful heart. *Thank you for protecting me against myself tonight. Thank you for sending Mr. Beck.*

Her dreams were not peaceful, but thanks to the presence of a tall roustabout, neither were they nightmares.

He had to stop watching for Miss Rousseau, had to stop thinking about her, and most definitely had to stop smiling at her. Even if she did smile back, Samuel told himself, he did not have time for such things. He might be on the river to find a woman, but the

131

woman he sought had red hair, not blond. Emma had pale eyes, not bright blue ones. Still, for all of Samuel's resolve, at night when he retired beneath the wagon, the last thing he remembered before he fell asleep was the faint scent of roses and the feeling of Miss Rousseau's hand on his arm. *Fannie's* hand on his arm. *Fannie's* smile.

Every time Samuel had reason to go up on the hurricane deck, his heart beat faster than it should. He tore his shirt one day while hauling wood, and Miss Rousseau noticed and Mrs. Pike mended it. The idea that Miss Rousseau was watching him haul wood drove him to distraction. *She's not watching you, you idiot. She's bored. What else is there to do? She's anxious to get to Fort Benton and begin searching for her aunt — and return home to civilization. Just because she watches the goings-on at the woodlots doesn't mean a thing.* And even if it did, he couldn't let it mean much.

From the number of yards of silk gathered into Miss Rousseau's mourning dress, she was obviously a lady of means. There might as well be an entire ocean between the two of them. But that didn't keep Samuel from thinking about her. Nights were the worst. Just when he'd developed enough callouses that his hands didn't hurt, just when he'd gotten used to the work and the aches and pains didn't keep him up anymore . . . thinking about Fannie kept him awake.

Every night he gave himself the same speech. *She's in a first-class cabin, you dolt. She's a lady. Ladies are polite. They return smiles. That's all it is. You wouldn't dare so much as walk up to her front door in St. Charles. You're a back door common laborer now, and the sooner you remember that, the better off you'll be. Even if you were still the heir of a wealthy man, it wouldn't matter. You're on the river to find Emma . . . not to fall in love.*

Tonight was no exception. Rain had raised the river a couple of inches, and Captain Busch had decided to navigate a stretch of river for just an hour or so after sundown. Just until they got to the next woodlot. The crew members were taking shifts sounding the depths, the river was calm, the evening perfect. But Samuel couldn't sleep for thinking of Fannie.

Grabbing his coat and retrieving his mother's Bible, he crawled out from beneath the wagon and made his way past the boilers and toward the front of the ship. Just as he passed the stairs leading up to the hurricane deck, the ship shuddered. Samuel paused. Listened. Jerked on his coat, stuffed

133

the Bible into an inside pocket, and called for Lamar. This was no sandbar. Something was ripping into the underbelly of the *Delores*.

In seconds the deck began to tilt. As the vessel listed toward shore, everything began to slide toward the water. Deck passengers and hands alike screamed and shouted. The wagon toppled. Samuel lunged to help Lamar, but then he caught a glimpse of the small man already scrambling toward the far end of the deck. *Of course.* Lamar's first instinct would be to free the panicked horses. Changing course, Samuel made for the crew lowering the mackinaws into the water. And then he heard the women screaming. *Fannie! Mrs. Pike!*

Grabbing the tilted railing, he managed to climb halfway up the stairs toward the hurricane deck. One of the smokestacks ripped free. As cables whipped through the air, steam escaped in a horrific burst of heat and vapor. Thrown off the stairs and against one of the capstans, Samuel barely avoided being thrown into the river. Before he could right himself, flames spewed from the firebox below the boilers and began to crawl across the deck, blocking the stairs.

One moment Fannie was asleep. The next

she was awake and terrified. Something in the saloon slammed against the opposite side of the wall at the head of her cot. The next thing she knew, her cot was sliding toward the deck-side wall, its progress stopped only when it crashed into her trunk. The force threw her out of bed. She tried to get up, but the floor was tilted.

She reached for the edge of Hannah's cot, shouting the older woman's name. The cot contained only rumpled bedding. At the sound of breaking glass, Fannie looked toward the deck-side door. As she watched, the transom window shattered. Her hand went to her face, but the glass fell outward toward the deck. Hannah's skirt! The hook on the door where she hung her skirt at night was empty! She must have been out on the deck when — *No! No! What's happening?*

Staggering back onto her own cot, Fannie snatched her dressing gown off the foot of the bed and pulled it on. Intending to open the door just a crack to peer outside and call for Hannah, she nearly fell out of the cabin when the latch gave way and the weight of the door yanked it all the way open. She clung to the doorjamb, staring in horror at the swirling water just on the other side of the hurricane deck railing. Her cabin door faced the water now. *Hannah! Where are you?! Where are the lifeboats?*

Her things — she needed her things. Planting one foot against the doorjamb, she pried her trunk open. The ship shuddered. When someone screamed *Fire!* Fannie peered over her shoulder and up toward the saloon. Oh, dear Lord . . . she could see it . . . crawling across the saloon floor . . . coming this way . . . a golden monster, licking up the wood.

She screamed again, panicked at the thought of flames in one direction and water in the other. She couldn't go into that water. No, wait . . . the ship had stopped moving. It had to be sinking, but for now . . . for now it was steady. She might not be thrown into the water after all . . . but the flames! Clinging to the foot of her cot, she watched the flames approach, mesmerized by the light and the smoke rising into the sky. Someone called her name. Someone behind her . . . near the water . . . She looked that way.

"Hurry, Fannie! There's no time! Come to me now!"

Mr. Beck . . . Samuel . . . in a lifeboat. *Her things . . . the letters!* She couldn't give the letters to the river. Rummaging through the pile tossed out of the tray and into the

136

open trunk lid when the steamboat pitched, she grabbed her mother's locket and pulled it over her head. Snatching up the leather envelope, she hesitated. It was odd to feel heat at her back.

Samuel screamed her name again and reached one hand through the railing. Fannie glanced over her shoulder. Flames were curling around the saloon-side cabin door. The transom window popped and shattered. Just as a burst of flames belched through the doorway toward the two cots, she let go of the doorjamb. The ship moved again. Clutching the envelopes to her breast, Fannie fell toward Samuel. The railing stopped her fall . . . pain . . . and the world went dark.

Cold. So cold.

"Fannie? Fannie . . . can you hear me? Please, Fannie, open your eyes."

He sounded so worried. He shouldn't worry. She was fine. Except for being cold. She needed a blanket. Where were the blankets? *Fire!* There was fire! Sucking in a breath, Fannie struggled to escape the fire, but a gentle hand on her shoulder settled her back. "It's all right. You're safe."

She opened her eyes. Samuel was looking at her with an embarrassing amount of tender concern. Hannah wouldn't approve of the emotion registered on his face. *Hannah.* Where was she? Turning away from Samuel, Fannie noticed some people huddled around small campfires. They were . . . on shore. They looked . . . so forlorn. Exhausted. Smudged faces. Torn shirts.

A dark face appeared beside Samuel's. Mr. Davis smiled. "There now, miss. You'll be fine, just fine. You rest now. Help's coming. It shouldn't be long."

"Wh-what happened?" Fannie croaked, but before either man could answer, she remembered. The shuddering crash, the rushing water, the fire. "Help me sit up," she said, but when she extended a hand, she realized she was still in her dressing gown. Horrified, she looked about for a blanket, but there was none.

Samuel shrugged out of his coat and drew it about her shoulders. "The envelope you were carrying is in my inner coat pocket. It's safe."

She curled her fingers around her mother's locket and thanked him as she peered at the river. A smoldering skeleton hovered over the place where the *Delores* had once floated. She looked up at the two men. "Hannah?"

Mr. Davis answered. "There's men searching both sides of the river, miss. They'll search until they've found everyone."

Fannie bowed her head. Fatigue washed over her.

The old man's voice soothed, "You lay yourself back down and close your eyes. Help's coming soon."

Terrified as she was, Fannie obeyed. Her head cushioned by a patch of thick prairie grasses, she curled up beneath Samuel's black coat and closed her eyes. The next thing she knew, shouts were ringing out from the river, and when she opened her eyes, a row of mackinaw boats were lined up waiting to carry everyone . . . where, she didn't know.

The silver light of a full moon had given way to morning gold. Fannie clung to Samuel's arm as he led her away from the landing. They'd been brought there by the mackinaws sent out from this place to rescue the steamboat passengers and crew. Samuel said they were at Sioux City. Fannie's side hurt where she'd hit the railing. Every pebble felt like a shard of glass against the tender soles of her bare feet. Determined not to cry out, she bit her lower lip, ducked her head, hung on to Samuel, and kept going. Everything seemed to be happening in the mists of a fog that wouldn't clear. What were bleeding feet in a world where ships burned down and people lost everything that mattered.

She slid her hand along the lining of the black coat still draped about her shoulders. She'd saved the letters, but the idea brought little comfort. Nothing mattered right now except that they find Hannah. *Please, God. Let Hannah be all right. She's all I have left.*

The levee bustled with activity. Townspeople clustered around, offering assistance, asking news of the wreck, offering opinions about Captain Busch's navigational skills, and generally adding to what Fannie considered a curtain of noise hiding the one thing she wanted to see: Hannah's smiling face. When a train whistle pierced the morning air, Fannie jumped. Looking behind her toward the river, she saw two steamboats at the landing. One was the *Sam Cloon,* the steamer Captain Busch had been determined to catch . . . and pass. Shivering, she clutched Samuel's black coat to her and looked toward the town. As far as Fannie could tell, Sioux City was little more than a collection of clapboard buildings and log huts strewn along streams of mud that people had aggrandized with street names.

When a tall, stringy-haired woman spoke to her, Fannie recoiled at first, but the woman's voice was kind as she spoke to Samuel about providing shelter. "Here now, dearie," she said, gesturing toward a false-fronted building up ahead. The letters above the door proclaimed the building to be a hotel.

"I'm Nellie," the woman said. "Nellie Tatum. My husband and me own the hotel and Captain Busch's mate has arranged for us to take you in. You're safe now. You come with me and we'll get you fixed up in no time."

Fannie hesitated and, it seemed, so did Samuel. She liked the idea of his being reluctant to let her go, but then she remembered she was wearing his coat. He was just waiting for her to take it off. Grabbing the envelope of letters, she started to shrug out of the coat, but Samuel stopped her. "Keep it for now. Lamar and I are going to go back to the river and see what news there might be of the others." He touched her arm. "You'll know as soon as I know."

Hannah. Blinking back tears, Fannie nodded. She swayed a bit, and was suddenly grateful for Mrs. Tatum's stepping up to take her arm.

"Now, dearie, you come with me. Nellie

will take good care of you." She nodded up at Samuel. "You rest easy, now. Time you get back, I'll have her all fixed up."

Nellie Tatum kept her word. Leading Fannie inside the hotel, across the splintered floor, and to a doorway that opened from beneath the stairs, Mrs. Tatum escorted Fannie into what she said — with a tone of pride in her voice — were her private quarters. "Mine and Hiram's, that is." She guided Fannie to a blue painted chair while she heated water on a tiny iron stove. "You just set there while I heat up some water. I'm thinking you'd like to wash up a bit, and we're gonna soak those tired feet, too. You can talk or not, whichever. It don't matter to me. Some like to talk when they been through a tough spot, some don't. You do what comes natural."

The woman seemed to think a monologue was appropriate whether Fannie spoke or not, and that was fine with her. She didn't know what "came natural" to her after a "tough spot." Right now she didn't have a thing to say other than to answer Mrs. Tatum's question about the name of the woman "her friends were looking for." She managed to answer, although her voice wavered when she pronounced Hannah's name. After that she sat, her hands in her lap, Samuel's coat about her shoulders, and tried not to shiver noticeably while Mrs. Tatum heated water. When, a few moments later, she slid her feet into a tub of warm water, she sighed with relief.

Mrs. Tatum nodded. "What'd I tell ya? Nothing like a good foot soak to make a body feel better." She stood back up and offered a blanket in place of Samuel's coat. "Thought I'd give it a brushing before he comes back."

Fannie took the envelope out of the pocket and laid it in her lap, surprised and more than a little pleased on Samuel's behalf when Mrs. Tatum found the Bible in the other pocket and laid it on the scuffed table. She didn't know very much about Samuel Beck, but she'd seen enough of him to know the book was important to him. She hadn't realized it was a Bible until this moment.

"Well, ain't that nice," Mrs. Tatum said. "A man of the cloth, I reckon."

Fannie frowned. *Was* Samuel Beck some kind of minister? If so, why would he be working as a roustabout?

Mrs. Tatum hung Samuel's coat on a chair and moved it toward the stove. "I'll let it dry while I fetch you something to wear." She handed Fannie a coarse gray washcloth.

"You can clean up while I'm gone. And in case you're wonderin', won't nobody bother you while you're in here. In the way of privacy, I mean. Hiram's far too busy gathering news of the sinking and pouring drinks for the survivors in the dinin' room. We've a full house thanks to the *Delores*." She broke off and changed her tone, shaking her head back and forth and *tsk*ing in sympathy. "I do hope that handsome young man and his friend find your Mrs. Pike."

Samuel and Lamar stood beside the river, looking down at the mackinaw and its sad burden. Samuel spoke first. "How am I ever going to tell her —" he gestured toward the mackinaw — "this?"

Lamar put a hand on his shoulder. "The best way to deliver bad news, son, is to just say it right out. Mrs. Pike is gone." He paused. "You want me to do it?"

Samuel shook his head. "No. But I wouldn't mind you coming with me. You can deliver Captain Busch's message."

Lamar nodded. Together, the two men stepped into the boat. Together, they bore Hannah Pike's body up the hill and around back of one of the clapboard buildings, where the hardware store owner had already commenced to building coffins for the three victims of the wreck of the *Delores.*

CHAPTER TEN

Two are better than one; because they
have a good reward for their labour.
ECCLESIASTES 4:9

"Well now," Mrs. Tatum said, "don't that just look fine, even if I do say so myself. Sets off your golden hair right nice." She rummaged in a box. "I've got me a spool of thread right here. We'll have it hemmed up in no time. Your young man will think you just went shopping at the dry goods store, even if I do say so."

Fannie looked down at the rich tones in the plaid underskirt. Where had Mrs. Tatum found such a lovely ensemble in a place like this? And where had she gotten the idea that Samuel Beck was her young man?

"Guess you're wondering about such finery in a place like this." Mrs. Tatum knelt on the floor and began to pin the skirt up. "Fact is, Hiram and me are opening a store.

146

Me being the best at cipherin', I keep the books and I been hiding the ladies things from him for weeks now. Don't want to hear him holler about it. But the way I figure, with the railroad and all, it won't be long and all kinds of ladies will be walking these streets. Putting something fine like this here dress in the window will draw 'em inside.

"Hiram don't like to admit it, but he knows I'm right. You get the ladies' business and you got a good chance of making it." She continued pinning. "That's why I work my hands raw scrubbing floors and such in this here hotel. Keep it clean and the word gets out. The ladies will all want to stay here, and with the ladies come children and that means good business for the dining room, now, don't it. We done sold several pans of my sweet rolls just today to folks comin' off the train."

Fannie looked down at her. "You do all that? Cleaning rooms, setting up for a new store, baking bread? Do you ever sleep?"

"I'll sleep when I'm dead." Mrs. Tatum chuckled. She gestured toward the box she'd carried in with her when she returned with the traveling suit. "I guessed about yer size. You can get yerself a pair of shoes outta that box. You don't see what you like, I got a whole barrel in the storeroom next door."

Fannie crossed the room and opened the box. She selected a pair, but then Mrs. Tatum shook her head. "No. That black won't look good with the gold. I shoulda thought of that." She tapped the black shoe in Fannie's hand. "Try that on. If it fits, I'll take it with me. Be back with brown in no time. Proper stockings, too. You can work on the hem while I'm gone."

Fannie did as she was told, but after Mrs. Tatum left, she sat, needle in hand, not having any idea how to hem her own skirt. Hannah had always done the hemming. Fannie tried to remember back to the lessons she'd had as a child about French seams and fancy stitches, but she hated sewing and Mother hadn't forced the issue. She poked the needle through the fabric, but instead of stitching she stabbed her finger hard enough to draw blood. She was blinking back frustrated tears when Mrs. Tatum returned with a pair of lovely brown high-buttoned shoes in hand. As she came in the door, she said, "Your young man and his friend are back. They asked to see you."

Fannie swallowed the lump in her throat. If the news was good, Mrs. Tatum would be bustling about to help Hannah the way she'd helped Fannie. She put her hand to her still-snarled hair.

"Here now," Mrs. Tatum said, and produced a hairbrush. "Let me help you get fixed up a bit more."

"It doesn't matter," Fannie said, and suddenly nothing did. She really was alone now in the world. The dark clouds she'd left behind in St. Charles had found her again — and there was no one to help her escape them this time.

Mrs. Tatum cleared her throat. "You know what? How about I just let your friends come on in and we'll see to the rest later." She put her hand on Fannie's shoulders and gave a gentle squeeze before crossing to the door. "I'll be just outside, miss. You need anything, you holler." She opened the door and spoke to the men waiting just outside. "She's ready."

No one was ever ready to hear news like that. Samuel and Lamar came into the room, hats in hands. Lamar crossed to her and knelt down on one knee. When she extended her hand, he took it between his calloused palms. "Captain Busch done said to tell you that whatever you need, he'll see to it. Hotel . . . food . . . passage home . . . everything first class." He squeezed her hand before letting go and standing back up.

Home. The word brought back the image of peeling paint and the seedling growing out of the sagging gutter. And a life-sized stone angel bending over two graves. Taking a deep breath, Fannie forced herself to stand. "Where is she? I need to . . . see her."

Samuel's deep voice soothed. "Word is there'll be a service at the cemetery. Later today or tomorrow morning. We could ask about a church service if you want one."

Fannie didn't think she could face a preacher's voice echoing in a mostly empty church. Tears welled up as she thought back to all the grousing Hannah did about what she called "putting on airs." She cleared her throat. "Hannah was a simple woman. She'd want a simple burial." She glanced at Samuel. "If you wouldn't mind reading a few words from your Bible, though. I think Hannah would like that." The tears she'd been trying to keep back spilled down her cheeks. "I'll want a proper headstone. She was more of a mother to me than anyone. I won't have her treated like she was no one."

Samuel nodded. "I'll be honored to read the service. Mrs. Pike was a good woman."

Lamar spoke up. "That she was. Gave me some liniment for my knees. It worked real good, too."

Hearing that Hannah had shared her precious liniment with Lamar wasn't a surprise, but something about that little bit of news broke through Fannie's resolve not to make a scene. Covering her face with her hands, she began to sob. Samuel pulled her into his arms.

He couldn't think of a single man in all of creation who could watch a beautiful girl cry and not want to comfort her. Human kindness demanded it. On the other hand, a great deal more than human kindness was going on inside of Samuel while he held Miss Fannie Rousseau. The longer she lingered, the more aware he became of the feminine curves of her body against his. He closed his eyes. She could cry for a millennium as far as he was concerned.

Eventually, she laid her palm against his chest and pushed herself away, apologizing in a flustered way that verified what Samuel knew to be true. Mrs. Tatum's arms would have served just as well for this moment. "There's a packet boat leaving midmorning tomorrow," he said. "The *Isabella*. She'll wait for the early train to come into town in hopes of picking up a few passengers bound for St. Louis. We can reserve a cabin for you." When Fannie didn't answer, he said, "If you aren't quite ready to decide, that's all right."

Lamar agreed. "There's plenty of boats on the river. There'll be another one tomorrow."

Fannie's hand traced the outline of the small lock on the leather envelope behind her on the table. "I just don't know." She curled the fingers of her free hand around her locket. "I'd like to see Hannah now, please."

If Samuel's heart hadn't already been broken for Fannie, it would have broken when he and Lamar took her to see Hannah Pike's body. He offered to wait outside, but she didn't want to be alone. She asked both him and Lamar to stay. Samuel's heart ached as tears flowed down Fannie's cheeks and dripped off her jaw. Lamar's tears flowed freely, too.

The undertaker arrived while they were there. He'd already taken his measurements, he said. The coffin was ready. He listed the services he'd performed in less than tactful terms and said that ten dollars would take care of things in full. "Payment before I plant," he said, then stood back and folded his arms across his expansive belly, a complacent smile on his face.

Samuel wanted to knock him out of the

room, but the man's insensitivity seemed to help Fannie in an odd way. She stopped crying. Bent to kiss Mrs. Pike's cheek and murmured good-bye. And then she asked for a pair of scissors. "A knife will do if scissors aren't available," she said.

With a confused frown, Samuel opened his pocket knife and handed it to her. He glanced at Lamar and then at the undertaker, who seemed no less concerned than Samuel when Fannie lifted the hem of Mrs. Pike's apron. Frowning, she looked up at the undertaker. Smoothing the apron back in place, she moved to the foot of the table and lifted the hem of Mrs. Pike's skirt. She handed Samuel's knife back and spoke to the undertaker. "I believe you have something that is mine."

He scowled. "I don't know what —"

"Yes," Fannie interrupted, "yes, you do." She looked up at Samuel. "I thought Hannah was being ridiculous when she sewed all our money into the hems of her clothing, but the house was burglarized not long before we boarded the *Delores,* and she insisted we not trust our traveling money to locks and keys." She glared at the man standing across the room.

The angle of the undertaker's jaw went from stubborn to determined. "I don't know anything about any money other than the reasonable fee I charge for my services." Fannie repeated the request for her money, but this time her voice wobbled. The wobble weakened her position. The undertaker stood firm. "I am sorry for your loss, miss. If someone took your money — and of course it would be ungentlemanly for me to question such a lovely lady's veracity — whoever took your money, did it before your friend's body came to me." He looked pointedly at Lamar.

One edge of the man's mouth curled up in what Samuel could only see as a mocking smile. A dare. And Samuel just had to wipe that smile off the man's face. He would do violence if necessary, but first he'd try another way. Putting his arm about Fannie's shoulders, he pulled her close. "I don't believe you're hearing what the lady is saying, sir. There is evidence that our dear friend's 'safe,' if you will, has been violated. Since the Missouri wields neither knife nor scissors, it's obvious humans were involved. Now, sir, I am a man of peace, and I do prefer peaceful resolutions to conflicts. But where the lady and our dear friend are concerned, if peace isn't possible —" He released Fannie then, held up one clenched fist, and headed across the room.

The undertaker's hands came up to ward off an expected blow. "Now, now." He took a step back. "There's no need for any of that. I understand your position. Perfectly." Pulling a wad of cash from his pocket, he thrust it at Samuel.

Samuel peeled one bill off. "I believe you said your fee is ten dollars." He handed the rest to Fannie.

Tears coursed down her cheeks as Fannie bent down to place a small nosegay against the white wooden cross marking Hannah's grave. "I'm supposed to head home on the *Isabella* today." She swiped at the tears. "What should I do, Hannah? Do I just give up? Go back to the empty house?" She began to sob. "What will I do back there? I said maybe we'd take in boarders in the fall, but I can't do that without you." She lowered her voice. "I can't do *anything* without you. Captain Busch is heading back to St. Louis to find another ship to pilot. Samuel and Lamar are only going as far as Fort Rice. If I keep going . . . I'll be alone." She paused. "I'm afraid, Hannah. Afraid to go home and afraid to go on. Could you maybe ask God to tell me what to do? He listens to you, Hannah. I know he does."

She stared down at the fresh earth.

Thought back to the cemetery in St. Charles. The absurdity of talking to Hannah now made her cry harder. What did she expect, anyway? A voice from heaven?

"I'm tired of crying at graves, Hannah. I cannot imagine facing Mr. Vandekamp and listening to him say 'I told you so.' I can't." Her voice wavered. "I thought this was important. I thought it was something I should do. I can't turn back now . . . can I?"

She glanced toward the cemetery gate and the two men waiting for her. Finally, she stood up. "I've ordered a gravestone for you, Hannah. A proper one. Mrs. Tatum promised to see to it for me. She's a good woman. At least I think she is." Fannie shook her head. "But then, I thought E. C. Dandridge was a good person, too." Her voice broke. "I need you, Hannah. I don't know what to do."

A riverboat whistle sounded. Fannie looked toward the river. It was time to go. Hannah loved her, but even Hannah wasn't going to speak from beyond the grave. She glanced up at the sky. *You love me too, God. I know you do. But I feel so . . . alone. Could you . . . please . . . help me know what to do.*

Lifting her skirts, she picked her way through the damp grass to the cemetery

156

gate. Lamar nodded, and Samuel offered his arm. They were supposed to go back to Mrs. Tatum's now, have something to eat — Mrs. Tatum insisted, since Fannie hadn't had an appetite that morning — pick up the new trunk she'd packed with things for Fannie's journey home . . . and say good-bye. She would head back to St. Charles. And Samuel and Lamar would become memories . . . just like Hannah.

"Edie? Edie LeClerc! What in *tarnation* are you doing in Sioux City?"

Fannie, Samuel, and Lamar had just stepped into the hotel dining room when a portly man with rumpled hair called out from across the room. Fannie turned toward him, just in time to see him wipe his spectacles and perch them back on his bulbous nose. He squinted at Fannie. Blinked. And sputtered, "I'm sorry, miss. I . . . I thought you were someone else."

Her heart hammering, Fannie reached in her bag and took out Aunt Edith's photograph. She didn't know what to say, so she just handed it over. The gentleman rose. Looked from the photo to Fannie, then back at the photo.

Finally, Fannie found her voice. "I — um — she's my aunt. My mother was her sister.

157

Her twin, actually." She swallowed. "We —
uh — I haven't heard from Aunt Edith since
last year, but her letter was posted in Fort
Benton." Fannie hesitated. How much
should she tell this man? How much could
he tell her? "Apparently she was headed to
Alder Gulch."

The man nodded. "Yes. That's . . . um . . ."
He glanced at Samuel. Cleared his throat.
"That's where I met her." Suddenly, he
seemed to remember a pressing appoint-
ment. "You give Edie my best," he said.
"Name's Elmer. Elmer Fleming."

And before Fannie could think of another
thing to say, Elmer Fleming had left his
half-eaten meal and bustled out of the hotel.
Samuel went after him, of course. But there
was no sign of the man. He'd disappeared.

After Elmer Fleming, Fannie lost all interest in breakfast. Not even one of Mrs.
Tatum's sweet rolls could entice her to eat.
All she wanted was a cup of tea. Samuel
didn't suppose he should be surprised, after
the morning she'd had. Samuel, on the
other hand, only got hungrier when he was
upset. He was halfway through his stack of
flapjacks when Fannie cleared her throat
and said, as calmly as you please, "I'm going to Fort Benton."

Samuel and Lamar exchanged glances.

Lamar spoke first. "Now, miss. I understand what it is to feel like there's someone out there you belong to. Someone who belongs to you." He paused. "Not a day goes by I don't hope that one of the dark faces I see on this levee or in that town is going to be some of my kin that was sold off the place before I got free. But, miss." He took a deep breath and sighed. "Fort Benton makes Sioux City look like high society. There's *nobody* like you in Fort Benton, and there's a reason for that. It's because Fort Benton is no place for a lady. It was a mite different when you had Captain Busch and Mrs. Pike looking out for you, but —"

"But you heard what that man said," Fannie interrupted. "He met Edie LeClerc in Alder Gulch." She reached for the leather envelope and withdrew the stack of letters. "Aunt Edith mentions me in every single one of these, and she talks about wanting to visit. But for some reason she never has." She looked down at the photo and murmured, "I've lost my entire family, but I still have her — if only I can find her." She looked across at Samuel. "I know what you're both thinking. You're thinking I should write a letter and trust the mailbag

159

to Fort Benton." She shook her head. "I can't. Not now. I can't give it up. I won't." She smiled at both of them. "You're good men, but this isn't your responsibility. You have your own worries." She glanced toward the door. "I have to speak with Mrs. Tatum. I . . . I'll need a few more things if I'm headed to Montana."

Lamar spoke the minute Fannie was out of earshot. "We can't let that girl go upriver alone."

"I don't want to, either," Samuel agreed. "But Emma's supposed to be at Fort Rice, and it's another thousand miles past Fort Rice to Fort Benton. What if Emma needs me?"

"Miss Rousseau needs you, too. We'll undertake for both of them, somehow, if need be. We both know what happens to pretty girls who venture into river towns alone. And we both suspect why Mr. Fleming didn't want to talk to Miss Rousseau about her aunt Edie. At least we think we do — knowing what kind of women are usually well-known in gold mining towns."

"I don't want to believe that," Samuel said.

"Neither do I, son." Lamar took a deep breath. "The way I see it, there's a duty to be done here. Neither of us will sleep well the rest of our lives if we don't see this through, and that's the truth. She's going, whether we help her or not. Maybe she's not thinking straight, but that don't really matter, either. She's going. And she can't go alone, son. Captain Busch never would've allowed it. He thought she was all fixed up with first class on the *Isabella.* It's up to us now."

Lamar was right, of course. God help him — and according to Mother's Bible, God would — Samuel couldn't let her go off alone. "All right," he said. "We're agreed. But that raises a new question. How do the three of us travel together without creating a scandal?"

CHAPTER ELEVEN

For the word of God is quick, and
powerful, and sharper than any
two-edged sword, piercing even to the
dividing asunder of soul and spirit, and of
the joints and marrow, and is a discerner
of the thoughts and intents of the heart.

HEBREWS 4:12

Dear Minette,
By now the news has reached St.
Charles of the demise of Captain Busch's
Delores. I am safe and well. But, oh,
Minette . . . I have lost Hannah. She is
buried on a hillside here in Sioux City, and
my heart is broken.

I don't know how I will ever forgive
myself, or even if I should. I have caused
you heartache as well — by leaving without saying good-bye — but I was afraid
your father (with only good intentions, of
course) would stand in my way. Obviously

I was only thinking of myself and how lonely I was and how everything was pressing in on me. I was even afraid you might try to stop me, and I knew I wasn't strong enough to stand against that. Me . . . my . . . I. Those were my only thoughts, whatever worry and grief I might cause others. I am so sorry, dear Minette. Please forgive me.

After the disaster, I was bound for home, defeated and hopeless, when a chance encounter here in Sioux City offered evidence that Aunt Edith is, indeed, in Montana. And so I must go on. If nothing else, I cannot let Hannah's death count for nothing.

I'm doing my best to grow up — to see life through a different lens and to try to stop blaming Mother for my unhappiness — perhaps even to understand her. Hopefully, Aunt Edith will be able to help with that, but even if she does not, at least I will have finished the quest and had the opportunity to make this journey, which cost my beloved Hannah her life, mean something besides a childish adventure taken up by a spoiled, self-centered girl.

The weather is warm and lovely, and I am to be ensconced in a beautiful cabin aboard the Far West, with kind traveling companions who daily become better friends. I will write more of them another day.

Please offer your father my sympathies on the loss of the Beauvais cargo aboard the Delores. While the value of my assurances may be small, I would be remiss not to mention that Captain Otto Busch is one in whom I continue to have the greatest confidence. I would trust any one of Papa's fleet to him without hesitation. The Missouri River was at fault in the disaster, not Captain Busch.

Should you wish to write — and oh, how I hope you will — address your letters to Fort Benton. I don't know how long I will be there, but I am more determined than ever to follow the trail to Aunt Edith.

I remain . . . I hope . . . your lifelong friend,

Fannie

Fannie blinked back tears as she stared down at the overflowing trunk Mrs. Tatum had repacked upon learning that Fannie would go on to Fort Benton. Two ready-made dresses — Mrs. Tatum suggested calico — "You can wash it out real easy and ain't that better fer a place like that?" — stockings, unmentionables, and even a flannel nightgown. She'd included hairpins, a brush and comb, a small mirror, even tooth powder. Finally, she produced a wool cape so lovely that Fannie would have worn it on the streets of St. Charles with pride.

But that wasn't all. When Fannie tried to pay her, Mrs. Tatum waved a hand in the air and shook her head. "This here's advertising, plain and simple. When people admire something, you tell them about Nellie's Mercantile in Sioux City. I'll be beholden to ya for it." She hurried to the back of her future store and returned with a thick comforter folded over her arms. Stuffing it inside, she closed the trunk, locked it, and handed Fannie the key.

"Now, you don't worry about a thing. I'll see to the tombstone just like I promised, and when you come back this way, you stop in and see me, y'hear?" She headed for the door. "I'll have Hiram take this trunk down to the levee and get it hauled to your cabin." She paused halfway to the door and turned back. "I know you're a mite nervous about another steamboat," she said, "but the *Far West* is one of the best on the river. I don't know as luxury is the right word exactly, but it's a far sight better than the *Delores*. Last I heard, they offered nearly a dozen different meats on the menu every night.

165

And four kinds of pie. You'll be just fine, miss. You'll see." Then, with a wink, she added, "I know it's not my place to say it, but that young man of yours is a good one. You keep him if you can."

The *Far West* pulled away from Sioux City in the predawn hours with a full passenger roster and a main deck so packed with freight that Fannie wondered if the vessel would stay afloat. The dull thunder of the paddles slapping the water, the rattling of tiller chains below, the panting roar of escaping steam all combined to create the familiar pandemonium that was steamboating. Fannie knew she'd quickly relegate it all to annoying background noise. In a day or so she'd barely notice it, but on this first morning back on the river, as she stood next to Samuel and watched the ribbon of water between boat and shore widen, her gloved hand tightened around the railing. When the ship shuddered, she gasped and grabbed on with both hands.

Samuel murmured reassurance. "Just the normal shifting of gears so we don't have to back our way to Montana. Nothing to worry about."

Embarrassed, Fannie forced a smile. "I didn't expect to be so nervous."

"I'm not all that relaxed, either."

As Sioux City faded in the distance, the gray skies cleared and sunlight dappled the shoreline. Fannie and Samuel turned away from the railing and meandered toward the prow. *Almost like flying.* That's how Hannah would have described this moment. The thought brought tears to Fannie's eyes. When she swiped at them, Samuel murmured comfort. She shrugged. "What does it say about a person when her housekeeper's passing hurts more than losing her own mother?"

"When did your mother pass on?"

"Several weeks ago." Fannie studied the far shore. "We weren't . . . close." She took a deep breath. "I'm not entirely sure why. We didn't really fight. We just didn't seem to belong together." She paused, and then, without really understanding why, she wanted to tell Samuel everything.

"Papa died a few years ago. It was just Hannah and me living in the house last month, when someone broke in. Nothing happened really . . . beyond my being frightened to the point of fainting." She shook her head. "But my advisors urged me to gather up Mother's valuables and put them in a safer place. That's when I found the letters and the photograph. And, because of some other pressures involving Papa's business . . . well, I convinced Hannah to come with me to find Aunt Edith." She watched the countryside slide past. "Anyway, Hannah said that traveling by steamboat was like flying. She loved it. I don't think I'll ever hear a whistle or a bell again without thinking of her."

Samuel took her hand and gave it a squeeze. She squeezed back, then pulled free. "I suppose I'm in flight, too, trying to escape the things I didn't like back home, hoping to find someone I've never met who, at least in her letters, seems warm. Loving." She forced a laugh. "How pathetic is that? Girl who feels unloved seeks long-lost aunt. What might Mr. Dickens do with that bit of drama?"

Samuel didn't say anything for a few moments, but when he did, his voice was gentle. Soothing. "Going in search of someone who cares about you . . . someone you care about . . . isn't anything to be embarrassed about." He looked down at her. "That's why I'm on the river, too. I'm looking for someone I love." He paused, waiting for another group of passengers taking the air to pass by. When they'd gone on into the saloon, he continued. "I'm afraid my sister's story doesn't involve anything nearly as romantic as mysterious letters. It's actually pretty terrible."

Fannie gazed up at him. The pain in his eyes made her reach out. "Tell me." He glanced behind them. Gesturing toward two chairs on the far side of the broad deck, he escorted her over. They sat down.

Taking a deep breath, Samuel began. "My Pa's nothing like the man I imagine you called *Papa.* Mine likes to drink. And when he drinks . . . his temper takes over." He leaned forward, resting his forearms on his thighs, staring down at the deck as he spoke. "I went fishing. There was a business loss, and I knew Pa would likely come home drunk. Ma had passed on by then. I knew I should stay home. But I went fishing and left Emma alone."

He took his hat off and ran a hand through his hair. Left the hat on the deck beside his chair. To keep it from blowing away, Fannie picked it up and set it on her lap. Samuel didn't even seem to notice.

"Emma was never one to back down from a fight. Pa came home and objected to . . . something." Samuel stared at the passing countryside. "Who knows what. It could have been anything. Or nothing. But instead of retreating like she should have, Emma stood her ground. I don't know what got into her, but they argued. Horribly." He paused. "The main floor of the house after —" He shook his head. "It looked like there'd been an entire company of men battling one another in those rooms."

He took a deep breath. "Anyway, Emma ran. Our father chased her to the barn. Later she said she thought he was going to kill her. She scrambled aboard one of the horses bareback, intending to run off. But Emma was never a very good rider. She fell off — and into one of the corral posts." Samuel's voice wavered. "And then I came home."

"Oh . . . Samuel . . ." Fannie reached for his hand, but he pulled away.

"She was at the well, trying to wash it . . . trying to hold her face . . ." He traced a line from eye to jaw. "I thought she was going to bleed to death before I could get her to the doctor. But she didn't." His voice broke. "And that . . . that was the end of my beautiful Emma. Everything changed after that . . . because I went fishing."

Fannie's eyes filled with tears. "I'm so sorry."

He shrugged. "Her fiancé wanted a beautiful wife. So he broke their engagement. She took up with the wrong sort."

"And your father? It must have been hor-

170

rible for him."

Samuel's fingers curled against his palms. "I hope so. I haven't seen him since it all happened. I left Emma at the doctor's long enough to go back to the house and pack some of our things. Pa was stretched out on the floor . . . snoring." Samuel reached into his pocket and took the Bible out. Opening it to the page recording marriages and births, he pointed to a name. "That's him."

Fannie looked down at the name. Her mouth dropped open. "Saul Pilsner is your *father?!*"

He nodded. "Sometimes people who have horrible reputations are just . . . misunderstood. In my father's case, everything you've heard about him is true."

They sat in silence for a few moments. Saul Pilsner owned a packet line, but his steamboats were only part of an empire that included warehouses in New Orleans, cotton fields in Georgia, and foundries back East. He'd tried to ruin Papa more than once. Fannie didn't know the details, but every time that name came up in conversation, Papa clenched his jaw and his face reddened with emotion.

"He's brutal in business . . . and no different at home," Samuel said. "I'm done with him and his name. Forever. Beck was

my mother's maiden name, and I'm determined to spend the rest of my life being as
different from my Pa as it's possible to be."
He cleared his throat. "Emma disappeared
a few weeks ago. Gone from her boarding
house room without a word to me or anyone
else. I finally found someone on the levee
who told me she'd taken up with a Major
Chadwick." He glanced at Fannie. "Not
married, mind you. Just . . . 'took up with.'
Then I learned Chadwick was headed upriver to Fort Rice. So —" He took a deep
breath. "Here I am."

Fannie didn't know what to say. Anything
she could think of seemed so . . . empty.
What did she know of trouble compared to
what Samuel and his sister had been
through?

Samuel reached for his hat and put it on.
"I failed Emma, but I won't fail you, Fannie.
I have to get off the *Far West* while we're
tied up at Fort Rice and try to find her. I
hope she's found a new life, but I have to
know." He leaned forward, then, and took
her hands in his. "But even if I do find her,
I'll come back to you. Lamar and I agree.
We're going to do everything we can to keep
you safe and to help you find your aunt. If
Emma isn't in a good situation, I'll convince
her to come with us. Either way, both

Lamar and I are committed to being the best friends we know how to be, for as long as you want us."

Fannie soon learned that Mrs. Tatum had been right about the fare on the *Far West*. Evening menus listed a dozen meats, half a dozen vegetables, pies, and cakes, along with an impressive wine list. And yet, Fannie had no appetite for food, and she just wasn't interested in polite dinner conversation with strangers. Too much had happened. There was too much to think about. Chatting with strangers about nothing wore her out.

She hated the truth behind Lamar's statement that even though he was booked on the *Far West* as Samuel's "manservant," everyone on board — including him — would be happier if he stayed on the main deck.

She was relieved when Samuel proved himself to be an able and charming conversationalist. People soon assumed the two of them were brother and sister. Samuel encouraged the ruse, saying it would ward off any hint of scandal. It would also let any scoundrels of the E. C. Dandridge type know not to trifle with Fannie.

When he mentioned Dandridge, she forced a smile. "I believe I've learned to be a little wiser in that regard. But just the same, I appreciate your concern." She was more than appreciative. She liked the idea that Samuel felt protective. Very much. Perhaps too much.

Tears seemed just below the surface for most of every day. Thinking of Mrs. Tatum's kindness brought tears. Writing to Minette made her cry. She cried for Samuel's sister, for Lamar, for the families affected by the *Delores*'s wreck. Once she even cried in sympathy for one of the servers who was scolded for dropping something. And every night, when she stared across at the empty space where Hannah should be, she cried some more.

"I miss you so much, Hannah. . . . I need you. . . . What's it like to fall in love? . . . How do people know?" She remembered what Minette had said about an echo. She hadn't heard one . . . yet.

Two weeks out of Sioux City, Fannie was standing at the railing just outside her cabin door when Samuel called to her. "Have you had breakfast?"

She turned around, surprised by an unexpected rush of joy at the prospect of breakfast with Samuel. When she shook her head, he grinned. "It's good to see you smile." He nodded behind him toward the dining saloon. "If we hurry, we'll just make it."

Samuel greeted several of the other diners by name as he poured coffee, and joined in their laughter when an older gentleman told about the child on board who'd kept everyone entertained the previous afternoon, playing with an imaginary rabbit. "At one point he had us all down on all fours searching under every table, every chair, in search of the invisible." He pointed at Samuel as he said to Fannie, "Your brother saved the day, though. Found the imaginary rabbit . . . nibbling on his slippers."

"I thought you said it was imaginary," Fannie said with a frown.

Samuel grinned. "So were the slippers."

After breakfast, they took chairs out onto the hurricane deck. Fannie opened *Great Expectations* and Samuel opened his Bible. Side by side, they read for a while. When the wind came up, they retired back inside. Once they were settled again, Fannie pointed to the Bible. "Read to me."

"Really?"

"My father was more given to the Greeks. Mother used the Scriptures as a weapon. As I recall, she had a verse to support everything and everyone she condemned."

Samuel looked down at the book in his

hands. "Mine had a verse to support everything she did to help people . . . and her reaction to my father's unforgivable behavior."

"Read me those, if you can find them."

"Easily." Samuel opened the book. "She had them marked."

When Samuel opened his mother's Bible, Fannie was astonished at how abominably Mrs. Pilsner had treated her Bible — at least by Mother's standards. "My mother would have had my head if I'd written in a book."

Samuel smiled. "This is the only book I ever saw mine write in." He began to read. " 'Trust in the Lord with all thine heart; and lean not unto thine own understanding. In all thy ways acknowledge him, and he shall direct thy paths.' " Looking over at Fannie, he said, "I imagine those comforted her more than once." He flipped a page. "She has a date written in the margin here.

" 'Although the fig tree shall not blossom, neither shall fruit be in the vines; the labour of the olive shall fail, and the fields shall yield no meat; the flock shall be cut off from the fold, and there shall be no herd in the stalls: Yet I will rejoice in the Lord, I will joy in the God of my salvation. The Lord God is my strength, and he will make my feet like hinds' feet, and he will make me to walk upon mine high places.' "

"Something terrible must have just happened," Fannie said.

Samuel nodded. "I don't know what, but I don't suppose it really matters. The sad truth is that it could have been any number of terrible things — all of them related to her being Mrs. Saul Pilsner."

Fannie reached out to him. She gave his arm a gentle squeeze. "Do the words give *you* comfort?"

He seemed to ponder that for a moment before answering. "Yes. I think they do." He turned a few more pages. "Because of this." He read aloud, " 'Now faith is the substance of things hoped for, the evidence of things not seen.' " He held up one hand. "Here's what I know," he said, holding his other hand opposite it. "Here's what I don't." He nodded at the space in between his two hands. "That's where faith lives. In the unseen space between the two." He smiled. "I think that's where hope lives, too."

Fannie waved her hand through the space between Samuel's. "All I see is empty air."

"I'm beginning to think that from God's side of things, there's no such thing as empty." He shrugged. "But then as soon as I think I have that figured out, I get confused again." He made a fist and rapped his own head with his knuckles. "And then I decide it's my *head* that's empty."

Fannie laughed with him. She glanced down at Mrs. Pilsner's Bible. What if that book really did contain words from the mind of the God who'd made the river they were on . . . and everything stretching away from it . . . and all the rivers of the world. Oh, everyone believed God created the world in an intellectual sense. But Samuel was talking about a belief that was more than that. It seemed that his mother had had a kind of faith that took the words out of that book and put them into the decisions she made in her life. That was a far different kind of faith than Fannie knew. She prayed . . . but she was never certain anyone was listening. What would her life look like if she were more certain? What if she actually sought out the words in the Bible and let them rule her life? The idea was at once fascinating . . . and terrifying.

Samuel bent his head and peered up into her eyes. "Where'd you go?"

She shook her head and took a deep breath. "Read some more," she said. She loved the sound of Samuel's voice, but there was more to it than that. She was beginning to love the *words*. What was that hymn Minette loved? Something about "beautiful words of life." Did the Bible really contain words of life? For the first time in hers, Fannie wished she had her own Bible.

CHAPTER TWELVE

For God so loved the world, that he gave
his only begotten Son.

JOHN 3:16

There was always a sandbar to be gotten
off . . . or over . . . or past. The weather
became a major topic of conversation.
Fannie wrote to Minette every few days,
gathering up the letters and posting them at
every opportunity as the *Far West* made its
way upriver. She explained "lightering" to
get off a sandbar and double-tripping to
avoid grounding in shallow water. Fannie
told Minette all about Samuel and Lamar
and . . . Indians.

One evening in Dakotah Territory, every
man on the boat with a weapon loaded it
and lined the deck, watching the distant
hills. Someone had reported seeing squads
of Indians in the high grass and on the sides
of the big hills. The captain ordered the

brass howitzer loaded.

Fannie and the other women on board spent a sleepless night together in the saloon, ordered there by the captain in case of an attack. When dawn arrived, nervous laughter followed the announcement that it had likely been a false alarm. Someone joked about imaginary bunnies in the dining saloon . . . and imaginary Indians on the distant hills . . . and the ladies all seemed relieved that at least now they would have something of interest to write in their letters and diaries.

A few days later, the steamer passed a large encampment of Indians. Fannie stood at the railing, wishing that Hannah could see the tepees and the campfires. A group of women stood at the water's edge. Fannie raised a hand in greeting. One returned the gesture. She grew increasingly nervous about what might happen at Fort Rice. She was going to go with Samuel to ask after Emma. The night before they were to land, she told Hannah about it.

"I'm worried for Samuel," she said into the emptiness of her cabin. "What if Emma's there? What if she isn't?"

Fannie didn't know which was more cause for concern. She did know that she cared about Samuel.

■ ■ ■ ■

Although she'd seen plenty of illustrations in various publications, Fannie had never seen a military fort firsthand. Fort Rice was impressive. Its stockade rose ten feet in the air on three sides and stretched for hundreds of feet on a side. The Missouri River was the natural defense for the fourth side, which was open to the water. When the *Far West* landed, Samuel and Fannie were among the first ashore. They walked the entire circumference of the parade ground, past company barracks and officers' quarters, the post hospital and storehouses, the powder magazine and the library. No one had heard of a Major Chadwick. The post headquarters stood apart from the east line of log buildings, and Samuel received the same news there. There was no Major Chadwick at Fort Rice.

Fannie and Samuel had just headed back toward the *Far West* when a soldier they'd talked to earlier flagged them down. "Any luck?" When they said no, he replied, "If you get a chance to telegraph territorial headquarters, give them the major's company and they'll be able to tell you where he's stationed."

"It isn't actually Major Chadwick I'm trying to find," Samuel finally said. "It's my sister." He cleared his throat. "I was told she was with him. Red hair, pale eyes. Pretty, except for a scar on her left cheek. Her name is Emma. Emma Pilsner. Unless they've married, that is."

The soldier nodded. "I have three sisters," he said. "Don't see nearly enough of them." He pointed toward a row of buildings in the distance. "If it was me, I'd ask over on Laundry Row. Most laundresses are married to enlisted men, but not all. Those ladies have a way of knowing just about everything that goes on here. If your sister was ever here, there's a very good chance one of the laundresses will remember."

And they did. The first one Samuel asked put her hands on her hips and said, "Is it *Major* Chadwick, now?" She laughed and called to a woman stirring lye soap in a huge cast-iron cauldron over an open fire. "You hear that, Charlotte? Johnny's gotten himself promoted to major!" She squinted up at Samuel. "I always wondered why Em took up with him. She seemed smarter than that."

"Can you . . . can you tell me where I might find her?" Samuel swallowed.

The woman seemed to sense the emotion

behind the question. Her expression softened. She sighed. "I'm sorry, but I'm not sure. The last I knew, Johnny had a terrible case of gold fever." She shouted to the other woman. "Was it Virginia City they were headed to?"

The other woman nodded.

"There you have it, then. Virginia City. I told Em she was a fool to go with him, but she wouldn't listen." She peered at Samuel for a moment, and then she reached out and patted his forearm. "Johnny seemed to have true affection for her, hon. He's good to his women. Even the ones he leaves behind have nice things to say about him."

After Fort Rice, Samuel realized something new about Mother's notes in her Bible. She'd underlined a lot of verses about worrying. Of course, they all said not to. Samuel hadn't realized that Mother worried, but thinking that she did made him feel closer to her. He drank in the Bible's "do not worries" like a man dying of thirst, trying to keep from worrying about Emma . . . Fannie . . . and what lay ahead for them all in Fort Benton and beyond.

One sleepless night when he was roaming the ship alone, he ended up sitting on the main deck, at the very tip of the prow, staring upriver. Lamar came to sit beside him. "You seem to be having a lot of trouble with sleeping lately."

"I can't stop thinking about Fort Benton. Alder Gulch. Virginia City." He shook his head. "Emma's tough. But Fannie? Fannie's got no business in Fort Benton, let alone in a place like Virginia City."

"She'll be all right, son. Worryin' won't help it, can't change it, don't fix it."

Samuel knew that what Lamar said was right. But it was easier to *read* "don't worry" than to stop worrying.

Fannie was talking to Lamar one evening in late June when Samuel rushed toward them, his finger in his Bible, his eyes alight with . . . something. As soon as he was within earshot he blurted out, "Did you know Jesus is coming back?!"

Lamar smiled. "I believe I remember a preacher or two who said as much."

"But that's . . . incredible!"

"Amen," Lamar said.

Samuel gestured toward the shore. "It changes everything. Everything over there. Everything about everything."

Fannie didn't quite see how a few Bible verses could change everything. Didn't everyone realize they were going to see God again someday?

"Everyone needs to know," Samuel said. "This book —" he tapped the Bible with his finger — "*matters.* Eternity depends on what we do with it. People need to know that!" His voice wavered with emotion. "If Emma had known, things might have been different for her." He looked over at Lamar. "Am I crazy to think that?"

"It's never crazy to believe what God says, son." Lamar smiled again. "But the world is a hard place, and like you said the other day, there's that space that sometimes feels like empty air. It can be mighty hard to hold on when a body feels like they're in that place."

Samuel looked down at the Bible. He nodded. "I think I see that. But it doesn't change the fact that, if this book is true . . . if God reached into the world with his own Son . . . if he's coming back to see that everything's made right . . ." His voice broke. He swallowed. "If that's all true, then he can make everything right inside of us, too. If we let him." Samuel paused. "People need to know how much God loves them. They need to know that Jesus is alive . . . and he's coming back." He pointed to the Bible. "God's love sings through this whole book. Even those *begats* that used to frus-

trate me show that he cares about everything. In every generation."

"Now you really are sounding like a
preacher," Lamar said, grinning.

Samuel laughed. "I'd be a terrible
preacher."

"Seems to me you've got the most important part of it down." Lamar pointed at the
Bible. "You love that book."

"I do. But there's still a lot of it I don't
understand."

"There's nothing more irritating than a
man that don't know he don't know. So you
just keep thinking that way. After all, when
it comes to the Almighty, it seems to me
there's always going to be a whole lot a man
don't know."

Samuel laughed. "Then I'm more quali-
fied than most." He settled back and began
to read to them. " 'For if we believe that
Jesus died and rose again, even so them also
which sleep in Jesus will God bring with
him. . . . For the Lord himself shall descend
from heaven with a shout . . . and the dead
in Christ shall rise first. . . . Wherefore
comfort one another with these words.' "

Fannie had to agree with Samuel. Those
were wonderful, amazing, comforting words.
The way he read them, his voice rang with
hope and joy. Lamar was right. Samuel

sounded like a preacher . . . and while she knew she should be thrilled, she wasn't. Preachers married women who quietly went about their duty without causing disruptions. Preachers' wives didn't ask challenging questions about God. They led staid lives in solid communities where people looked up to them. They stayed in the background and did what they were told. Preachers' wives were admirable.

And Fannie would never be able to be like that.

Dear Minette,

I apologize for the long gap between letters. There hasn't been much to say that would be of interest. Samuel's sister was not at Fort Rice, but there was news of her, and now Samuel has even more reason to venture out in search of Aunt Edith, for it seems that the two ladies may be in the same place, or at least in the same part of Montana. It is called Alder Gulch. Virginia City, the territorial capital, is there, as are a number of other gold camps. It seems that anyone in search of gold in Montana ends up there. It is over two hundred miles from Fort Benton, and I will admit that the idea of going there frightens me, but then, I have been frightened for weeks now, and still somehow I manage to continue. I have decided to try my hand at praying and hope that God will undertake to guide the next phase of this journey.

The days seem long. I am eager to be finished with the river. I can quote large passages of Mr. Dickens's book now, for I believe I have read it over several times. Social life is an important part of steamboat travel, and a group gathers in the dining saloon every evening after the meal. Some ladies sew, others play cards. For a short part of the trip, there was a passenger who played the violin beautifully, but he has since disembarked.

Samuel leads a brief Sabbath service now, and the passengers seem quite taken with his earnest words. Even though he is untrained, his manner is not unlike that of Reverend Garrison of the First Church. What I mean is, he is passionate about the words that he shares from his dear mother's Bible, always emphasizing that they are not his, but that they come from the very hand of God and should bring us comfort and hope. While he is very poor in worldly possessions, Samuel is rich in kindness, and if wealth were measured in love for God, I believe he would be the richest man in the world.

And so are my days filled. We see buffalo and antelope, wolves and eagles. We glide past Indian villages and sometimes, in the evening, we can see their campfires and their shadowy forms. On occasion, the mackinaws take us to call on ladies on another steamer, and that is a welcome relief to the monotony.

Not an hour goes by but that I think of dear Hannah and wish she were with me, but I am doing my best to be mindful of her residence in heaven, which is a far better place than aboard a steamer on the Missouri.

I will write again once we have reached Fort Benton. I hope this finds you less angry than you were the day Walker brought you my note . . . and willing to forgive. Sometimes I think I may be hearing an echo, Minette . . . and then I tell myself it is only loneliness and my imagination. Tell me . . . when did you know for certain that Daniel was your echo?

Ever your friend . . .
Fannie

Finally, fully ten weeks after leaving St. Charles, after a terrifying, lurching rush over rapids and a course that took them

190

between soaring palisades of bare cliffs, Fannie lost count of how many wood stops they'd made and sandbars they'd cleared, finally, the *Far West*'s whistle blew, announcing their arrival at Fort Benton in early August.

Once again, Fannie stood next to Samuel on the hurricane deck above the ship's prow, doing her best to remain calm. Whatever she had imagined, whatever nightmares she had about Fort Benton . . . the reality of the place was worse. No wonder she was the only woman still on board the steamer. Even Nellie Tatum would be taken aback by the place.

First, there was the levee, a stretch of barren earth crowded with crates and barrels, wagons and teams, and a virtual army of filthy, rough-clad men whose scraggly beards probably contained enough vermin to populate a good-sized town. As the *Far West* inched closer to land and it became obvious that the levee itself was actually even with the hurricane deck, Fannie backed away from the railing.

Samuel reached for her and looped her arm through his. "Don't be afraid. You're the prettiest thing most of these men have seen in months. You can't blame them for looking."

"I was just — I hadn't thought — What if Mr. Dandridge — He said he was opening a business here."

"You don't have to worry about him," Samuel said, covering her hand with his. "When Captain Busch put him off the boat, he made it more than clear that your well-being was of special concern." He paused. "So did I, for that matter. He's a coward, Fannie. You should have heard him stammer assurances and apologies. If you see him, look him in the eye and wish him a good day — then continue on your way. That will give notice you're not to be trifled with. Not anymore."

Fannie pondered the advice as she gazed along the row of buildings toward the buttes in the distance. "I don't know why, but I expected mountains."

"So did I." Samuel smiled as he pointed to the isolated range far off to the south. "I guess that's them."

Fort Benton stood on the west side of a wide north-south loop of the Missouri. The terrain stretching away from the water's edge was relatively flat and bereft of trees. The horizon in every direction featured rolling uplands. To the west, an isolated butte projected upward out of the earth.

The adobe fort Dandridge had described

all those weeks ago was a great disappointment. The wall facing the river didn't seem to be much longer than the *Far West*. A small door set into a massive log gate admitted entrance, but the larger gate was closed. Fannie had no idea what might be inside in the way of buildings. Certainly, unless the side walls were longer than what she could see, the interior wouldn't house much more cargo than the *Far West*. Two bastions at opposite corners of the high adobe walls boasted narrow slit windows. The obvious reasons for high walls and bastions reminded Fannie of all the talk about the Blackfeet. Her heart lurched.

Finally, the boat stopped moving and Samuel said they should disembark. The men on the levee stopped whatever they were doing to watch her pass by. She wished she'd packed the silk traveling suit away and donned a simple calico. Maybe it wouldn't have made any difference, but the golden plaid had to be the most color that had been seen on this levee in a while. Samuel covered her hand with his in a protective gesture. Still the men stared. A few doffed their hats. One or two whistled. Fannie heard more than one comment about her blond hair, and wished she'd tucked it further out of sight. By the time she and Samuel crossed the threshold into the Macleod Hotel, Fannie was trembling.

The place reeked. She'd smelled slops and outhouses before, but the smell of Fort Benton was worse than anything she'd ever encountered. How she longed for one of Mother's rose-scented kerchiefs.

Thinking of picking her way to whatever necessary might be available behind this hovel posing as a hotel made her shudder. She would never have expected to think back to the *Delores* with fond memories, but from what she had seen of Fort Benton thus far, the *Delores* was a palace.

Tugging on Samuel's sleeve, she nearly dragged him back outside. "Couldn't I stay on the *Far West* for now?"

"You probably could tonight. But they'll be pulling out tomorrow."

Fannie's gaze landed on an overflowing brass spittoon just inside the door. "I won't complain tomorrow. But I need a little time to . . . prepare." She paused, peering up the street. "Do you think there's anything else?"

"Only one way to find out." Together, they headed off up the main street, a broad swath of earth running parallel to and very near the river. As she picked her way through the dust, Fannie thought back to St. Charles's brick-paved streets. It was difficult enough to navigate around the puddles there when it rained. She couldn't imagine what it would be like to try to plot a course through this place after a shower, let alone a few days of steady rain. Thank goodness Mrs. Tatum had suggested those calico dresses. Fannie had never paid much attention to how Hannah did the wash or ironed . . . but clearly she would have to learn.

A string of mostly unpainted false-front clapboard buildings trailed along the dusty street, boasting outfitters and hardware stores, blacksmiths and saloons. It might be midmorning, but the saloons were obviously doing a good business. Piano music wafted out into the street from every doorway. It was amazing how many men in Fort Benton couldn't seem to walk straight.

Fannie's presence was no less noted here than it had been on the levee. Samuel joked about her power to part the Red Sea. She forced a smile and tried to ignore the men who stared at her, openmouthed, waiting for her to pass by before they whistled or muttered something behind her back. She concentrated on the business signs, hoping for another hotel that might promise something besides lice and filth. E. C. Dandridge had mentioned a dozen women in Fort Benton. Where were they? Where was *he?*

CHAPTER THIRTEEN

Let your light so shine before men, that
they may see your good works, and
glorify your Father which is in heaven.

MATTHEW 5:16

"Harlan Henley, git yer backside down
here!"

The screech emanated from inside a one-
room shack wedged in between a saloon and
a barn. Before the last word faded, a small
figure dropped to the barn floor from the
loft above and shot around the corner and
out the back. A woman appeared in the
doorway of the shack, although it was no
kind of woman Fannie had ever seen. A
cigarette jutted from one side of her mouth
and a collection of scabs and open sores
dotted her face. Just as Fannie looked her
way, the woman removed the cigarette, bent
over, and hacked something into the dirt at
Samuel's feet.

"Is Harlan about this high?" Samuel asked, holding his hand about four feet from the ground.

When the woman nodded, he gestured. "I think he just ran out the back barn door."

The woman opened her mouth to respond, just as a bearish figure appeared behind her spouting the most creative string of epithets Fannie had ever heard. The essence of the man's sentence was that the boy was needed and if he kept running off he was going to get what he had coming. Fannie could only imagine what the man thought the boy had coming, because as he swore at the boy, he was grabbing the woman by the strands of stringy hair trailing out from beneath her stained kerchief and preparing to "teach her what happens when the boy don't do what he's told."

And then Samuel moved. Before Fannie even realized he'd let her hand go, he'd forced the man to let go of the woman's hair and placed himself between them. When the man raised a first, Samuel stopped it. When he lunged, Samuel stepped aside. The man's momentum carried him into the dirt. He sprang up like an enraged bear, and all the while the woman screeched until an entire circle of men had gathered to watch. Fannie backed away until her back was pressed against the front wall of the barn. The angry man kept lunging and Samuel kept dodging. At one point the man lunged so hard that when Samuel dodged away, he floundered headfirst into the corner of his own doorway. Blood streaming, he still staggered his way at Samuel.

"I'm not going to fight you," Samuel said. "I just didn't want you hitting your wife."

"Who said anything about her being my *wife,*" the man growled. "You think I'd marry a sorry, stringy-haired, plague-ridden piece of trash like her?!"

"Now, Henry," the woman whined, "you ought not talk like that. You and me get along fine. And Harlan's a good boy, he just —"

"Harlan ain't mine!" the man roared. "And don't think I don't know it!" At that, he barged back inside the shack. Fannie could hear him rummaging about, and presently he came to the doorway and tossed a bundle of rags out the door. He waved a hand at Samuel. "There! You think so much of her, you take her! I'm done. And you can have the brat, too. Neither one of 'em ever did me any good."

He took a step back and slammed the door. Weeping, the woman knelt down and picked up the bundle. She wiped her nose on her sleeve as she surveyed the circle of onlookers. One by one, they drifted away until only Samuel and Fannie and the woman remained.

"I . . . I didn't mean to make things worse for you," Samuel said. "I just — I couldn't let him —"

The woman squinted up at him. She shook her head. Looked away.

"I've got some money," Samuel said. "I could get you a room. Until you have time to decide what to do. But how would the boy find you?"

"Won't be hard," she said, gesturing toward the closed door. "This here'll be all over town before sundown. He'll know not to come home, that's for sure." She hesitated. "What you mean you got money for a room?"

"Just what I said. Room and board for you and your boy. Until you can decide what to do."

The woman looked at the closed door again. "He ain't bad when he's sober."

Samuel smiled. "Then room and board until he's sober."

She tilted her head. Looked him up and down. "You and the missus meanin' to start a rescue mission here in Fort Benton?"

Samuel glanced at Fannie. "This is my

friend, Miss Rousseau. She's here on a family matter. So am I, although my business will take me to Alder Gulch."

The woman scratched at one of the scabs on her face as she stared at Fannie. "You want to keep them high-toned looks, you best get away from this place as fast as you can." She sniffed. "Time was I wasn't all that bad lookin' myself. That was afore a couple of the rougher sort got holda me." She looked back to Samuel. "If she stays in these parts, she'll want a gun."

Noise from inside the house caught their attention. The woman turned around. "He's fixin' to head up to the saloon. That scrapin' sound? That's his boots coming out from under the bed." She nodded. "You two dandies best be getting on to them family matters. You don't wanna be here when he comes out."

Samuel offered her his arm. "Come with us."

The woman looked at Fannie. "Is he crazy?"

"No . . . he means it." *But please don't take him up on the offer.* She couldn't help it. Everything about this woman repulsed her. All she wanted was to get away.

"Listen, sonny," the woman said. "You keep yer money and don't worry about me or Harlan. We'll get by." With that, she headed through the barn in the same direction the boy had gone.

Samuel peered after her. Fannie tugged on his arm. "Let's go back to the *Far West*. I'll ask the captain about a place to stay."

The screeching woman was right. The news of what Samuel had done beat them back to the *Far West*. Fannie saw more than one face from the crowd that had gathered to watch the fight . . . and then drifted away. As she and Samuel crossed the levee, men muttered to one another, nodding at Samuel and shaking their heads.

When they set foot on deck, Lamar walked up, smiling. "What's this I hear about a tall stranger defending some woman up the street and almost getting himself killed?"

Samuel shook his head. "I was never in any danger. You must have heard about some other fight."

"Word is you offered to rent her and her child a room," Lamar said. "Makes you sound like a high roller."

"Anyone who thinks that will know the truth soon enough." Samuel grinned. "Had she taken me up on the offer, I'd have been embarrassed to inform her that she could only stay one night. That's about all that's left of my pay from the *Delores*."

Fannie looked at him in disbelief. "You offered your last penny to house a — to house *her?*"

"It seemed the thing to do."

Lamar spoke up. "While you were gone, I asked about another place to board. There's a place behind the fort. Fewer fleas, good food, and an honest owner." Lamar paused. "Some even thought he might let *me* have a room."

Samuel glanced down at Fannie. "How about you stay here while Lamar and I investigate?"

She hesitated. Fort Benton was like a foreign country where she didn't speak the language, but if she couldn't so much as take a walk in Fort Benton without needing to retreat, how would she ever stay long enough to look for Aunt Edith?

"I see what you're thinking," Samuel said. "There's no dishonor in being rattled by this place. Anyone would be."

Fannie relented. She had had enough of Fort Benton for the moment. Back in her cabin, she retrieved Aunt Edith's photograph and stretched out atop Mrs. Tatum's comforter. She wondered if the woman in the photograph had had the same reaction to Fort Benton as she had. *Probably not.*

She'd traveled all over the world by then. She's adventurous by nature. I'm . . . what?, Fannie wondered. *What am I, exactly? If Aunt Edith ran into a woman like that on the street . . . would she react like Samuel did and want to help her . . . or would she stand with her back pressed against a wall, just waiting to get away?*

Fluffing her pillow, Fannie turned on her side. Once again, she wished for Hannah to reassure her, to say something wise, to tell her she was going to be all right. Her mind raced from letters to steamboat wrecks, and finally landed where it usually did . . . on Samuel. His kind eyes . . . his deep voice . . . his patience . . . understanding . . . sense of purpose . . . faith . . . She would never have tried to help that creature on the street. Never would have stood up to that awful man. Never would have offered her last dollar to help any of them. Maybe she never should have come here. She would never be as good as Samuel, never be good enough to deserve him. . . . She drifted off.

Samuel and Lamar returned just as Fannie awakened from her nap and stepped out onto the hurricane deck for some fresh air. If Samuel's height didn't catch a person's eye, his long black coat most certainly did.

Knowing he was coming to her made Fannie smile. *"Land sakes,"* she whispered to herself, "he is a handsome man." Reaching up to smooth her hair, she descended to the main deck.

"Lamar found a good place," Samuel said. "Come see for yourself."

"I'll see to your trunk," Lamar said, then hesitated. "You all packed up?"

Other than Mrs. Tatum's comforter, Fannie was. Lamar said he would see to it, and Fannie and Samuel headed across the levee in the direction of the fort, then past it. Once past the fort, the noise from the levee faded into the background.

"That's it," Samuel said, pointing to a log structure with an overhang shading the front wall. The first thing Fannie noticed on the rustic porch was the pot of wild flowers propping open the front door. She paused to read the regulations posted to the left of the open doorway and smiled. Whoever ran the place obviously had a sense of humor.

FORT BENTON HOSTELRY
ESTABLISHED SEPTEMBER 1, 1868,
A.D.
HONEST ABE VALLEY, PROPRIETOR

HOUSE RULES

IF YOU CAN'T KEEP 'EM DON'T COME
THROUGH THE DOOR

- SPIKED BOOTS AND SPURS MUST BE
  REMOVED BEFORE RETIRING.
- TOWELS CHANGED WEEKLY. FREE
  BATHS PROVIDED BY THE MIS-
  SOURI.
- NO MORE THAN ONE DOG ALLOWED
  TO BE KEPT IN EACH SINGLE ROOM.
- ASSAULTS ON THE COOK ARE
  STRICTLY PROHIBITED.
- GUESTS ARE FORBIDDEN TO SPIT
  ON THE CEILING.
- EVERYTHING CASH IN ADVANCE.
  BOARD $25 PER MONTH. BOARD
  AND LODGING $50 PER MONTH.
  BOARD AND LODGING WITH BED
  $60 PER MONTH.
- A DEPOSIT IS REQUIRED ON ALL
  CANDLES CARRIED TO ROOMS. DE-
  POSIT REFUNDED AT CHECKOUT
  ON ALL CANDLES OR PARTS OF
  CANDLES NOT BURNED OR EATEN.
- IF YOU DON'T KNOW ASK HONEST
  ABE. IF HE DON'T KNOW HE'LL
  MAKE SOMETHING UP. HONEST.

One look at the man standing behind the
counter just inside explained Honest Abe's

nickname. He was taller than Samuel and sported a Lincolnesque beard, a very worn top hat, and a large wart on his left cheek. Fannie liked him immediately, both for his humorous sign and because, above the beard and below the brim of the top hat, his brown eyes looked almost as kind as Samuel's. Another thing that recommended Mr. Valley was the fact that, in the midst of a place with ubiquitous dust and filth, he was sporting an impeccably clean blue-and-white-striped shirt.

Fannie wanted to see the rooms for herself, of course, but she had hopes based on that striped shirt, and her hope was not disappointed. Behind the large log cabin, Mr. Valley had built two rows of single rooms that faced each other across a space he laughingly called "the commons." Down the center of that open space, a series of planks atop sawhorses provided "meeting place, dining room," he said as he doffed his hat for Fannie, "or sewing circle. Whatever the lady pleases." He'd strung a rope from roofline to roofline "for airing the bedding" and placed the necessary a good distance away from the rooms. The rooms themselves were minuscule, but they boasted tiny stoves and washstands equipped with a bowl and pitcher.

As Mr. Valley handed Samuel and Fannie keys to two rooms, he smiled and said that they were "just what the territory needs — good young people. What brings you to Fort Benton, if you don't mind my asking?"

Fannie spoke up. "Family."

"Family in Alder Gulch," Samuel added.

Valley frowned. "Now, son, it's none of my business, but you don't want to take this little lady anywhere near there. It's rough, dangerous country all two hundred some miles of the trip. The Blackfeet are fierce, and they're none too happy about what's been going on up here." He nodded at Fannie. "You both need to just stay here in Benton where it's safe." He leaned toward Samuel and said in a stage whisper, "If I had me a young lady as pretty as that, you wouldn't catch me looking for trouble up Alder Gulch way."

Samuel smiled. "I'll keep that in mind, but I'll be looking for neither trouble nor gold. I'll just have to trust the good Lord to smile on the trip and see it to a good end."

Valley arched one eyebrow. "You a gospel grinder, son?" When Samuel looked confused, he nudged him. "A preacher. You mentioned the 'good Lord' like the two of you might be acquainted. And I guess the black coat should have given it away, now, shouldn't it." He shook his head. "Can't imagine you'll find much of a congregation where you're headed. You stay here. Fort Benton needs a church. In fact" — Valley pointed toward the far end of the room — "we can clear out those tables and chairs on the Sabbath and you can hold your first service right here."

"If I'm still in town on the Sabbath, Mr. Valley," Samuel said, "I'll take you up on that offer. I don't think I'm what you'd call a gospel grinder or a preacher, but I'd be happy to offer a few words and lead some hymn singing."

Valley winked. "Well, the ladies will swarm like flies to honey when they get a look at you, son, and that's the truth. We haven't had a real preacher up this way in a long while, and they didn't last. The missuses didn't take to the territory one bit." He glanced Fannie's way.

She cleared her throat. "Just out of curiosity, Mr. Valley, I haven't seen but one other woman in all of Fort Benton. What 'ladies' would come to hear a sermon?"

"There's a few," he said. "And I'm speaking of real ladies, if you know what I mean." He winked. "You never know, you just might take a liking to Fort Benton."

Fannie smiled, even as she thought, *I just*

208

might. Right about the same time I don trousers and go to work on the levee.

"You going out dressed like that?" Mr. Valley asked the next morning, standing at the far end of the boards forming a rustic porch across the face of his boarding house. He'd been sweeping, and as Fannie and Samuel came out the front door, he set the dustpan down and stood up, broom in hand.

Fannie glanced up at Samuel before she answered. "We're going to find Mrs. Webb. Didn't you say she might help us?"

"Yes, ma'am. I believe she'll be happy to help you and delighted to meet another lady of your quality in this part of the territory." He paused before adding, "It's like having a beautiful bird flitting about Fort Benton, seeing the morning sunshine reflect off that fancy outfit. You are going to turn some heads. Folks up this way haven't seen fashion like that since . . . oh . . . since the after-dark gals paraded through town a few weeks ago."

After-dark gals? Fannie stared at Mr. Valley. He returned her gaze . . . intently . . . as if there was more to be said, but he wasn't going to say it. Fannie looked down at the gold plaid traveling suit. What could be wrong with it? Slowly . . . very slowly . . .

209

what he was saying without saying it . . . dawned on her. She glanced up at Samuel, who didn't seem to have any idea what was going on, and then back at Mr. Valley.

"Thank you. Very much." She dropped her hand from Samuel's arm and said, "I believe I'll try to save this for the trip home. The mud and dust here are going to be really hard on this silk, and without Hannah to help, I don't know if I'd ever be able to clean a really serious stain." She glanced Mr. Valley's way. "I've a blue calico I brought from Sioux City. Mrs. Webb won't be insulted if I don't wear my best silk, will she?"

"Mrs. Webb is a woman of simple means and tastes," he said with a gentle smile.

As Fannie retreated to her tiny room and changed into the blue calico, she chuckled aloud. "Well, Hannah, I've just had a lesson in putting on airs . . . from a man in a worn-out top hat, if you can believe that."

The woman who introduced herself to Fannie as Susannah Webb adjusted her spectacles as she examined the photograph Fannie held out. "When did you say the letter was posted?"

"Last year. I've heard that she was intending to go to Alder Gulch with a freighter named Babe Cox. An Elmer Fleming in Sioux City recognized her and said that was where he'd met her."

Mrs. Webb studied the picture. "Mr. Webb and I haven't been here long. I'm afraid I don't recognize her." She looked up. "But most everyone knows Babe Cox. He freights between here and Virginia City on a regular basis. He's up that way now, but he'll be back soon enough." She paused. "Let's see now . . . he pulled out last week. It's three weeks there and three weeks back . . . so . . . he'll be back in town I'd say in about five weeks."

Fannie couldn't hide her disappointment.

Mrs. Webb glanced over at Samuel. "You might have your young man ask in some of the places a lady shouldn't go, if you know what I mean. Not that I'm saying the lady in the photograph would frequent them, mind you. What I mean is, beautiful women up here . . . the men remember them . . . talk about them over drinks for months." She smiled at Fannie and patted the back of her hand. "You can bet you're already the subject of more than one tall tale in this saloon or that. That's just how the men up here are. Some can create an entire saga from a smile. They don't mean a thing by it." She paused before adding, "I was afraid of my own shadow when Mr. Webb dragged me off the steamer. You know what, though? I've been surprised by how many of these rough old boys seem to take to a smile from a lady. Turns them into gentlemen most of the time — even if it's only for a minute."

It wasn't polite to argue, and Fannie wasn't about to relay her own experience with a supposed "gentleman." She meandered to the far end of the counter as they talked, finally pausing before a glass case filled with hair pins and combs . . . some of them as elegant as anything Fannie had ever seen in St. Charles.

When she expressed surprise at the offerings, Mrs. Webb smiled. "Wherever women are, and whoever they are, they appreciate nice things. Men don't care as much. Take my husband. When we first put this place up, he thought I was a fool for cutting scallops along the edge of my shelf paper." She pointed toward a shelf stacked high with bolts of cloth. "I told him that even God himself cared that things be pretty. Why, when he gave instructions for how the tabernacle was supposed to be made, he ordered all kinds of beautiful things. Isn't that right, Reverend?" She looked to Samuel for affirmation.

Samuel didn't bother to correct her about

the title. He merely nodded and said, "Yes, ma'am. I believe it is."

"So there you have it. God likes things to look nice. And so do we ladies." She picked up a comb decorated with a delicate twining vine set with tiny red stones. "One of the girls from out on the edge of town has her eye on this," she said. "I expect one day soon some hapless miner will buy it for her, and then she'll have a bit of finery that'll make her smile." She shook her head. "And Lord knows those girls can use a reason to smile."

CHAPTER FOURTEEN

Hope deferred maketh the heart sick.
PROVERBS 13:12

Samuel spent the first few days in Fort Benton inquiring after Emma and Edith LeClerc in the establishments Mrs. Webb had whispered about. By chance he had heard that E. C. Dandridge's business prospects in Fort Benton had fallen through when his partner found out Dandridge was swindling him. Fearing for his life, Dandridge left Fort Benton on an overloaded mackinaw headed back to Sioux City and hadn't been heard of since.

No one remembered Emma, but several seemed to recognize the woman in Fannie's photograph, and they all told Samuel to head for Alder Gulch. All except one.

Just as Samuel exited a saloon one night, a gambler seated at a table in the back shoved a sporting girl off his lap and followed him out, muttering, "Got somethin' for you."

Samuel stepped to one side of the door and then followed the gambler to the opposite side of the street and a corral alongside a livery. The man was quiet at first, taking his time about lighting a cigar and watching two horses and a team of mules mill about in the moonlight. Finally, he glanced at Samuel. "About that picture you've been showing around . . ." He held out his hand and waggled his fingers. "Let's see it." Samuel reached into his coat pocket and pulled it out. The man lit a match and surveyed the photo. He handed it back, drew on his cigar, blew a trail of smoke into the night air. Finally, he growled, "What do you want with Edie? And what's that fancy little blonde staying at Abe Valley's got to do with anything?"

"Her name is Miss Rousseau," Samuel said.

The gambler took the cigar out of his mouth and turned to face Samuel. "Let's try this again. What do you and the blonde want with Edie Bonaparte? And who's the redhead you're looking for?"

"The redhead is my sister. And Miss LeClerc — we know her as Edith *LeClerc* — is Miss Rousseau's aunt."

The gambler snorted. "Well, isn't that sweet." He puffed on his cigar. "Nothing better than a family reunion. That's our motto here in the territory. We just love it when Pinkertons and parsons start asking questions. Especially about people who seem to have changed their name. Can't imagine they wouldn't want to be found."

"I don't know what to say." Samuel leaned against a corral post, hoping it would make him look relaxed. "I'm not hiding anything. I'm neither detective nor parson. I really am a brother looking for his sister." He paused. "Her name is Emma Pilsner. I've followed her all the way up the river from St. Louis where we grew up, and I don't intend to give up on finding her. She ran off with a Johnny Chadwick — who was posing as an army major, by the way. Someone at Fort Rice told me they'd headed up here. I just want to know my sister's safe — relatively speaking, at least. I don't want to cause trouble for anyone."

"Don't know a thing about your sister." The man flicked ashes onto the ground. "What's your business with Edie?"

"You know her?"

"That sounds an awful lot like another question, Parson. I believe I asked for an answer."

"I don't have anything to hide. And like I said, I don't want to cause any trouble for anyone."

"Then answer the question."

"I met a girl —"

Raucous laughter erupted from the saloon across the street and the man interrupted. "All the sad stories tend to start that way."

"I met Miss Rousseau on board the *Delores*. She and her maid were on their way up here looking for the woman you call Edie Bonaparte. Fannie — Miss Rousseau — found letters from Edie and the photograph I showed you in her mother's things after her mother passed on. It seems her mother was Miss LeClerc's twin sister, but Fannie didn't know anything about her. She just wants to meet her."

The gambler thought for a moment. "This Miss Rousseau," he said. "She was traveling with a maid? So Edie came into some money?"

Samuel shook his head. "I don't think so. I don't think Fannie's wealthy. It's more that she's lonely."

After another moment or two of silence, the man finally said, "Your Miss Rousseau is the talk of Fort Benton right now. All kinds of rumors going around about her." He dropped his cigar stub in the dirt and stepped on it. "I'm inclined to believe what you're saying. But, Parson . . . there's a reason folks stop writing home after they've come to a place like this." He paused. Cleared his throat. "The thing is, Miss Rousseau may *think* she wants to find her Aunt Edith, but she doesn't . . . at least not as long as she's looking for the woman in that cabinet photo. Do you hear what I'm telling you?"

"I believe I do."

"Good." One of the livery ponies shoved a nose through the corral poles, and the gambler stroked its muzzle as he said, "I'll tell you what I'm going to do. From what I hear, the little blonde is nice enough — just needs to get over being afraid of her own shadow. As for Edie, well, I always did like Edie. I'll let her know her niece is looking for her — and before you ask, I'm not telling you where to find her." He paused. "What happens next is up to Edie. Is that clear?"

Samuel nodded. "I can't see any good coming from my giving Fannie false hope. Like you said, a person who doesn't want to be found has their reasons."

The gambler slapped Samuel on the shoulder. "I knew you'd see things my way." He headed back inside.

He was halfway across the street when Samuel called out, "I know you said not to thank you, but thank you anyway. You might be saving Miss Rousseau more grief. She's already had her share."

The gambler gave a two-fingered salute. "You know, Parson, if I was sweet on a gal as pretty as her, I'd tie her to the bedpost before I let her head up that trail to the gulch. That gold hair of hers? High trading value as a scalp. Not that she'd last long enough for that. The trip itself will likely kill her. She's no pioneer, son. Best thing for her? Put her on the first steamboat headed back to civil-i-zation." He drawled it out . . . *civil-EYE-za-tion.*

He made a good point. The guy was observant, but then, gamblers had to be observant to stay alive, didn't they. Samuel stayed by the corral for a while, watching the animals mill about in the moonlight, obliging the friendly pony with a pat on its muzzle and a scratch behind its ears, listening to the music and laughter flowing into the night from the dozen or so saloons strung along the main street.

The gambler might be right about what was best for Fannie, but Samuel knew there was no way to get her on a steamer headed home yet. At least no way he could think of short of dosing her with laudanum and locking her in a cabin. He'd have to find a way to tie her to a boarding house bedpost . . . figuratively speaking, of course.

For days on end the only good news Fannie heard was that E. C. Dandridge was no longer in Fort Benton. There was no news at all of Aunt Edith, until over a plate of Abe Valley's scrambled eggs one sunny morning, Samuel said that he'd finally run into someone who thought they recognized the woman in the photograph. "Don't get your hopes up," he added quickly. "I didn't really learn very much. But I think it's time to head to Alder Gulch."

Fannie leaned forward. "That's wonderful! When can we leave?"

Samuel and Lamar exchanged glances. He shook his head. "*We* aren't leaving. You need to wait here."

"Wait here? Why would I do that? There's nothing here for me. If Aunt Edith is two hundred miles away, that's where I need to go."

"You don't belong on the trail to Alder Gulch, Fannie. Or in a gold mining town. And if you'll just think about it, you'll know I'm right." Samuel covered her hand with his. "Please, Fannie. Trust Lamar and me to do this."

Suddenly aware of the room full of Abe Valley's boarders and of how quiet that room was, Fannie set her fork alongside her plate, pushed back her chair, and excused herself. Once outside, though, she didn't quite know what to do with herself, and so she kept walking, alongside the fort's adobe wall and toward the levee, already teeming with activity in the morning light.

Samuel caught up with her. "I'll consider finding her just as important as finding Emma. I'll do whatever it takes. But, Fannie —"

She stopped and looked up into his handsome face. Sincerity shone in his dark eyes.

"This is good news, Fannie. Don't you see?" He reached for her hand. She let him take it. "But we don't have the money to buy horses, let alone a wagon. We're going to have to walk, and I know you'd try, but Fannie . . . think how far that is." He forced a laugh. "For all I know, Lamar will have to carry *me* part of the way. We may run into trouble. Indians . . . grizzly bears . . . who knows what else. Mr. Valley gave us the names of a couple of freighters he thinks we can hook up with. Lamar's good with horses, and I can wrestle freight with the best of them." He squeezed her hand.

221

"Please, Fannie. You have to stay here."

She didn't know whether she wanted to kiss him from relief or slap him for calling her weak. He was right, of course. Everything he was saying made sense. Not only couldn't she walk that far . . . she didn't want to. The idea terrified her.

She'd heard plenty of stories from other boarders this past week. Fort Benton's main street was nothing compared to what she'd encounter in a gold camp. And when it came to danger, the Missouri River was nothing compared to the trail to Alder Gulch. She still wanted to find Aunt Edith, but she wasn't cut out for Montana.

Even though Samuel was right, facing it called the dark cloud back overhead. Fannie pulled her hand away. To keep from crying, she began to walk again, this time along the perimeter of the adobe fort.

She was sorry she'd ever left St. Charles. Homesick and frightened. She missed Hannah. She missed Minette. Worst of all, if she couldn't handle Montana, it probably meant she wasn't cut out for Samuel, either.

"I never meant to be a burden to you." Her voice wavered. "I never should have left home."

"You aren't a burden," Samuel said. "You're . . . please, Fannie . . . please don't cry." He cupped her cheek in his palm and swept a tear away with his thumb.

She turned away and swiped at her own tears. He reached for her, but with a little shake of the head she stepped away. "I'll be fine. And you're right."

"I . . . am?"

"Of course you are. I'm not an idiot, Samuel. I don't belong here." She took a deep breath. "I'll speak with Mr. Valley about staying on at the boarding house for a few weeks. Mrs. Webb said it was three weeks up to the gulch and three weeks back. I'm assuming you can send word with another freighter headed this way if you find anything?"

He nodded. "I'll write. As often as I can."

"Then I'll wait."

Back at the boarding house, after Lamar and Samuel had headed for the levee, Fannie reread Mr. Valley's posted rules. *Sixty dollars a month for room and board.* She would need over a hundred dollars to stay here for eight weeks, and that only gave Samuel and Lamar two weeks to search a gulch teeming with thousands of people.

A needle in a haystack. Finding either woman would likely prove impossible . . . in spite of the man in Sioux City and whomever Samuel had talked to last night. As for his finding his sister? He was admirable to hold out hope, but . . . *Faith is the substance of things hoped for . . . the evidence of things not seen.*

Fannie thought over the verse she'd memorized as a child. She was something of an expert in hoping for "things not seen," but she was quickly losing faith. Mother's passing had ended any hope of knowing her love. Belief in a secure future had faded before she left home. As for the faint hope she'd harbored about Samuel and her — it was better not to think about that at all.

Pacing to the edge of Abe Valley's boarding house porch, Fannie stared toward the west. It was time she faced reality. Not a whisker of any of the big things she'd hoped for seemed possible. And now . . . now even the little things were a challenge. A hundred dollars and more to pay for her room might as well be a thousand. Of course Samuel had no idea she was nearly out of money. And he didn't need to know. If Samuel and Lamar could earn their way to Alder Gulch, then she would find a way to earn her keep in Fort Benton while they were gone. Somehow, she would hang on to a glimmer of hope in regard to Aunt Edith . . . even if it seemed she should let go of others.

■ ■ ■ ■

Abe Valley told Samuel and Lamar to seek out a freighter named Dick Turley. "He's a frightful-looking man, but he's survived things that would have killed a dozen lesser men. His father was a fur trapper. Married into a Piegan band, then got himself killed, leaving Dick to grow up with his mother's people. Since they've let it be known they won't take kindly to his being harassed, Dick's bull trains tend to make it through without any Indian troubles. I can't guarantee he'll welcome you with open arms, but if I was headed to the gulch, I'd want to be with Turley's outfit. Tell him I sent you his way." Valley paused. "Tell him I'll vouch for you."

Valley's warning didn't prepare Samuel for the snaggle-toothed, one-eyed, bald-headed mountain of a man that was Dick Turley. They found him sitting on an up-ended stump just outside of E. G. Palmer's store, whittling a bit of wood with the biggest knife Samuel had ever seen. Abe Valley's name didn't seem to do much at first.

Turley eyed Lamar and grunted, "Don't need a cook."

"I wasn't thinking to cook," Lamar said.

"I was thinking you might need an extra hand with your animals. I tended a fine batch of southern Thoroughbreds on the place where I grew up. I can trim hooves, tend cuts, repair harnesses, cure colic . . . handle just about anything that pesters four-footed critters." Lamar looked toward Turley's mules. "And while I'm partial to Thoroughbreds, I've tended my share of mules, too."

Turley grunted. He eyed Samuel. "What *you* got to offer?"

Lamar spoke up. "Sam can shoulder more freight than any man you've ever seen. And he preaches a fine sermon. Held Sabbath services on board the *Far West* all the way up from Sioux City."

Turley stopped whittling. Squinted at Samuel. "There's nobody in Alder Gulch wants to be preached at."

"Can't say that I'm surprised," Samuel said. "I don't really like being preached *at*, either."

Turley grunted. "You know the Shepherd's Psalm?"

"Sir?"

"You heard me. Do you know the Shepherd's Psalm?"

"Well . . . yes. I . . . uh . . ."

"Let's hear it."

"Now? Here?"

"Naw," Turley said, and spat. "Why don't you wait until next week sometime?" He swiped his mouth with the back of his hand. "Yes, Preacher, I mean right now. Let's hear it."

Samuel recited the psalm. Turley listened. "Well now, that wasn't so hard, was it?" He paused. Spat again. "Been some time since I've heard that. I like it." Folding his whittling knife, Turley stood up. "All right, then. Let's see how hard you two can work."

Samuel and Lamar had one of Turley's massive wagons loaded by noon. The man seemed pleased enough. He said they'd pull out at first light the next morning. When he offered to buy them a drink, Samuel had just opened his mouth to make an excuse when Turley made a face and said, "Sorry, Parson. Shoulda realized you'd be a teetotaler." He pointed in the direction of the boarding house. "Tell Abe I'll make good on it if he puts a steak on yer dinner plates. How's that?" Turley headed off without waiting for an answer.

Samuel found Abe Valley elbow deep in bread dough in the lean-to kitchen attached to the main room. He seemed surprised that Samuel was asking after Fannie. "I thought

227

she was with you. She headed toward the levee a while ago. Said something about Mrs. Webb's store and getting one of them calico bonnets." Valley held his dough-encrusted hands up to his face to mimic a sunshade. "Said something about style not mattering as much now." He grimaced. "She'll likely be just fine, long as she doesn't get lost." Valley chuckled. "She asked me for a job."

"A job?"

He nodded. "Asked if I'd be willing to let her serve tables and help with clean up and such in return for her board."

"What did you say?"

"Told her if she really meant it, I'd be more than obliged." He chuckled. "Word gets out that little gal is serving tables here, folks will line up halfway to the fort just to get a look at her." When Samuel frowned he shook his head. "Now, don't get yer dander up, son. A man can't help it that he likes pretty scenery. I'll see to it they behave themselves. You can't expect her to just stay in her room waiting for you to come back, can you?"

Of course he couldn't expect that. He just didn't like the idea of all those men staring at Fannie. On the other hand, the idea that she'd asked for work was admirable for a girl who'd been raised in one of the biggest houses in St. Charles. He had to smile, though, at the thought of Fannie pushing a broom.

"I had to ask her if she even knew how to sweep a floor," Valley said. "I think it made her a little mad . . . but then she said she thought she was smart enough to learn." He laughed again. "Tell her when you find her she's due for her broom lesson with Abe."

Valley's lack of worry relaxed Samuel some. Still, the farther he and Lamar got from the boarding house, the more unsettled he felt about Fannie's setting off on a shopping excursion alone. At least she wasn't wearing the silks and carrying that parasol. He hoped she'd tucked that gold locket out of sight. And she'd know to avoid the strip of saloons on Main . . . wouldn't she?

"This is a heck of a place for her to decide she has gumption," Samuel muttered as he and Lamar broke into a lope. What passed for gumption in Missouri could be dangerous in Montana.

Was that a scream? *Lord . . . NO!*

CHAPTER FIFTEEN

If it be possible, as much as lieth in you,
live peaceably with all men.
ROMANS 12:18

Their aroma preceded them, but it wasn't
unwashed bodies . . . it was liquor. Fannie
was nearing Mrs. Webb's mercantile when
three braves stumbled out from behind a
livery. She backpedaled immediately, intending to duck into the barn, but she was too
late. They saw her. A combination of para-
lyzing terror and fascination stopped her in
her tracks. The three men were tall and, if
she could just get past the panic she was
feeling, she might even call them impressive
— except for the whiskey bottles. Long
braided hair . . . leggings . . . beaded moccasins. Apart from the fact they couldn't
seem to stand still, they might have been
subjects for a painting.

All of that flitted through Fannie's mind,

but in its wake the fear returned, for they'd stopped staring. Now they were conferring with one another, and the way they kept looking at her, Fannie knew she was the subject. Her hand went to the place Mother's locket usually hung. Thank goodness she'd tucked it inside her dress.

The tallest of the three braves tilted his head. Took a step forward. Fannie took a step back. The other two moved to block her retreat. She spun to look at them, and just as she did, the tall one poked her back. She spun back around. The three men laughed. One waved his bottle in the air and did a shuffling kind of two-step in a circle.

The one who'd poked her reached out again. This time, he touched the bun at the back of her head. Pulling his finger away, he looked at it. Held it up to the light. Said something to his friends, and reached for her again as they all began to talk at once.

One of them must have caught a glimpse of the locket chain. Fannie winced when he inserted his finger between her neck and the high collar of her blue dress and yanked. Hard. The chain broke, and the locket fell between her breasts. When Fannie put her hand to her chest, the men laughed again. She crouched down, wrapped her arms about her knees, and began to scream.

Rough hands clawed at the bun at the back of her head. Voices yammered. She heard rather than saw a whiskey bottle fall to the earth. And then . . . footsteps . . . men yelling her name . . . and darkness.

She woke suddenly, still terrified, gasping for breath, holding her hands out and flailing madly against what proved to be only air.

Someone grasped her hands, and an unfamiliar male voice soothed, "It's all right, Miss Rousseau. You're safe. No one's going to hurt you."

Wherever she was, she was no longer at the mercy of *them.* She opened her eyes. The man who'd just spoken had a slight accent. Curly dark hair and a well-trimmed beard framed hazel eyes. She blinked in the dim light. She was lying on . . . a table? And the stranger was standing next to her, although at a respectful distance. "Where's Samuel?"

"He's just outside," the stranger said. "I'll get him as soon as you're fully awake . . . and ready."

Ready? What was there to get ready about? She wanted Samuel. She sat up and looked around the room. Some kind of framed certificate hung on the far wall above a desk sporting overflowing cubby holes and a mountain of papers. Another wall boasted a shelf cluttered with glass bottles in various sizes and colors, mortars and pestles, and a small scale.

"Where am I?"

"In my clinic, such as it is," the man said. "Dr. Edmund LaMotte at your service, *mademoiselle*."

French. That was the accent. "Clinic? H-How did I get here?"

"You fainted and Mr. Beck carried you here after your unfortunate . . . encounter."

It all came back. When she reached for Mother's locket, the doctor said, "It fell free when Mr. Beck picked you up. He told me you'd be worried about it. Your friend Mr. Davis has it. It's safe." He motioned to the mirror hanging on the wall near where Fannie sat. "Once you take a moment to fix your hair, you'll be good as new. There's a brush and comb in the holder on the wall by the mirror. They're clean. Feel free to use them."

Her hair. She reached back to feel what was left of the neat bun, shivering as she remembered how those men had treated her.

"I'm afraid you're going to have to put up with my hovering," the doctor said, "until

I'm certain you aren't going to faint again. It wouldn't do for you to be rescued only to fall and break your neck in my clinic. Very bad for a doctor's reputation."

Scooting to the edge of the table, Fannie dangled her feet over the edge as she removed what was left of her hairpins. As her hair tumbled down her back, the doctor said, "They didn't mean to hurt you. Sadly, they were drunk, or they would have been much more respectful. They merely wanted to see your hair. It really is lovely, and as you can imagine, blond hair is something of a rarity here."

Reaching out to cup her elbow in his palm, he said, "Now get up slowly. If you don't feel faint, I'll retreat and occupy myself with that mound of infernal paperwork over on the desk while you put yourself back together. Your friends will be greatly relieved to see that you're no worse for the wear."

"The way my hands are shaking," Fannie said as she stood up, "I don't know that I'd agree about not being any the worse for wear." She pressed her lips together to keep the tears back. What would have happened if Samuel and Lamar hadn't heard her scream?

"They didn't mean any harm," the doctor

repeated. He caught her gaze in the mirror. "I know those three, and" — he shook his head — "it's terrible for them. Smallpox has killed half their friends and family, and interlopers are killing off game at an alarming rate and telling them to stop the very behaviors that have measured their manhood for generations."

"Is terrifying women part of the way they measure their manhood?"

The doctor sighed. "Of course not, *mademoiselle*. As I said, they didn't mean any harm . . . and even if they had, they were too drunk to cause any." He retreated to his desk.

Fannie's voice dripped with sarcasm. "It makes me feel so much better to think they were too inebriated to follow through with . . . whatever they might have wanted to do." With a shiver, she tucked the last hairpin in place and turned away from the mirror.

"Enfin," the doctor said with a maddeningly charming smile. "It's obvious you're fully recovered." He shrugged. "As to my ability to read minds, it isn't necessary." He nodded toward the door. "Lame Bear is waiting outside to apologize for his sons' behavior. And their fascination with your

hair? It's true. But he'll tell you that himself."

Samuel and Lamar rushed in the moment the doctor opened the door. When Samuel opened his arms, Fannie went to him gladly, reveling in his warmth while he scolded her mildly for going off on her own. Fannie glanced at the doctor. "Dr. LaMotte assures me I was never in any real danger." When she asked the smug physician about a fee, he shook his head.

"It was my pleasure to be of service. And I didn't really do anything but reassure your young man here that he could expect a full recovery." His eyes crinkled at the corners when he smiled. "And now, I believe you have someone waiting to see you." He led the way outside, where an imposing Indian with gleaming black hair waited astride a beautiful gray horse. As Fannie approached, he dismounted.

"This is Lame Bear," Dr. LaMotte explained. "I'll translate for him."

"I have come with a gift to show the sadness I feel at what my sons have done. They were blinded by whiskey and your golden hair. They only meant to see if the gold would wipe away and make their hands shine in the sun. They meant no harm. But they frightened you with their drunken

dance. I wish peace. I offer you this gift."
He stroked the pony's sleek neck. "When
my sons have slept away the drink, they will
come to you and offer gifts of their own.
They will not harm you. I, Lame Bear, say
it is so."

Speechless, Fannie turned to look at Dr.
LaMotte, who explained. "He doesn't want
you to file a complaint with the army. He's
well-known here in Fort Benton, as are his
sons. The boys are rabble-rousers, but
harmless. They're related to Mrs. Culbertson, a true lady of the Blackfeet Nation,
whose husband is one of the most respected
traders in this part of the country." He
paused before saying, "Lame Bear is a good
man, Miss Rousseau. He's too proud to beg
with words, but that horse is his way of begging you not to make trouble for Owl,
Eagle, and Bear."

"That's a fine animal," Lamar murmured.

Lame Bear spoke again.

"The animal's name is Smoke," the doctor translated. "Lame Bear says he is sure-
footed and gentle. A good horse for a
woman."

Fannie didn't accept the hackamore Lame
Bear tried to hand her, but she did step
down off the porch and go to the pony,
which snorted and danced away. Lame Bear

spoke to the horse, and soon Fannie was running her hand over the horse's cheek and, finally, down to his muzzle.

"I won't make trouble for your sons," she told him, "but I have no need for a horse." When Lame Bear's voice changed and he began to gesture and shake his head, Fannie didn't need the doctor to translate. She glanced his way. "He clearly thinks I need a horse. What should I do?"

"Take the horse," the doctor said. "It's an insult to refuse a gift. I've been trying to talk Lame Bear into selling me one of his ponies for weeks now." He grinned. "I'll happily take him in trade for perpetual medical care as long as you're in Fort Benton."

Fannie spent the rest of the day, after her encounter with Lame Bear and his sons, ensconced in Honest Abe's dining room reading through Aunt Edith's letters and drinking endless cups of coffee. She wanted to write a letter for Samuel to have on hand in the event he actually found her, but she didn't know what to say. How did one answer twenty years of letters? After several false starts, she came up with a letter that she hoped would lure Aunt Edith to Fort Benton before too much time passed.

Dear Aunt Edith,

If you are reading this, it is because Samuel Beck and Lamar Davis have found you. I've dreamed of meeting you, and I've come to Fort Benton in hopes that you will want to meet me.

In last year's letter you wished for Mother to share your greetings with me. Sadly, she never did. She rests beside Papa now, beneath a weeping stone angel in the church burial ground. In my efforts to gather up some of her things and put them in Mr. Vandekamp's safe, I discovered both your letters and the cabinet portrait you had taken in Paris. Mother may not have shared them with me, but she treasured them. I know this because she kept them all together in her dressing table. I don't know why she never shared them with me, but I've read the letters so many times now that I almost have them memorized.

Is it too much to ask you to come to Fort Benton before the last steamboat of the season leaves in October? I should be on it, returning home to attend to what is left of Papa's estate and to resume the life I left. But first . . . can we make amends for these twenty years?

Fondly and with hope, your niece,

Fannie LeClerc Rousseau

Samuel and Lamar met Fannie in the candlelit dining room at the hostelry before dawn. Much to Samuel's amazement, Fannie had made coffee and breakfast.

"Don't look so surprised," she said. "Abe gave me coffee and egg lessons just after sweeping lessons yesterday afternoon." She forced a smile. "By the time I see you again, I may have graduated to piecrust and corn bread." She held out the letter she'd written to her aunt. Samuel tucked it into his mother's Bible, and then he and Lamar sat down to breakfast. He did his best to force the eggs down. They were surprisingly delicious, but he didn't have much of an appetite that morning.

Their good-bye was . . . awkward. Just when he intended to take her in his arms, Fannie remembered that Abe had suggested she send a couple of loaves of bread with them on the trail. She skittered into the kitchen. When she returned with a towel knotted around the loaves, she tucked them into the carpetbag Samuel had left sitting on one of the tables, then handed him the bag. She hugged Lamar first, then stood on tiptoe and kissed Samuel on the cheek.

"I don't want to cry," she said, and physically propelled him out the door.

They were halfway to the levee when he turned back to see Fannie silhouetted in the hostelry doorway.

"You're doing the right thing," Lamar said.

Samuel took his hat off and raked his fingers through his hair. "That doesn't make it easy."

"Nothing much worth doing is easy, son," Lamar said. "You'll write her. She'll write you."

"I don't understand why God would let me fall in love with a girl like her."

Lamar chuckled. "I can't imagine, either. A man'd be crazy to want a woman that beautiful and smart."

"Citified . . . afraid of the wilderness . . . high-toned . . . downright stuffy at times."

"Be careful, Sam," Lamar chided. "It's good to be holy. Holier-than-thou? Not so much."

"All I'm saying is —"

"— you wish she wasn't what she is. I know. Maybe she wishes you were different, too. Last I knew, only God changed hearts. So you be who you are and do what you need to do . . . and let her be who she is

241

and do what she needs to do. And trust God with the rest."

Dear Minette,

Letters can find me now. Everyone in Fort Benton seems to know that Miss Fannie Rousseau of St. Charles, Missouri, is staying at the Fort Benton Hostelry. You'd think they'd never seen a woman with blond hair before, although Mr. Valley — who insists I call him Abe now — says that it is more than the blond hair. Which of course makes me blush.

I enclose a copy of the placard hanging outside the establishment for your amusement. Abe's is actually quite acceptable when it comes to accommodations. My room is just large enough for a small bed, a washstand, and a tiny stove. There is a window opposite the door which affords me a view I would rather not have, since Abe's is on the far northern edge of Fort Benton tucked in behind the fort. From my window I see a disconcerting wilderness. I thought that Montana meant mountains, but it is all prairie here. I expected it to be colder, as well, but the days are mild.

You will wonder at this next statement, but Minette . . . I am working for my keep! It is actually enjoyable, although Abe has had to teach me the most ridiculous things. I didn't know how to sweep a floor! You may think that is a simple task, but initially I stirred up more dust than I swept. I am in charge of keeping the coffee flowing now, and Abe has promised to teach me to make bread soon.

Serving in the dining room (which is essentially the only room of the establishment save the lean-to kitchen and the rows of rooms out back) provides a never-ending supply of humorous anecdotes. Perhaps I'll begin to write them down for posterity. Recently I have served a former opera singer, a college professor, and a newspaperman. Of course by looking at the three, I would have guessed farmer, miner, thief. But that is to my shame.

I remember you telling me once that a person can learn more about others if they forget what they can see. I didn't believe you then. Being here has taught me the truth of what you said. It's more than a little humbling to realize I've spent years misjudging people based on their appearance. I always thought of Hannah as far more than a maid. Why didn't I extend the same grace to everyone?

In recent days, I have learned that many of the rough-looking men here give what they receive. If I smile and address them as if they were gentlemen, they usually respond by behaving as such. Don't fear for my safety. After one foolish mistake (which involved Indians!) I feel much better suited to guard my ways.

Mr. Beck and Mr. Davis departed for Alder Gulch a week ago. They earned passage by working for a frightful-looking freighter who, Samuel says, has a soft spot for the Shepherd's Psalm. Do you see what I mean? People are not what they seem.

The journey to Alder Gulch is one of three weeks' time, and so I am certain to remain in Fort Benton for many weeks to come. The last steamboat down the river leaves here in October, and of course I won't take any chances of missing it. To be truthful, I don't think about it very much because I don't want to consider the end of the journey without success, and while there are whispers of Aunt Edith, she has yet to materialize.

I am ever hopeful that one day soon a mailbag will arrive with a word from you, my dearest friend.

With true affection and hope,
Fannie

CHAPTER SIXTEEN

Fear ye not therefore, ye are of more
value than many sparrows.
MATTHEW 10:31

Fannie was scrubbing tables in the boarding house dining room one evening when
Abe trundled in and handed her a coffee-
stained piece of paper. "Found this blowing
around out back."

Fannie looked down at the paper. *Dear
Minette.* She blushed, laid the page on Abe's
counter, and went back to scrubbing. Abe
reached into the bucket of water on the
floor, squeezed out a rag, and joined her at
work. "Sending mail from here to Missouri
costs a pretty penny."

Fannie nodded and said nothing. She'd
written to Mr. Vandekamp requesting
money, but there was no telling how long it
would take that letter to reach him, or if he
would even reply, and she couldn't afford to

mail any more letters. Still, she kept writing. When she ran out of paper, she went back and made additions in the margins. It felt good to write to Minette, even if she couldn't mail the letters.

Abe pulled a chair from beneath a rustic table and swiped at the seat. "Soon as we're done here, what say I give you a paper and a pencil and you make a list of what you need. Start with more paper and ink — pen nibs if you need some — for those letters, and postage to send them on their way." He slid the chair back in place. "There's no reason folks back home should be losing sleep because of letters sitting here in my hotel. We'll keep an account and you can pay me back when your money comes from that Mr. Vandy fellow. Fair enough?"

"I don't know if it's fair to you," Fannie said, blinking back grateful tears, "but I think it's wonderful of you to offer."

Abe crossed to the counter, opened a drawer, and pulled out a piece of paper and a pencil. He set them on the counter. "You got any idea what things cost up here?"

Fannie shook her head. "I didn't really pay attention to the prices of things at Mrs. Webb's store. At home I just got what I wanted and signed a paper. Mr. Vandekamp took care of everything."

"Well now," Abe said, putting his hands on his hips. "I had no idea you were that fine of a lady." He grinned. "Can't imagine what your fancy friends would think if they saw you sweeping floors and scrubbing tables."

"They'd be proud of me and grateful to you for putting up with me." She smiled. "Don't think I don't appreciate it, Abe. I just hope Mr. Vandekamp answers in a hurry."

"Have you noticed how busy I've been since your presence started decorating my dining room?" Abe tapped the paper with his finger. "You make your list. I'm not rich, but I can front you a grubstake for a bit." He paused. "I don't mean to worry you, but it's August and winter comes early here. Once the river closes, we won't get mail again until spring."

Fannie had been watching the calendar in recent days with the same sense of concern, but she didn't know what she could do about any of it. Whether she found Aunt Edith or not, she couldn't imagine leaving Fort Benton without seeing Samuel again. Minette had said that falling in love was like hearing an echo. What did it mean that she couldn't echo Samuel's intense feelings about God? Next to Samuel, she almost felt like a heathen. And yet, when she thought about how safe she felt in his arms . . . the kindness in his dark eyes . . . no. She couldn't leave.

"I might not like Fort Benton in winter," Fannie said, "but right now I'd like leaving even less."

Abe nodded. "I understand. But, Fannie, you haven't felt cold until you've been through a winter up here." He shook his head. "My wife was from hardy stock, but it only took one Montana winter to do her in."

Fannie stopped scrubbing. She stood up and looked across the room at Abe. "I'm so sorry. I didn't know you'd been married." She paused. "Oh, Abe . . . losing a wife . . . that must have been so hard for you."

He grinned. "Not after she left, it wasn't. First peace and quiet I'd had in years." He lit a lamp on one of the tables. "Don't feel sorry for me. I get along just fine." He transferred paper and pen from the counter to the table. "You get to work on that list. I'm just going to set the sponge for the morning's bread. Then we'll talk."

With Abe's generous loan, Fannie was able to send Minette's letters on their way and buy more writing paper and envelopes.

Thinking of Samuel, she bought herself a Bible. At the last minute, she indulged in knitting needles and a generous supply of yarn. How she'd groused at Hannah over knitting on board the *Delores*. Now she hoped she could remember enough to make Abe a pair of mittens, even as she hoped answers would come about Aunt Edith long before she needed a pair for herself.

As she settled into a routine of sorts and got to know a few more people in Fort Benton, Fannie began to feel better about taking short walks away from the boarding house on her own. Abe said she could trust Lame Bear's apology in regard to his sons. "Half the men in town have eaten here at one time or another since you started work. I think they'd take it personally if they saw anyone bothering you. Sort of like having someone tromping through a rose garden they all enjoy." He handed her a walking stick. "Stay in this part of town between my place and the levee and I think you'll be fine. Anyone who doesn't respect you, you just hit 'em where it hurts."

Fannie blushed, but she accepted the walking stick and began to venture out for midmorning walks to and from the river. Abe had been right — again. As they got used to seeing her, men on the levee began to call out greetings and doff their hats. Once, when someone Fannie didn't recognize said something rude, another roustabout grabbed him and gave him such a talking-to that Fannie almost begged for mercy on behalf of the one who'd been so rude. She made sure to thank her defender personally the next time he ate at Abe's — and gave him an extra helping of biscuits and gravy.

Eventually she realized that she was subconsciously waiting for mail. She didn't know what she wanted most, a letter from Minette or money from Mr. Vandekamp. She felt a desperate longing for both, for different reasons. And then there was the longing to hear a word from Samuel. Hadn't they met a freighter coming *toward* Fort Benton in that time? Couldn't Samuel have at least . . . Well, of course he could have written. If he wanted to. Maybe he didn't miss her as much as she missed him.

One day Fannie skirted along the back wall of the adobe fort, and when she came around to the front, the wide gate facing the river stood open. It was the first time she'd seen the interior of the old building. Walking stick in hand, she headed inside, impressed anew by the high walls nearly three feet thick. No wonder it had taken years to build the place. She hadn't realized that the fort walls doubled as the back wall for each of the long buildings spanning nearly the entire length of each side of the interior square. Glancing up at the corner bastions, she tried to imagine what it would have been like in the days before steamboats, when the only things plying the river were mackinaws and flatboats.

She saw this place as a wilderness, but to the men who'd built the fort, the wretched town represented progress. Had the Blackfeet who first brought furs to trade realized how things were going to change?

As she admired the history behind the fort, Fannie glanced down at the bare earth and wondered at the thousands of other feet that had walked there before her. A shadow fell across the earth. Then moccasins came into view. Her heart pounding, Fannie looked up, only somewhat relieved when she recognized Lame Bear. He spoke to her, then crouched down and drew the outline of a horse in the dirt.

"Please don't be offended," she said. "I don't ride well at all, and I'd have needed a sidesaddle. Smoke is a fine animal, but —"
It wasn't doing a bit of good. From the way he argued and gestured, the man clearly

didn't understand. Fannie glanced toward Dr. LaMotte's clinic, where half a dozen men waited on the log bench outside the door. Dr. LaMotte was clearly in. Maybe he could help by translating. Motioning for Lame Bear to follow her, Fannie headed for the clinic.

She and Lame Bear were halfway there when a steamboat whistle echoed in the distance. Fannie looked downriver toward the steamer, wincing when someone on the levee fired a welcoming volley from the cannon pulled out of the fort and poised near the river for just that purpose. The instant the cannon fired, a team of bays harnessed to a wagon waiting at the levee screamed in panic. Rearing up, they lunged forward, unseating their driver. He landed in the dirt, and to the cries of "Runaway!" the horses charged off. Fannie watched them go, horrified when she saw a boy in the path of the spooked bays.

It happened so quickly, Fannie didn't have time to think. And yet, in some ways, things seemed to slow down. She saw pure terror on the child's face. Heard the wagon clattering as the team charged toward him. Registered the shouts. Realized that fear had rooted the boy in place. He wasn't going to move. In a flash, Fannie launched herself in his direction, but instead of pushing him out of the way, all she managed to do was knock him down. She fell atop him just as the crazed team lunged past, so close she felt a tug as a wheel rim ran across the edge of her calico skirt. Dazed, she sat up just as a wild-eyed Dr. LaMotte came tearing out of the clinic and raced toward them.

"Patrick! Oh, dear God . . . *mon Dieu* . . . please be all right . . . Patrick!" He scooped the boy into his arms, smoothed his dirty face with the flat of his hand, held his chin up, felt his arms and legs, and then, re-assured by the boy's sobs that he was only afraid, not injured, he turned his attention to Fannie.

"I'm all right," she said. "Really, I'm . . . fine." She got back to her feet and began to dust herself off. Lame Bear limped up. Handing her the walking stick she'd dropped, he began to pat her arm and mutter what she chose to believe was sympathy and concern. "I'm fine. Really, I . . . I —" She looked back down at the boy. "Are you sure you aren't hurt? I landed right on top of you. I'm so sorry, but —"

Dr. LaMotte stifled a sob. "You saved his life." After another crushing hug, he held the child away from him and scolded, "You were supposed to wait for me to come for you, young man." His voice wavered. "You were supposed to *wait*."

"I've walked from the store home at least a million times. I don't always need help." The boy wrestled free. Bending down, he felt for his own stick, found it, and stood back up. He looked at Fannie with beautiful but, she realized, sightless blue eyes, and smiled. "Thank you, miss. Are you as pretty as you smell?"

"Patrick!" the doctor scolded.

"I didn't realize you had a family here in Fort Benton," Fannie said. *And may I call on your wife . . . please? Is she as lonely as I am?*

"He doesn't have a family," Patrick said. "He has me. Ma died." He paused. "She had measles. So did I. I got well, but now I can't see." He forced a weak smile. "But I remember colors. Ma's eyes were brown. What color are *your*s?"

Dr. LaMotte spoke for her. "Miss Rousseau's eyes are blue, and you and I should be getting back to the clinic." Once again, he turned to Fannie. "I really don't know how to thank you. But I'll think of a way."

Lame Bear interrupted, and the doctor answered him, nodding and turning to Fannie. "Lame Bear is concerned that you didn't accept his gift. You said you didn't need a horse because you were leaving. He says that obviously you *do* need a horse, since you're still here. And he says that perhaps I should thank you by providing the saddle you need in order to be able to ride Smoke."

Fannie turned to the old man. "I didn't think you spoke English."

Lame Bear shook his head and gestured to the doctor, who said, "He doesn't *speak* English. That doesn't mean he doesn't understand it."

For the first time, Fannie thought she noticed a faint glint of humor around the old man's dark eyes. How had she not noticed that before? She cleared her throat. "I'm waiting for news from a friend, but I don't need a horse — even though I realize Smoke is a very fine one."

The doctor and Lame Bear spoke for a few minutes. Finally, Lame Bear nodded and, with a hint of a smile, headed back toward the fort.

"I've promised Lame Bear that you can ride Smoke whenever you like." The doctor smiled. "And I've agreed to get you a saddle."

Fannie gazed after the old man. "He certainly is . . . persistent."

"The Blackfeet are a generous people."

Putting a hand on his son's shoulder, Dr. LaMotte smiled. "I can't imagine what a man gives a lady who's already received — and rejected — a horse. A saddle you don't really want doesn't seem like an appropriate thank-you, either."

Fannie laughed, then nodded toward the men waiting outside the clinic. "Don't let me keep you. You're clearly needed." She glanced at Patrick. "I realize that you don't need an escort, Patrick, but I wouldn't mind one. What if we send your father back to work and you and I take a walk?" She reached for his walking stick. "You can show me how you use this, and I'll tell you how my blind friend at home uses hers."

Patrick looked her way. "You have a friend who can't see?"

"I do. Her name's Minette."

"Pa says your eyes are blue. What about your hair?"

"Patrick!" the doctor scolded.

Fannie laughed an answer. "My hair is blond and today I have on a green dress. Any other questions?"

"Will you have supper with us? I want to hear more about your blind friend. Did she go to a special school? Pa says they have schools for kids like me."

"They do. In fact, there's a very good one

not far from my home in Missouri. Minette was a student there for three years."

"And can she do everything? Did they teach her to do everything?"

"Well, she can do almost everything. She's not very good at driving a team — but then some sighted people can't seem to do that well, either." When the boy laughed, Dr. La-Motte looked at Fannie and mouthed the words *thank you* with such sincerity it made her blush.

"Do people treat her like she's stupid?" Patrick asked. "Sometimes they treat me that way. They yell. I can hear just fine."

"It's just something people do. Minette said that at school they told her to look calmly at the person yelling and say . . . very quietly" — she dropped her voice almost to a whisper — "you don't need to yell. I can hear you" — she raised her voice to a shout — "perfectly fine!"

Patrick laughed again. He looked up at his father and said, "Can't you *please* make this lovely lady join us for supper?"

Fannie teased, "Patrick LaMotte, you cannot know that I'm lovely."

" 'Course I can," the boy chided. "I can tell by the way Pa talks to you."

"You," Fannie said, blushing, "are far too accomplished at flirting, young man. And while I would enjoy joining you for supper, I have a previous engagement serving over at the Fort Benton hostelry."

"Then lunch," Patrick said.

"How old are you?"

"I'm ten. Why?"

"Because, you're quite charming. The girls at school are going to fight over you."

"Until I spill peas down my shirt," Patrick muttered. "Or knock over their milk."

"There will be no spilling of peas and no sloshing of milk," Fannie said. "I can show you how it's done."

"You can?"

"With your father's permission, yes, I can. Minette used to make me eat blindfolded."

Dr. LaMotte smiled. "I have a hunch that Patrick would be amicable to your joining us for a late lunch after you help Mr. Valley."

"Yes!" Patrick enthused.

Fannie agreed and Dr. LaMotte smiled. "I have to make a sling for the patient who's likely going to give me an earful for making him wait so long in the clinic," he said. "But after that, when you're finished at the hostelry, Patrick and I would be honored if you joined us for lunch." He smiled and glanced at his son. "*I*, however, will *not* be dining blindfolded."

Fannie returned the smile . . . and it stayed on her face all the way back to Abe's, as she wondered how it was that she didn't remember Dr. LaMotte as anything but an aging doctor who could translate for the Blackfeet. He wasn't old at all. Oh, he had a bit of gray showing at his temples, but he probably wasn't much past thirty. All in all, Dr. LaMotte was . . . well.

Surprising.

CHAPTER SEVENTEEN

But God commendeth his love toward us,
in that, while we were yet sinners, Christ
died for us.

ROMANS 5:8

Dick Turley's bull train lumbered into
Virginia City in a pouring rain three weeks
after leaving Fort Benton. The Montana
scenery he saw on the way set Samuel to
inwardly praising the God who'd created
such grandeur. The mining camps, where
the Sabbath meant going into town to
gamble and drink and enjoy a little attention from the ladies on display, set him to
praying. Today, as rain poured out of the
sky, the women posed beneath overhangs
along the street like a flock of painted birds,
raising their ruffled skirts to scandalous
heights and occasionally calling out to
passersby. They seemed to take particular
notice of Samuel, and some of the things

they called out made him blush.

More than just the women seemed to notice him, though. As he and Lamar clomped alongside the bull train, Samuel watched more than one man put his hand on the pearl-handled weapon at his side. A couple even swept their own long dark coats back behind their holsters. Casting a somewhat panicked prayer toward the heavens, Samuel tugged his hat farther down on his head and, as soon as the rain stopped, concentrated on helping unload the freight. Finally, he asked Dick Turley, "Do people up here always consider newcomers the enemy? I feel like I'm under a microscope."

Turley shrugged. "I told you to buy a gun. Only two kinds of men dress in long black coats up here. Preachers and gamblers. Nobody expects a preacher, for obvious reasons, so they figure you're a gambler. They're taking your measure." He slapped a few dollars into Samuel's palm with the words "fer you and your friend. You're both welcome on my train any time." Turning away, he crossed the muddy street and went into a saloon a few doors up from where Samuel stood, feeling conspicuous and unsure.

Lamar said in a low voice, "From the look on some of the faces staring at us, I'd best keep my head down. White folks have a way of thinking a black man who makes eye contact is asking for trouble. You decide what's next. I'm right behind you."

Just then, a feminine voice called, "Hey, sweetie."

Samuel was of a mind to ignore it, but as it turned out, the woman wasn't talking to him.

"I like molasses. Why don't you come on up here and visit Rosalie?"

"Lord, have mercy," Lamar muttered.

"Come on, now. Don't be shy. Come on and step outta the rain. Rosalie don't bite, and it looks to me like you and the tall one could both use a friend."

He was tired, soaking wet, and more than a little afraid, and so Samuel stepped underneath the nearby overhang and made eye contact with the smooth-skinned beauty wearing the lowest-cut, brightest yellow dress he could have imagined. Then he surprised himself by snatching his hat off and asking — more loudly than he intended — "Is there any place in the gulch where a man could hold a service? It's the Sabbath, you know." He took a step toward the woman named Rosalie to make room for Lamar to duck out of the rain.

Rosalie leaned to her right so she could

see around Samuel to smile at Lamar. She put her hands on her shapely hips, then looked up at Samuel. "I've been asked for an entire dictionary full of things since opening, but a place to hold a church service? That's a new one." She looked Samuel up and down. "I guess I should have realized the truth when I didn't see a holster strapped around that leg." She ran the flat of her hand along Samuel's belt and down his leg where a holster would normally be as she fluttered her long eyelashes at him. When he stayed still and stared straight ahead, she chuckled and shook her head. "A preacher. Will wonders never cease."

When she glanced behind her through the doorway to the saloon, Samuel followed her gaze. The makeshift bar made of roughhewn boards thrown atop rickety sawhorses was lined elbow-to-elbow with men. If he'd been counting, Samuel figured he'd probably just seen no fewer than two dozen shots of whiskey thrown back, glasses slammed back down onto the bar, and refills poured. When the woman lingered before him, the scent of roses made him think of Fannie. Thank God she wasn't here.

"You serious about wanting to hold a service?" the woman asked.

"I . . . I suppose I am." If it would keep

him and Lamar from getting shot by some territorial gambler calling out the new blood, he'd preach in every saloon in the gulch. He nodded. "Yes, ma'am. Yes I am. Serious."

Her laughter was mellow. Amused, not unkind. "Well, then. Follow me." Latching onto his coat lapel, she pulled Samuel through the door, calling to Lamar as she moved, "It's all right, honey. You come right on in. This is my place, and everybody's welcome at Rosalie's." She hauled Samuel to the far end of the bar, where a man sporting a white apron was standing next to a cash register. Releasing Samuel's lapel, she leaned across the bar and said something to the man in the apron. With a bemused smile in Samuel's direction, he put two fingers to his mouth and let out a screeching whistle that instantly transformed the saloon from pandemonium to silence.

When Rosalie held her arms out to him, the man came around and lifted her onto the bar. Every eye in the place was on her as she said, "Ladies and gentlemen, Rosalie's is pleased to present, for the first time ever in Alder Gulch, probably for the first time ever in all of Montana Territory, a genuine preacher." She bent down toward Samuel. "What's your name, honey?"

264

Looking away from the woman's décolletage, Samuel stuttered, "S-Samuel B-Benjamin Beck."

Rosalie considered the name and then stood back up to address the crowd. "His name is Brother Sam." She winked down at Samuel and then said to the crowd, "Everybody keep quiet until he's through. Bar's closed for the next hour, but if you stay through the sermon, Bill, here, will pour you a free shot." She looked toward the back of the saloon and called, "Rachel! Tell the girls to get on out here and listen, too. If they don't like what they hear, they will most definitely enjoy what they see."

With a grin, Rosalie leaned back down, braced one hand on each of Samuel's shoulders, and hopped off the bar. Looping her arm through Lamar's, she pulled him to the opposite side of the room and then, with a nod, called out, "All right, Brother Sam. Let's hear what you've got."

What Samuel had, as he surveyed the waiting crowd, was a dry mouth and no idea what to say. When he'd asked about conducting a service, he was expecting to be taken to some town hall and given a few minutes to find a passage in his mother's Bible and to maybe even scrape the mud off his boots. His motivation was more about

265

getting off the street and out of the line of sight of the men with guns than preaching. What could he possibly say to this crowd? This was embarrassing. *God, help me.*

Expectation hung almost as thick as the smoke in the room. Female tittering caught his attention. He looked toward the row of brightly clad women, their eyes flirting as they murmured behind fancy fans. He could feel himself blushing. He looked away.

You said my Word sings about my love. So sing.

He wished he'd paid more attention in church. Maybe he could remember the hymn they'd sung at Mother's funeral. *God — help!!* Clearing his throat, Samuel began to sing. " 'There's a land that is fairer than day . . . and by faith we can see it afar . . . for the Father waits over the way . . . to prepare us a dwelling place there.' " To his amazement, as he began the chorus, the piano player joined in with chords and, by the end of it, was adding impressive flourishes and embellishment. " 'In the sweet by and by . . . we shall meet on that beautiful shore. . . . In the sweet by and by . . . we shall meet on that beautiful shore.' "

Miraculously, Samuel remembered two more verses, and when the last strains of the song died away, the crowd applauded.

Cheered. And bellowed for more. So he sang the only other two hymns he knew, and still they wanted more. The piano player began a familiar melody. It wasn't a hymn, but Samuel knew it, so he sang "When I Saw Sweet Nellie Home." The crowd hooted and stomped and clapped. A few sang along.

Finally, Samuel pulled the Bible out of his pocket, thumbed over to a favorite passage, and read about man's unworthiness and God's love. It was, he decided, probably the worst sermon that had ever been preached in the history of preachers. But the crowd listened. Some even swiped at tears, and when the hour was up and the bar reopened, Rosalie snatched Samuel's hat off his head and handed it to the bartender, calling out, "I'm passing the hat for Brother Sam. Be generous, boys. Think of your mother and how she'd feel about someone chasing down their wayward sons and daughters to tell 'em God still loves 'em." Sam started to protest, but Rosalie held her hand up in a way that said *Hush.*

Calling to her piano player for a waltz, she turned to Lamar. "What d'ya say, handsome. Give Rosalie a dance while they pass the hat."

With Lamar dancing, Samuel couldn't exactly leave, but he felt decidedly out of place. More than one of the "congregation" offered to buy him a drink. Finally, the bartender handed him a sarsaparilla, assuring him it was nonalcoholic.

A doe-eyed girl he considered far too young to be in this line of work sashayed up, loud with praise for the sermon. "You should come every Sunday," she said. "Even if you start a church, you'll get more business here at Rosalie's than you ever will in the pew." She smiled. "Is that what you're doing? Starting a church up this way?"

Samuel shook his head. "Actually, I'm looking for someone."

"Aren't we all," the girl said with a laugh.

"That's not what I meant." Was he blushing again? "I'm looking for my sister."

"Your *sister* works in a saloon?"

Samuel barely avoided blurting out *I hope not.* Instead, he shrugged. "I just want to make sure she's all right. I haven't heard from her in a while. The last I knew, she was with a man named Johnny Chadwick and they were on their way up here."

The girl frowned. "Johnny Chadwick, you say?"

His heart lurched. "You know him?"

She motioned for Rosalie, who undraped herself from around Lamar and, taking his hand, crossed to where the girl and Samuel stood. "He's looking for his sister," the girl said. "Thinks she might be with Johnny."

Rosalie's face clouded over. "Oh, honey," she said. "I'm sorry."

"And here she is now," Abe said when Fannie got back to the boarding house. "The heroine of Fort Benton." He smiled. "Heard you saved a life today. Not bad for a prim little city gal."

Fannie blushed. "Trust me, if I'd stopped to think what I was doing . . ." She shuddered.

"Well, now you'll be famous and that means even more business. You're going to have to start helping me cook."

Fannie laughed. "You want to encourage business or poison people?"

"Well now, I taught you to sweep and scrub. I bet I can teach you to cook."

Fannie hurried into the kitchen and pulled an apron down off the hook. "I'll take you up on that, Mr. Valley. Hannah and I were thinking —" She broke off. Stopped. Stared at the floor. Swallowed. "I was thinking I might have to take in boarders this fall at home." She looked up at Abe and forced a smile. "So the people of Missouri will owe you a debt if you teach me to cook."

Abe waved her over. "All right, then. A

lesson in beans," he said, and removed a lid from the pot on the stove. "Smell that? You don't get that mouth-watering aroma unless you add a nice ham hock and an onion." He had Fannie measure dried beans into a second bean pot.

By the time she had graduated from Sorting, Rinsing, and Soaking, Fannie could hear boots clomping in the front door. It was time to serve lunch.

It was midafternoon before Fannie agreed to leave a grinning Abe Valley to finish up while she made her way back to the clinic. Patrick was waiting on the porch. When Fannie called hello, he led her around to the back door and inside a combination parlor/kitchen/bedroom.

"Do I really smell pot roast?" Fannie asked hopefully as they stepped inside.

The doctor chuckled. "Yes. Buffalo though — not beef."

"Pa's patients pay him in meat more than money," Patrick explained.

Fannie inhaled again. "It smells heavenly."

"Pa's a good cook." Patrick felt his way to a cupboard nailed to the wall across from the stove. Counting out three plates, he turned around, took three steps, and put the plates on the table.

"Please," Dr. LaMotte said, "be seated. It will be our pleasure to serve you." First, he washed his hands in a pail of water on the floor beside the stove. Patrick followed suit, and while he was drying his hands, the doctor said, "I was surprised to learn you were still here. You seemed fairly set on leaving Fort Benton as soon as possible when we first met."

"And I was surprised to learn that you have a son."

The doctor smiled. "*Touché, mademoiselle.* Patrick was helping out at Palmer's store the day —" He glanced at Patrick. "The day you came to see me."

"Mr. Palmer pretends I'm a huge help," Patrick said. "He's really just being nice, but he pretends to need help sorting the penny candy. I can do that because of the shapes. And he pays me in kind."

Dr. LaMotte chuckled and rumpled his son's russet hair even as he spoke to Fannie. "Before he left Fort Benton, Mr. Beck stopped in to show me your aunt's portrait. The family resemblance is remarkable, by the way. You look very much like her."

"She was my mother's twin," Fannie explained.

"That's what Mr. Beck said. It's a shame about his sister. I was sorry I couldn't give

271

him any news."

"Two different people have recognized Aunt Edith from the photo," Fannie said. "I'm hoping to hear news from Alder Gulch any day." She glanced at Patrick. He was far too intelligent for her to say much more about Aunt Edith or Emma Pilsner's being in the gold camps. Abe and Samuel and Lamar had all talked *around* it, of course. Surely not every woman in the gold camps was *that kind* of woman. Her heart broke for Samuel if he discovered such news of his sister. At least Fannie didn't *know* Aunt Edith.

"I'm just hoping for the best," she said, realizing even as she said it that she didn't sound very convincing. Feeling self-conscious, she glanced around the room. "You've a very comfortable living arrangement, it seems." She could just see the lower part of a trundle bed below the bottom edge of a ragged quilt partitioning part of the room off as a bedroom. The rest of the decent-sized room contained a large table, the stove, a cupboard, and a surprisingly beautiful rocking chair next to a marble-topped table and a shaded kerosene lamp.

"We do all right," the doctor said as he poured coffee. He nodded toward the door behind him. "It's convenient for the practice and keeps me from worrying — most of the time."

"It seems that you like to read," Fannie said, nodding at the rocking chair and the lamp.

"Look up, Miss Rousseau," Patrick said.

Fannie did. Dr. LaMotte had a few dozen running feet of books on shelves running the entire circumference of the living area about a foot below the ceiling.

The doctor smiled. "I have a fondness for the Greeks. And, on occasion, a Puritan or two. I also enjoy Dickens, especially when the snow flies."

"Pa *loves* winter," Patrick said. "He gets more time to read when the river traffic stops and people hunker down and stop shooting one another." He sat down across from Fannie and folded his hands. Feeling embarrassed, Fannie followed suit. She'd forgotten about saying grace in the days since Samuel and Lamar had left for the gulch.

"Why don't you say grace today, son," the doctor said.

"Thank you, Lord, that I didn't get trampled today. Thank you that Fannie was there and that she has a blind friend and she can teach me. Thank you that Pa knows how to cook and that it tastes real good.

273

Thank you for schools where I can learn how to do things and please let me go there soon. Thank you that Miss Rousseau smells like roses, because Pa —"

"We thank you, our heavenly Father," Dr. LaMotte interrupted, "in Jesus' holy name. Amen."

When the doctor said *Amen*, Patrick joined in. Stifling a smile, Fannie followed suit, opening her eyes just as Dr. LaMotte put a slice of meat on his son's plate. When the doctor reached for his own knife and fork and began to cut it up, Fannie frowned. The doctor noticed. "Is there a better way?" When Fannie nodded, he withdrew his knife and fork. "Please," he said. "Show us."

Fannie went through a brief lesson for Patrick in cutting meat. She sat back. "At least that's how Minette does it."

His face beaming with joy, Patrick forked a piece of meat he'd just cut for himself into his mouth.

While he chewed, he said, "What about milk? Show me how to keep from spilling it. I know where it is, but I'm always knocking it over."

"First," Dr. LaMotte interrupted, "show Miss Rousseau that you have been taught *some* manners."

Patrick swallowed. "Sorry. I know not to

274

talk with my mouth full. I just forgot."

"Do you know how to tell time?" Fannie asked. "What I mean is, do you know what the face of a clock looks like?" When Patrick nodded she told him his glass of milk was precisely at two o'clock, and then gave a few other pointers before looking across at Dr. LaMotte and saying, "It will be very important that you set the table exactly the same way every day or this won't work."

"Obviously," the doctor agreed.

"All right, then," Fannie said to Patrick. "You already know it's at the two o'clock position. Instead of just reaching out, though, use the edge of your plate as a guide. How about pouring your own, too." She put the pitcher in his right hand and then showed him how to judge when the glass was full. "The only thing that's hard about any of this is reminding yourself to pay attention and take your time."

Sliding his index finger along the rim of his plate to the two o'clock position, Patrick encountered the glass. Following Fannie's instructions, he poured his own milk and drank it down. When he went to set the empty glass back on the table again, he hit the rim of his plate. He made a face, then smiled. "But that was better."

Fannie agreed. "And it will only continue

to get better. All you have to do is practice. And be patient."

"I feel stupid sometimes," he said.

"So do I." When Patrick looked doubtful, she said, "Not very long ago, Mr. Valley had to show me how to sweep a floor." She joined Patrick laughing, and then said, "You think I'm joking, but I'm not. It's true."

"Everybody knows how to sweep a floor."

"Everybody doesn't, until they've learned." She put her hand on the back of Patrick's hand. "You aren't stupid, Patrick. You just haven't had a chance to learn from people who understand what it's like to be blind. I'm not stupid, either. But I never had a chance to learn some things others take for granted."

"Don't people where you're from sweep floors?"

She chuckled. "I never did. Others did it for me."

"Are you rich?"

"No, but my parents were. They hired people to sweep so I could do other things."

"Like what?"

Fannie hesitated. She didn't think Patrick would be too impressed with her knowledge of the proper form in the quadrille or which of the four forks at the dinner table one should use to eat shrimp. "Well," she said instead, "my papa loved the Greek philosophers. He used to read Aristotle to me. He had the outrageous notion that it was all right for a girl to learn those things."

"Really?" Dr. LaMotte said.

Fannie smiled. "Yes, but please don't expect me to be able to discuss his method of logic. I listened . . . but I didn't really understand." She patted Patrick's hand. "You, on the other hand, will undoubtedly understand every word of it. You'll be able to read it for yourself, you know."

"You're talking about Braille."

"I am. Minette's school has an entire Braille library."

Patrick turned to his father. "Then that's where I want to go."

Dr. LaMotte smiled at Fannie. "Where is this wonderful place with the library?"

"In St. Louis."

The doctor mouthed the question *"Can we talk later?"* When Fannie nodded, he asked aloud, "I wonder, Miss Rousseau, if while you're here in Fort Benton, you'd have time to teach Patrick some of the things you learned with your friend Minette. I'm afraid I can't offer much in the way of a salary, but I could canvass the area regarding your aunt while you tutor Patrick. Mr. Beck made a thorough search of Main

Street before he left town, but I make regular calls to some of the more remote locations. I don't think Patrick would mind my leaving him behind to spend time with you."

Patrick turned to Fannie. "Please say you'll do it, Miss Rousseau. Tell Mr. Valley I'll scrub tables. Wash dishes. Do anything he asks. A boy can only spend so many hours waiting in a carriage before he goes mad." He sighed dramatically and put the back of one hand to his forehead.

Fannie laughed. "I certainly cannot be responsible for a young man's going mad. And as for Mr. Valley, I don't believe he'll mind having an extra hand. He's been very busy lately."

"So I heard," the doctor said. "My patients keep talking about how good the food is since Mr. Valley hired help. I've been meaning to see for myself. Now it appears I'll have even more of a reason than ever."

Patrick sighed loudly. "You know what I hate? I hate when grown-ups talk but what they're saying isn't what they're really saying." He turned to Fannie. "Will learning Braille help me with that, Miss Rousseau?"

Fannie didn't know what to say. Dr. La-Motte laughed and got up to refill their coffee mugs.

CHAPTER EIGHTEEN

Teach me thy way, O Lord, and lead me
in a plain path.

PSALM 27:11

"What do you mean Chadwick's dead? When did he die? How? Did he have a woman with him?" Samuel stammered questions even as Rosalie grabbed his lapel and led him to the rear of the saloon, through a doorway, down a hall, and into a room no man of the cloth with any kind of self-respect would be caught dead in.

Rosalie raised the window shades. Gray light seeped in through the dirty windows, but light didn't improve the scenery. "Sit down, honey." She motioned to Lamar. "You too. Come on in and sit." Her voice grew stern as she said, "The bed's clean, Reverend. What was that you said out by the bar a little while ago? Jesus is no respecter of persons? I brought you back here to talk in private. If you think you're too good to sit down in my room, we can go back out front and the whole saloon can hear what I'm about to tell you about a woman with red hair and an ugly scar."

Samuel sat down. Lamar followed his example, while Rosalie perched opposite them on a stool. "Johnny Chadwick came into town with a woman that has to be your sister, although Johnny called her Estella. Anyway, it had to be her. He was good to her. At first. He said he knew a secret about a vein of gold so big it would birth a town named Chadwick. I heard him tell Estella/ Emma more than once that she was going to be the queen of Alder Gulch." Rosalie shrugged. "Imagine everyone's amazement when Johnny's secret didn't pan out. Oh, he had a few good runs, but he lost every cent he made chasing better stakes. The worse his luck got, the worse he treated Estella." She paused. "I think your sister really loved him, Brother Sam. She put up with a lot."

Just like Mother. Emma attached herself to a blowhard, and when life disappointed him, he took it out on her. It was Saul Pilsner and Mother all over again.

"But the day finally came when Emma had had enough."

280

"She left him," Samuel said.

Rosalie shook her head. "No, honey. She shot him. Deader than dead."

Dear Minette,

Do you remember Pastor Garrison's telling us that everything happens for a reason? Well, if that is true, I believe I may have met the reason I am still in Fort Benton. His name is Patrick LaMotte. He is ten years old and very bright . . . and he is blind.

Fannie wrote about Patrick that evening in the dining room after having lunch with him and his father. She talked about his longing to attend a school for the blind and how excited he was to learn the few things Fannie could teach him. She wrote and wrote and wrote . . . and then, suddenly, she realized that she had barely mentioned Samuel at all. Barely thought to mention him. What did that mean?

"You've a caller, Miss Rousseau."

Fannie started at the sound of Abe's voice. When she looked up, he was smiling and pointing at the doorway where Lame Bear stood waiting, with an envelope in his hand. Fannie opened it and read:

I have been called to Bonaparte's on an emergency. Patrick is with me. We may be gone for a day or two. I didn't want you to worry when you found the clinic locked up. When we return, we'll stop by the boarding house. I have news for you.

Most sincerely,
Edmund LaMotte

For a long moment, Fannie stood speechless, staring down at the bit of paper. When she looked back up, Lame Bear was watching her with an expression she could only interpret as concern. "He's gone to Bonaparte's," she said. "He didn't want me to worry when Patrick didn't come tomorrow." She frowned. "He says he has other news for me, but . . ." She shrugged. "I suppose I'll just have to wait." She turned to Abe. "Who are the Bonapartes?"

Abe hesitated. "Can't say," he finally said. "Guess you'll just have to wait for the doc to get back to town."

Fannie sighed. It was going to be a long couple of days.

Emma had committed murder. Of all the things Samuel had ever imagined or feared, he'd never entertained the idea of murder. Rosalie left to get him a cup of coffee. When she came back, she ordered him to drink it, and he did — before he realized the drink wasn't all coffee. He coughed his way through a scolding protest, but when the warmth of whatever it was spread through his midsection, he decided to just let it go.

"There now," Rosalie said with a satisfied nod. "For a minute there, I thought you were going to faint on me. And don't take that the way it sounds. There's not a thing about you that's anything but all man, but you've had a shock." She smiled at Lamar. "As for you, handsome . . . I just thought you might like a drink."

Lamar finally asked the question Samuel couldn't. "What do they do with a woman who's done something like that up here?"

"They cheered," Rosalie said. Samuel looked up at her. She nodded. "You heard me, handsome. Johnny Chadwick didn't have a friend left by the time it happened. He'd turned so mean that every single person who knew him agreed he had it coming. None of us could figure why Estella stayed as long as she did. The way I heard it, Johnny went after her one night and . . . well, if she hadn't done what she did, I'd be showing you her grave."

"Where is she?"

Rosalie shook her head. "I can't help you

with that. I know she was alive when she left Johnny's claim, but I don't know where she headed. She could have gone anywhere. With a freighter, with another miner . . . she could be working at a place like mine." She reached over and patted Samuel on the shoulder. "I'm sorry, Brother Sam. No brother wants to think of his sister —" she paused — "well, of his sister turning out like me." She looked away, then forced a smile and stood up.

"But hey. For whatever it's worth, honey, it seems to me your sister is a survivor. I hope you find her. If you're going to keep looking, you're going to be visiting a lot of places like mine." She winked. "Lots of chances to preach to the mean and lowly. That's somethin', Brother Sam." She went to the door, then turned back around. "I doubt you'll think this is a good offer, but if you two need a dry place out of the rain tonight, you're welcome to stay right there." She nodded at the bed. "I won't tell a soul."

Samuel could hear her laughing as she retreated up the hallway toward the saloon. He looked at Lamar. "What should I do?"

Lamar shook his head. "I don't know, son. I really don't."

"Do you think Emma could still be up here somewhere?"

"The lady said nobody was holding it against her."

"Did I hear her right? Did she honestly say people *cheered* when they heard what happened?"

"You heard right."

Samuel put his head in his hands. What kind of person had Emma become in this place . . . among these people? Without looking up, he said, "I don't know what to do."

"Sleep," Lamar said. "The good Lord provided a bed. Use it."

For the first time, Samuel realized just how bone tired he was. "What about you?"

"Don't worry about me," Lamar said, and headed for the door.

Samuel woke sometime in the middle of the night to piano music, the smell of stale whiskey, and a woman's laughter just outside the door, but fatigue weighed him down. He listened for a moment and then fell back into a deep sleep that lasted until dawn. When next he woke, there was no piano music. He sat up and went to the door. Peering out the door and into the saloon, he saw an empty room with displaced chairs and empty glasses scattered on tabletops. And Lamar, stretched out atop two tables pushed together, his face covered with his hat. When Samuel walked up, Lamar spoke without moving the hat.

"Sleep well?"

"Like I've never slept before." Samuel plopped into a chair. "I'm sorry."

Lamar lifted the hat. "For what?" When Samuel gestured at the tables, Lamar shrugged. "No different than the deck of the Delores, son. No need to apologize." He stood up. Stretching, he looked around the room. "Doesn't look quite as alluring in the light of day, does it." He scooted a chair back in place and then crossed to the bar and, reaching behind it, produced a broom. "What say we do a little housekeeping by way of thanking Rosalie for her hospitality? That'll give you time to think about what we're doing next. And where we're getting breakfast."

Samuel stood up and began to gather glasses. He had no idea what he was going to do now . . . except for one thing. He had to show Rosalie the photograph of Fannie's aunt.

"Well, well."

Rosalie's voice sounded from the back hall and she stepped into the main room, her body wrapped in a bathrobe, her sleek black hair falling down her back. She was holding a rifle. When she saw Samuel and Lamar, she crossed to the bar and set the rifle down. "I was wondering who was out here stealing my liquor." She surveyed the room. "You boys interviewing for a job as butlers?"

"We just wanted to show our thanks," Samuel said, and nodded at Lamar. "It was Lamar's idea, actually."

"Nice of you." She looked up at Samuel. "You decide what you're going to do now?"

"We'll keep looking. At least for a while. It isn't just about my sister, anyway." He went to the coat he'd hung on the back of a chair and pulled out the cabinet portrait of Fannie's aunt.

Rosalie studied it for a moment. "Who'd you say this is again?"

"A friend's aunt." Quickly, Samuel recounted how he'd met Fannie and how she'd found the photograph.

"And your friend — what did she say her aunt's name is?"

"Edith LeClerc," Samuel said. Something was wrong. He went back to his coat and withdrew Fannie's letter, then handed it to Rosalie. "I was supposed to give this to Miss LeClerc if I found her."

Rosalie read the letter. Finally, she glanced over at Lamar, then back at Samuel. "You are telling me the truth about all of this. Right?"

"Yes, ma'am," Samuel said.

She handed the letter and the photo back. "I knew her, but not by that other name. To me and everyone else up this way, that's Edie Bonaparte." Rosalie gestured around. "I bought this place from her last year. She was headed — somewhere. I don't really know where. She and some of her best girls." Rosalie shrugged. "I've heard whispers of a place down Fort Benton way, but none of my regulars talk about it, and in this business . . ." She paused. "This is not a business where people are given to discussing their plans, Reverend Sam. Only fools like Johnny Chadwick do that. And you know how that went."

After a restless night, Fannie managed to stay busy through most of the morning. She took a walk after lunch. Read her Bible. Wrote another letter to Minette. Still, the hours dragged. That afternoon she went into the kitchen and, nodding at the mountain of spuds piled on the worktable, asked Abe, "Do you think I could graduate to peeling potatoes today? I'm going to go crazy waiting for Edmund to get back and tell me his news."

288

When Abe agreed, she donned an apron. He handed her a knife. "It's sharp," he warned, "and the doctor's not here to sew you up, so you take your time."

Fannie nodded. She picked up a potato and held it out to Abe. "Please don't roll your eyes at me. Just show me how." He did, and Fannie perched on the stool beside the table and went to work massacring the mound of spuds.

"I've got to fumigate one of the rooms out back," Abe said. "Take all afternoon if you need it." He put a bean pot on the table. "Once they're peeled, cut them into quarters and put 'em in here. When the pot's two-thirds full, cover them with water and set them on to boil."

While she worked, Fannie's thoughts flitted in every direction. She worked steadily, but when she had the first pot of potatoes settled on the stove top and the fire going, she went in search of Abe. He was hauling the bed ticking out of a room. When he caught sight of her, he held his hand up.

"Don't come any closer." He pointed to the ticking. "Fleas. Can't decide whether to treat it or burn it." He dropped the ticking in the sun and headed back her way.

Taking Edmund's note from her apron pocket, Fannie read it aloud. "Are you sure you've never met the Bonapartes?"

"I think you need to wait until you hear from the doc."

It took Fannie the rest of the afternoon to peel her way through Abe's mound of potatoes, and she was grateful. The hours still dragged while her mind raced from possibility to possibility, from Aunt Edith to Mother to Emma Pilsner to Samuel and back again, but at least she had something worthwhile to do while she obsessed. Once, she thought she heard Edmund's buggy and raced to the front door. Lame Bear was sitting in the shade beneath the boarding house overhang, but there was no buggy.

The sun went down and the moon came out, and still there was no word.

"He told you he might be a day or two," Abe said when Fannie worried aloud. "Take this out to Lame Bear." He handed Fannie a plate of food.

Later, when she went back to get the plate, Lame Bear was licking it. For the first time, Fannie realized how thin he was. The idea that she hadn't ever noticed made her feel ashamed. How could she have seen the man as often as she had and not wondered if he might be hungry?

Fannie waited up reading by lamplight until she began to nod off. Finally, she turned down the lamp and went to bed. Whatever was going on out at the Bonapartes', it must have been a difficult case. She couldn't help but think about Patrick. Maybe the Bonapartes had children. Hopefully he wasn't terribly bored.

The outrageous idea arrived halfway through Fannie's sleepless night, and it would not be argued away. Abe knew more than he was saying about the Bonapartes. The longer Fannie waited for Edmund to return, the more obvious it became. Something about the word made Abe uncomfortable. Fannie thought she knew what it might be . . . but he was never going to admit it. It was going to be up to her. Her idea was outrageous, but not nearly as outrageous as climbing aboard a steamboat headed into the unknown. Finally, Fannie gave in to it.

She got dressed in the dark and made her way toward the front of the boarding house. Lame Bear was still there, leaning against the boarding house wall. His head was bowed when Fannie first stepped onto the board porch, but at the first creak, he was on his feet.

"I want to go to Dr. LaMotte," Fannie said. "Will you take me?"

The Indian shook his head.

She pulled Dr. LaMotte's note out and read it to him. All of it. "The news he has is about my aunt." She spread her hand on her chest. "My mother is dead. She has a sister. Here." Fannie gestured around. "Possibly at the Bonapartes. I need to see her."

"Bad place." Lame Bear shook his head again. "Bad for you."

For a moment, Fannie was so shocked that Lame Bear had actually spoken English, she didn't know what to say. But finally, she found her voice again. "Edmund is there with Patrick. I'll be all right. Please, Lame Bear. Take me to them."

"Too far," he said, and pointed to her feet.

"Let me try," she said. "Please."

Finally, the old man motioned for her to follow him, but when he headed toward the fort, Fannie protested. "Isn't the Bonapartes' —" she gestured toward the west — "isn't it that way?"

"Too far," Lame Bear repeated, and kept walking.

If she was going to ask him to take her somewhere, Fannie supposed she was going to have to trust him. Her heart pounding, she followed him, alongside the high fort walls, across the moonlit expanse between the fort and . . . Edmund's. Lame Bear hadn't understood a thing she'd said. He thought she wanted to go to the clinic.

Fannie had just opened her mouth to protest when Lame Bear headed past the clinic and toward the small shed out back. Smoke whickered a greeting and nosed Lame Bear's arm, while the old man whispered something in the pony's ear. Finally, fashioning a hackamore from the woven lead he'd used when he'd tried to give the pony to Fannie, Lame Bear led Smoke into the moonlight and gestured for her to climb aboard.

Fannie looked about in desperation. "I don't . . . I can't . . . ride," she said.

Lame Bear repeated the gesture. Fannie hesitated. This was insane. *But it might work.* Edmund was there . . . and if they met him coming back, she could just climb into his buggy and learn whatever news he had the way he had intended in the first place. He'd be surprised, perhaps angry, but Patrick would be a buffer. How dangerous could it be?

"You won't let go, will you?"

Lame Bear grasped the hackamore firmly in hand. Fannie searched about for something to climb up on. Motioning to a stump by the woodpile, she went to it and, lifting her skirt, stepped up. Lame Bear walked Smoke up beside her, and she scrambled

CHAPTER NINETEEN

A man's heart deviseth his way: but the
Lord directeth his steps.

PROVERBS 16:9

Oh, dear God. What have I done? When
Fannie realized what Lame Bear had in
mind, she panicked. They were still within
sight of Fort Benton, and she very nearly
slid off Smoke and ran back, but at that moment a wolf howled. And so she stayed on
the pony, trembling with fear as Lame Bear
loped ahead and ducked into one of the
handful of tepees pitched in a clearing.

When Lame Bear emerged, he was accompanied by three other Indians . . . the
same three who'd tried to rub the gold from
her hair. Fannie took in a sharp breath.
Smoke must have sensed her terror. Snort-
ing, he danced sideways. Somehow, she
managed not to fall off.

"Please, Lame Bear," she croaked. "I —"

She looked back toward Fort Benton.

Lame Bear held up a hand to silence her. He gestured to the others, and Fannie realized they were armed. With rifles. But they were also standing at a respectful distance. "They guard the way." Taking Smoke's hackamore in hand, he headed off again.

The wolf howled again. Another animal screamed . . . *screamed.* Fannie shivered, realizing once again how stupid she was. How could she have thought they would just walk across the landscape at night, undefended? She should have known. She didn't think. Once again . . . she didn't think. Thankfully, Lame Bear did. He'd promised that his sons would bring her gifts to apologize. They never had. Lame Bear had just seen to it that they made amends.

As the sky grew light, Lame Bear turned around and gestured to his sons, and together, the three turned around and headed off at a lope. Up ahead, in the midst of a stand of trees, stood a two-story log structure surrounded by half a dozen smaller buildings. Edmund's buggy was parked next to a large corral, and his old horse stood inside it, looking off toward something in the distance.

Smoke whinnied and the horse turned its

head and answered. When Smoke began to dance, Fannie grasped his mane, suddenly aware of just how sore her legs were. Lame Bear spoke to the horse and motioned for Fannie to put her hand on his shoulder and slide off. She obeyed, but lost her balance when her feet struck the earth and landed on her backside instead of her feet. A combination of exhaustion and raw nerves helped her laugh — much more loudly than she should have. Smoke snorted.

"I don't know how to thank you," she said.

Lame Bear shook his head and motioned for her to go. She was halfway to the house when she turned to look behind her. Astride the pony now, Lame Bear waited. Watched. Fannie raised a hand in thanks. Lame Bear returned the sign.

As Fannie picked her way toward the front door of the log house, smoke began to curl into the sky from one of the two stone chimneys. A rooster crowed. One of the outbuildings was a substantial chicken coop, its yard enclosed in wire. There was a large barn and what had to be a bunkhouse. Or . . . maybe . . . not exactly a bunkhouse in the traditional sense. Fannie's stomach clenched.

Now that she was there, she wished she

were anywhere else. This might have been the worst idea of all the horrible ideas she'd ever had. Maybe she should have just climbed into Edmund's buggy and gone to sleep and waited for him to come out. She had no business — A door slammed and a man emerged from the back of the house and headed for the necessary. It wasn't Edmund. Fannie's heart thudded. She'd just about decided to hide in the buggy when movement at the window to the right of the front door caught her attention. She'd been seen. There was nothing to do now but follow through with her plan.

She glanced behind her one more time. Lame Bear was gone. Shivering and rubbing her arms, she wished for a shawl to wrap herself in . . . something to do with her hands, at least. She picked her way to the door. It opened just a crack and a husky voice said, "Who are you and what d'ya want?"

"I . . . I'm looking for Dr. Edmund La-Motte and his son, Patrick. They . . . he — Dr. Lamotte — sent a message telling me they were coming here. I'm Fannie. Fannie Rousseau." She thought she heard someone stirring about inside. Voices? Someone swearing. "They aren't exactly expecting me, but . . . could you please tell the doctor . . . or Patrick . . . that I'm here?"

After a long silence, a voice said, "Wait," and the door closed again.

Fannie waited. And waited. She looked around at the place again. Was it — had it been — a ranch? It seemed so far from town. It didn't make any sense, actually. It was too far from town to get any business, wasn't it? Pondering the "business" brought new dread. She should never have come. Where was Edmund? What was she going to say? *Oh, God. Do you see me? I think I've made another mistake . . . and it's too late to take it back. Help! Please help!*

She had stepped away from the door and was staring at the horizon sending panicked prayers toward the heavens when the door behind her opened. She turned around and with a sharp intake of breath, looked at . . . Mother. Not Mother, of course, but still . . . the resemblance removed any possibility of Fannie's saying a word. She stared, speechless.

She couldn't remember ever seeing her mother's hair down. Had it been this pretty? Except for gray at the temples, the cascade of hair around this woman's shoulders shone like spun gold. But this clearly wasn't Mother. This woman was smoking. A cigar. Odd that in spite of the cigar and the somewhat annoyed expression, there was also something regal about her. She looked Fannie up . . . down . . . and then up again. And then she removed the cigar from between her pale lips and said, "I don't think you're really here to see Edmund. Or Patrick."

The voice wasn't anything like Mother's. Husky. Almost masculine. In fact, Fannie realized, this was the same person who'd told her to wait at the door. She'd thought it was a man. Amazing. And, Fannie realized, probably alluring to the kind of men — *God in heaven. Help. Help me get through this. I'm so sorry I came.* How could she be sorry and fascinated, regretful and excited all at once? The emotions racing through her made Fannie tremble. She clutched at her skirt with both hands, then let go. Reached up to smooth her hair. Finally, clasped her hands before her. And all the while, the woman in the doorway watched.

Finally, after what felt like a millennium, the woman's expression softened a bit as she said, "Hello, Fannie. I'm Edie."

Edie didn't invite Fannie in, but when she stepped back and retreated into the room behind her, she left the door open, and so Fannie assumed she was meant to follow.

The moment she crossed the threshold, Edie said, "Edmund said you have a photograph of me."

Edmund had known all along . . . and hadn't said a word. He let Samuel and Lamar go on a wild goose chase . . . and he never said a word. Anger with Edmund LaMotte distracted Fannie for a moment. She only managed to nod in reply.

"It was a good likeness at the time," Edie said. "I must admit I'm surprised Eleanor kept it."

"I . . . I f-found it in her dressing table." *Do I smell . . . roses?* She glanced around the room. A glass bowl on a small table brimmed with dried rose petals. Mother had one just like it.

Edie arched one eyebrow. "You found it, you say? In her dressing table?" She waggled a finger in the air. "Snooping is naughty, Fannie."

Who did she think she was to waggle a finger? She had no idea. Fannie lifted her chin. "I wasn't snooping. I was gathering up her jewelry for safekeeping. To take it to Mr. Vandekamp." As she said the name, Fannie looked for a reaction. There was none. She flung out the words, "Mother's dead."

Something changed in Edie's expression. Her voice softened. "I see. I'm sorry." But

301

then the icy façade returned. "And Louis? How is he managing without his beloved Eleanor?"

The edge of sarcasm in Edie's voice made Fannie angry. She'd come thousands of miles to this? "Papa's been gone for three years." Was it a coincidence that, when Edie put her cigar out, she kept her hand on the table? Had news of Papa's death finally broken through? Fannie realized that the aroma of the cigar reminded her of Papa. *Cigars and roses.*

"I'm sorry for your loss."

"It's your loss, too," Fannie said. Where was the woman who'd written those letters? She hadn't come all this way to be held at arm's length. Again. "When I was gathering up the jewels, I found your letters in Mother's dressing table." She paused. "All twenty of them."

Edie blinked. "If your mother wasn't going to let you know I existed, I can't imagine why she kept them." She fingered her cigar. "There doesn't seem to be a point to it, does there?"

"I think . . . I think it means she cared. About you."

Edie pursed her lips. "A lovely sentiment. Do you find comfort in fairy tales, Fannie?" She paused. A realization seemed to dawn.

"Ah . . . I see. You read *my* fairy tales. Kings. Princes. Gold." She gestured around. "Well, here it is. What part of my 'happily-ever-after' would you like to share?"

Fannie looked around at the room. *Periwinkle blue.* The log walls were painted Mother's favorite color. The two chairs next to the tea table by the fireplace were like the ones in Mother's room. And Edie had a gilt-rimmed mirror hanging on the wall opposite the window. It was so much like Mother's it felt . . . almost haunted. She shivered again. Shook her head.

Edie sighed dramatically. "So sorry to disappoint you, my dear. I'm certain you wish you'd kept the fairy tale intact." She seemed about to say something else, but instead, she turned to go. "I'll see that Edmund and Patrick know you're here. Edmund's patient is doing better. In fact, he'd planned on returning to town this morning." She nodded toward the door. "I'm sure you'll be more comfortable waiting in the buggy."

Edie was just like Mother, after all. The warm woman in the letters didn't exist. Determined not to let her see the pain she'd caused by dismissing Fannie so easily, Fannie hurried to leave, blinking back the threatening tears. She'd just gotten to the door when Edie called after her.

"I wonder, Fannie. In your mother's things . . . did you find an amethyst ring? It would have matched a necklace and earrings Eleanor used to wear."

"It was there." Something in Fannie wanted to strike out at the stone-faced woman rejecting her. "I don't recall ever seeing her wear it."

"Well, of course not, dear. I sent it to *you.* But obviously she didn't tell you that. Obviously . . . she didn't tell you anything."

Fannie whirled around and lashed out. "Now that I've met you, I'm glad she didn't."

But Edie was gone. She probably hadn't even heard the words.

She'd hurried out to Edmund's buggy to get away from Edie, crying as she climbed aboard, and then hunkered down to wait for him, finally falling into an exhausted sleep. At the sound of Edmund's voice, she opened her eyes.

"Fannie. Fannie, wake up. I've brought you some water. We'll be heading back into Fort Benton soon. You need to drink something."

Fannie blinked, saw Edmund's kind face, and began to cry again.

"You're a foolish, foolish woman," he scolded.

"And you lied to me!" Fannie spat the words out. "You *knew.* All this time you knew. You let Samuel go looking for her . . . and all the while —" Edmund touched her arm. She jerked it away. "Leave me alone."

"No," Edmund said. When Fannie looked back his way, he repeated it. "I won't leave you alone. Stop behaving like a spoiled child who didn't get what she wanted for Christmas." He looked back toward the house. "Do you have any idea what it did to Edie to open the door and have you just . . . standing there?"

"I have an excellent idea," Fannie said. "It didn't mean a thing."

"Oh, Fannie . . ." He shook his head. "Think, Fannie. *Think.* Put yourself in Edie's shoes. You've left home and written twenty years' worth of letters that read like fairy tales. And then . . . everything falls apart. You do the best you can, but the best you can do is something everyone in your past would find heinous. And then, just when you feel that you're finally beginning to dig your way back out, someone young and innocent . . . someone you long to know . . . arrives on your doorstep. And you aren't ready. You want her to admire you.

But you can see exactly what you don't want to see in her eyes. And your heart breaks."

Fannie gazed back toward the log house.

Edmund cleared his throat. "As to my being a liar . . . I never lied. Not to you, and not to Mr. Beck. I do owe you both an apology. Of course I recognized Edie when Mr. Beck showed me her photograph." He glanced toward the house. "I've been the doctor for Bonaparte's since the beginning. I told Edie about you the first time I saw her after Samuel showed me that cabinet portrait. But I also promised her I wouldn't say anything to you, at least for a while. To give her time to decide what she wanted to do."

"You let Samuel go on a pointless search."

"No I didn't. He was going anyway, in search of his sister. And, quite honestly, I knew he'd probably run into someone who knew Edie. They'd tell him where Edie's establishment was located, he'd run into the new owner . . . and maybe find Emma as a result." He scrubbed his beard with the back of his hand. "I also thought that perhaps Mr. Beck would come back with evidence that would help you understand Edie. Evidence that would show you what I meant when I said she was starting to dig her way back out."

Fannie frowned. Shifted in the buggy seat and turned toward him. "Bonaparte's is a *brothel,* Edmund. I know what a brothel is, I know what Edie is, and you can please stop trying to talk around it."

"Except that Bonaparte's *isn't* a brothel, Fannie. Not anymore." When Fannie snorted disbelief, he smiled and opened his mouth to explain, but just then Patrick came trotting out from behind one of the "bunkhouses." The man who was shuffling alongside the boy waved a greeting, and Edmund hurried to finish. "We'll talk later, but, Fannie — none of us is completely who we seem. There's a great deal of pain beneath Edie's icy demeanor. It's a defense. I don't know all the reasons, but I suspect your family plays a part." He put a hand on her arm. "I've never seen Edie cry, Fannie. She was crying when she told me you were out here."

"Fannie?" Patrick asked in disbelief. He looked toward his father. "But how did Fannie get to Mrs. Bonaparte's ranch?"

"Exactly the question I was about to ask," Edmund said, even as he helped Pete hitch the little mare to the buggy for the drive back to Fort Benton.

"Lame Bear brought me," Fannie told them. "He led Smoke and I rode."

Pete's gray head popped into view from the off side of the mare. "You come all the way out from Fort Benton with that old Injun? In the *night?*" He shook his head. "Wonder you didn't all turn into wolf bait."

Fannie cleared her throat. "Well . . . we weren't alone." She glanced at Edmund. "Those sons of his — he rounded them up first. They walked behind. With rifles."

Edmund and Pete exchanged glances. When both men burst out laughing, Fannie sniffed. "I don't see what's so funny. I was nearly frightened to death the entire way."

"Fannie Rousseau," Edmund explained, "you have got to be the only white woman in all of Montana who calls up four Blackfeet warriors to escort an expedition."

Pete joined in. "Yes, ma'am. That's something all right." He grinned. "You might want to have your answer ready when one of Lame Bear's sons proposes marriage."

Fannie shot both men a horrified look that set them both to laughing again. For his part, Patrick seemed impressed by the whole idea. "Do you think Owl and his brothers would come hunting with us sometime, Pete?" He glanced Fannie's way. "Wouldn't *that* impress the girls at school?"

"Patrick LaMotte," Edmund scolded. "You just get in the buggy and stop thinking so much about how to impress the girls you haven't met at the school you haven't been accepted to in a place we haven't gone." He thanked Pete for his help, waved toward the house, and then climbed aboard.

Fannie sighed with relief when Edmund settled beside her on the buggy seat. She was going to be stiff and sore in places she didn't realize she had come morning. What she wouldn't give for a soak in a tub of hot water. Thinking about baths set her to thinking about the bathhouse at the far end of Main in Fort Benton. Bathhouses . . . brothels . . . her eyes grew heavy as Patrick enthused about camping out with Pete at the ranch, and the ancient gelding Pete let him ride . . . and then she was waking and realizing she'd been using Edmund's shoulder for a pillow.

The minute she lifted her head, Edmund leaned down and said in a low voice, "Someone's upset." Fannie followed his gaze toward the clinic, where Abe Valley was waiting. The minute they drove up, he was at the buggy helping Fannie down, but all the while wanting to know what in tarnation she thought she was doing sneaking out in the middle of the night without so much as a "fare thee well."

"I . . . I'm sorry, Abe," Fannie stammered

as she looked up at him. "I guess I didn't think."

"Yer darned tootin' you didn't think!" Abe sputtered. "Lucky you didn't get pulled apart by wolves."

"Wolves would never have gotten Fannie," Patrick said from the buggy's back seat. He told Abe about Lame Bear and his sons.

Abe looked doubtful until Edmund chimed in. "It's true," he said, barely stifling a chuckle.

"Well, at least she's got the sense to know better than to head off into the wilderness without a gun." He waxed colorful regarding the aftermath of such an event and swore his way through an imaginary funeral and then, after telling Fannie he expected her to be back in time to serve supper and help with cleanup, he stormed off.

"Mr. Valley was mad," Patrick said with wonder. "I never saw him so mad."

Fannie glanced at Edmund. "I should go. Help him with . . . everything."

Edmund nodded. Glanced Patrick's way. "Maybe we'll bring Abe some business for supper." He smiled. "I'll buy you a cup of coffee and a piece of pie later."

"That means I'll have to bake some pies," Fannie said with a grin.

"You know what I hate?" Patrick interjected. "I hate it when grown-ups talk about coffee and pie but they're really talking about something else."

Edmund laughed. "Would you rather I just said, 'Patrick, find something to do. I want to talk to Fannie and I don't want you to hear it'?"

Patrick shook his head. "No, I guess not. Then I wouldn't get pie."

"Pie it is, then," Fannie said.

"And I'll offer to go to bed early so the grown-ups can talk," Patrick sighed.

CHAPTER TWENTY

Delight thyself also in the Lord: and he
shall give thee the desires of thine heart.
PSALM 37:4

Edmund and Patrick lingered over supper at Abe's, and when the last diner left, the two helped transform the dining room into a sitting room by scrubbing tables and lighting lamps. Four boarders started up a card game at one table, and Patrick offered to help Abe wash dishes "so the grown-ups can talk about something besides pie."

As Fannie and Edmund walked toward the levee in the moonlight, Fannie pulled her shawl about her shoulders and folded her arms across her torso. "I don't think I really know how to have this conversation."

"Well, I know how to begin it," Edmund said. Stopping short, he touched Fannie's arm and, when she turned toward him, he repeated his apology. "I truly did not mean

312

to deceive anyone. My intent was only to give Edie time to adjust to the idea that a past she obviously finds very upsetting has caught up with her."

He leaned toward her slightly. "Please say you believe me."

His sincerity was undeniable. "Of course I do." She took his arm. "What I don't understand is Edie. She's nothing like the woman she created in her letters. Were they all lies? And if they were, and Mother knew it . . . why did she keep them?" Fannie shook her head. "I don't understand any of it."

Edmund covered her hand with his. "All I know is that Edie was visibly shaken when I told her you were here. Stunned, really."

"That, I do understand," Fannie said. "Her letters created a fantasy. When I showed up at the door, she'd been found out." She paused. "And honestly, Edmund . . . what woman wants her family to know she's running a brothel?"

"Except, as I said earlier, she isn't. She did . . . but she doesn't anymore." They were near the clinic, and Edmund guided her there, motioning for her to be seated on the front porch bench while he leaned against an upright. "The Bonaparte's up in the gold camps was just what you say. And a successful one, apparently. But last year,

313

something terrible happened. One of Edie's favorite girls took her own life. The patient I drove out to see — Mollie — said that, for a while, they were all afraid Edie was going to follow suit. She was that distraught. Then Edie closed down. She sold out and came here. Five of her girls came with her when she told them she wanted to provide a haven of sorts — if they were interested." Edmund looked out toward the river. "She had the ranch built, and very quietly, word has traveled in the territory that if a sporting girl needs a way out, she can come to Bonaparte's."

Fannie looked up at him. "But that's . . . that's a wonderful thing to do. Why on earth wouldn't she want me to know about that?" She answered her own question. "Of course . . . knowing that would mean knowing the rest." She sighed. "I should never have gone out there."

"It was . . . premature," Edmund agreed. He came to sit beside her. "Your aunt is something of an enigma, Fannie, but there's a good woman beneath the ice. I've met that woman — the one who cares deeply about others and wants to make life better for them."

Fannie looked out on the town. She thought of Emma, Samuel's sister. Had she been forced to work in a place like the ones up on Main? Would she have done that if she'd known of a place like Edie's ranch? "How many women are living at Edie's?"

"Half a dozen."

"The one you were called to treat — is she all right?"

"She will be. Her baby was early. Too early." His voice wavered. "It was a little girl. Mollie named her Edie. I imagine they had a little service after we left. They were lining a box with fabric for a coffin."

Fannie closed her eyes. She couldn't imagine that kind of heartache. She turned to look at him. "Would you have stayed for the service if it hadn't been for me?"

"No. It would have been too difficult to explain to Patrick." After a moment, he said, "I'm sorry things didn't go differently out there today. But I don't think you should abandon all hope."

"That's going to be hard. My mother was . . . remote . . . like Edie was today. I'd given up trying to break through it by the time I was fourteen, but I never stopped hoping things would change between us. When I found Edie's letters, I suppose I thought it was like getting a second chance with Mother." She studied her hands, feeling rather than seeing the results of weeks of washing dishes and scrubbing tables at Abe's. "I can't help but think it's all been a waste. Of time. Money. And" — her voice wavered — "and it cost Hannah her life."

Edmund reached for her hand. "What happened to the *Delores* wasn't your fault."

"I know that. And one day, I'll think differently about all of this. But right now —" She shook her head. "Right now, I just want to go home."

"Please don't." He said it abruptly, and with such emotion that Fannie turned to look at him in the moonlight. He shrugged. "I still think there's a good chance Edie will relent." He smiled. "And besides that, if you were to leave now, Patrick would be heartbroken. Abe's business would fall off horribly . . . and I'd be . . . bereft of someone to discuss Mr. Dickens with over coffee."

He stood and pulled her up beside him. Fannie's heart thudded as she looked up into his eyes. For just a moment, she thought he might kiss her. For a moment, she wanted him to. But then he looped her arm through his and said, "You can't leave. There's an entire committee of people against it, not the least of whom is Samuel Beck."

Fannie took some time in mid-September

to sit down and catch up on some letter writing.

Dear Samuel,

Dr. LaMotte says that Babe Cox is good about helping letters find their way. When Mr. Cox saw who this letter was for, he told us about the preacher in the gold camps that people are calling Brother Sam. I remember that day on the Far West when, Bible in hand, you said, 'We have to tell people about this!' And now you are. Samuel, I'm so happy for you.

You can be happy for me, too. I've found Aunt Edith. She has a ranch a short distance from Fort Benton ("short" as distance is measured here, that is). She expressed only shock at meeting me. No joyful reunion. I am holding on to hope that I will see her again and that, after she has had a chance to get used to the idea that I'm here, we will be able to have a real conversation. When I do, I will ask about Emma for you. Edie has spent time in the gulch, but her ranch is a kind of "home for the friendless." Edmund says that she has about six women staying with her now.

Do you remember when I told you that I might have graduated to piecrust and corn bread by the time you returned? Well, Abe is an excellent teacher and he seems to think I may have a knack. Hannah would be amazed. Abe's boarders like my pie! Have you ever eaten huckleberry pie?

In addition to working at the boarding house, I've been tutoring Dr. LaMotte's son, Patrick, who is a charming young man of ten — and blind. I am certain I told you about my best friend at home, Minette, who lost her sight when we were children. I've been teaching Patrick some of the things Minette forced me to learn. (She used to make me play blindfolded.) Edmund hopes to enroll Patrick in the very same school next year. He plans to establish a practice in St. Louis so he can be near Patrick.

Fannie hesitated. She didn't know what else to say . . . or how to sign the letter. Did "Brother Sam" still have feelings for her? What did she feel for him? The more time she spent with Patrick . . . and Edmund . . . the more confused she felt. But then, neither man had expressed anything beyond friendship. Had they?

She signed the letter *Fondly.* And added Lamar's name to the greeting.

Edmund and Patrick began to dine at Abe's more often, and one evening Fannie produced the locked leather envelope containing Aunt Edith's twenty letters and asked Edmund to read them. She watched his face as he read, smiled knowingly when he looked up a time or two, and finally said, "And now you know why I was so shocked when I met her."

Edmund nodded . . . and said nothing.

And then . . . finally . . . word arrived from home. Fannie sat at one of the tables in Abe's dining room and opened Minette's letter first. She was soon sighing with relief. It was just as Hannah had predicted and Fannie had hoped. Minette was incensed that Fannie had gone off without her . . . and forgiving.

Mr. Vandekamp's letter, on the other hand, was neither forgiving nor helpful. Fannie read it with trembling hands, and by the time she'd finished, Edmund and Patrick had joined her, Edmund's hand on her arm, his brow furrowed with concern. Without a word, she handed him what amounted to a cryptic note ending life as she'd always known it.

We received the news of Mrs. Pike's tragic death and offer our condolences, even as we rejoice that you did not suffer a similar fate. As to the journey itself, you

319

have no need of further comment from this office as to our opinion of the matter.

I regret to inform you that the house on Main was struck by lightning and caught fire on the 30th of May. Every effort was made, but to no avail. The damage was extensive. It is my opinion that the house is a total loss and that the property should be disposed of as soon as possible. Of course this cannot be done absent your directive and that of your other advisors. We have seen to the securing of the contents while we await word from you.

As Mr. Beauvais and Mr. Hennessey are absent St. Charles on a business trip, and since your directive forbids me to act alone, I am unable to release funds as you request.

We await your reply, but would be most glad for your presence. I remain your faithful servant.

When Abe set a mug of coffee before her, Fannie took a sip. The hot liquid steadied her.

"It's gotten really quiet," Patrick said. "Should I be asking to go to bed now?"

Fannie forced a laugh. "That's very sweet of you, but no . . . you don't need to excuse yourself."

"There's been a fire at Fannie's house in Missouri," Edmund explained.

Patrick's brow furrowed. "That's terrible." He bit his lower lip, but then his face lit up with a smile. "Does that mean you'll stay in Fort Benton?"

"You know you can," Abe agreed. "Right here at the finest hostelry in the territory."

"Thank you, Abe, but —" She read aloud, " 'As Mr. Beauvais and Mr. Hennessey are absent St. Charles on a business trip, and since your directive forbids me to act alone, I am unable to release funds as you request.' "

"Well, what in tarnation does that mean?" Abe asked.

"It means —" Fannie sighed — "that Mr. Vandekamp is choosing to be difficult and that I'm not going to have any cash at my disposal for a very long time."

"That's all right," Abe said. "You more than earn your keep now."

Fannie thanked him even as Edmund murmured the name Vandekamp. "Didn't I read that name . . . ?"

Fannie nodded. "Yes. In Edie's last letter. But when I asked Mr. Vandekamp about Edie . . ." She glanced at Patrick. "It was one of those experiences Patrick talks about. Where people speak but don't say what they really mean."

She put the letter down on the table. "He wasn't willing to tell me a thing about Edie. Then I discovered serious financial problems in Papa's business, and I thought they might be because of Mr. Vandekamp's mismanagement. And then . . . he was pressuring me to marry someone . . . unsuitable." She shrugged. "I left St. Charles on a whim. I didn't tell him because I didn't want another confrontation. But I also didn't quite trust him anymore, and so I left instructions forbidding him to do anything without approval from my friend Minette's fiancé and her father, both of whom are very well respected businessmen. So now . . . Mr. Vandekamp has an opportunity to get his revenge. And there's really not a thing I can do to force his hand. I'm too far away."

Edmund's face flushed with emotion "How can he do such a thing? What if you were in dire straits? What if you didn't have friends to help? It's unconscionable to the point of being evil."

"Calm down, Edmund," Fannie said, patting the back of his hand. "I'll admit to being surprised that he's decided to be this vindictive, but I'll be all right."

I'll be all right. For the first time since leaving home, she believed it.

CHAPTER TWENTY-ONE

And be ye kind one to another,
tenderhearted, forgiving one another,
even as God for Christ's sake hath
forgiven you.

EPHESIANS 4:32

Rosalie had joked about Samuel's finding his calling in her saloon. The longer he stayed in the gold camps looking for Emma, the more he wondered if she was right. He began to feel downright bold about walking into places and asking to preach. He didn't even wait for Sundays in some places.

The day a barkeep looked at him and said, "Are you the one I heard about? The one they call Brother Sam?" Lamar laughed out loud. Clapping Samuel on the back he said, "Preach it, brother."

Later that night, the two men were bedded down in a barn when Samuel spoke up. "What the heck am I doing, Lamar? I'm no preacher. I've got no training at all."

"You've got the most important things a preacher needs," Lamar said. "You love people, you love God, and you love his book. I don't see a reason to be confused. Seems plain as day, doesn't it? There's a calling on your life, Brother Sam."

"All I do is sing some hymns and say a few words. Sure, people listen, but then they go back to whatever they were doing as if nothing happened. That's not how it's supposed to be."

"You know for a fact they all go back to being the same people?" The straw rustled as Lamar shifted around. "Seems to me God promised his Word would never go out but what it would do its work."

"You think I should keep preaching, then?"

"I think you should get some sleep. And tomorrow morning we should decide just how long we're going to wander these hills. Once you've got a plan about that, the rest will fall into place."

After a while, Samuel said into the darkness, "I worry about Fannie." He looked toward the bit of sky visible through the open haymow door. "Part of me wishes I'd never learned anything about her aunt."

Lamar was quiet for a long while. "I've

lived a long time, Sam. Watched people. Some of 'em, life gets hard and they just kind of fold in on themselves and fade away. Others take on the load and get stronger. Oh, they might stumble about awhile, but eventually they learn how to shoulder the load and they keep going."

"Which kind do you think Fannie is?" Samuel asked.

"You really need to ask that, son?"

"She fainted when those Indian braves frightened her."

"True," Lamar agreed. "But then she made us breakfast and joked about learning to cook while we're gone." He paused. "She's had bad news before, son. Her parents are gone. She lost Miz Pike, and still she kept on. You respect her enough to tell her what you learned about her aunt. I'm not saying she won't wobble a bit, but if you think on it awhile, you'll see the same thing I do in that little gal. She's stronger than you think."

Fondly?! She signed her letter *fondly.* Seated across from Lamar in a hotel dining room, Samuel fingered the letter Babe Cox had handed him with a teasing wink and a comment about the "fine hand" that had addressed it. He read it again, then handed it to Lamar. "Read that. Tell me what you think."

He'd preached his way all the way to Virginia City, and now they were staying at a hotel while they asked after Emma Pilsner and Edie Bonaparte, who might also call herself Edith LeClerc. They'd had no word of either woman since Rosalie's. "Well?" he asked when Lamar had finished reading Fannie's letter. "What do you think?"

"What do I think about what?"

Samuel leaned back in his chair and made a face. "She's spending a lot of time with Dr. LaMotte."

"She's teaching his son, Sam. The doc helped her find Edie." Lamar looked back at Fannie's letter. Finally, he said, "As long as we've been up here, plenty of people know about Brother Sam and the redheaded sister he cares so much about. If Emma turns up, I believe the news will find you, no matter where you are in the territory."

Samuel nodded. "But I can't give up on her."

Lamar leaned forward. "Nobody who knows you believes you ever will." He reached for the Bible Samuel had taken out of his pocket and put on the table when they sat down. Thumbing through the pages, he read softly, " 'Delight thyself also in the

327

Lord: and he shall give thee the desires of thine heart.' "

"I do delight in the Lord."

Lamar laid the Bible down. "I know you do. I've been watching the proof of it for a long time. But, Sam, why is it you seem to think the only time it's God's will is if it's hard — something you got to force yourself to do?" He held up a hand. "Now, I know — sometimes that's how things are, and then we just lean into the wind and trust the hand of God to keep us from blowing away. But it seems to me that when a man listens to God's voice as sincerely as you do, Sam . . . couldn't God be putting the desire to take a break in your heart, too? The Lord himself rested on occasion."

Samuel looked from Fannie's letter to his Bible and back again. The idea that God might think it was all right for him to leave the gulch for a while set his heart to thumping. He smiled. "You mean my wanting to see Fannie again might be all right?"

"Maybe more than just all right. After all, there's plenty of saloons in Fort Benton to preach in."

Sam and Lamar were in trouble before they knew it, with no way out. One minute they were thanking God for the near miracle that had landed them good horses for the journey back to Fort Benton, and the next they were caught up in a storm of flying arrows. One minute the way was clear, the sky bright, and the fall air filled only with the sounds from a creek crashing through a ravine below the trail, and the next war cries sounded from every direction.

Lamar's horse bolted. Samuel's reared up, slashing the air in a frenzy of terror. Instantly unseated, Samuel shouted a meaningless "Whoa!" as he went down. The last thing he remembered was the sight of Lamar clinging to the saddle horn as his horse charged down the trail. The last thing he heard was shouting in a language he didn't understand. The last thing he saw was a sea of painted faces.

He didn't know how long he'd been unconscious, but his head felt like it just might be splitting open. With a groan, Samuel opened his eyes. Everything looked blurry . . . smelled rancid. Where was he? Blinking, he lifted his head, then groaned and reached up with both hands to feel what surely must be a gaping wound along his hairline. He felt a ridge of dried blood. At least he wasn't still bleeding. He opened his eyes again. Stared straight up. He was in a tepee.

Campfire light flickered just enough to reflect off the long poles visible around the circle of starlit sky visible through the smoke hole above.

How long had he been there? He felt so sick. He closed his eyes. Drums pounding. Or was that his head? And where was Lamar? Maybe Lamar got away. Away from . . . what? Were the Indians after their horses? He'd been warned that might happen, but he didn't listen. He was in too much of a hurry to get to Fort Benton to see Fannie. Thought they could make it through if they traveled mostly at night. It had worked for a week, but then they'd decided to chance a few hours by daylight. Just a few hours.

"L-lla . . ." His throat was so dry he couldn't talk. Moistening his lips with his tongue, Samuel tried again. *I can't . . . talk . . . what's . . . wrong . . . ?* The drumbeats grew louder. He closed his eyes. Put his hands over his ears to block out the sound. He felt so dizzy. He was going to vomit. What was wrong with him?

On a crisp fall evening, Fannie and Patrick finished cleaning the dining room at Abe's and made their way back to the clinic. Fannie carried a warm loaf of bread and a crock of soup for Edmund, who'd been kept busy all evening stitching up the victims of a barroom brawl. She'd just set the soup at Edmund's place and reached for a knife to slice the bread when he opened the door between the clinic and his living quarters.

"Still not finished?"

He shook his head. "I've a new patient. A couple of Dick Turley's men found him on the trail this morning." He paused. "It's your friend Lamar, Fannie."

"But what — ?" Fannie gulped. She took a step toward the clinic, but Edmund held her back. "I'm not sure you want to see. Give me some time to get him cleaned up."

"Tell me what you need. I'll be fine."

Edmund studied her for a moment, then nodded. "First . . . water."

"I'll get water," Patrick said, grabbing a bucket and heading for the door.

"What happened?" Fannie asked.

"Turley says Indian trouble."

Fannie followed Edmund back into the clinic, where two men were waiting by the front door. "He couldn't have been alone," she said to them. "There had to be another man with him. You have to go back."

The shorter of the two men spoke up. "All due respect, ma'am. We don't have to do anything . . . and we're not going back." He glanced at his partner, who nodded his agreement. "We darned near got ourselves killed as it was. There's somethin' goin' on between the Bloods and the Piegan up that way, and this feller musta got caught in the worst of it. His horse got shot clean out from under him. Lucky he didn't get his neck broke in the fall. We got more 'n our share. And there wasn't anybody else on that trail."

Edmund thanked the two men for bringing Lamar in.

"Samuel would never leave Lamar alone," Fannie insisted. "He was there. He had to be."

"We can't do anything for Samuel right now," Edmund said. "Help Patrick get more water." He turned away and, grabbing a pair of scissors, began to cut Lamar's shirt away. For the first time, Fannie noticed three arrow shafts protruding from the shirt. *Three.* His right cheek had been grazed. And his earlobe . . . was it gone? She couldn't tell for the blood. His face was swollen almost beyond recognition.

"His arm's broken," Edmund muttered.

Feeling weak, Fannie retreated to the kitchen and sat down. Took some deep breaths. Patrick returned. After they carried two buckets of water in to Edmund, Fannie got the fire going in the stove and made coffee to help Edmund through the long night ahead. And all the while, behind her concern for Lamar, behind her busyness, behind her outward calm, an unsung litany hung in the air. *What happened to Sam?*

It was three long days and nights before Edmund ventured a positive comment. Lamar might get to keep his arm. The arrow wounds looked like they would probably heal. But he couldn't understand why Lamar hadn't regained consciousness. The bump on his head just didn't seem that serious.

On the fourth day after Lamar was carried in, Fannie was sitting, half asleep, beside Lamar's cot when he groaned. Lurching awake, she put her hand on his forehead. "It's Fannie, Lamar. You're in Fort Benton. Safe. You're going to be all right."

Lamar grew still. For a moment, Fannie thought he'd slipped back into unconsciousness, but then he muttered something. Fannie leaned closer. Took his hand. "Did you hear me, Lamar? It's Fannie. You're at Dr. LaMotte's clinic and you're safe." She paused. Was it her imagination, or was he listening? "If you hear me, if you under-

stand, squeeze my hand." Almost impercep-
tibly, he responded. "The men who found
you . . . said you were alone. Do you
remember what happened? Was Samuel
with you? Was Emma there? Were you on
the way back because you found her?"

The dark eyebrows drew together, almost
as if it hurt to think. Lamar's lips parted.
"Sssss . . ."

"Yes?" Fannie said. "Samuel? Where is
Sam?"

"Gone," Lamar said. "Sam's . . . gone."

"Fannie."

At the sound of her name, Fannie started
awake. Edmund was on one knee beside the
chair where she'd been keeping vigil over
Lamar. She smiled and reached out to
touch his cheek. "You're back."

He took her hand. "I'm taking you to the
boarding house and I want you to sleep
until you awaken naturally. And if you're
still tired, I want you to sleep some more.
Do you hear me?"

Fannie opened her mouth to argue. She
had to stay there. By Lamar's side. Didn't
Edmund understand? What if Lamar awakened and she wasn't there? What if he said
something about Samuel and they missed
it? But instead of protesting, she leaned into

him as weariness washed over her.

Dear Edmund. He cradled her head on his shoulder and stood up with her in his arms. She was vaguely aware of low voices and things being moved around in the clinic, but she was safe with Edmund . . . and so tired. And then . . . she was in her room at Abe's . . . sleeping.

Fannie burrowed into her pillow and tried to ignore the sunshine pouring through the tiny window on the back wall of her room. Caught between sleep and wakefulness, she inwardly groused at Hannah for failing to draw the drapes. She wanted to sleep. Didn't Hannah realize. . . . She heard men's voices just outside her door. Her eyes flew open. And she remembered. She was back at Abe's and the voices were other boarders headed toward the dining room for breakfast.

She lifted herself up on one elbow and looked through the window. Surely not breakfast. Perhaps lunch. What time was it? And Lamar — was there news? Throwing back her comforter, she sat up, then shivered and snatched the comforter back around her. She could see her own breath rising in the cold air. *The last boat . . . what am I going to do if the last boat is leaving and Lamar's still . . . and Samuel . . .* Closing her eyes, she willed herself to stop worrying.

The comforter still wrapped around her, she reached for her shoes and stockings, perched atop her trunk. *Did Edmund take them off?* She had a flannel nightgown on. Apparently he'd taken her dress off . . . and petticoats . . . and tucked her in. Her cheeks blazed. Pulling her stockings out of her shoes, she pulled first one, then the other on. Finally letting the comforter go, she hopped up and scurried to the washstand crammed between the doorway and the wall and poured water from pitcher into bowl. *How long will it be now, before the water in the pitcher has a crust of ice over it every morning?* The idea made her shiver even more as she bent to splash her face. She peered into the cloudy mirror above the washstand. She looked horrible. Pale. Tired. Frazzled. *And Edmund took down my hair.*

Poor Edmund. He had to be exhausted. She'd gather up some victuals and hurry back to the clinic. Making quick work of her toilette, Fannie made up the bed and reached for her shawl, then thought better of it and pulled the hooded wool cape Mrs. Tatum had provided out of her trunk. *Thank you, Lord. Thank you, Mrs. Tatum. I didn't know I'd need it, but I'm so glad I have it.*

Thoughts of Mrs. Tatum made her think about the grave in Sioux City. Did Hannah have a grave marker by now? *Hannah. I still miss you . . . do you see me? Lord . . . I need help. With everything. Samuel's missing . . . Lamar's hurt . . . and Edie. I don't even know what to say about her except . . . help. Nothing's happening fast enough. I can't stay here through a winter . . . I can't . . . can I?*

Draping her cape over her arm, Fannie closed and locked the door to her little room, then made her way across the yard, past the long tables, and in the back door of Abe's lean-to kitchen. Her stomach growled. She inhaled with appreciation. *Stew for lunch . . . maybe for supper, too.* Reaching into a basket of biscuits, she took one, poured herself a cup of coffee, and then set to gathering up food to take over to the clinic. But then she heard someone calling for her from the next room. Peering around the doorjamb into the dining area, she saw Patrick sitting at the table in the corner, a pad of paper before him, a ruler in one hand and a pencil in the other.

"How did you know it was me?"

"You were talking to yourself," he said with a grin. "And Abe doesn't clatter around as much when he's in the kitchen."

"Clatter?! I do not clatter," Fannie teased.

"And since you mentioned him, where is Abe?"

"Helping Pa with his other patient. They left me here to tell you to come over but to eat breakfast first."

Another patient? Fannie thought back. Vaguely, she remembered other voices and things being moved around as Edmund carried her out the door. "Have you been here since breakfast? I didn't realize how tired I was. But I feel better now. I'm just gathering up some food to take over. Since Abe is over there, too, maybe we'll just take the whole stew pot. Your father probably hasn't eaten. You know how he is sometimes."

Patrick nodded.

A few minutes later Fannie and Patrick headed for the clinic. They were halfway there when Patrick said, "Pa said I could tell you the rest once we were on our way over."

Fannie only heard one word of "the rest." *Samuel.*

Edmund met them at the clinic door. Abe appeared and took the stewpot out of Fannie's hand. He and Patrick retreated to the kitchen with the food. Edmund insisted Fannie sit down beside him on the bench where patients usually waited. He had to keep repeating things. Fannie couldn't seem to take it all in with only one telling.

Lame Bear's sons had found Samuel unconscious at the bottom of a ravine below the trail. His horse must have thrown him in the melee. When Edmund called the horrible fall a blessing, Fannie looked at him in disbelief. But then, as he went on to explain what had happened, Fannie began to realize he might be right. Samuel and Lamar had gotten caught up in the middle of a skirmish between two different bands of Blackfeet. If the Bloods had found Samuel, they would have taken his horse, scalped him, and left him to die.

"But Lame Bear's sons were on the other side of the battle," Edmund said. "They didn't recognize Samuel because it got dark, but when they picked their way down into the ravine to head back toward their own camp, they found him and remembered him from that day here in Fort Benton.

"They said their father wouldn't have wanted harm to come to one of 'White Sparrow's friends,' so they couldn't just leave Sam out there to die."

White Sparrow? Lame Bear called her White Sparrow? Fannie shook her head. "But they ignored Lamar? He's my friend, too."

"Bear took a horse back up the trail to get Lamar, but he was already gone. Turley and Bud must have come along by then. When they all got back to camp, Lame Bear wanted to bring Samuel here, but Owl, Eagle, and Bear refused. They made a good case for what would happen if the three of them were seen with an injured white man who'd obviously been in a scrap with Indians. So . . . they compromised. They took Samuel to Edie's."

"Edie's?!"

"Uh-huh. They dumped him on her doorstep and then made a lot of racket to get someone to come to the door."

"I want to see him." Fannie started to get up. Edmund put his hand on her arm. "Remember how swollen Lamar's face was a few days ago? Samuel looks worse. His fever is high and he isn't making a lot of sense right now when he tries to talk, but I don't think he has any broken bones. He's young and strong. He has all that . . . and our prayers . . . in his favor."

Fannie nodded. She understood exactly what Edmund was saying. *I don't know if he's going to live.*

The left side of Samuel's once-handsome face looked as white as death. The right sported a ridge of swelling and the blackest eye she'd ever seen. A neat row of stitches ran just under the curve of one eyebrow. Another row began at the edge of Sam's scalp and disappeared somewhere near the crown of his head.

Edmund did his best to reassure her. "A few nasty scars are a small price to pay after what he's been through."

Fannie looked across Samuel's still body to where Lamar lay, sleeping peacefully, the swelling in his face almost gone, his wounds healing.

"Arrows?"

"Only one," Edmund said. "In his right thigh. A flesh wound."

"Then . . . why . . . why does he look so . . ."

"He fell a long way, Fannie. A very long way." Edmund cleared his throat. "I don't like the fact that he hasn't moved his legs since he came in. There could be other damage we can't see. The brain is a complex organism. We just have to wait."

Patrick came to the door between the clinic and the living quarters. "Edie helped me," he called softly. "There's food ready, if anybody's interested in eating."

Fannie whirled about. Edie stood silhouetted in the lamplight, standing just behind

341

Patrick. When Fannie met her gaze, she turned away and retreated into the kitchen.

Fannie glanced at Edmund for an explanation.

"Pete drove the wagon and Edie rode in the back with Sam." He paused. "The team was about to drop in their traces when they pulled up." He took her hand. "Come into the kitchen. Eat something."

She shook her head. "I'll wait here. You go ahead. You must be ravenous."

"All right then, don't eat. But Lamar and Samuel don't need you right now." He squeezed her hand. "She came all this way, Fannie. She's stayed, and you're a big part of the reason. So talk to her."

With a little nod, Fannie followed Edmund through the door. Her heart pounding, she stepped into the room. Edie was standing at the stove, stirring the pot of bubbling stew Fannie and Patrick had brought over from Abe's.

"Pete already downed a bowl and headed out back. He's real worried about the team."

Edie kept talking, reporting on the whereabouts of Abe — gone back to the hostelry — and Patrick — with Pete — in a tone of voice Fannie hadn't heard. Edie had been calm and seemingly in complete control before. Now she seemed nervous and somehow less imposing than Fannie remembered. While Edie chattered, Fannie glanced at Edmund. He nodded toward the table. Fannie recognized Samuel's Bible and, lying atop it, a letter. The letter Samuel had carried with him for Edith LeClerc. Fannie glanced at the nervous woman standing at Edmund's stove.

Edmund said he was going to head over to Abe's and make arrangements for Lamar to recover at the hostelry. He asked Edie to check on both men in a few minutes.

"I'll send Pete for you if there's any change," Edie offered, as she put the lid back on the stewpot and shoved it to the back of the stove.

Edmund thanked her, smiled what Fannie took as encouragement her way, and left.

Finally, Edie turned around and said, "Would you like coffee?" She reached for two mugs in the makeshift cupboard. "Personally, I'd like a drink, but I suppose coffee will have to do." As the dark liquid flowed from the pot into her mug, she said something about how long it had taken her to learn to make coffee. "I warn you," she said, as she poured a second cup, "I make it strong."

"There's no such thing as strong coffee," Fannie said, repeating a mantra she'd heard from Papa, surprised when Edie joined in with the words, "there are only weak men."

"If I've heard Louis say that once," Edie said, "I've heard it a thousand times." She smiled. A sad smile, Fannie thought, as she accepted the mug of coffee.

Once seated opposite Fannie, Edie picked up the letter Samuel had been carrying with him. Unfolding it, she read aloud, " 'I've read the letters so many times now that I almost have them memorized. . . . Is it too much to ask you to come to Fort Benton before the last steamboat of the season leaves in October?' " Edie looked up and swept an errant blond curl off her forehead with the back of her hand. "Were you really willing to wait until October just for a chance to meet me?"

When Fannie nodded, Edie sighed. "It must have been a huge disappointment when you finally did."

Fannie shrugged. "I might have even waited through winter if I'd known spring would mean meeting the woman who wrote those letters to Mother." She took a sip of coffee, wincing at the bitter flavor of what was more sludge than drink. She got up and went to the cupboard after sugar. As she crossed the room, she recited a passage from one of the letters about Edith

LeClerc's dancing with the emperor of France. Back at the table, she sat down again and stared across at Edie. "Did any of the things you talked about in those letters really happen? Or was it all a fantasy? You seemed to suspect Mother wouldn't ever let me read them, and it's obvious she never answered them. So . . . why did you continue to write? What did you mean by 'proving your devotion' through Mr. Vandekamp? And why was Mother so . . . angry with you that I never even knew you existed?"

Reaching for something on the floor, Edie produced a small bag, brought out a cigar, and lit it. Closing her eyes, she drew in the smoke. When she exhaled, Fannie once again thought of Papa. It *was* the same tobacco. It had to be. Instead of answering Fannie's questions, Edie said, "Tell me about the life you left. The one you'll be going back to."

Fannie glanced behind her, into the clinic and toward Samuel and Lamar.

"They're resting," Edie said. "I'll check on them in a minute."

"I've told you everything that matters. Papa and Mother are both gone."

"And Hubert," Edie said, flicking ashes into an empty mug. "Is he still handling things for the Rousseaus?" She chuckled

345

softly. "I can just imagine what he had to say about your coming up here." She smiled. "It speaks well of you that he didn't talk you out of it, by the way."

"I didn't tell him I was coming," Fannie said. "In fact, when I showed him the letter with his name in it, he . . ." She toyed with her coffee cup. "Let's just say he wasn't thrilled."

"That would be Hubert," Edie said. "He never was interested in anything remotely out of the ordinary."

"It sounds like you knew him fairly well."

Edie took a sip of coffee, then circled the rim of the mug with her index finger as she said, "To answer your question . . . yes. Every single one of the things I wrote about really did happen. The emperor's name is Louis, and he favored me with a dance because I slapped someone at court who was particularly rude to the Empress Eugénie."

Fannie frowned. She gestured around her. "And then you came *here?*"

"Only after going to St. Charles, hoping to see you and give you an amethyst ring."

She took another drag on the cigar, blowing the smoke toward the corner of the room.

"But Hannah . . . told me she'd never met

you. Didn't know anything about you."

"She didn't." Edie swallowed. "I'm sorry about your losing her, by the way. She was lovely."

She looked up then, and met Fannie's gaze. "I saw her once. You were with her. I was in my room at the little inn on Main, looking out the window. And there you were. Walking with that blind friend of yours. And Hannah. You all three went into Haversham's. And I hurried to the house to see Eleanor." She cleared her throat. Looked away. "It did not go well." She put her cigar in the ashtray. "And so I left. I sent the ring with a messenger and a note begging Eleanor to give it to you on your wedding day." She gestured around her. "And then I came to fabulous Montana."

With a trembling hand, she opened the letter again and read, " 'Can we make amends for these twenty years?' " She gazed at Fannie. "Edmund tells me you know about Bonaparte's. *Both* of them." She paused again. "So I'd say that whether or not we can make amends depends entirely on you. I know I'm a great disappointment. As time goes on, you'll find even more things to dislike. The letters aren't lies. But still, I'm not the woman you thought I was."

Fannie thought of E. C. Dandridge, pretending to be a gentleman . . . and men from all walks of life pretending to be miners . . . and Mother . . . pretending nothing was wrong financially when, in fact, the Rousseaus were on the brink of losing everything. Was anyone ever exactly who they seemed to be? She forced a smile. "I've come a very long way to find you." She reached across the table and grasped Edie's hand.

Edie gave a nervous little laugh. Tears gathered in her eyes. "Well, then. That's fine." She stood up. "Let's go in and check on the patients." As she and Fannie headed into the clinic, Edie said, "You know, Fannie, you could do something even more outrageous than leaving St. Charles in the first place. You could spend the winter here in Fort Benton." She paused. "You could even stay at Bonaparte's if you thought you could bear it. Who knows . . . given time, you might decide you like me."

Voices . . . whispers . . . his name . . . Samuel could tell they wanted him to answer. And he tried. But he was at the bottom of a well and the weight of the water on his chest wouldn't let him rise . . . wouldn't let him breathe. He was too weak to even open his eyes. Where was he? What day was it?

Indians! There'd been . . . arrows. War cries. And that half-wild cayuse had reared up and that was all he could remember until the voices . . . and drums.

Pain . . . such pain. He grimaced. Something cool on his forehead. Something moist pressed against his lips. That felt . . . good . . . soothing . . . but it didn't last.

The pain swallowed everything.

CHAPTER TWENTY-TWO

I will look unto the Lord; I will wait for the
God of my salvation: my God will hear
me.

MICAH 7:7

Samuel didn't know how long he'd been in
and out of consciousness. Reality came in
snatches of light and voices he recognized,
but he still didn't have the energy to as
much as open his eyes. He was alive. For a
while he'd wondered if he was dead and
trapped in some limbo state the Bible didn't
talk about. The Bible said absent from the
world . . . present with the Lord. Didn't it?
It hurt his head to think about it. To think
about anything but . . . sleep. He slept.

Lamar. Where's Lamar? Lamar was . . .
talking. Somewhere. Just across the room?
To who? A woman. Fannie! No . . . not
Fannie. Someone . . . older. He'd heard that
voice. Humming. Songs. Hymns. He sighed.

Opened his eyes.

He and Lamar were in a room. He looked around in the flickering lamplight and recognized the clinic where he'd brought Fannie the day she fainted. Fannie . . . where was Fannie? He wanted to ask for her, but he couldn't say her name. He squinted at the woman helping Lamar get a drink of water. She wasn't Fannie, but her voice was kind. He felt . . . empty. Was it hunger? Maybe. He parted his lips and tried to moisten them with his tongue. Nothing but cotton there.

"Hey, my friend," Lamar said, and the woman leaning over him turned quickly to look at Samuel.

She looked so much like Fannie . . . only . . . older. Her voice was low. Almost masculine. "Look who's awake." She smiled. She had a nice smile. He could hear water trickling back into the bowl when she wrung out a cloth and pressed it to his lips. He sucked eagerly.

"Whoa there, Parson," she said. "Let's see if I can do better than this rag." She filled a glass and then helped him lift his head. He coughed most of the water right back up, but some of it slid down his throat. He'd never tasted anything more wonderful. And never worked so hard. He was exhausted.

Just from swallowing a little water? It made no sense, but he was too tired to worry about it. He closed his eyes and slept.

When someone knocked on Fannie's door in the middle of the night, she started awake, instantly terrified . . . Samuel was . . . *no. Don't think it.* Flinging back the covers, she scrambled to the door and opened it.

"The parson's coming to," Edie said. "Doc's with him. I thought you'd want to come see for yourself."

Fannie threw a dress on and grabbed her wool cape. Her hair cascaded down her back, but she let it be. The cape would hide it anyway. As she and Edie scurried back to the clinic in the cold, she glanced toward the river. Her heart sank as she saw the golden glow of lamplight illuminating the transom windows of the newly arrived steamboat. She looked away. She couldn't think about that now . . . all that mattered right now was Samuel.

He couldn't talk. Everything came out wrong. Garbled. He tried to say "water," but what came out didn't sound a thing like the word *water.* Everyone was trying to act like it didn't matter, but he knew better. He could see the fear in Fannie's eyes and the worry in the other woman's. *Edie Bonaparte.* He blinked and looked from her to Fannie and back again. Like seeing Fannie in twenty years. She'd still be beautiful. Something had obviously changed between the two of them. Fannie's letter had said Edie didn't want to know her. What had happened? He had so many questions . . . and he couldn't talk. He grabbed the doctor's arm. Gestured around the room, furrowed his brow.

Dr. LaMotte asked, "Do you remember being on the trail?"

Samuel nodded. Glancing at Lamar, he mimicked drawing a bow back and releasing an arrow.

"That's right, son," Lamar said. "You and me, right in the middle of a war. I thought they were trying to steal our horses, but Doc here talked to Lame Bear the other day — he came in to see about you and me. Seems we were just in the wrong place at the wrong time. Some argument between the Bloods and the Piegan."

Dr. LaMotte nodded his agreement. "Two freighters found Lamar up on the trail and brought him in. But they didn't see any sign of you. Your horse must have thrown you and taken off. Lame Bear's sons found you at the bottom of a ravine. They were afraid to bring you into town, so they took you to Bonaparte's. Edie and a wrangler named Pete nearly drove a team into the ground bringing you here."

Samuel looked for the woman, but she'd apparently left the room. He winced as he reached up to touch the side of his face that hurt the worst.

"I'm sure everything hurts. From what Lame Bear described, you fell a long way."

He rubbed his lips with the side of his finger. He tried to ask, "Why can't I talk?" Nothing came out but a few disgusting-sounding grunts. The doctor got a chair and sat down beside Sam's cot.

"What you're experiencing is called *aphasia*. Your brain knows what it wants to say, but your mouth can't follow through. There's some minor evidence that bloodletting has helped in a couple of cases. In my opinion the evidence was inconclusive, and I consider bloodletting barbaric. I'd rather have you rest and give it some time." He peered closely at one of Samuel's wounds. "I can only imagine how frustrated you are — and honestly, you're probably at least a little afraid, but it's very good that you are obviously understanding what people say to you."

Samuel nodded, then touched the wound

along his eyebrow.

"You have stitches there. And here." The doctor traced a line from the edge of his own scalp toward the crown of his head. "An arrow caused a flesh wound on your right thigh. Everything's healing nicely, although you are very . . . colorful . . . at the moment. To be honest, I've never seen so many bruises on a body as well off as yours."

When Samuel pointed at the mirror hanging on the far wall, Fannie took it down and handed it over, then held up a lamp so he could see himself. Between the rainbow of color splayed across one side of his face, the swelling, and the stitches, he looked . . . monstrous.

"Do you remember anything after the horse threw you?" the doctor asked.

Sam held his thumb and forefinger apart. *A little.* He remembered being in a tepee. He thought someone had given him some water. He must have passed out when they moved him. He didn't remember a thing about a wagon ride. How long had he been here? He pretended to scribble on his palm. When the doctor produced paper and a pencil, he managed to write the words *How long.*

"I don't know how long it will take. Only

God knows."

Sam shook his head and gestured around the room again, then tapped the paper.

The doctor's eyes lit with understanding. "You've been here a week, floating in and out. If you don't remember, consider it part of God's gift of healing. There's very little to remember but pain."

Sam turned his head to look at Lamar, surprised at how much it hurt. With a grimace, he pointed at his friend.

"Don't worry about me, son. I'm old, but I'm tough." Lamar put a hand on the sling around his neck. "My arm's broke. The doc says to be glad the bone didn't break the skin. He thinks I'll be all right." He grinned. "One thing good about it, I haven't thought to complain about my knees in a while."

Samuel nodded . . . and then he fell asleep.

Abe sent soup over from the boarding house the next evening, along with a message that he wouldn't need any help serving supper. Samuel had spent a painful amount of time throughout the morning trying to talk and managing only unintelligible sounds. Fannie could see his mood slipping toward despair with every passing hour. Finally, he gave up. He hadn't uttered a sound for the rest of the day. Over supper, she peppered Edmund with questions. "He wants to be a preacher. He has to be able to talk. There must be something you can do."

"I've pored over every medical book in the clinic, and all I can tell you is what I already have. Sometimes the healing is remarkable. Sometimes the damage is permanent."

"It hasn't been that long," Edie offered. "I know it's hard, but . . . we all have to be patient."

Fannie shook her head. "That's not good enough." She glanced toward the river, feeling her frustration grow. "Are there specialists? Is there someone else?" She knew she was practically yelling but was too frustrated to care. "Should we take him downriver?"

Edmund took a deep breath. "If you're asking me if there are doctors who know more than I do about aphasia, the answer is yes. There's likely a doctor who knows more than me about just about everything." He pulled the napkin out of where it had been tucked into his collar and, folding it, laid it beside his soup bowl. "I've told you everything *I* know about it, Fannie. I don't know if Sam will talk again. I think he will, but I don't know. Unfortunately, God doesn't visit me at night and discuss my patients' prognoses."

He stood up. "I'm sorry I'm such a disappointment to you. You're welcome to read my medical books if you think I've missed something." He took a step toward the clinic, then paused. "It isn't much, but I do know one thing. Hauling Sam Beck aboard a steamer is a terrible idea. He's stuck with the best I can do." He disappeared into the darkened clinic.

Awkward silence at the table made Fannie feel self-conscious. She pulled her piece of bread apart and dropped the fragments into her soup bowl to soak up the last bit of broth, then realized she had no appetite. She got up to refill her coffee mug.

Patrick broke the silence. "Don't worry, Fannie. Sam's going to be all right. Pa will take good care of him."

Fannie crossed back to the table and put a hand on the boy's shoulder. "I know he will. I don't know why I said those things."

"It's because you're scared," Patrick said.

Fannie agreed. "I'm scared for Sam. He loves God so much . . . and telling other people about him . . . he loves doing that. What will happen if he can't preach?"

"But that's not why you yelled at Pa," Patrick said. "You yelled because the last steamboat is at the levee and you don't want to leave, but you're scared of staying here all winter." He reached for her hand. "You don't have to be scared, Fannie. Winter's not so bad if you have stuff to do and enough to eat. You and I can play checkers. Pa has a lot of books you can read. Abe likes having you at the boarding house. Sure, it gets cold, but you won't freeze. We'll be all right." He turned as if looking at Edie as he said, "Edie wants you to stay, too."

Fannie glanced at Edie, but the older woman was concentrating on spreading butter on a slice of bread and didn't seem to have heard a word. "Why do you say that?" she asked.

Patrick mulled the question for a moment. "When you can't see faces, you listen better. Sometimes listening lets a person see in a better way."

Fannie couldn't suppress a smile. Minette had an amazing sensitivity to nuances that sighted people often missed, but she'd been taught much of it at school. Apparently Patrick had a natural intuition. "Tell me, Patrick, what do you 'see' when you listen?"

The boy sighed. "Well . . . like I said. Edie likes you. So does Abe." He smiled. "And of course, Pa."

"I'm glad to hear that," Fannie said. "Because what I just said to him was unkind." She got up and, retrieving the coffeepot from the stovetop, poured both herself and Edmund another cup. "I think I'll go in the other room and apologize. I just hope he'll hear me out."

"Of course he will," Patrick said. "Don't you hear it when he talks to you? He keeps liking you more all the time."

Fannie hugged him. "And I keep liking *you* more all the time, Patrick LaMotte." She kissed him on the cheek.

"I'll clean up here," Edie said quietly. "Patrick and I have a date with the Greeks." She pointed to a book on the reading table by Edmund's rocker.

Patrick nodded. "We're almost to the part where Jason finds the fleece."

Fannie grabbed the two coffee mugs and stepped into the clinic.

Edmund had lit the shaded kerosene lamp at his desk and was seated, his head bowed over yet another medical tome. He didn't look up when Fannie came in, just murmured that Samuel and Lamar were both asleep and kept reading.

Fannie went to him and set the coffee down. She put a hand on his shoulder. "Patrick just gave me a lesson in listening. Sometimes I think he's better at understanding people than those of us who have our sight." She paused. "He said that you like me, and that you'd forgive me for what I said just now." She crouched down beside him and put a hand on his arm. "Please, Edmund. Forgive me. You're a wonderful doctor and I know you're doing everything you can."

He looked down at her. "Do you really believe that?"

"I do." She glanced toward Samuel. Shook her head. "I just hate to see him suffer. He didn't find his sister, but he seemed to have found his calling in life. And then . . ." She shrugged. "It seems so unfair."

Edmund agreed even as he thanked her for apologizing. He got up and, retrieving a chair, set it next to him at the desk. Fannie sat down and he showed her a diagram of the human brain and began to explain what he thought was going on with Samuel. "The truth is, we don't know a lot about how the brain works. There's disagreement over even the most basic things, like where, exactly, the capacity for speech resides. From the cut on Sam's scalp, it would seem most likely that that's the part of the brain where speech resides. But there's just as much evidence from others that it's not there at all." He paused. "Obviously, someone like me who practices in a remote area —" He broke off. "I haven't exactly kept up with the latest findings. So you're probably right. There are probably all kinds of doctors who know more than I do about any of this."

"Please," Fannie said, putting a hand on his arm, "stop." She reached for her coffee mug and cupped it in her palms, gazing down at the golden arc from the lamp reflected in the surface of her coffee. "Just now, Patrick said that I was really upset because I don't want to leave, but I'm afraid to stay." She forced a smile. "He said I shouldn't be afraid." She took a sip of coffee. "When I left St. Charles this spring, I expected to be back by fall. And then . . ." She shook her head. "Patrick's right. It's not just that I don't want to leave. I can't *imagine* it. I've just found the reason I came. Edie isn't at all what I'd envisioned, but she's all the family I have. As for Sam and Lamar . . . I know they'll be fine. They don't *need* me — but I can't imagine being cut off from knowing how they are."

Edmund reached over and took her coffee mug out of her hands and set it on the desk. Taking her hands in his, he lifted them to his lips and deposited a kiss on the back of each one. "We *do* need you," he said. He released one and, tracing the line of her jaw, lifted her chin so that she met his gaze.

"Please, Fannie. *Stay.*"

And suddenly . . . it wasn't such a difficult decision after all.

The doc had turned down his lamp and he and Patrick had retired long ago. By now, Fannie was asleep over at the boarding house. Edie had taken to keeping watch at night. She was in the kitchen now. Every once in a while, Samuel heard a quiet footstep or a creak as she got up to get another cup of coffee and then settled back into the doctor's rocker. She'd asked Samuel if he minded if she read his mother's Bible. He'd smiled and she'd teased him, "If I'd known you had such a pretty smile, Parson, I'd have asked to read the Good Book as soon as you woke up."

Samuel lay on his side staring at the square of pale light on the board floor where moonlight shone in the window by the doc's desk. Praying for a miracle. Praying to heal so he could return to the gold camps before snow closed the trail. Wishing he hadn't heard the doc begging Fannie to stay. Wishing he hadn't seen how easy it was for her to say yes . . . to *him.* Doing his best to believe that in that space between what he knew to be true and what he didn't understand . . . that somewhere in that empty space . . . he'd have the faith to be happy for Fannie and Dr. LaMotte . . . and to hold on to hope for himself.

Dear Minette,

There is so much to say — so much to explain — and I haven't nearly as much time as I need. I want to write pages and pages, but the steamboat departs this morning and this letter has to be in the mailbag on board, because I won't be. Too much has happened for me to leave now.

Oh, Minette, I've finally found Aunt Edith! And while at first she seemed less than happy to have been found, now we are spending time together. We've just begun to get acquainted, and I don't want to put our relationship at the mercy of either the river or a mailbag.

The next reason I need to stay is for Samuel's sake. He has not found his sister, but he and Lamar were headed back to Fort Benton when they were caught up in an Indian skirmish. They were helped into Fort Benton and are recovering, except for the fact that Samuel cannot speak. He makes noises, he can swallow, he can understand, but he can't form words. Yet. Dr. LaMotte is hopeful, but I can see the fear in Samuel's eyes. He is my dear friend, and I cannot abandon him.

Lastly, I want to stay for Patrick and Edmund LaMotte. Patrick is a dear. He reminds me of you in that he has a sixth sense about people. He told me that listening carefully sometimes helps him see. I can't explain it all, but suffice it to say that Patrick helped me to see that I cannot leave yet.

And so, dear Minette, I will be spending a winter in the northernmost trading outpost of the Missouri River. Abe's boarding house is nearly empty, and so there is little work to be done, but he assures me I am welcome to stay, even though I am bereft of a way to pay him. Which leads me to another topic.

I am enclosing a letter to Mr. Vandekamp. It is essential that both your father and Daniel read it before it is delivered.

I hope this finds you well. I am fine, although changed in ways I don't quite understand myself. I have always believed in God, but I've needed my faith more since leaving home. It is as if a seedling is sprouting stems and leaves. Perhaps by the time I see you again it will be in full bloom. I know that I will never be the same because of Fort Benton and all it represents.

Please know that my devotion to you remains as strong as ever. I love you, dear friend. In the midst of the shock this letter will undoubtedly cause, I pray that you can still find it in your heart to love me as well as ever.

Always yours,
Fannie

Dear Mr. Vandekamp,

Having received your letter, I find it necessary to express my deep disappointment at your taking advantage of my situation in order to follow the letter of the law rather than its spirit. In the absence of your goodwill, God has seen fit to provide for me in other ways. I send this letter in care of friends who will see that it is delivered and my wishes executed without the disappointing taint of the vengeful spirit evidenced in your communiqué.

At her request, I forward greetings from Miss Edith LeClerc . . . my own Aunt Edie.

Sincerely,
Fannie LeClerc Rousseau

Fannie folded the note to Mr. Vandekamp and reread the accompanying document that would hopefully provide Daniel Hennessey and Mr. Beauvais everything they needed to manage her affairs. She couldn't help but feel what was probably a sinful bit of satisfaction as she envisioned the effect the document would have on Mr. Vandekamp. Those two bright spots of color would have already appeared on his face when he read her note. But, as he stood in the presence of Daniel Hennessey and Mr. Beauvais and read the document, his entire face would burn bright with rage. The only person he had to blame was himself. And now . . . now Fannie could face the winter knowing that things in St. Charles would be all right until she returned in the spring. Faith was the substance of things hoped for and the evidence of things not seen, and as she sealed the envelope, Fannie realized that she was at peace with her decision to stay . . . and hope . . . and see.

To all parties involved in businesses and private matters related to the estate of the late Mr. and Mrs. Louis Rousseau of St. Charles, Missouri:

As the sole heir of the parties herein mentioned, I, Fannie LeClerc Rousseau, wish it to be known that in my absence from St. Charles, Missouri, however long that may be, and until further written notice from me or by verbal instruction from my own person, Mr. Daniel Hennessey and Mr. Claude Beauvais are my appointed agents. Their decisions are to be considered final and binding on all parties concerned. I hereby instruct Mr. Hubert Vandekamp to make available to the aforementioned gentlemen any and all financial records, accounts, etc., necessary in order for Mr. Hennessey and Mr. Beauvais to conduct matters in such a way as they see fit.

Regarding the property on Main Street, which I understand was damaged in a fire in my absence, I request that everything possible be done to prevent further damage to both the house and its contents until I return to inspect the property. Mr. Amos Walker has my full confidence in the matter of upkeep and, along with his assistant, Tommy Cooper, should be paid for his services in that regard. If Mr. Walker sees fit, he is to take up residence in the carriage house apartment. If he does not wish to do so, appropriate measures should be taken so that a trustworthy watchman remains on the premises. Nothing is to be disposed of unless this is deemed necessary by Mr. Hennessey and Mr. Beauvais, who have my utmost confidence and trust.

Hereto I assign my signature on this twentieth day of October, 1869.

Fannie LeClerc Rousseau

Witness: Edmund LaMotte, M.D. Fort Benton, Montana Territory, U.S.A.

Witness: Abraham Valley, Proprietor of the Fort Benton Hostelry, Montana Territory, U.S.A.

CHAPTER TWENTY-THREE

In whom we have redemption through his
blood, the forgiveness of sins, according
to the riches of his grace.

EPHESIANS 1:7

As October waned and the prairie browned,
Fannie saw Fort Benton transformed. Only
a few crates and barrels remained on the
once bustling levee. The last bull train left
for the gold camps, and with that, many of
the saloons closed down to wait for spring.
While business didn't completely die, the
nights were no longer punctuated with
music and gunfire.

Lame Bear and his sons rode into town
one day in a display of feathers and finery
that took Fannie's breath away. They were
headed to their winter camp, but Lame Bear
wanted to see how Lamar and Samuel were
doing, and now that White Sparrow was going to stay the winter, he thought she might

change her mind about riding Smoke. After an impressive speech, he waved at Owl, who jumped off his pony and presented Fannie with a beautifully tooled sidesaddle.

Even as she ran her hand over the burnished leather, Fannie protested. "We're the ones who should be giving gifts. They saved Samuel's life. In fact . . . I'm ashamed I haven't done so."

When Edmund translated the message, Lame Bear smiled at her and gestured to his sons. Edmund laughed. "He's willing to accept you into the clan if you'd care to go into winter camp with them."

Fannie shook her head even as she smiled at Lame Bear. "I see the smile around your eyes. You're teasing." Putting her hand to her heart, she nodded her thanks to the three braves. The men returned the gesture and then, in a whirl of color and a chorus of yells, charged out of town toward the north.

Fannie looked down at the saddle. "Do I dare wonder how on earth they came up with this?"

Edie deadpanned, "There's a saddler right up the street. I imagine they stopped in and bought it right before they had tea at the mercantile." She laughed. "If you know what's good for you, Miss Rousseau, by the time spring rolls around and Lame Bear comes back this way, you'll be ready to demonstrate how well you can ride that gray horse he gave you."

"But I sold Smoke to Edmund."

"Did you, now?" Hands on hips, Edie glared at Edmund. "For cash?"

"For perpetual medical care," Edmund said. "A fair trade."

Edie nudged Fannie. "Take the horse back, honey. A woman who has to wait on a man to go where she wants to go is a woman who spends far too much of her life waiting." She tilted her head. "Now that I think about it, we need to teach you how to shoot. Then you'll be all set."

Later that evening, Fannie took her time washing dishes in the lean-to boarding house kitchen while Patrick and Abe played checkers and Edie, Lamar, and Samuel played poker with bits of paper for chips. Samuel was feeling considerably better, and was now able to sit up and play a game for a half hour at a stretch before the exhaustion caught up with him again. The laughter sounding from the room should have made Fannie happy, but somehow it made her feel lonely.

He might not be able to speak clearly, but

Samuel seemed adept at making people feel comfortable with him. Patrick especially liked him, and Edie . . . Sam seemed to have a special fondness for Edie that Fannie couldn't quite understand. It was almost as if the two shared a secret no one else knew about. Sam seemed to take special care to play the gentleman around Edie, and she seemed to have an affection for him that bordered on mothering. Fannie was glad for Samuel's sake, but she felt left out. Which was petty, and she knew it, but she couldn't seem to help it.

Samuel himself was the cause of part of her loneliness. His speech was coming back, but it was painfully slow. Fannie had noticed a streak of impatience and anger in him when he tried to talk to her that hadn't been there before. Sometimes he just plain gave up, and that left her feeling helpless. There was so much she wanted to talk to him about, but he didn't have the words. She wanted to hear all about the gold camps and how he'd been invited to give a sermon in a saloon. Lamar said it wasn't his story to tell, and she'd just have to wait until Sam was able. She wanted to hear about Emma. Mostly, she wanted to offer comfort, but Sam didn't seem to want that. At least not from her. He was more than willing to try to talk with Edie, but every time Fannie tried to join a conversation, Samuel turned to writing cryptic notes. He wouldn't even try to talk to her.

Edie appeared in the doorway. "Want some help out here?" She picked up a dish towel. "I've won the house so many times those two are sick of playing with me. They've gone to bed. Abe and Patrick are still at the checkerboard. He said he'd keep Patrick occupied while I talked to you."

"About what?"

"About taking Lamar and Sam to my place for the duration. I thought I'd see if Lamar might take on some of Pete's work — as soon as his arm heals, of course. Pete's not getting any younger. He can fix just about anything, but he's slowed considerably. As for Sam. . . . if I ever had a son —" She broke off. Shrugged. "He makes me believe there's a slim possibility God hasn't written off old Edie after all."

"Why would you say such a thing?" Fannie protested. "God doesn't do that."

"I just might be the exception to his willingness to put up with mistakes."

Fannie shook her head. "You've given six women a home, Edie. Anyone would admire that."

Edie concentrated on drying a plate. "You

have no idea just how many mistakes I have to make up for. Bonaparte's in its present incarnation is little more than a speck of dust in a whole desert of sins."

"Don't I remember something in the Bible about forgiveness being free? I don't think we have to earn our way with God. Everybody falls short."

"Some of us fall shorter than others." Edie forced a chuckle. "I know he's no priest, but Sam's easy to . . . confess to." She put a stack of plates on the shelf. "No matter what I say about people I've left behind, people I've hurt, Sam keeps sending me to that Bible of his and saying just about the same thing you just did. He describes it as more forgiveness than any person could ever need, no matter what they've done or who they've hurt."

"Sam . . . *says* that?"

"Well . . . not out loud. But he keeps pointing me to the same verses, and when I try to tell him I'm the exception, he shakes his head and writes *You can't sin more than God can forgive.*" She reached for another plate as Fannie lifted it out of the rinse water, but then held on to it until Fannie looked up at her. When their eyes met, Edie asked, "Do you think that's true? That anything can be forgiven?"

Now, why did that question make Fannie feel . . . unsettled? What was Edie getting at, anyway? Fannie released the plate and plunged her hands back into the dishwater, forcing a lighter tone into her voice as she said, "If it isn't, everyone's in what Hannah used to call 'a heap o' trouble.' "

They worked in silence for a while. Finally, Edie gave Fannie's shoulder a squeeze. "I'm sorry I let Eleanor chase me away, Fannie. Sorry she couldn't find a way past her anger to make you feel loved." Her voice wavered. "You're a beautiful, kind, honest, delightful girl." She cleared her throat. "And I'm about to say something that's going to make you really angry, but I have to say it."

Fannie steeled herself to hear something terrible even as she realized she liked the idea of Edie treating her the same way she treated Samuel — as a close friend.

"Edmund's going to propose to you. And you have to say no."

"What?" Fannie turned to look at her. "What are you talking about? Edmund's. . . . We're friends. That's all."

"Maybe so, but that doesn't mean he isn't going to propose. You're wonderful with Patrick, and the boy loves you. He needs a mother, and you'll be a superb mother." Her voice lowered as she insisted, "You mustn't do it, Fannie."

"What — why would you say something like that?"

"Because you're in love with Sam." Edie put one hand on Fannie's arm and gave it a squeeze, then let go. "He loves you, too, although he's being ridiculous and refusing to acknowledge it because he's not well. He's terrified he never will be, and he's being tragically noble. Which is stupid . . . but what are you going to do? Men are stupid."

When Fannie said nothing, Edie added, "Don't be angry with me, Fannie. Once you think about what I've just said, you'll know I'm right."

"I'm not angry. I'm . . . amazed." She swept her forehead with the back of her hand. "How did we get from Samuel and Lamar going to Bonaparte's to God's forgiveness and then on to whom I should marry — which, by the way, isn't really any of your business. But, since you brought it up, I'm no match for Samuel Beck — not when he's going to be Reverend Samuel Beck someday, and I believe with all my heart that he will be."

"So do I," Edie agreed. "But you're wrong about not being a match for him. You're exactly right. The truth of it shines in his eyes every time he looks at you."

"Why don't *I* see it when he looks at me?"

"Because he's a beautiful-but-bullheaded son of a willy-walloo."

Fannie laughed in spite of herself. "Captain Busch used to call himself that."

"Yes, well . . . unless he's changed, Otto *is* a son of a willy-walloo." Edie smiled. "There's more than one in the world, honey. And some of us are women."

Samuel had taken to rising before dawn and forcing himself out the door to take a walk, which had begun as mostly a torturous limp that barely carried him to the fort before he was exhausted, but now carried him all the way to the river and back. He was getting stronger. Dr. LaMotte had taken out all the stitches, and while Sam still didn't like what he saw in the mirror, he reminded himself that vanity wasn't a very attractive character quality. He should be thankful to be alive, and he was.

And so, on this frigid morning when frost had painted the landscape white, Samuel dragged himself out of bed and limped toward the levee. As he walked, he recited the Shepherd's Psalm. Or tried to. Mostly he mumbled. Edie said he was getting better every day. He couldn't hear it. All he could hear was a garbled mess.

Edie. There was a fascinating woman. There was something . . . he couldn't figure it out, but once or twice he'd caught her watching Fannie when Fannie was unaware. And all of Edie's talk about how he didn't know just how much God would have to forgive if he forgave her. He was sure at least part of that was connected to Fannie some-how. Sam just couldn't quite untangle it. He wanted to see Edie finally give things up to God and stop trying to fix them herself. He wanted to tell Fannie . . . so much. But he needed to talk to do any of that. Didn't God know that? Dr. LaMotte said to give it time. Everyone did. Sam was doing his best to believe them, to not to give up, but it was getting harder by the day.

Fannie woke just as dawn spilled in her bedroom window. She'd almost mastered getting dressed beneath the pile of comfort-ers, but she was still shivering by the time she made it into Abe's kitchen to start breakfast. She'd just gotten the fire going in the cookstove when a shadow in the door-way made her jump.

"Sss . . . me."

"Were you sitting in the dark?"

Sam shrugged. Nodded. "Praying."

Fannie smiled. "Well, I don't suppose you

need a lamp to pray, do you."

He shook his head and retreated.

"You don't have to leave. I'm just going to mix up some batter for flapjacks."

He lingered in the doorway, watching her work. "You grad— grad—"

"Yes." Fannie smiled as she measured flour and soda into a mixing bowl. "I told you I would. Graduate." She scooped coffee beans into the grinder and handed it to him. "Earn your keep."

While Samuel ground the coffee beans, Fannie finished mixing up the batter and began to fry flapjacks. She'd just put a stack of hot ones on a plate when someone opened the front door.

"That's Edmund and Patrick," she said, wiping her hands on her apron and hurrying to greet them. One look at Edmund and she knew something was wrong. "What's happened?"

He shook his head, rubbed his neck.

"Patrick, there's an entire plate of flapjacks in the kitchen. It's on the right side of the work table. Think you could get it out here without a disaster? If you need help, Mr. Beck is there making coffee."

As soon as Patrick was out of earshot, Edmund told her, "Dick Turley came to see me last night about a cough. The old fool

380

hasn't listened to a thing I've said for months. And now . . . there's nothing I can do."

Fannie put her hand on his arm. "I'm so sorry."

"When I offered him laudanum to keep him comfortable, he waved it off. Said he'd drink his way to hell and that I shouldn't feel bad for him." He plopped into a chair.

Fannie went to stand behind him. Placing her hands on his shoulders, she began to knead the knotted muscles.

"That feels . . . wonderful."

"That's the general idea."

He reached up and took her hand just as Patrick and Sam emerged from the kitchen.

So that's the way it was. It made complete sense. If he'd ever had a chance with Fannie, Sam realized he'd lost it. And it hurt. A lot. But then . . . what did he expect? He'd been off in the mountains for weeks, then unable to talk for himself since he got back. And Edmund LaMotte was a good man. In fact, now that Samuel really thought about it, Fannie would be much happier with him anyway. Hadn't she said something about LaMotte taking Patrick to that school in St. Louis? It was obvious the boy loved her. Who wouldn't? Fannie's best friend was blind. It was almost as if God was preparing her to be Patrick's mother all along. It really was perfect. Fannie wouldn't have to adapt to Montana, although Samuel had to admit that she'd done an amazing job of that, too. She was a different woman from the one who'd looked up at him that long-ago day on the levee at St. Charles and asked about passage to Fort Benton. A different woman altogether. More mature, stronger, and clearly meant for someone else. It was God's will and he, Samuel Beck, would learn to accept it. Of course, acceptance didn't mean he had to sit there in Abe Valley's dining room and eat breakfast while Edmund LaMotte courted her . . . did it?

"You'll eat with us, won't you, Samuel?"

Sam shook his head, nodded at the doctor, tousled Patrick's hair, and retreated to wait in the commons for Edie Bonaparte to open her door. The minute she did and offered him a good morning, Sam said, "R-ready to go. With . . . you. Home."

Edie looked him over. "What's happened?"

Samuel shrugged and tilted his head toward the dining room. Edie headed that way. He heard her greet the diners. She lingered awhile. When she came back to where Samuel sat huddled at one of Abe's rustic outdoor tables in the cool morning air, she handed him a mug of coffee and said, "I understand what you think you're seeing, but I don't think you should give up." She retrieved a shawl from her room, then returned and sat down across from him. "I am right, aren't I? You do love her?"

Samuel nodded.

"Well then." Edie smiled. "As I just said. Don't give up."

He shook his head. "Noth . . . ing . . . to offer."

"That's not true."

He tapped his chin with his open palm. "A preach . . . r . . . who . . . c-c-an't —"

"You're getting better every day."

He looked toward the dining room. "She . . . doesn't . . ." He stopped. "He's b-better."

"You're wrong." Edie's voice was firm. "The one who loves *most* is the one who's *better.*"

Sam frowned. "He l-oves."

"As a friend, yes. As a mother for Patrick, of course. But, Sam, Fannie deserves to be loved with the passion I see in your face every time you look at her." She leaned forward. "Listen to me. I know what I'm talking about. There is nothing noble about being too much of a coward to tell someone the truth." She broke off. Sat back. "Just risk it, Sam. Tell her. Let *her* decide."

He searched her expression. What did she mean . . . she was speaking from experience? What was it about Fannie . . . He looked toward the dining room and then back at Edie. And he knew. Suddenly, the puzzle pieces fell into place, and he knew. He put his hand on her arm. Swallowed. "You s-see . . . me love . . . her. I . . . w-watch . . . n . . . s-see . . . you . . . love . . . h-her . . . too." He patted her arm and held her gaze. "E-Edie . . . are . . . y-you . . . F-Fannie's . . . real ma?"

Edie pulled back. She looked away. Her hands clenched in her lap. She sat so still it almost seemed she had stopped breathing. Finally, she took a deep breath and gave a short, half-hawking kind of laugh. She swiped at the tear trickling down her cheek. "Well . . . what d' ya know." She cleared her throat. Her voice was husky when she said, "It seems I've lost some of my skill as an actress. I'll have to be more careful." She brushed at the tears now spilling down her cheeks. Nodded. "Yes, Parson. As a matter of fact, I am."

"Tell m-me . . . how . . . why." He smiled. "Good lis-ner." For a moment, he didn't think she was going to take him up on it, but then, Edie began to talk.

"Eleanor and I were always rivals. When Louis chose her, I took it as a personal challenge." She paused. "I've already told you that I'm not a nice person, Sam. But compared to when I was twenty? I'm a saint. Back then, I just wanted conquest. And when it came to Eleanor, I wanted revenge. I pretended to be interested in someone else. Hubert Vandekamp. But that was just to give me a reason to be around Louis. They were in business together . . ." She stopped again.

"When I found out I was expecting Louis's child . . . well. By then Louis and Eleanor had been married for long enough that they'd learned there was little hope Eleanor would ever be able to have children. And Louis desperately longed for children. When I realized, once and for all, that he would never love me, I had to get away. I convinced myself that loving the baby meant giving it a home with a loving mother and father. Because she loved Louis, Eleanor agreed to raise the baby."

Edie rocked back in her chair. "People thought of Eleanor as cold. Can you imagine the kind of love it took for her to raise Louis's and my baby as her own?" She shook her head. "Eleanor loved deeply . . . but she never forgave me. She forbade me to see Fannie. The last time I tried, Fannie was fifteen. I went to the house when Fannie was gone. Eleanor . . . well. There was quite a scene. I left town, but I continued writing letters, even though I knew Fannie might never see them."

"Un . . . tilll . . ."

"Yes. Until this spring when Eleanor died, and Fannie found them." Edie reached for Sam's hand. "Don't make my mistake. Don't give up on yourself. Or her." She swiped the last of her tears off her cheeks. Stood up. Staggered . . . and seemed in danger of fainting.

Sam moved to steady her, and that's when he realized Fannie was standing in the doorway of the lean-to kitchen. And the look on her face told him she'd heard every word Edie just said.

CHAPTER TWENTY-FOUR

Lord, I cry unto thee: make haste unto
me; give ear unto my voice, when I cry
unto thee.

PSALM 141:1

Edie reached out, her tone pleading. "Fannie . . . I'm so sorry . . . oh . . . please . . ."

Fannie held up both hands, palms out.
No. Don't. She backed away. Into Abe's
kitchen. Leaned against the worktable, grip-
ping the edge with both hands to steady
herself. She felt sick with a jumble of emotions she couldn't control. Shock. Amazement. Denial. And finally, anger. Anger so
hot it melted through all the other emotions, burned away the nausea and sent her
reeling into the dining room. But Patrick
was there, too, and so she stopped in her
tracks and waited for Edmund to look her
way. When he did, he jumped to his feet
and came to her side. She folded into herself

and collapsed against him, burying her face in his shoulder as she murmured in his ear. "Edie . . . I heard her talking to Sam. . . . Edie Bonaparte is my *mother*."

Edmund pulled her close even as he called to Patrick. "Fannie's not feeling well, son. I'm going to take her over to the clinic and make a toddy. Would you tell Abe she's with me?"

The boy's brow furrowed. "She'll be all right, won't she?"

Fannie cleared her throat and managed to reassure Patrick that she'd be fine. She let Edmund wrap her in his coat and guide her toward the clinic. The cold air cleared her head. Still, when Edmund swept the quilt that served as a room divider in his living quarters out of the way and insisted she lie down, she obeyed, happy to let him take care of her.

He stirred up the fire in his stove and stepped into the clinic. Fannie could hear the clink of glass as he removed stoppers from various bottles, and a faint crunch as he worked with mortar and pestle. By the time he'd brewed what he called a "calming tea," she'd wrapped herself in one of his coverlets and moved to his rocker. When he offered her the steaming concoction, she shook her head. "I feel calm. I'm so calm, in fact, I'd probably be fast asleep if I hadn't moved over here." She tucked her hair behind one ear and snuggled deeper into the wrapper.

"You're trembling." He pulled up a chair and sat opposite her. "Just take a sip." He forced a grin. "It's not nearly as horrific as some of my concoctions."

Fannie relented, grimacing as the hot liquid went down. "It's horrible enough." She took another swallow. Leaned her head back and closed her eyes. "I've wondered why Mother didn't care more. Why she didn't act like Minette's mother did. But never in my life did I ever, for one moment think maybe she wasn't really my mother." She took another sip of tea. "Even when I found Edie's photograph and those letters . . . I never thought . . ." She sighed.

"I knew life would never be the same for me after Hannah died. I realized it again when I got Mr. Vandekamp's letter telling me the house was damaged in a fire . . . but this?" Tears spilled down her cheeks. "My whole life is based on a lie." She shivered. Edmund motioned for her to take another drink. She obeyed.

Someone banged on the clinic door. Fannie pulled the coverlet closer. "I don't want to see her. I can't. I need time."

Edmund headed into the clinic. There was a commotion. A woman cried out. More commotion and Edmund directed someone to "get her onto the table."

Fannie cast off the coverlet, set her mug on the table, and went to the door. Edmund looked her way. "Can you heat up some water? Are you —" The woman screamed.

The poor thing. Barely visible in a tangle of filthy rags and yet writhing in pain. "I'll get it," Fannie said. Her own problems forgotten, she hurried to grab a bucket and pump some water out back. Back inside, she added fuel to the stove and set a pan of water on to boil. Again, the woman cried out. Fannie hurried into the clinic and to the cupboard where Edmund kept clean bandages.

"I'd just helped her up in the wagon when the pains started," a man said. Fannie pulled bandages off the shelf. She turned around and recognized him. *Pete.* Edie's Pete from the ranch.

Edmund looked her way. "You've got the water on?" She nodded. "Go get Edie. Tell her I need her help with a delivery. Ask her to bring a nightgown — a clean anything she can spare."

"But I can —"

"I want Edie," Edmund snapped, then

told Pete to pull his coat off and see to bringing in the hot water. "She's half frozen. We've got to get her warmed up. Where'd you say you found her?"

"Just outside of town. I was coming into town to see about Edie. The girls have been missing her and wondering how things were going with the parson." He nodded at the woman. "She was stumbling along the trail."

"Left me —" the woman gasped. "Didn't know — didn't want — baby." She grunted and yelled her way through a contraction. That's when Fannie saw the blood seeping through the woman's skirt.

Edmund roared her name. "Fannie! Get Edie *now!*"

She tore out the door.

Samuel was with Edie, who'd obviously been crying, when Fannie charged through the hostelry door and called to Edie, "Edmund needs you! There's a girl — a baby —"

Edie grabbed her cloak off the hook by the door and ran into the cold morning. Fannie watched her go, then realized she'd forgotten to say anything about a nightgown. Hers wasn't clean, but it would be better than the rags the poor thing had on. She glanced at Samuel. "I have to get something Edmund was asking for." She hurried to her room for the nightgown, returning by way of the kitchen in search of Patrick. He was elbow deep in bread dough while Abe and Lamar stood nearby cheering him on.

"That's it," Abe said. "All the great cooks in the high-tone cities are men." He took a pinch of dough. "Another few minutes."

Patrick groaned in mock protest, but he smiled as he called a greeting to Fannie. "Are you feeling better?"

"I . . . yes. I'll be fine." She paused. "Your father's delivering a baby."

Patrick made a face. "That means I'll be here for a long time."

Abe put his hand on the boy's shoulder. "Then you can shape and rise and bake and see this bread through to the end. I'll make a first-rate bread baker out of you yet, son. You don't need to see to do bread. You already know how to measure everything. The real knack is how it feels when you're kneading. That tells you when it's ready to rise more than anything." He smiled at Fannie. "You tell the doc not to worry about Patrick. He'll be busy all afternoon at least. If need be, he can bunk in one of the rooms."

Fannie nodded. "So, Patrick, we'll be

counting on you for fresh bread for supper." She turned to go, almost colliding with Sam. "I feel so . . . helpless. The poor thing . . . she's dressed in rags."

"Never help . . . less." He clasped his hands as if he were praying. She glanced at Lamar, including him as she said, "Yes. Please. Please do pray. She was in so much pain. . . ." Fannie was halfway to the clinic when she met Pete headed her way.

"Going after the parson," he said. "The girl's calling for Sam. Says her name is Emma."

Back at the clinic, Fannie handed the nightgown to Edie. She looked so worried. And Edmund . . . Edmund's expression sent a shiver of fear up her spine. *Oh, God . . . please.* At times like this, she wished she understood prayer better. God controlled everything, and yet people were supposed to pray. Would God change things if they did? She'd never seen Edmund so concerned . . . not even when Lamar and Samuel were hurt. *Father . . . please.*

Sam lurched through the door. Bible in hand, he fell to his knees beside his sister. Tears streamed down his face as he brushed her burnished hair out of her dirty face and bent to whisper in her ear.

"The bleeding's stopped," Edmund said. "It could be the labor was premature. Brought on by stress. Things may settle down . . . we'll see."

Was it Fannie's imagination, or did Emma turn toward Sam? He obviously thought so. A faint smile flickered across his face and he set the Bible aside. Fannie couldn't discern his words, but the tone spoke hope and encouragement. He looked over at Edie, then at Fannie. Finally, he got off his knees and moved a chair to the head of the table, sitting down and taking Emma's pale hand in his.

Edie laid the nightgown aside. Edmund had retreated to the kitchen. Now he returned with a pan of warm water which he settled on a table holding a frightening array of instruments that hadn't been there when Fannie ran to get Edie. Edie dipped a cloth in the warm water and began to wipe the dirt from Emma's scarred cheek.

"The poor dear must have been on the trail for a long while," she murmured. Once she'd wiped the grit from Emma's face, she paused. Looked over at Fannie. "You don't have to talk to me . . . but I need your help." She turned her gaze on Edmund. "If you and Sam will give us a moment, Fannie and I will cut Emma out of these rags." She looked back toward Fannie, an unspoken question in her eyes. *Will you help me?*

Terrified at the prospect and ashamed that the idea repulsed her, Fannie still nodded. She'd do it for Samuel. Emma stirred. Grimaced. Edie took her free hand. "It's all right, honey," she said. "You're safe now." Edmund and Sam retreated to the kitchen. Edie reached for the scissors.

They worked in tandem, one on either side of the examining table, Fannie merely shadowing whatever Edie did. Edie made short work of what was left of Emma's faded calico dress. The layer of unmentionables closest to her body was surprisingly fine. Edie sliced through them all, clucking her tongue softly and muttering to herself as she worked. She was tender . . . respectful . . . and it wasn't long before Fannie's embarrassment faded and she simply concentrated on the task at hand. Poor Emma. She was dangerously thin, her body distorted by pregnancy.

Wondering about lice and other vermin, Fannie obeyed Edie's directive to try and comb through Emma's tangled red hair. She sat at the head of the examining table while Edie finished washing Emma's prone body. By the time Fannie had worked her way through the last of what she thought was a hopeless snarl, Edie was holding the nightgown aloft. "I'll lift her shoulders and hold her against me. You work the nightgown down over her head."

Feeling awkward, Fannie obeyed. Edie had obviously done this before. Many times. Fannie blocked out thoughts of how and why with a question. "Were you ever going to tell me?"

Instead of answering, Edie busied herself gathering up the fragments of Emma's clothing. Fannie repeated the question.

Finally, with a sigh, Edie sat down. She shrugged. "I don't know. I thought I could be content to remain 'Aunt Edith.' " She took one of Emma's hands in hers. "You already knew enough horrible things about me. But you seemed willing to look past it." She concentrated on rubbing Emma's hand. "Got to get some circulation back into this girl," she said, swiping at a tear while she worked. Finally, she said, "With you coming to find me, I already had more than I'd dared hope for. I didn't know what would happen if I admitted to the rest."

Emma stirred. Grunted. Edie put a hand on her swollen abdomen. Waited. "It's all right, Emma. Baby's taking a rest. You should, too. Sam's here and we're all going to take good care of you." When she stroked the girl's arm, Emma settled.

Fannie didn't know what to feel. Edie was so tender . . . so caring. And yet, she'd given her own child away. How could she do that? *It was twenty years ago. People change.* She began to brush Emma's hair. Emma sighed.

Edie smiled. "That's good. It'll calm her." Finally, she said, "You didn't quite believe me when I told you that my business up in the gulch was only a grain of sand atop an entire desert of sins." Her voice wavered. "Well . . . now you know I was telling you the truth. I'm . . ." She strung an entire dictionary of epithets together. The names Edie called herself made Fannie's cheeks burn with shame.

After a moment, Edie took a deep breath and said, "I've awakened to regret every single morning for a big part of my life. The first regret was always connected to leaving you. I wondered where you were, what you were doing, and I wished . . ." She shook her head. "I have wished countless times that I wasn't who I am. That I could somehow go back and . . . change. I am so very sorry, Fannie. Sorry I was too much of a coward to stay. Sorry you didn't —" She broke off. "I'm so sorry."

Fannie worked at another snarl in Emma's hair. Her emotions wobbled from

397

anger to hurt, from resentment and, finally, she recognized an unexpected emotion. Relief. Somewhere, in the middle of everything, she felt relief. Knowing the truth explained so much. She moistened her lips. "At least I finally know why Mother never seemed to . . . quite . . . *want* me." It was silly that those were the words that finally brought her own tears to the surface. She'd thought them a thousand times. Giving them voice made it real. Made it hurt more than she thought it would.

"No. Don't ever think that." Edie seemed about to reach for Fannie, but instead, she gathered up the filthy rags and, crossing to the stove in the corner, took up a handle, removed a burner cover, and began dropping the remains of Emma's clothing into the fire. "Eleanor and I . . . we were so very different. She used to say I was the hummingbird and she was the sparrow. I wore my feelings on my sleeve. Emotions were always harder for Eleanor. I don't know why." She glanced across at Fannie. "I think you may be more like her in that." She sighed. "She always said she wished she had my courage. I wished I had the love of a good man like Louis." She put the last rag into the fire and put the cover back on.

"Eleanor was the good one, Fannie." She

came back and sat down. "Think of all the love it took for her to raise you. Think of the love she must have felt for your father. And for you. Louis and I both hurt her so very badly. It could have destroyed her." She paused. "If it were me? I would have kicked Louis out of my life. But Eleanor? Eleanor *loved.* Even when it hurt. She loved."

So many things Fannie had never understood made sense — if she accepted what Edie was saying. Hannah had tried to tell her the same thing, but Fannie wouldn't have it. Now, knowing what was behind Mother's sorrow . . . *Oh, Mama. I'm so sorry for you.* She was glad she'd planted those roses at Mother's grave. Glad she'd chosen Mother's favorite color. *I hope they bloomed for you this year. I hope you saw them. Thank you for loving me. I'm sorry it hurt so much.*

Edie's voice wavered as she said, "Can you ever forgive me?"

Fannie set the brush down. She wanted to be angry. But the truth was, Edie hadn't had such a glorious life, after all. She'd lived with pain, too. And still . . . still she shone kindness. She'd treated Emma like a precious jewel just now, murmuring comfort, showing tenderness. Edie wasn't a terrible person.

Compassion. It seemed impossible, but that's what finally emerged in Fannie's heart. Compassion and a deep sorrow for all that Edie had to regret and the joy Mother had allowed to be robbed by bitterness. She let her own tears come, weeping for all the brokenness hanging over lives that could have been different. For what was lost that could never be reclaimed. And for Edie. Mostly, in the end, Fannie wept for Edie. Finally, she reached out and took the older woman's icy hands in hers.

"It's . . . done," she said. Edie lifted her head. Disbelief shone in her eyes. Disbelief and desperate hope. Fannie swallowed. "Mother's gone. It's too late for me to understand her. She never let me in. But now . . . now I've found *you*. And it's not too late for us."

It had been nearly twenty-four hours since Pete scooped Emma up off the prairie and brought her into Fort Benton. Labor pains came and went, but Emma hadn't opened her eyes once, and the look on Dr. La-Motte's face and the worry in Edie's eyes enclosed Sam's heart in iron bands of fear that made it hard to breathe.

He'd prayed until he didn't have any more of his own thoughts. And so he turned to the Scriptures, reading Psalm 139 and silently praying it over Emma. *O Lord, thou hast searched me, and known me. . . . Thou hast beset me behind and before, and laid thine hand upon me. . . . Yea, the darkness hideth not from thee; but the night shineth as the day. . . . Thou hast covered me in my mother's womb. I will praise thee. . . . Search me, O God. . . .* He read on into the next psalms, savoring phrases like *I know that the Lord will maintain the cause of the afflicted. . . . Lord, I cry unto thee: make haste unto me; give ear unto my voice.* He stroked Emma's scarred cheek and tried to encourage her, but all he could manage was an occasional word. It took so much effort to talk . . . and there was no sign that Emma even knew he was there.

Samuel stayed with his sister for most of the day, and labor returned with a vengeance that night. With every contraction, Emma grunted and moaned, and with every passing hour Dr. LaMotte said it would be "just a little longer now."

Edie and Fannie came in to help and encouraged Samuel to take a break, but he wouldn't leave his sister's side.

Finally, Emma opened her eyes and screamed Sam's name.

"Here," he said. "I'm . . . here."

She blinked, looked at him and, with terror in her eyes, clung to his hand.

"Just a little longer, Emma," Edmund said. "Push now. Push with all your might." Emma struggled and strained. She yelled a man's name . . . pushed for all she was worth . . . and finally, a baby slid into the world, squirming and squalling, red-faced and sticky . . . with a thatch of bright red hair.

Dr. LaMotte cut the umbilical cord and laughed aloud as he held the baby up for Emma to see. "You've a beautiful daughter." He smiled. "A bona fide miracle." He laid the baby in Edie's outstretched arms and went back to work, one hand on Emma's abdomen while the other reached out for . . . gauze. Bandages. Anything Fannie could find.

Sam swept Emma's sweat-soaked hair back off her forehead. Then with a deep sigh, she closed her eyes.

The doctor called Sam's name. When Sam looked his way, Edmund shook his head. "I'm so sorry, Sam."

With an anguished cry, Sam pulled Emma into his arms. He cradled her against his chest, rocking and weeping. The terrifying sight rooted Fannie in her place. With the baby snuggled in her arms, Edie stepped up behind her. "Let him wail," she murmured, and nodded for Fannie to follow her into the kitchen.

Edmund retreated with them and slumped into his rocker, pale and listless. Fannie handed him a mug of coffee. He took it but didn't drink it, just balanced it on one knee and sat, staring at the back door.

"Edmund." When Edie spoke his name, he looked her way. "You did everything you could. And you saved a beautiful baby girl."

The baby whimpered. Fannie gazed at the pink cheeks, the flaming red hair. . . . *What's to become of her?* Her heart thudding, she spoke the question aloud.

"Mollie," Edie said, looking to Edmund for confirmation. "It's possible . . . right? It's only been a few weeks."

He nodded. "If she's willing, yes. It is possible. Her body will respond once she begins to nurse the baby."

"We also have a goat and a milk cow at the ranch," Edie said.

"But what do we do until then?" Fannie asked. "She's hungry now."

"I'll write some instructions for you. We can get by with sugar water for a few hours, but you dare not linger in town." With a sigh, he got up and headed back into the clinic.

Sam stroked Emma's hair. Her beautiful red hair, glowing in the lamplight. He'd failed her again. Failed to protect her . . . failed to find her . . . failed to save her. Failed in everything. Why had God allowed it? Why hadn't he answered Sam's prayers? He lifted Emma's hand to his cheek. *I don't understand. I prayed so hard. I asked day and night. I begged. You knew where she was. Why didn't you take me to her? Or bring her here sooner? Why?*

"Sam."

He looked up. Edie crossed to where he was sitting beside Emma. Without asking, she thrust a bundle into his arms. He stared down at the baby. Her face puckered and she let out a wail pathetic enough to pierce a heart of stone. Sam fell in love. Edie handed him a bit of cloth with something tied up in the corner. When it touched her mouth, the infant smacked her lips, suckling with gusto. Sam smiled in spite of himself.

"She'll be all right," Edie said. "We'll take her to Mollie at the ranch. Edmund says it will take a week or so, but in no time things will be fine. She'll have a wet nurse and all the love she can abide. We'll take very good care of her, Sam."

He nodded. "I-I . . . want . . to come."

"Of course," Edie said. "You must." She stroked the baby's cheek.

He nodded. "I'll . . . wait . . . to come
of course," Edith said, "you must be
around the baby's clothes

Chapter Twenty-Five

Let us run with patience the race that is
set before us, looking unto Jesus the
author and finisher of our faith.

HEBREWS 12:1–2

The wind had picked up by the next afternoon, blowing bits of dried grass and debris
along the hard earthen streets, rattling loose
boards, and driving nearly everyone indoors.
The team pulling the wagon to the graveyard lowered their heads and laid back their
ears as they faced the wind. Fannie held
Patrick's hand as they walked along behind
the wagon. With her free hand she clutched
at her black cape lest it blow open. Every
few steps she glanced over at Samuel, but
he was looking straight ahead, his eyes fixed
on the rough wood coffin in the wagon
ahead of them. His shoulders were stooped
and he walked with a shuffling gait that had
nothing to do with the fall he'd taken up on

the trail. Emma's death had done something to him, something that frightened Fannie every time she looked at him. He seemed interested enough in the baby, but he hadn't eaten a thing all day, and Lamar's attempts at conversation had been even more one-sided than usual.

Abe had known where to procure a coffin. Fannie and Edie dressed Emma's frail body in the silk walking suit Mrs. Tatum had given Fannie in Sioux City. And now Pete drove the wagon toward the burial ground while Sam and Lamar, Edie and Fannie, Edmund and Patrick and Abe trailed along behind through the cold, bleak day.

Just as the men lowered the coffin into the grave, Emma's baby began to cry. The service was short. At the last minute, Samuel handed his Bible to Lamar and stood, tight-lipped and expressionless, as Lamar read from the New Testament about Jesus' return and how the dead in Christ would rise.

And that . . . was that. The men filled in the grave and everyone walked back to Abe's together. No one said more than two or three words. Fannie held the baby while Edie and the others gathered their things from their rooms. Abe brought an Arbuckle coffee box into the dining room. He'd put a thick layer of straw in the bottom, nestled hot stones he'd been heating in the oven into the straw, then folded a coverlet atop the stones. "That little darling's going to be warm as can be," he said with a determined nod.

Fannie settled the sleeping baby atop the comforter. They covered her with yet another, and then Samuel loaded the box into the back of the wagon, coming back inside to help Lamar with carpetbags and Edie's things.

Edie drew Fannie aside. "Are you certain you won't come with us?" She glanced at Edmund. "You haven't forgotten what I said?"

Fannie shook her head. "I haven't forgotten, but —" *Samuel doesn't want me.* "I promised to teach Patrick the basics of Braille — if I can remember them." She forced a smile. "I'll be busy punching holes in paper for the next few days."

Edie turned to Edmund. "You'll come check on the baby?"

He nodded. Smiled Fannie's way. "We'll drive out next week."

Lamar hugged Fannie, murmuring, "He'll be all right, little miss. He just needs some time." Fannie looked over at the wagon. She wanted to believe what Lamar was saying, but Sam seemed so broken. So lost.

Right before Sam climbed into the wagon bed, he came and kissed her on the cheek. She kissed him back, murmuring, "God bless you, Sam." He didn't smile, just climbed into the wagon bed and settled opposite Edie, the makeshift cradle between them.

Lamar climbed up beside Pete, and with that, they pulled out. Edie waved. Fannie waved back, barely resisting the threatening tears. As the sound of the wagon faded in the distance, Patrick turned to Fannie. "Bet I can beat you at checkers."

Edmund tousled the boy's hair. "It's not the best day for checkers, son."

Abe spoke up from the doorway of the boarding house. "But it's always a good day for gingersnaps. Want to help me make some?" Patrick headed off with Abe.

Edmund put an arm around her. "You look exhausted. Why don't you come back to the clinic with me and take a nap? I promise to be quiet as a mouse. I'll busy myself in the clinic and when you wake up, we'll have a quiet dinner and I'll read to you. Anything you choose."

It sounded comforting. Perhaps even restorative. Fannie nodded. "Thank you. I'll just get my knitting from my room."

"You . . . knit?"

"Thanks to Mother's insistence and Hannah's never-ending patience, yes. I noticed a hole in one of Abe's sweater elbows the other day. I offered to mend it for him, and now that I think of it, he was surprised, too. At any rate, now that there's little work at the hostelry, Abe agreed to let me earn my keep by knitting him some socks — maybe even a new sweater — once he sees proof I know what I'm doing."

Edmund smiled. "I like the idea of an evening of reading and knitting."

The look on his face made her think of Edie's warning. *He's going to propose. You must say no.* Perhaps going back to the clinic wasn't a good idea. On the other hand, why should she spend an evening alone?

"I won't be long," she said, and headed for her room. Someone had shoved what looked like a letter beneath the door. She bent to pick it up and perched on the edge of her bed as she read.

Dear Fannie,

I realize I should have known when you wrote me in Virginia City that something was different. Now that I've seen the special affection you have for Patrick, I can only assume you feel the same for Dr. LaMotte, and that that is why things seemed different, both in your letter and when I returned. I'm assuming you are not yet officially engaged, although I cannot imagine it will be long before the doctor speaks the words.

Things have not turned out the way either of us expected, but please know that I wish only the best for you. If you think of me, please pray for me. I thought that I had found my calling, but in light of recent events, I find myself questioning everything. Of course, if my speech doesn't improve, it will be even more obvious that I have been mistaken about a great many things.

Lamar tells me that everyone must endure a "dark night of the soul" and that I will endure mine. I hope he is right. He is a good friend, as are you. I wish for you, dear Fannie, great happiness.

Yours respectfully,
Samuel

P.S. I write this note so that you can visit Edie without any awkwardness regarding my presence at Bonaparte's.

Fannie sat on the edge of her bed for a very long time looking down at Samuel's letter, reading it over and over again, until someone rapped sharply on the door.

"Are you all right, Fannie?"

Edmund. She put the letter down. "Yes," she called. "J-just a minute. I'll be there in a minute."

She sat alternately looking at the letter and gazing at the work bag that held blue yarn and knitting needles from which dangled a half-finished sock. Finally, she went to the door and opened it a crack. "I'm sorry, Edmund, but I just . . . I'm exhausted. I think I'll stay here."

"Are you sure?" He glanced toward the dining room. "Patrick's counting on our savoring the cookies he's baking."

"I know . . . and I don't like disappointing him, but really . . . I just want to be alone for a while."

He nodded. "I understand."

But he didn't understand. Fannie could hear the truth in his tone of voice. She could see it in the way he turned away. He didn't understand . . . and it made him angry.

Poor Edmund.

The moment the wagon came to a halt at the side door to Edie's ranch house, a gaggle of chattering women gathered around the wagon to welcome Edie home. Edie introduced Sam as he was lifting her out of the wagon. "This here's the parson that Roberta found on our doorstep. As you can see, he's almost fit as a fiddle." She smiled up at Sam, then looked back at the girls. "He took a bad bump on his noggin and the doc says to take it easy on him, so if he doesn't talk much you all just leave him be, you hear?" She turned to Lamar. "And this is Lamar. He's staying on if he takes a liking to it." She grinned. "So let's do what we can to see that he does."

"I'll do my best," a mahogany-skinned beauty said.

"*Saints above,* Ruth," a buxom brunette teased. "You'll make the poor man blush. We're not in that line of work anymore." She nudged Lamar's good arm. "My name's Fern. I'll do my best to keep her in line."

Feeling himself in danger of blushing, Samuel reached into the box for the baby.

"And this is our newest boarder," Edie said. "But let's get inside for the rest of the introductions." With that, she spread her arms and, like a sheepdog driving its flock, herded everyone toward the door.

Sam noticed that one of the women stayed behind with Pete, apparently intent on helping him with the team. "That's Lily," a petite blonde said as she came up behind him. "She loves animals. And Pete. But he doesn't seem to know it." She smiled. "I'm Roberta. You nearly scared the life right out of me that morning, by the way. I've seen a lot of things in my life, but I never tripped over a dead body before." She grinned. "Of course, you weren't dead. Which was real nice to find out." She nudged Sam's arm. "Didn't realize you were so handsome."

Once inside, all the girls gathered around to exclaim over the baby's red hair, admire her dimpled cheeks, and coo over her perfect, tiny hands. Edie spoke up. "This is Sam's little niece," she said. "Born just this morning." She cleared her throat. "Her mama's gone on to heaven."

In the chorus of sympathy, the one girl who had yet to say a word squeezed past Roberta and stood on tiptoe to peer into the baby's face.

"This is Mollie," Edie said as she put her arm around the girl. Mollie touched the sleeping baby's cheek. She looked at Edie then and said abruptly, "I could try and feed her. My ma was a wet nurse. I could try." She looked up at Sam. "If you want."

"That's exactly what we and Doc La-Motte were hoping you'd say," Edie said. "God bless you for offering."

Mollie held out her arms. When Sam

414

handed the baby over, she leaned down and nuzzled her cheek. "Hello, little one," she murmured, then wrinkled her nose.

Edie laughed. "Well, I'd say that's the official word that both ends work. You want me to change her nappy?"

Mollie held the baby closer. "No, ma'am. I'll do it." She sighed happily as she looked up at Sam. "I never expected God to care one way or the other when I told him I missed my baby." Her voice wavered. "I know she isn't mine, Parson, but I'm so *glad* you brought her out here."

Sam swallowed. "Thank . . . you."

"What's her name?" The question came in a chorus. Sam had been thinking about the problem of a name since he stood at Emma's grave. "Nnnn." He closed his eyes. Pursed his lips and shook his head.

"It's all right, Parson," Edie said. "Nobody here's in a hurry. Take your time."

Taking a deep breath, he finally managed to say the name. "Josephine." Opening his eyes, he looked first at Lamar, then at the women. "She was . . . my . . . moth . . . errrr." He reached into the pocket of his black coat and pulled out her Bible. Held it up and said, "This is all I h-have . . . of . . . her."

"Not all," Edie said, smiling. "Now you

have her granddaughter."

Sam nodded and blinked away tears. He put the Bible back in his pocket and, together with Lamar, followed Edie up the stairs at the back of the house and into the room that Edie declared theirs for as long as they wanted to stay at Bonaparte's. "Including forever," Edie said, then glanced at Sam. "Although I think once you've had a chance to pray on it, you'll realize you belong somewhere where you can tell a lot of people about the One who wrote that book you love."

She headed back out into the hall. "Supper should be about ready, so you two come on down to the parlor soon as you can. I imagine it'll be a bit overwhelming until the girls get used to having you around, but they don't mean anything by all the joshing they do. They're good girls."

When Sam put the Bible in his carpetbag, Lamar got it back out and put it on the nightstand by the bed. Sam shook his head. "Don't . . . need it."

"You need it now more than you ever did," Lamar said. "I know you're hurting, son. You prayed as hard as you've ever prayed for anything, and God didn't take you to Emma. And then he brought her to your doorstep and let her die." He tilted his head and looked up at Sam. "Is that about right?"

Sam shrugged.

"Answer the question, son. Do you know of anybody in the Bible who begged God for something and didn't get it?"

An entire flood of names cascaded into Sam's mind. He wouldn't be able to say them anyway, so all he said was, "Lots."

"That's right." Reaching for Sam's Bible, Lamar thumbed to a passage and pointed to a verse. "Read it," he said.

Sam sat down and began to read.

"No . . . read it out loud."

Frowning, Sam shook his head.

"How are you going to ever learn to talk again if you don't talk?" Lamar stood up. "Tell you what, Sam. I'm going to go on downstairs. But I don't want to see you until you've read from verse 32 all the way to the end of the chapter. That's only eight verses. Might take you half an hour. That's not much. You've got a whole lifetime of talking to do. Get to learning how again." Lamar went to the door. "I'll see you at supper." He left, closing the door firmly behind him.

Sam sat on the bed, listening to him clomp down the stairs. For a while, he ignored the open Bible on his cot. Finally, though, he decided it wasn't worth the argument to resist what Lamar wanted him to do. He'd ask if Sam had read the verses, and Sam couldn't lie to Lamar. He reached for the Bible.

Hebrews. Frowning, Sam stared at the verse Lamar had pointed out. He looked back to the beginning of the chapter. *By faith Abel . . . by faith Enoch . . . by faith Noah . . . by faith Abraham . . .* Hmph. It seemed like his own faith had dropped into the hole they'd dug for Emma's coffin. With a sigh, he found verse 32 and started to read aloud.

" 'An' wut shallll I mmore say? F-For the time would fail me to tell of —' " *Great.* A long list of names. Bible names he probably couldn't say even if he could talk right. He limped through them as best he could. At least he knew how to say one of them. *Samuel.* He kept reading. The first verses were all about amazing things men had done "through faith." But then . . . " 'They were stoned, they were sawn asunder, were tempted, were slain with the sword . . . destitute . . . afflicted . . . tormented . . .' " And they " 'received not the promise.' "

It probably did take half an hour for Sam to mangle the entire passage aloud. By the time he'd finished, he'd broken out in a cold sweat and was in no mood for supper. His jaw and throat ached with the effort. Still, something drew him to reread the passage, and when he came to the end he kept going into the next chapter. *Wherefore . . . let us run with patience the race that is set before us, looking unto Jesus . . . who for the joy that was set before him endured the cross . . . consider him . . . ye have not yet resisted unto blood, striving against sin. . . .*

Sam closed his eyes. He felt so weary. So filled with anguish . . . anger . . . confusion . . . grief.

He glanced at the quilt on the bed and the pillow covered with a pristine white pillowcase. He set the Bible back on the table. Pulling off his boots, he stretched out on the bed. And fell asleep.

A baby . . . wailing . . . Sam started awake. When had it gotten dark? He sat up and looked around the room. Lamar was asleep in the other cot, snoring softly. Footsteps sounded in the hall outside the door. Whispers. And the baby . . . still wailing.

Someone had covered him with a patchwork quilt. Sam threw it back. He padded toward the door and opened it, then continued on downstairs in his stocking feet, pausing at the base of the stairs and peering up the hall toward the parlor. The baby wasn't crying anymore. Someone had lighted a lamp, though, and Sam made his way toward the light. As he neared the parlor, he realized that Mollie was sitting in the rocker, her back to the stairs, her shoulder bare. Samuel couldn't actually see Josephine, but he knew she was there in Mollie's arms, for she was suckling with enough gusto that he could hear it halfway across the house.

"You're a greedy little girl," Mollie whispered, "and you aren't mine . . . but I'm going to love you, Josephine. You are God's gift to me for a little while, and I am going to love you." She began to hum.

Sam sat down on the bottom step. The psalm he'd read over Emma came to mind. *Thou hast beset me behind and before, and laid thine hand upon me. Such knowledge is too wonderful for me; it is high, I cannot attain unto it.* As he looked toward the golden circle of light in the parlor, and listened to Mollie humming to Josephine, something changed. He didn't know what it meant. He was still angry about everything. He still had the same questions, and he was more certain than ever that he wasn't going to find an answer to some of them. And yet . . . something had changed.

Mollie lifted Josephine onto her shoulder. The baby's red hair fairly glowed in the lamplight.

Sam retreated to his bed and fell asleep, delighting in the beauty of the newborn baby girl.

CHAPTER TWENTY-SIX

There be three things which are too wonderful for me, yea, four which I know not . . . the way of an eagle in the air; the way of a serpent upon a rock; the way of a ship in the midst of the sea; and the way of a man with a maid.

PROVERBS 30:18-19

Fannie stood at the window of the boarding house dining room, staring off toward the west. She'd expected things to be strange for a few days, but she hadn't expected this. She felt empty. Listless. Like nothing really mattered all that much. And she worried. Samuel's note mentioned "a dark night of the soul." The idea that sweet, gentle, brave Samuel Beck might have to endure such a thing terrified her. What if he lost his faith? What if he never regained it? What if — She sighed. What if things were never the same between them again? And what did that mean anyway. *The same.* What was it she wanted?

Abe's voice sounded from the kitchen. "They probably heard that sigh all the way to Bonaparte's." He came to the doorway holding a steaming mug of coffee. "You gonna be all right?"

"Is it that obvious?"

"About as obvious as the wart on my face." He smiled. "You'll see them in a few days. And things are going to be fine. If there was anything wrong, Pete would have come tearing back into town."

"It's so quiet compared to before."

"I told you the winters were long. My wife —"

"I know." Fannie nodded. "But I'll be fine." She forced a smile. "It is an adjustment, though." She sat down at the corner table and, taking up a pin, began to prick holes along the lines she'd drawn. It wasn't Braille, but if Patrick could learn to discern even a few letters this way, he'd be a natural when it came to learning the real thing next year at school.

"That boy's crazy about you, ya know," Abe said.

Why did he have to say that? Every time she thought about Patrick, she felt guilty. Every time Edmund tried to take her

423

hand . . . and she pretended not to notice . . . she felt guilty. She thought it would help, not seeing Samuel every day. It wasn't helping at all.

"You going over to the clinic today?"

Fannie shook her head. "Edmund's bringing Patrick here around lunchtime." She looked up at Abe. "What?"

He shrugged. "Nothing. Just asking."

"Is there something you want to tell me?"

"I told you about my wife . . . right?"

"And I said that I'm going to be fine."

"You didn't let me finish."

Fannie waved a hand in the air. "Then . . . finish. You have my undivided attention."

"There was somebody else," Abe said. "She really loved somebody else, but she got tired of waiting for him and so she took me instead." He paused. "And I was crazy for her and I thought I could make her love me. All I did was get us both caught up in something that made us miserable. So that's what I wanted to say. You want a cup of coffee or not?"

Five days. It had been five days, and Fannie had taught Patrick everything she knew about Braille, finished knitting two pairs of socks, listened to Edmund read half of *Great Expectations* aloud . . . and with every passing day she was growing more on edge, because Edmund seemed to be growing more . . . determined.

As she lay in bed late one night, Fannie stared through the window at the starlit sky, and all she could think of was Samuel. Was he looking at these same stars tonight? Was he talking to God? Was he *talking?*

For the first time in weeks, she found herself talking aloud to Hannah. She missed Sam. She loved Patrick. She liked Edmund . . . but this just wasn't working out. And what could she do about any of it? She wasn't sorry she'd stayed, but what was the point if she couldn't spend time with Edie? And how could she spend time with Edie when Samuel . . . when Patrick. . . . Finally, she began to talk to God instead of Hannah. And she counted the days until she would go with Edmund to check on the baby.

On the morning they were to head to Edie's, Fannie rose early. She brushed her hair until it shone. Staring into the mirror, she held up the lamp and wished for a bit of ribbon to weave through the braid. She nestled fresh bread and huckleberry jam into a basket to take with them and had breakfast ready when Edmund and Patrick arrived at the boarding house. She had no appetite, but she forced herself to eat a little. Finally, Edmund was helping her up into the buggy. Abe settled a heated stone at her feet. She insisted Patrick sit on the front bench. "It's much too cold for you to be all alone back there. Come up here between your father and me." Edmund spread a buffalo robe across all their laps and at last they were on their way.

The wind stung her cheeks and made her eyes water. Edmund turned his collar up. Fannie and Patrick huddled together beneath the buffalo robe. It seemed to take half the day before the ranch house came into view. As Edmund handed Fannie down from the buggy and retrieved his medical bag, Pete led the little mare toward the barn. Instead of going off with Pete as he usually did, Patrick begged to come inside to see the baby.

Edie flung open the door and offered a hearty greeting, pulling them all inside. "We've got lunch ready." As Edmund helped Fannie out of her cape, then hung his own coat up alongside it, Edie drew them aside and said in a low voice, "Would you believe it? Mollie's milk's already coming in. Josephine's going to be a little butterball in no time. And it's doing Mollie a world of good. I've never seen her smile so much."

Just then Mollie came in, her face wreathed in smiles, and held the baby out to the doctor. "The parson named her Josephine for his mother."

Where is "the parson"? When he finally came in to say hello, he was surrounded by "the girls." Fannie's heart lurched. Introductions revealed that Ruth favored Lamar, but the others seemed to think that Samuel was the center of the universe. Sam barely acknowledged her. Oh, he kissed her on the cheek and said hello, but she might as well have been his elderly aunt. Actually, she thought, he'd likely have displayed more warmth toward his elderly aunt.

He said grace over lunch, though, and while he had to stop a few times and repeat a few beginnings, it seemed that the time at Bonaparte's was agreeing with him. Of course, he had an entire bevy of women kowtowing to him. Fannie supposed that would be good incentive for any man to learn to talk.

They were halfway through lunch when Pete knocked on the door. "Don't mean to rush the doctor off, but there's a storm coming in. It's moving mighty fast."

As it turned out, the storm was moving too fast. By the time Pete had the buggy hitched up and they were ready to head back to Fort Benton, it was obvious they'd be fools to try. The temperature had dropped noticeably. The black clouds scudding across the sky promised a storm. Were they about to be snowbound?

Samuel watched as the storm piled snow up against the bunkhouse after supper that night and rattled the windows, making things miserable for Lamar and Pete when they headed out to tend the animals. They were shivering when they came back in, and set up the checkerboard as close to the woodstove as they could until the women began to tease them about scorching their faces. Pete and Lamar traded chairs and joked about being "evenly done."

Roberta kept Patrick busy holding a skein of yarn so she could wind it up into a ball. Sam never would understand why that was necessary, but it served its purpose, because it kept Patrick entertained as Roberta told him an outrageous version of Hansel and Gretel.

Samuel settled himself in a chair near the kitchen, where Edie and Fannie were baking cookies and talking. Sam told himself the light was better for reading there, but the real reason was that he liked the sound of Fannie's voice.

The evening hours went by quickly. Edie introduced them all to a game she'd learned in France called charades. Samuel took perverse delight in his ability to excel at the game. After all, he'd been trying to express himself without talking for weeks. "So now," he said with a smile, "you know . . . how it f-feels."

As the evening wore on, he wondered if it was his imagination that Fannie seemed able to guess whatever he acted out. When Roberta asked if Fannie was a mind reader in disguise, she blushed and shook her head. As soon as the game was over, she bade everyone good-night.

Oh, Lord, I couldn't wait to get here . . . and now I can't wait to leave. Fannie stood at the window of the room she was sharing with Lily and stared out at the snow. The storm had left a few inches in its wake, but nothing like the blizzard they'd feared. Part of her longed to be snowbound . . . and part of her wished she'd never come. It was just too hard to be around Samuel and have him be so . . . friendly.

For all her ridiculous talk about friendship, she'd realized the moment he walked into Edie's parlor that she didn't want to be

Samuel's friend. She wanted him to sweep her up in his arms and kiss her until she couldn't breathe.

Even now, just standing there thinking about it made her tremble. And made her want to cry. He hadn't said three words to her all day. And he'd written that note to tell her good-bye.

Oh, Lord, I couldn't wait to get away from her . . . and now I can't wait for her to leave. Samuel stood at the window of the room he was sharing with Lamar and stared out at the snow. The storm had left a few inches in its wake, but nothing compared to the blizzard they'd feared. Part of him wished to be snowbound . . . but mostly he wished Fannie had never come. It was just too hard to be around her and have her be so . . . friendly. For all his ridiculous writing about how he wished her and Dr. LaMotte well and how he'd always value their friendship, he'd realized the moment she walked into Edie's parlor that he didn't want to be her friend. He wanted to sweep her up in his arms and kiss her until she couldn't breathe. Even now, just standing there thinking about it made him tremble.

Minette said love was like an echo . . . like

having an empty place inside of you filled . . . a place you hadn't even realized was empty. It was silly, but tonight when they'd been playing charades, Fannie had remembered that conversation . . . and gotten goose bumps at the idea that she and Samuel were echoing each other's thoughts. There was no point in trying to sleep tonight. She crept downstairs in the dark, quiet house — only to discover that she wasn't alone after all.

"It seems the whole house is filled with insomniacs tonight."

Fannie startled and looked toward the fireplace. A hand was just visible on the arm of one of the overstuffed chairs facing the fireplace. A hand holding a cigar. "Edmund and I were just having a talk," Edie said. She waved Fannie over. "And now, I believe I'll leave you two alone." She glided from the room, leaving the aroma of her cigar in her wake.

Edmund spoke up as Fannie sat in the chair Edie had vacated. "Patrick asked me something tonight after we retired. I didn't know how to answer him." He leaned forward onto his elbows. "He asked me why you've been so sad. I told him he was imagining things, but he said no. That he sees with his ears sometimes, and that we've both been sad. That it wasn't the same as being sad because of the lady who died. He wanted to know if he'd done something to cause it."

Fannie sighed. "I blamed myself for my mother's sadness. It makes me heartsick to think Patrick might blame himself for my moods." She paused. "I'll talk to him in the morning. I'll make him understand."

"What will you say?"

"That we're all . . . sad. We feel terrible about what happened to Samuel's sister. I've been worried about the baby. And I've been missing my friends back home."

"I know that's all true, but it doesn't explain what Patrick senses about you and me."

He turned toward her. "What Patrick senses is something I've been too selfish to admit. I can't make you happy, Fannie. However fond of me you might become over time, you will never look at me the way you looked at Samuel Beck tonight."

"I never — I didn't —"

"You can't help it. You *shimmer* when he looks at you. It's as if he's holding up a light and you reflect it back to him. Everyone in that room tonight could see it, and Patrick sensed it. He asked me what made the sadness go out of your voice tonight."

"Samuel doesn't love me. He wrote a note saying good-bye. He even wished you and me well."

"He's being noble. Denying himself. And, I fear, confusing the issue by trying to decide what is best for you without consulting . . . you. You'll have to be patient with him, Fannie. It may take a while for him to admit he's been an ignorant son of a willy-walloo about a few things. It's taken me most of the year." He knelt before her. "I love you for Patrick's sake, Fannie. I don't love you the way you deserve to be loved. And Samuel does."

"But Patrick —" Fannie's voice wavered. She couldn't hurt Patrick.

"*Patrick* isn't giving you up. I am. I still expect you to teach him for as long as you are in Montana. I want you to play checkers and bake cookies and be the best friend you can be to him, right along with Abe Valley and Lamar and Samuel and Edie. And when the time comes that you leave Fort Benton or he and I do, so that he can go to school, I expect you to write. Often." He kissed her on the cheek. "Neither of us is letting you go when it comes to friendship, Fannie."

He couldn't do it. He'd said good-bye enough. It was weak and perhaps even despicable, but as the morning dawned, and Samuel felt the reality of Fannie heading back to Fort Benton with Edmund and Patrick LaMotte, he realized that he just didn't have it in him to pretend it was all right. He'd been noble and done the right thing by her, but enough was enough. He dressed without lighting a lamp, grabbed his boots, and headed down the stairs.

Pausing just inside the door to pull on his boots, he headed outside, through the barn, and to the massive pile of wood behind the barn. Bonaparte's used a prodigious amount of wood. Nothing like a steamboat, but enough that Pete was beginning to have trouble keeping up. Edie had mentioned it as part of the reason she would welcome Lamar as a permanent resident. Pete needed help. Today, Samuel would give it. In fact, he welcomed the work. It would give him something to do besides chasing after Fannie, because he was very near making a fool of himself over her. *Help, Lord. Keep me from doing anything stupid.*

He began to chop wood. When he got hot,

he took off his coat. When his hands hurt, he ignored it. When he realized Pete was hitching up the doctor's buggy, he ignored that, too. *Let her be happy.*

Finally, he heard the crunch of buggy wheels on snow as Pete led the mare toward the house.

He stopped chopping wood . . . sank the ax into a stump . . . and looked up toward the sky. *Let her be happy.*

The door to the ranch house opened, and LaMotte and Patrick . . . and Fannie . . . with Edie . . . emerged. Hugs. Last words.

He couldn't do it. He couldn't let her go. *God forgive me. . . .* He called her name.

LaMotte looked his way. Waved. Patrick followed suit and then climbed into the buggy.

"Fannie! Wait!"

The buggy headed out. Sam started to run. *Let me make her happy. Let me. . . .* And that's when he realized . . . she hadn't gone. He looked back at the house. She was standing there . . . alone. Looking his way. Then running . . . into his arms.

He looked down into her eyes and saw love echoed there.

"I . . . don't . . . have . . . words."

"I don't need words," Fannie said. "I only need you."

Now unto him that is able to do
exceeding abundantly above all that we
ask or think, according to the power that
worketh in us, unto him be glory in the
church by Christ Jesus throughout all
ages, world without end.
Amen.

EPHESIANS 3:20–21

EPILOGUE

1874

Fifteen-year-old Patrick LaMotte stood just outside the door of the Missouri School for the Blind. When he heard a carriage roll up and a familiar childish voice shouting his name, he smiled, stooped to pick up his valise, and with the help of his ever-present white cane, made his way down to the street.

"Paddy! Paddy! Climb in!" Elizabeth called. "Wait till you see my new puppy! He's all golden and he has a black nose and floppy ears and he'll lick you to pieces!"

Patrick laughed as his little sister flung herself into his arms for a hug. She helped him climb aboard, and as the carriage wended its way through the streets toward home, Patrick learned that the puppy's name would be Plato because Papa liked the Greeks. Jake, the daddy dog, was big and friendly, and he and the mama dog

437

lived in St. Charles with the Hennessey family.

"Mrs. Hennessey saved the best puppy of the litter especially for us because Mama was her favorite teacher ever at the blind school!" Elizabeth gushed. "Mrs. Hennessey's house has red bricks and black shutters, and it has the prettiest rose garden ever!" She went on to tell him that Mrs. Hennessey had a little girl and a brand-new baby, and Elizabeth was quite sure she was the most beautiful woman she had ever seen . . . except for Mama, of course.

At which point Papa spoke up with what could only be called resounding agreement. And kissed Mama, right there in public. Which was embarrassing, but Papa didn't care.

Concordia Theological Seminary in St. Louis, Missouri, celebrated its spring graduation with a ceremony on the lawn. The student chosen to give the graduation address was a handsome, square-jawed man with a scar running the length of his left eyebrow. As he rose to speak, a blond beauty seated in the front row swiped a tear with a gloved hand. As for the newly ordained Reverend Samuel Beck, he grasped the lectern and took a moment to smile down

438

at his wife before beginning.

"I first met God in the face of a mother who forgave what, at the time, I considered unforgivable. After she passed on to her reward, I pored over her Bible, trying to find the secret to her peace of mind. I found not only what had given her peace of mind, but also I found what this book" — he held his mother's Bible up "— calls 'the peace that passeth understanding,' the peace God promises to everyone who bows the knee at the foot of the cross."

He looked out at the rows of his classmates. "I have met God in many places since reading my mother's Bible: in the lives of friends of other races who showed me kindness . . . on a river . . . in the gold camps of Montana Territory . . . and in the face of the woman he miraculously enabled to love me, in spite of the many faults she must endure every single day." Sam smiled down at Fannie before continuing. "And now, she and I are looking forward to seeing how God will help us use what we've learned here at Concordia to share a simple message: Jesus loves us. This we know, because the Bible tells us so."

As Samuel concluded his address, Fannie swiped at more tears. She couldn't help it.

She was so proud of how hard he'd worked to regain his speech and how hard he'd studied. She was so in love with him she thought her heart might burst. And she was afraid. They were going back to Montana. Back to Fort Benton and its rowdy, stinking, mostly lawless streets. Fannie knew Samuel was right when he said that Fort Benton needed to hear about Jesus. She also knew there was no better person to talk about Jesus in that place than a man like her Samuel, a man willing to preach in a saloon. As for her . . . she was living in that place between what she knew and what she didn't. The place where all she had was faith that God knew what was ahead and she could hang on to him.

People who'd known Fannie for years had been shocked to learn she was marrying a man intending to be a minister. "A most unsuitable match," they called it. Foolish woman to think she was suited to such a life in such a place as Montana Territory. And in so many ways, they were right. She *was* unsuitable. But then, Hannah had always said that if the good Lord couldn't use fools and foolishness, he wouldn't get much done.

Fannie smiled as she contemplated all the "unsuitable" people God had used. The

Bible was full of such people. And she was so glad, because finally, she had come to understand that God's business was one of taking the most unsuitable and using them in spite of themselves. Of course, she still had moments when she felt overwhelmed by what the future held for them in Montana. Even with Mother there making a home for Josephine and "the girls," even with the friendships of Lamar and Abe, things weren't going to be easy. She would never be a perfect preacher's wife. But with God's help, she would be the best, most loving daughter and auntie and wife and helpmeet she could be.

Land sakes . . . it was going to be an adventure.

A NOTE FROM THE AUTHOR

While working on this book, I've learned once again that God's grace is never ending, his mercy never fails, and while he doesn't spare us trials, he walks with us through the darkness, redeeming every broken thing and making it new. I received the joyous news that my garden of grandchildren will blossom in 2011 (adding another granddaughter and two grandsons), and then had to grieve over the news that I'll have to wait until heaven to hold sweet Barrett in my arms. (I envision him waiting at the gate, holding onto his grandpa's hand, ready to show me the way through the golden streets.) Whatever heaven is like, I know it includes joyous reunions, and the older I get, the more heavenly reunions I anticipate.

While working on this book, I've come to the end of myself yet again, and found Jesus waiting with outstretched arms, ready to carry me and mine until we had the strength to take up the journey on our own two feet once again. And so . . . I offer you another story forged in the fires of my own life.

My books aren't always about the things I think I'm writing about. I learned late in this book that the "most unsuitable match" I was *really* writing about was the fact that we often don't see ourselves as suitable to do or be what God seems to want us to do and be. I've been reminded that as we offer ourselves up to him, he can *make* us suitable "for every good work" (2 Timothy 3:17).

I hope you are encouraged as you make the journey with Fannie and Samuel up "Old Misery" to Fort Benton. I hope you have a Lamar or a Hannah to help you along life's way. May our adventures land us all at the throne of grace someday, where we can rejoice together in what God has done.

My deepest gratitude goes to editor Ann Parrish. Just when I have decided I should turn in my computer and promise never to attempt a novel again, Ann's kind words convince me to keep trying. If you are blessed by this book, Ann and the Bethany House team get much of the credit.

As always, my beloved Daniel deserves

thanks for the untold hours he had to fend for himself while his wife wrote and rewrote to meet the ever-looming deadline.

I can't imagine the writing life without my writing friends, most notably the Kansas Eight and Chi Libris. Dear friends, you are such a blessing . . . and you challenge and teach me every day.

And readers, I wouldn't have this writing life without you. Your willingness to "come and play" with me and my imaginary friends brings me endless joy and enables me to serve the Lord in ways I never dreamed possible. Thank you.

UNTIL HE COMES,
STEPHANIE GRACE WHITSON
LINCOLN, NEBRASKA
APRIL 2011

DISCUSSION QUESTIONS

- For the person who chose this book for book club discussion: What made you want to read it? What made you suggest it to the group for discussion? Did it live up to your expectations? Why or why not? Why do you suppose works of historical fiction are so popular with readers? What appeals to you the most about these types of books?

- The story is told from two points of view, Fannie Rousseau's and Samuel Beck's. How do you think the book might have been different if another character told part of the story?

- Share a favorite passage with the group. Why did it resonate with you?

- Talk about the time period in which the story is set. Is this a time period that you

447

knew a lot about before you read this book? If so, did you learn anything new? If not, did you come away with a greater understanding of what this particular time and place in history was actually like? How well do you think the author conveyed the era?

• Would you say that Fannie has experienced facets of 1 Corinthians 13 love in her life? If so, from whom? How did this person or these people manifest their love? Do you think Fannie feels differently about Eleanor at the end of the book? Would she say Eleanor loved her? What about Edith?

• Can you think of a time in your life when you felt you were an "unsuitable match" for a task God placed before you? What did you learn from that experience? Do you think Fannie will be a good preacher's wife?

• In chapter 4, Fannie says, "I guess it's time I grew into the life I've been handed." What events help Fannie do that?

• In chapter 7, Hannah says that "if the good Lord couldn't use fools and foolishness, he wouldn't get much done." Can you think of a time when the Lord used a fool or foolishness to accomplish something grand?

- If you were casting the film version of *A Most Unsuitable Match,* who would you have play the various roles? Where would you *begin* the film? Describe the setting. Where would you *end* it?

- What is Fannie's greatest flaw? Is it still a problem when the book closes? What is the greatest challenge she faces? In chapter 21, Lamar tells Sam that Fannie is "stronger than you think." Do you agree?

- Several kind people end up playing significant roles in Fannie's life. Who is your favorite? Why?

- What do you think will be your lasting impression of the book? What spiritual lesson will stay with you?

ABOUT THE AUTHOR

A native of southern Illinois, **Stephanie Grace Whitson** has made a career out of playing with imaginary friends. It all started in an abandoned Nebraska pioneer cemetery on a corner of land near where the Whitson family lived in the 1990s. That cemetery provided not only a hands-on history lesson for Stephanie's homeschooled children but also a topic of personal study. When she began writing scenes in the life of a pioneer woman, Stephanie had no idea it would become her first novel. Nor did she ever dream that God would place her books on bestseller lists, bless her with Christy Award nominations and other awards, and provide a writing career that now includes nearly two dozen published books and a busy speaking schedule.

In addition to keeping up with five grown children and several grandchildren, Stephanie enjoys motorcycle trips with her blended family and church friends and volunteering at the International Quilt Study Center and Museum. She loves pioneer women's history, Paris, Florence, and the Big Island, and is in graduate school pursuing a Master of Historical Studies degree. Learn more at *www.stephaniewhitson.com* and *www.foot notesfromhistory.blogspot.com.* Contact her at Stephanie@stephaniewhitson.com or write to P.O. Box 6905, Lincoln, NE 68506.